DARKNESS STIRRING

A TROUBLED SPIRITS NOVEL

J.R. ERICKSON

COPYRIGHT

DEDICATION

For Hannah, Nicholas and Maddison.

AUTHOR'S NOTE

Darkness Stirring is inspired by a true story. To avoid spoilers, that story is briefly retold at the end of this book.

1

June 1998

"**B**everly, wait up," Lorraine called as her friend zigzagged through the trees, long red hair flowing behind her. The bell she wore around her neck rang as she ran ahead.

A stitch had worked its way into Lorraine's side, and she stopped, leaning against a tree and rubbing the sore spot. She wasn't a runner. She hated mile day in gym class when the teacher led them out to the track with his stopwatch and whistle. Everyone would take off, sneakers pounding on the rubber-coated asphalt, and Lorraine would be at the end of the pack, huffing and puffing, desperately counting the steps in her head, though every footfall seemed impossibly far from the one that came before.

Bev was a runner. She ran long-distance on the track team and even did those races where she leaped over hurdles. Lorraine had gone to a couple of her meets, watching enviously from the stands as Bev's sneakers slapped the pavement in dizzying blurs. Lorraine had munched on the energy bars her mother had shoved into her bag, eating away the feeling she'd never be able to run like Bev or be as pretty as Bev or as popular as Bev. The energy bars were supposed to help Lori snack on healthier foods, but she often scarfed down two or three of them in one sitting, chasing that full feeling that never seemed to arrive with ingredients like whey protein and cashew butter.

"Lor, come on!" Beverly shouted. "We're going to miss the sunset."

She walked back, slightly exasperated. Lorraine had paused, breath hitching in her lungs. Bev lifted the silver charm that rested against her white t-shirt and shook it. The silver ball emitted a pretty tinkling sound that reminded Lorraine of the little metal triangles some students used in the band. Lorraine played the tuba, which was delicate neither in appearance nor sound.

"What is that?" Lori asked her, stepping closer to peer at the spherical pendant.

"It's a harmony ball," Bev said, shaking it. It released its dainty tinkle. "Or a Mexican bola according to my mom. My yaya called it 'llamadores de ángeles,' which I guess means angel caller or something like that."

"Okay," Lorraine said slowly, wrinkling her nose.

"It's a charm Yaya wore when she was pregnant with my dad. She said they're used to summon a baby's guardian angel. She passed it to my mom when she was pregnant with me, but my mom never wore it. When my yaya visited last month, she told my mom she needed to find it and give it to me. My mom came across it last week when she was cleaning out our attic." Bev shrugged. "I like the way it sounds."

"It's kind of ugly though," Lori said, and maybe it was with its strange designs etched into the silver orb, but really, she didn't find it ugly at all. She thought it was beautiful and unique, much like Bev with her yaya and her big family from Mexico that she went to visit twice a year, at Christmas and on the Day of the Dead, which was kind of like American Halloween, but sounded far more exotic than dime-store costumes and a pillowcase full of candy.

"No, it's not," Bev argued, lifting it up. "Well, maybe a little. It sounds pretty, though. Come on."

She grabbed Lorraine's hand and dragged her along. The cramp in Lorraine's side had abated, but she still lagged behind Bev. Lorraine's shoulder-length brown hair stuck to the sweat on the back of her neck.

"Did you ask your parents about Milton's party this weekend? His dad is hosting it and he has an indoor pool. You have to go, Lorraine."

Lorraine hadn't asked her parents about the party, and she did know that Milton's dad was hosting and that he had an indoor pool. Which was exactly why she hadn't asked to go. The thought of donning a bathing suit in front of the entire eighth grade made her stomach feel like it was dropping out of her body into an alternate dimension. A vision of her pale flabby thighs pressed together, dimples deep in the soft flesh beneath her ugly purple bathing suit, made her want to die from shame. The soft marshmallows that were her upper arms flapping as she jumped into the pool? No, thank you very much.

"I don't think I can. My mom said something about visiting my grandma."

This was a lie, though it held a kernel of truth. They visited Lorraine's grandma almost every other weekend. This weekend would likely not be any different, especially if Lorraine's dad worked late Friday night and her mom got so wound up she packed Lorraine and Henry in the car and took off for the hour-long drive to Grandma's house. Lorraine loved visiting her grandma. She always had a plate of fresh-baked chocolate chip cookies in the center of her kitchen table. She and Lorraine's mom would sit around and clip coupons while Henry tried to catch her fluffy Persian cat named Trixie, and Lorraine read or watched hours of television and munched cookies.

Grandma Mavis was her mom's mom. Lorraine's dad referred to her as Miserly Mavis, which often resulted in scowls from her mother. Lorraine had looked up 'miserly' once in the dictionary at school and found out it meant 'having the character of a miser' or 'small and inade-quate,' which left her no closer to understanding what her dad meant.

Either way, Grandma Mavis was her favorite, and not just because her dad's mom was a grouchy old lady who chain-smoked and ignored Lorraine and Henry whenever they visited her. She had two Chihuahuas she called her babies, and when one of them bit Henry, she'd snarled, 'Serves you right, you little brat.' Lorraine's mom referred to her as the 'wicked witch,' but never in front of her dad.

"That sucks," Bev announced, dragging Lorraine through the forest. "You go to your grandma's all the time. Can't they leave you behind this once? You could spend the weekend at my house. My mom loves when you come over. She says you're the only person who compliments her cooking."

"I don't know why," Lorraine said. "That fire chicken she makes is so good, and the corn soufflé, that's like my favorite."

"Ooh, look. Let's climb that one." Bev stopped, pointing at an oak tree that rose toward the sky. The trees in this part of the forest were big and bushy.

Lorraine couldn't see the top from where she stood at the bottom, which meant the climb would be hard, not to mention scary. "It's pretty tall," Lorraine said.

"Isn't Machu Picchu in the mountains?" Bev asked. "How are you ever going to go there if you're afraid of heights?"

Lorraine scowled. "There's a difference between being high up with feet on solid ground compared to standing on a twig that might snap at any moment."

Bev wasn't afraid of heights. In gym class, she always scrambled the rope to the ceiling without even looking down. She'd skip along the highest bleachers, arms stuck out, barely aware of the drop on either side.

Bev ran toward the tree and jumped, grabbing the lowest branch that hung a foot above their heads. She kicked her legs and hoisted herself up, wriggling up onto the limb.

By the time Lorraine was beneath the branch, Bev had already crawled up two more. Soon she'd be in the leaves.

Lorraine jumped up and grabbed the tree-limb. The bark bit into her palms. She strained upward, trying to lift herself up. The muscles in her arms shrieked and her hands burned. Lorraine let go, dropped back to the ground, and wiped her raw palms on her jean shorts. They were cut-off shorts, but they went nearly to her knees, unlike the cute cut-offs most of the girls wore, Bev included. She had cut-offs on too, but hers were white and stopped high on her lean thighs.

Lorraine looked up to see Bev disappearing into the dense leaves, easily stepping from branch to branch as if she weren't twenty feet off the ground. Her harmony bell tinkled as she climbed. Lorraine thought if she couldn't see Bev and merely heard the bell, she'd imagine a little magical fairy crouched in the dense leaves above.

Lorraine took a few steps back and got a running start, jumped and planted her hands on the limb. She gritted her teeth and swung her leg up, hooking one foot on the branch.

"Come on, Lorraine," she muttered, eyes crossed as she struggled to heave her weight up. She was almost there, so close, but then her right hand started to go numb. She let her leg fall and then her hands jerked free. She landed on her feet, but her right leg buckled and she went down on one knee.

Lorraine sat heavily on her butt, kicking her legs out into the leaves.

"Whatever, who cares," she snapped, though her throat had grown sticky as tears pooled behind her eyes. She grabbed a handful of leaves and ripped them into shreds on her bare knees, gathering more until she'd concealed all of her pasty skin beneath the prickly vegetation. The tears dried, and she stood, brushing the leaves off and staring up into the tree.

"I'm not coming up," Lorraine yelled. She almost added it was too hard or something less lame like she'd seen a deer and wanted to follow it, but she said nothing, searching for Bev in the branches. She couldn't see her.

The shadows on the forest floor had grown longer, casting the world beneath the canopy into expanding darkness. The sun was setting, and Lorraine imagined Bev perched high in the oak, watching the dazzle of pink and orange flare at the edge of the world. A knot twisted in her gut, but she ignored it.

"Who cares about a stupid sunset," she snapped, reaching down for a stem of milkweed. She jerked it out, root and all, and tossed it aside. She could watch a sunset from her bedroom any night of the week if she wanted, and she wouldn't have to worry about falling and breaking her leg.

She walked a few paces away from the tree and examined a log, where a scattering of plump oyster mushrooms poked from the crumbly bark. She broke one off and sniffed it, wrinkling her nose. It smelled like mud and black licorice. She dropped it and squished it beneath her shoe, smearing the white flesh across the leaves. She pulled off another mushroom and crushed it between her palms before picking up another one. The texture was spongy and damp and she thought of the mushrooms from *Alice in Wonderland*. The hookah-smoking caterpillar had told Alice if she ate from one side of the mushroom, she'd grow larger and if she ate from the opposite side, she'd grow smaller.

"Smaller, please," Lorraine murmured. She looked at the mushroom in her hand and considered touching it against her tongue.

"Good way to end up in the emergency room," Grandma Mavis liked to say anytime Lorraine did something she considered dangerous, which more than once had been suggesting sampling wild mushrooms or berries during their walks in the woods.

She chucked the mushroom at a tree and watched it splatter on the gray bark.

Further into the forest, Lorraine heard Bev's harmony bell tinkling.

She turned and gazed at the tree Bev had climbed into ten minutes before. How had she climbed down without Lorraine hearing her?

"Bev?" she called, stepping toward the sound of the bell.

Bev didn't answer, but Lorraine heard the crunching of leaves and walked toward the sound.

In the distance, something darted behind a tree.

"Bev?" she called again, hesitantly. It hadn't looked like Bev. But then she heard the ting-a-ling once more. Lorraine ran forward, leaping the last few feet to the tree the figure had disappeared behind.

No one stood there.

Lorraine paused, listening, but didn't hear the bell or her footsteps now.

"Come on, Bev. I don't want to play this game." Lorraine didn't know exactly what game they were playing, but she figured it ended with Bev bounding out from behind a tree and scaring her half to death.

Bev didn't answer.

"Bev! I'm serious. It's going to be dark soon. Let's walk back."

Nothing.

Lorraine shoved her hands into her shorts's pockets, irritated but also primed for the scare she suspected was coming. She walked back toward the tree Bev had climbed, kicking at the leaves, spinning a full circle every few seconds in case Bev crept up behind her.

She didn't.

"Bev!" Lorraine hollered, directing her voice toward the top of the tree, though she surely wasn't up there.

Lorraine had heard the bell in the woods. Bev must have climbed down when Lorraine wasn't looking. She could practically feel Bev watching her, crouched behind a bush, waiting for the perfect moment to jump out.

Goosebumps rose along her forearms as she studied the darkening woods. Lorraine truly did feel as if someone were watching her—only it didn't quite feel like Bev.

She scowled and kicked the tree. "Come on, Bev. I'm not kidding around. I seriously will walk back by myself if you don't come out in five seconds. One, two, three."

A twig snapped behind her and Lorraine spun around, eyes searching the gloom.

No Bev.

Lorraine almost said, 'Four,' but her throat had gone dry. She needed a drink of water. She drew in a breath and squinted into the murky woods. The trees had taken on menacing shapes, big and black—perfect for concealing anyone or anything.

The Dogman flashed into her thoughts, an urban legend that had been the subject of Brady Malcom's English paper. He'd stood in front of the class two weeks before reading aloud from said paper, accentuating the stories of the Dogman as if he stood beside a crackling campfire in the night woods regaling his riveted audience with details of the half-man, half-dog beast who stalked the northern Michigan woods.

A strange sound ripped through the trees, a shriek of pain and terror snuffed out before it could reach its peak. Lorraine gasped and stumbled back against the oak.

'Some witnesses have described the Dogman's cry as a humanoid shriek,' Brady had told the class, a leering grin revealing his brace-encased teeth.

Lorraine pressed her back against the tree as she remembered the details of that hideous monster, and she wanted suddenly, desperately to be home sitting in front of the television, eating microwave popcorn, talking with Bev about which *Buffy the Vampire Slayer* character they'd most like to go on a date with.

"For real, Bev. I swear I'm going to leave without you." Lorraine's voice had lost some of its boom. It barely echoed through the trees before it faded and disappeared.

Gathering her courage, she stepped away from the tree, back in the direction she'd heard the bell earlier. She walked forward. "Bev!"

Lorraine continued walking and calling Bev's name, going ten yards in one direction, circling back to the tree, ten yards in another direction, back to the tree.

No Bev. Every minute that passed, her spine stiffened and the thump of her heart grew louder in her ears.

"Bev?" she called again, and now Lorraine's voice cracked and hot tears spilled down her cheeks. She didn't even care now if Bev saw her crying, if she jumped out and Lorraine was blubbering like a baby. She just wanted Bev to jump out.

"Bev?" Lorraine whimpered her name one last time, and then she ran.

Her feet cracked over sticks and leaves as she fled through the trees. She'd come back for Bev later.

Something, someone was behind her. She could feel it. She could imagine it growing larger, looming, the darkness swallowing her up, a hand reaching out to grab hold of her shapeless t-shirt.

Lorraine didn't even call Bev's name as she tore through the woods. She couldn't. The cramp in her side ballooned ferocious and hot, a hundred times sharper than it had been when they walked in. Her breath whistled through her dry lips, but she didn't stop. She didn't catch her breath. She couldn't. If she did, she'd never make it out.

2

Lorraine didn't stop running until her feet hit Tanglewood Drive, the dirt road they'd walked that afternoon. She turned south and half-jogged, half-limped toward her house, rubbing at the burning sensation in her side. When she reached her road, Cypress Avenue, Lorraine picked up the pace again, darting into the grassy ditch and across her front yard. She burst through the door into the kitchen where her mom was feeding Henry at the kitchen table. Henry, though five, refused to eat vegetables unless their mother fed them to him.

"You need to put your laundry away, Lorraine," her mother scolded. "I asked you three times yesterday, and what did I find in the basement this afternoon? Your basket full of laundry."

"Mom—" Lorraine huffed.

"I mean it. I wouldn't have let you and Beverly wander off if I'd have known—"

"Mom," Lorraine shouted.

Rebecca paused, spoonful of peas halfway to Henry's mouth, and turned to look at her daughter. Her mouth opened as she prepared to scold Lorraine for yelling, but her expression shifted from irritation to concern.

"What's wrong?" she asked, standing and putting a hand on Henry's shoulder as if to make sure nothing had happened to her youngest, who sat perfectly safe in his chair as he watched his big sister try to speak.

"Lor yelled," Henry announced. "Kids can't yell at mommies." He looked expectantly toward their mother as if waiting for her to agree.

"It's..." Lorraine struggled to spit it out. She hadn't caught her breath, and her mind had shifted into warp speed, thoughts ricocheting through her head like exploding fireworks. "Beverly's in the woods. I couldn't find her," she managed.

Their mother frowned—first annoyance, a typical reaction to the antics of teenage girls. Then exasperation, as if Lorraine had merely not looked hard enough. And then the final expression, one Lorraine would remember for years to come. Fear.

"Can I play with trucks now?" Henry asked as if sensing the forced pea feeding had come to an end.

"What do you mean she's in the woods? Did she fall and get hurt?" But Rebecca didn't wait for her daughter to answer. She stepped away from Henry to the black phone that clung to the wall beside the doorway into the sitting room. She put the receiver to her ear and dialed a number.

"Lor, look!" Henry slid from his chair, squatted and grabbed a blue truck from beneath the table. "Vrooooom." He walked around the kitchen as if driving the truck on an invisible highway.

"Charlotte, it's Rebecca," their mother said into the phone. "Can you come sit with Henry for a bit? Lorraine's friend got lost in the woods. Thanks. I appreciate it." She hung up the phone, untied the yellow apron wrapped around her waist, and stuck it on a hook in the pantry.

"She... she didn't fall," Lorraine breathed. "She went up a tree, and I never saw her come back down, but..."

Rebecca walked to Henry and washed his face and hands with a clean cloth. He tried to swat her away, but she persisted. She wiped down the table and then squatted in front of Henry, taking his shoulders in her hands. "Charlotte from next door is coming over, Henry. I want you to be a good boy."

"I will, Mama," he said, side-stepping her and continuing to zoom his truck through the air.

"Is she stuck in the tree?" Rebecca asked Lorraine.

Lorraine shook her head. "I called for her. I didn't hear her. I yelled and yelled."

Rebecca looked toward the window where the sun had already set, leaving a pale purple sky in its wake. "We don't have much daylight. Run out to the garage and grab a couple of flashlights just in case."

When Lorraine returned, their neighbor Charlotte stood in the kitchen. She'd brought her daughter Daisy with her. The little girl had just turned six the month before and, despite her mother's best efforts to civilize her, she wore her usual stained dungarees and a t-shirt streaked with mud and grass. Her dark hair lay tangled on her shoulders. She marched to Henry and grabbed the blue truck from his hand.

Henry's mouth fell open, but before he could erupt into a scream, Charlotte grabbed the truck from Daisy's hand and gave it back to Henry. "Daisy, no. We do not take toys our friends are playing with. Go find a toy in the living room."

Daisy and Henry glared at each other for another moment and then Daisy stalked through the doorway into the living room.

"Mine!" Henry announced triumphantly to her back.

"Henry, remember to share with Daisy." Rebecca turned her attention to Charlotte. "Thanks, Charlotte. If Brian calls, will you let him know we're in the woods off Tanglewood Drive?"

"Of course," Charlotte promised. "Hi, Lorraine. How are you today?"

"I'm okay," Lorraine murmured, except she wasn't okay. Her knees had begun to quake at the thought of returning to the forest.

"We better go," Rebecca said.

"Listen, Mark's home," Charlotte told her. "I'm sure he'd be happy to go with you—"

"No, that's okay. We'll be fine," Rebecca assured her, pushing open the door.

Lorraine followed her.

"Did you get in a fight?" Rebecca asked as she started off briskly down the road toward Tanglewood Drive.

"No. Bev wanted to go up a tree to watch the sunset, so she climbed it, but I..."

"You what?"

"I couldn't get into the tree. I couldn't pull myself up, so I just waited at the bottom."

Her mom pursed her lips. "And she never came back down?"

Lorraine picked at the hem of her shorts, pulling at the strips of fabric. "I didn't see her, but, umm... she was wearing this bell thing, like a necklace that was a bell. I heard it in the woods, so I thought she must have come down, and somehow I missed her."

"But you didn't see her?"

Lorraine shook her head, tears welling up. The stitch in her side had returned the moment they'd left the house, and she struggled to keep pace with her mom. Rebecca said nothing more as they left their street and turned onto Tanglewood Drive. There were few houses on Tanglewood and none at this end of the street, just forest lining the dirt road.

"Where were you?" Rebecca asked.

"Umm… a little further," Lorraine said, pointing to a spot down the road. "Maybe right around here."

Rebecca turned and strode into the trees. Lorraine wanted to grab her hand and jerk her to stop, insist they not go into the woods. Something terrible would befall them. But she didn't. She followed her mom, biting her bottom lip so hard between her teeth she tasted blood.

Rebecca turned to face her after several minutes. "For God's sake, Lorraine. Are you crying? You're fourteen years old." She swiped at Lorraine's cheeks with her hand, frowning as she looked at her daughter's mouth, where a bead of blood coated her lower lip.

She shook her head and turned away, scanning the forest. "Beverly!" she shouted, walking forward. "Beverly, this is Rebecca Hicks. It's time to come out, young lady."

Rebecca's tone was stern, but Lorraine heard the tremor in her voice. Lorraine stayed close to her, so close that when she stopped abruptly, Lorraine walked into her back.

"Lorraine," Rebecca said, annoyed. "Show me which tree she climbed."

Lorraine stared around the forest, which looked alien in the approaching nightfall. She took a few steps forward, making sure her mom followed.

"That one," she said, spotting it through a break in the trees. She was sure it was the right one when she saw the remnants of the oyster mushrooms she'd smashed on the ground several feet away.

Her mother glanced at the mushrooms and then walked to the base of the tree, staring up into the dark branches. "Beverly Silva! Are you up there? This is Lorraine's mother. It's time to come down."

No sound emerged from the tree and no Beverly.

Lorraine stared at the ground, at the pale mushrooms like flesh. She could smell their acrid odor and her stomach turned.

"Mom," she whimpered. "I'm scared."

Her mom said nothing, merely stared into the tree, but when she looked back at Lorraine a moment later, she too looked scared. "How long ago did you see her climb into the tree?"

Lorraine shook her head. "I don't know, a half hour maybe."

Rebecca turned on a flashlight, though darkness had not completely fallen. "Beverly," she yelled, walking ahead of Lorraine.

Again, Lorraine felt the irrational urge to grab her hand and scream, 'Run!' She wanted them both to turn and race from the trees. Instead, her feet leaden, she followed her mother deeper into the woods.

Eventually the crunching of branches underfoot met their ears. Lorraine perked up as her mother swung the flashlight toward the sound.

"Beverly," Lorraine croaked, stumbling forward, but it was not Beverly who stepped into the beam of light.

Mark, Charlotte's husband, appeared in front of them, his own flashlight, the long heavy-duty black kind, clutched in his hand. "Charlotte said one of Lorraine's friends is lost out here?" he asked.

Rebecca sighed, reaching for Lorraine's hand. Her palm felt cold and slick.

"Yeah, thanks, Mark," she told him. "Her name is Beverly Silva. I figured we'd walk in here and find her right away, but..."

"Where did you last see her?" He was looking at Lorraine now.

Lorraine pointed back the way they'd come. "She climbed into a big oak tree back there."

"And never came back down?"

She shook her head. "I never saw her come back down."

"Can you take me to the tree?" He clicked his flashlight on.

Lorraine walked past him, her mother's hand slipping from her own.

When they reached the tree, Mark easily swung onto the lowest branch and started up, hopping from branch to branch. "Beverly?" he shouted.

Lorraine and her mom stood on the ground watching as he disappeared into the same dense leaves Beverly had climbed into. For a moment, Lorraine thought he wouldn't come back out. Like Beverly, he'd climb up and up. She imagined the tree as the plant in Jack and the Beanstalk. It led to a giant's castle in the sky.

Several moments later, his jeans-clad legs stepped out from the leaves. He climbed back down and dropped to the forest floor.

"She's not up there," he said. "Best if we walk home and make some calls, get more searchers out here."

"Maybe she'll already be there," Rebecca said hopefully. "Might have found her way to the road and doubled back and we missed her."

"Very possible," he agreed.

Lorraine wanted to share their optimism, but as they trudged out of the forest, she felt sure they would not find Beverly waiting for them.

∾

That night Lorraine fell asleep to the sound of voices downstairs. Outside her window, beams of light from people's flashlights crisscrossed the yard and the road.

The police had come and Beverly's parents too. Lorraine had told them all the story, repeating the details again and again. She never reported the odd shriek she'd heard, fearing if she mentioned the Dogman, she'd lose all credibility.

It was midnight when Lorraine's mother had finally ushered her up to bed. Though Lorraine argued, she fell into a deep sleep when her head hit the pillow.

In Lorraine's dream, she was back in the forest once more. Everything was quiet, and a red mist rose from the ferns. In the distance she heard the tinkling of Bev's harmony bell. Lorraine stumbled forward, hands out, as she pushed through the fog.

"Beverly," Lorraine screamed. She could barely walk, feeling as if she moved against the rushing current of a warm stream. The tinkling of the bell grew further away.

Lorraine woke in her bed, whimpering, one hand reaching in the darkness.

Near her window, Lorraine heard the tinkling of Beverly's harmony bell. She bolted to her feet and lunged toward the window. Lorraine's toe caught on her bookbag and she pitched forward, missing her bureau by only a few inches, throwing out her hands so she didn't land on her face.

She held her breath and listened. The sound had vanished, but as she raised her eyes to the glass, she saw that it was wide open despite her mother having closed and locked it when she put Lori to bed.

∾

The searches went on for weeks.

Three weeks from the day that fourteen-year-old Beverly Silva went missing, the searches were called off. More than five hundred people had scoured the woods. Divers had gone into a pond. Tracking dogs had followed Beverly's scent to the tall oak, but could not find it from there.

In the months that followed, few leads arose regarding the where-abouts of Beverly Silva—few save one.

Those who continued searching for the missing girl reported hearing the haunting tinkle of a bell somewhere in the forest on Tanglewood Drive.

3

Fifteen Years Later

"Come on, Lori," Stu argued. "Everyone is going. The whole crew for a weekend of camping. How can you not want to go?"

Lori looked at her boyfriend, Stu. He wasn't pleading. Instead, he looked irritated that she'd even consider saying no.

"I don't camp, Stu. Go, have fun. I'm going to stay here. There's an HR webinar I wanted to attend that focuses on dealing with aggressive or violent staff."

"Are you kidding me right now? You're going to pass up a weekend of floating down a river to learn a skill you will literally never use? You work for a marketing company. That place is as dry as an old woman's panties."

Lori shifted back to her planner where she'd been filling in her work schedule for the next two weeks. "I'd rather you saved your bad metaphors for Ronny and Mitch."

"Both of whom will be camping this weekend."

"Well, that gives me two more reasons I won't be going."

"That's horseshit, Lori. We haven't taken a vacation in months and you've barely left your apartment. You cancelled our trip up north so you could dogsit for that spaz, Naomi, who probably just took off shopping or some shit."

"Her grandfather died, Stu. She didn't go shopping and she needed the help."

"Well, I wanted you there with me. Is that so wrong?" He got off the couch and walked to where Lori sat at her desk, spinning her around in the computer chair to face him.

He knelt and pulled her closer, forcing her knees apart so he could squeeze between her legs, stopping with his face inches from her own. "I'm asking you to go with me, Lori. I think we need this. I know we do."

Lori studied his eyes, green with bits of gold. They'd been the first thing she noticed when she'd met Stu five years before at the Steak Pit, where they were both waiting tables. Stu had been a year graduated, but working at the Steak Pit while he searched for a teaching job. Lori had been graduating in the spring and trying to save up money for an apartment. Despite the passage of years, Stu still worked at the Steak Pit, as a manager now rather than server. And Lori still lived in the same apartment she'd found the summer after they met.

He cocked an eyebrow and leaned in, keeping his eyes locked on Lori. "Come on, baby. For me."

She loved and hated when he called her that. Loved it because it made her feel special, chosen. She hated it for the same reasons and for that gaping void of fear that lay on the other side of that feeling. The chasm left if those feelings ever departed.

Lori glanced toward the bay window, where her cat Matilda slept in a pile of calico fur. Her paperback copy of *Something Wicked This Way Comes* by Ray Bradbury sat unopened beside her. Lori had bought the book the day before from a mobile book truck that had been parked in the lot outside her work building. She'd purchased it on impulse and had been fantasizing about a weekend reading and drinking coffee in her window.

Lori closed her eyes and opened her mouth to say no. She couldn't go camping. She had reasons she couldn't explain because she'd shut that part of herself away. She couldn't talk about it to anyone, not even to herself in the solitude of her own mind.

But Stu pressed his mouth against hers so hard that their teeth clacked together. He ran his hands through her long dark brown hair and then she felt his hands on her shirt, tugging it up and off. His mouth moved to her neck.

He grabbed the elastic of her sweatpants and pulled. Lori lifted upward long enough for him to yank them free and then he was picking her up and carrying her to the bedroom. Somewhere in the haze of grasping and kissing, she said yes.

~

"Lori!" Mindi shrieked when Lori climbed out of the passenger side of her car. Mindi bounded across the space between them and grabbed Lori in a hug. "Stu said you weren't coming. I'm so excited."

Lori hugged her back, noticing another of her former co-workers over her shoulder.

Nicki, inappropriately dressed in a tube top and jean shorts so high her pockets hung out the bottom, had stopped as she lifted a bag from her trunk, eyes narrowing in Lori's direction. Nicki's smile turned into a frown, and then her eyes slid over to Stu and brightened. She feigned struggling with the bag. Her keys hung from the trunk lock, a hot pink stiletto keychain dangling from the set.

"Need help with that?" Stu asked, walking toward her.

Nicki giggled and tucked one strand of pale blonde hair behind her ear. "Guess I should have packed lighter."

Mindi released Lori. "Cole and I brought a huge tent if you guys want to sleep with us. It's one of those beasts with three separate rooms. Apparently his mom bought it for some big camp-out they did a few years back in Yellowstone."

Lori shifted her gaze away from Stu and Nicki, trying not to notice Nicki's impossibly shapely tan legs that extended from her jean shorts.

"Who wears that camping?" Lori mumbled, considering her own camel-colored hiking shorts and baggy athletic shirt.

Mindi turned and eyed Nicki. "Oh, you know, Nicki. The fewer clothes the better even if we are hiking into poison ivy-infested woods."

"Really?" Lori frowned, wishing she'd opted for long pants after all.

Mindi laughed. "No, of course not. Not on the trail anyway. If you wander into the wilderness, well, that's another story, isn't it?"

Lori nodded her agreement and walked around the back of the car to the trunk where Stu had packed a tent, two sleeping bags, a cooler that she feared was mostly filled with beer, and a bag with camping supplies. For Lori's contribution, she'd packed only two pairs of clothes, extra socks, her copy of *Something Wicked This Way Comes*, her planner and a bag of trail mix.

Lori had tried to back out of her agreement to attend the camping trip after she'd come down from her climax, but Stu had given her such a look of frustration that she'd eaten her words and said she'd go.

For three days, Lori had done little more than dread it, barely sleeping at night, silently willing her body to get stricken with the stomach bug that had been circulating at work the week before. Lori had even gone so far as praying the night before for a freak thunderstorm. No such luck.

Friday morning had dawned bright and sunny, with Lori feeling perfectly healthy other than the nausea that stemmed entirely from her nerves.

Ronny and Mitch careened into the dirt parking lot in Ronny's truck. Ronny's girlfriend Ginger was crammed in the seat between him and Mitch.

Six other people they'd worked with at the Steak Pit had already arrived, including Trinity and Heather Stout—sisters who had both waited tables along with Lori, Stu and Mindi—Greg the line cook and Eric, the once-general manager who'd been promoted to regional manager and now oversaw eight Steak Pits. Three additional employees Lori had never met arrived as well.

Eric had organized the trip.

"All right, listen up, team," Eric called, blowing a red whistle that hung around his neck.

"You have got to be fucking kidding me," Stu muttered, much to the delight of a giggling Nicki. "This isn't summer camp, Eric," Stu shouted.

"For real, bro," Mitch joined in.

Eric rolled his eyes. "You're right, Stu. Most of us are well into our thirties these days. Time to grow up, wouldn't you say?"

Stu flipped him the finger and continued drinking from the can of beer he'd already cracked open.

"Anyway," Eric continued. "I brought a bag of these whistles because once we hike in there's a lot of woods and if you step off the trail to pee and get turned around, you'll be glad to have one. The camping bluff is two miles out. Which is why I recommend drinking water right now rather than alcohol." He looked pointedly at Stu. "So you don't get dehydrated. We'll camp tonight and float the river tomorrow. Sound good?"

"Where's the strip club?" Mitch called, grabbing a beer from Stu's cooler and popping the top.

"This is starting to feel like the set-up for a bad horror movie," Mindi murmured, nudging Lori, who nodded tightly in response.

Every ounce of her wanted to walk back to her car and tell Stu she'd pick him up tomorrow. She had a migraine, a stomach ache, a work thing she'd forgotten about. Any excuse would do. She just needed to get out of those woods.

Instead, as the group picked up their stuff, following Eric along the path into the woods, she trudged reluctantly behind.

The further they walked away from the car, the more Lori's muscles tensed and her thighs burned with lactic acid, not from the hike, but from her own clenching.

"Want a beer?" Stu asked her, after he broke away from Mitch and Ronny, or Tweedledee and Tweedledum as Lori thought of them.

She thought of Eric's comment about dehydration and knew of her own tendency to get tipsy off of one beer. She nodded anyway. "Yeah, please." She needed something, anything, to calm the rising panic.

They set up camp on a sandy bluff above the river they'd tube down the following day. Lori erected their tent with little help from Stu, seeing as Nicki had begged Stu to help with her set-up. She simply couldn't figure out how to get the poles into the nylon sheaths.

Mindi joined Lori after helping her boyfriend set up their own tent. "Everything okay?" Mindi asked. "You look pale."

Lori bit her lip, driving a stake into the ground. "Yeah. I'm just… I'm not a big fan of camping."

Mindi's eyes darted toward Nicki and she shook her head. "Don't let her get to you. She flirts with everyone like that."

Lori nodded, though it wasn't Nicki who was getting to her. It was the tall dark trees crowding around the clearing.

"How's work going? You're still at that marketing agency?"

"Yep, Synergy. I'm still working as an HR assistant. It's good— predictable, at least—and I like my co-workers."

"That makes all the difference in the world. I just got promoted to the event director at the retirement home and I have such an amazing staff, not to mention the residents. I couldn't ask for a better job."

"Congratulations on the promotion. That's awesome."

"Yeah, it feels good."

"Hot dogs on the fire over here," Eric yelled. "I brought some veggie dogs too if anyone isn't into meat."

"Sounds delicious." Mindi laughed. "I've got s'more stuff," she called out. "Do you like s'mores?" she asked Lori.

Lori's stomach growled at the thought of the gooey chocolate marshmallow on graham crackers. She'd loved s'mores as a kid, but now they fit into the category of forbidden foods. "No, not really. I'll stick with a hot dog."

~

After they'd eaten, Eric built a roaring fire. They sat around the fire drinking beer and soda and telling spooky stories.

Stu, already thoroughly intoxicated, kept reaching his hand up the back of Lori's shirt and tickling her. She squirmed away from him, trying not to focus on the long dark shadows pressing in from the forest.

Kurt, or Jafar as Lori had come to think of him with his stringy goatee, stood and leered at the group across the campfire.

"This is a true one," Kurt announced, "but it didn't happen to me. I heard it from my older brother and it happened to one of his buddies back in the day, but it's one that stays with you. His name was Ben, and this happened to his sister, Carmen. One evening, Carmen and her best friend Summer went for a walk in the woods. Ben and Carmen lived in a house about a mile away from the Manistee National Forest, which is like a huge forest on the west side of the state.

"Anybody who grew up near the woods knows it's pretty typical to play in them as a kid and it wasn't any different for Ben and Carmen. Anyway, Carmen and Summer went for a walk in the woods, and Summer had on this bracelet that was like a tambourine. When she shook it, it made those funny clanging sounds."

Lori pulled the sleeves of her sweatshirt over her hands and wrapped her arms across her chest.

"So they're walking and walking and they find this old hut. It was a hunting cabin, but totally rundown—no doors or windows, half collapsed. Summer wanted to go look inside, but Carmen was like, 'Hell, no, that roof will probably fall on our heads.' Summer didn't think so. She went in.

"It was dark in there, so like the minute she stepped inside Carmen couldn't see her anymore. Carmen heard her for a minute, you know, because of that bracelet, and then the sound kind of stopped. Carmen knew Summer was trying to scare her. Summer was like that, so Carmen backtracked a little bit and hid behind a big maple tree.

"A few minutes later, Carmen heard the tambourine sound further away, like Summer had slipped out of the cabin and was maybe trying to sneak up on Carmen. Carmen yelled out, 'I'm over here, Summer.' But Summer didn't answer so Carmen started walking in the direction she'd heard the tambourine, but she didn't hear it anymore and it was getting later and Carmen was someone who freaked out pretty easily so she started screaming Summer's name and crying and really getting worked up.

"Eventually she peaced outta there and went home and got her brother Ben because he was the only one at home. They went back out with flashlights and scoured those woods, but no sign of Summer, so then they called their parents and the police. The police came out and this massive search went on for like two weeks. They never found Summer, but people who searched that night said they kept hearing the sound of this bracelet just for like a second and then it would disappear."

4

Lori didn't know when she'd stood up, legs spread, hands clutching her biceps so tight they'd lost feeling.

"Hey, are you gonna tell a story?" Stu grinned up at her, rubbing her calf.

"Did someone put you up to that?" Lori demanded, glaring at Jafar and then down at her own boyfriend as if he were to blame, which didn't make sense because she'd never told anyone about Beverly Silva. No one after she'd moved away to college.

Jafar wrinkled his forehead. "Uh, no one. Who gave this chick weed? I think the paranoia's kicking in."

The group laughed, and Jafar snickered before sitting.

"The person standing tells the next story," Mitch shouted, laughing and tapping his beer can against Ronny's.

Lori stared at the faces around their fire, searching for who had betrayed her, but they all stared at her expectantly as if nothing out of the ordinary was happening, as if she might start sharing her story at any moment.

Tears threatening, Lori turned and ran back to her tent, yanking the zipper so hard it got caught on the nylon fabric and stuck halfway open.

"Hey." Stu grabbed her shoulder. "What's up? Why are you wigging out?"

Lori's hands shook as she fumbled with the fabric, desperate to get the tent open and climb inside, crawl into her sleeping bag, and shove headphones over her ears. She needed to not be in the woods anymore, but she couldn't leave, not at night, not alone, so she'd do the next best thing, listen to music and fall asleep. In the morning, she was out of there. No way she'd be spending another night in the woods. "I don't want to talk about it. I'm going to bed."

Stu stared at her, not bothering to help with the zipper. "Fine. Whatever," he snapped, turning and stalking back to the bonfire.

L ori woke to the cool damp of early morning in the woods. Gray light trickled beneath the rain flaps on their tent. The interior of the tent stank of beer and cigarettes. Stu had quit smoking years before, but still indulged on nights when he got especially drunk, usually those where Ronny and Mitch were involved.

Lori sat up and wiggled out of her sleeping bag. Stu didn't stir. A low grumbling snore poured from his half-open mouth and he hadn't even bothered climbing into his sleeping bag, but instead collapsed on the top. Lori could see a beer can on its side next to him and wondered if it had been half-full when he'd climbed in and the contents had leaked out during the night. From the smell in the tent, it had.

She got on her knees and unzipped the tent, shoved her head into the damp cool air and sucked in a breath as if she'd been on the verge of suffocating. It smelled of pine and dirt and for half a second a memory of her childhood playing in the woods, camping with her own parents in the years before her dad left, rushed back and enveloped her. They were almost immediately stolen by her final memory of the woods, watching as Bev's sneakers disappeared into the oak tree and then running, terrified, as the shadows lengthened and nightfall approached.

Lori climbed out, not bothering to zip the tent behind her. It needed to air out. Some of her terror from the night before had abated, but not all of it. Pale sunlight broke through some of the overhead clouds and set the leaves and pine needles shimmering, but beyond the sparkling green, the woods were dense and dark, much of it still in shadow as the sun made its leisurely eastern climb.

The group was supposed to go tubing that day, hiking to some spot that Eric knew of where they'd ordered tubes to get delivered for their float down. Lori didn't want to do it. She didn't want to spend another hour in the forest, and though she knew Stu would be mad if she refused to force herself through another day and night in the woods, she would lose it. She'd start ripping down people's tents and screaming and throwing their bags into the river and then not only would she have to leave the woods, Stu would have to leave too so he could check her into a mental institution.

"He'd probably just toss me in the river," she murmured, trying not to examine the thought.

She packed quietly, slipping her clothes into her backpack and zipping it up. She wouldn't bother with her sleeping bag. Stu could manage it.

The next step was the hard part, walking the trail alone back to her car. She stood and surveyed the array of colorful tents. No one else stirred. It was barely seven a.m. and they'd been up late. Stu still hadn't been in the tent when Lori had woken briefly at two a.m. It might be an hour or more before anyone else woke and if she waited for that, they'd try to talk her out of it. Or Stu might wake up and pull the guilt trip on her.

She shook her head, mind made up. She'd go alone. Thirty minutes and she'd be climbing back into her car, the warm leather behind her back, the familiar songs of Annie Lennox on the CD she rarely took out of her player carrying her back to the safe world.

Lori walked out of the campsite, but startled at a rustling sound behind her. She turned to see a small green tent shivering. The door flap fell open. Jafar, the storyteller from the night before, lumbered out in only a pair of boxer shorts. His goatee was matted and his eyes were half open as he stumbled toward the edge of the campsite. She heard the rush of pee on leaves as he relieved himself and noticed the pale top of his butt cheeks. She almost turned away, but then she remembered the story and rushed across the campsite toward him.

"Jafar," she hissed.

The guy yelped and nearly fell forward. He turned to face her. "Jesus. You almost made me fall-face first into my piss," he said, shaking his head. "What did you say? Afar?"

She searched for his actual name. "Kurt. Sorry, I meant to say Kurt. The story you told last night... that was real?"

"Duh. I said it was."

"Well, I need the phone number of Ben. The guy you talked about. Do you have it?"

Kurt yawned and blinked at her. "I'll find it later. I need to catch some more z's."

"No." Lori reached out and grabbed his arm. "I need it now. I have to leave and I need it now."

His eyes widened and he wiggled her hand off. "Fine. Hold on."

He crawled back into his tent and several minutes passed. Afraid he'd fallen back asleep. she started toward the tent.

His arm poked through the flap. "Here, it's on my phone," he grumbled from within the tent.

Lori took out her own cell phone and punched the number into her contacts, saving it under the name 'Ben—Missing Girl.'

"Thanks," she said.

Kurt said nothing, but pulled his arm back in and Lori heard the zipper close the door of his tent.

Tucking her phone into her bag, she started onto the trail that led back to the parking lot. Unlike the campers, the forest was already awake. Birds chirped and called. Squirrels darted across the damp ground, chasing each other across Lori's path. She smiled as some of the tension ballooning in her chest seeped out.

Everything was fine. She was simply taking a short walk in a sunny forest on a Saturday morning. There was nothing to be afraid of.

As she walked, she hummed the tune to *Somewhere Over the Rainbow* softly to herself. Not all woods were scary. She'd played in the woods for years, often alone, before Bev vanished. She'd never been afraid then. Now she was an adult woman. Even less cause to be afraid.

Even as she told herself these things, she noticed the tiny hairs rising on the back of her neck. She didn't feel alone in the forest. But of course she didn't, she was surrounded by birds and little forest animals. She wasn't alone. But that realization didn't soothe her because the eyes she sensed watching didn't seem like the vaguely curious eyes of an animal. She felt hunted.

Hunted.

The word popped into her head like an ugly hairy spider crawling up from the sink drain while she brushed her teeth. Once the word arose, she couldn't unthink it. It hovered there, danced and twisted and demanded she follow the thought further. Hunting for what? For her?

She quickened her pace and shot a look over her shoulder, then froze when she caught a shadowy figure on the path behind her. She whipped all the way around and realized it was only a tree, but when she turned back forward, she broke into a slow jog.

It was early and she'd not had even a sip of water, let alone given her muscles time to warm up. A cramp immediately seized her side and she massaged it while she ran, her backpack flopping wildly on her back, her breath bursting from her mouth. She gulped for air and sensed the eyes travelling over her, getting closer, slipping through the woods silently... hungry.

Her body felt like the body of fourteen-year-old Lorraine from fifteen years before. Side cramping, gulping for breath, barely able to keep her legs pumping as terror seized her.

She tried to repeat the mantra 'there's no one there,' but the word 'hunted' popped in—ugly and looming and more real than any comforting lie she told herself.

Through the trees, she spotted the color red. It was the top of someone's pickup truck in the parking lot. She ran harder, fingers jammed into her side to lessen the pain. The lot came fully into view. She saw her own car ahead and then a hooded figure stepped from behind a tree.

5

Lori screamed and jumped back as the figure lifted their head. It was a man who looked at her, surprised, and gave a start of his own. He swept the hood back from the puff of white hair on his head.

"Sorry, miss. Gave you a scare, did I?"

Lori stared, words evading her, and gave him a little nod.

"Just out here trying to catch the morning fish." He leaned over the side of a little gray pickup and pulled out a pole and tackle box. "Stream's about a quarter mile yonder if you'd like to join me."

"No, thank you," Lori stammered, hurrying to her car. "Sorry I screamed."

The man shrugged. "Gives you the willies when you think you're strolling through the woods alone and find out you're not. Have a good morning."

"Thanks. You too." Lori climbed into her car, dropped her backpack on her passenger seat and released a long shuddering breath.

It was a relief to be in the car, but she still wanted to put more distance between herself and the forest. She started her Prius and peeled out, sending a plume of dust into the air as she made for the highway.

Lori dropped her bags inside the front door to her apartment and walked to the bay window, where Matilda lay curled in a nest of calico fur.

"Hey there, sweet girl," Lori told her, running her fingers over Matilda's head and spine. The cat shifted, emitting a low purr, but didn't stand to greet her owner.

Lori sat beside the cat, leaning against the wall and gazing into the backyard where her downstairs neighbor, Kenny, apparently had thrown a party the night before. Beer cans lay strewn around the firepit and in the grass. The glass-topped table was also scattered with beer cans and a large plastic funnel that was likely a beer bong.

Kenny, who rented the apartment below Lori's, had moved in the previous fall. He was a junior at CMU and his presence had caused Lori to wonder why she was still living in the apartment she'd been renting since her own junior year at Central Michigan University eight years before. Many of the people she'd graduated with had moved away or bought houses and condos.

Stu had suggested more than once that she move in with him, but she'd always said no. He rented a small two-bedroom house within walking distance to the restaurant they'd all once worked at and Steak Pit employees regularly crashed at his place after hanging around after work and getting drunk.

There were days when Lori wondered if her life had gotten stuck. Despite the passage of years, she still worked for the same company she'd started at after graduating from college. She still dated the same guy she'd met during her senior year at MSU. They were going on four years, but oddly she felt no closer to him than she had in the initial months. They'd never moved in together, talked about marriage or children. They lived in a state of suspension.

"Bev..." Lori whispered the name that really occupied her mind. The name she'd not uttered in years, not allowed herself to remember in any meaningful way in more than a decade.

After Bev had vanished, Lori had been consumed with fear and grief. That had transformed when kids at school started whispering she'd murdered Bev because she was jealous. Then her life had been uprooted with her parents' divorce. Her mother had packed up Lori and Henry and they'd moved to Clare and into Grandma Mavis's house. New school, new life. Bev had become a figment of her past, her former reality, a scary story that she'd stopped talking about and eventually stopped thinking about.

She might have gone on doing that forever, living as if Bev had never existed at all, except Jafar had told his story and she couldn't unhear it. The similarities were uncanny, the situation made ever more disturbing by the proximity of the disappearances. Both girls had gone missing in the Manistee National Forest. It was a big forest, sure, but… it felt connected.

But surely police were aware that more than one girl had vanished in the same general area under the same circumstances. And Lori knew if she opened all that back up again, only to run into the same nothing-ness, no closure, it could derail her.

"Derail what?" she asked out loud, laughing dryly. "Derail my perfect life?"

Matilda lifted her head and then rolled onto her side, raising one leg in the air and curling up to lick her side.

Lori stood and walked to the little work station beside her kitchen counter. Her desktop computer, also a relic from her days of undergrad, sat on an antique writing desk that had once belonged to her grandma Mavis. Mavis had given it to Lori when she'd moved into the dorms at CMU more than a decade before. Lori turned the computer on and waited for it to churn to life, watching the little time wheel spinning. She'd had the computer upgraded several times. More than one techni-cian had asked her why she didn't just buy a new one and she'd never had a suitable response beyond not wanting to learn a new system.

When the screen saver appeared, Lori gazed at a photograph of Matilda as a kitten. She stood on her cat tree batting at a dangling furry mouse that hung on a string. Lori clicked the internet browser and then paused with her fingers above the keys, considering the blank search bar.

She typed 'Beverly Silva' and clicked 'search.'

Her cell phone rang in her purse, startling her. Lori stood and walked to the bag, fishing out the phone. Stu's name was on the screen.

She pressed 'answer' and held the phone to her ear. "Hi."

"Hey, where are you? I woke up and all your shit's gone."

"Yeah, my grandmother had a little fall last night," she lied. She'd decided on the story on her drive home, knowing anything less serious would have Stu fuming.

"Oh, damn. Is she okay?"

"Yeah, she's okay, but I'm heading up there this afternoon."

"Okay, yeah. Well, we'll miss you."

"Thanks. Have fun." Lori hung up the phone and returned to her computer.

Thousands of results had come back, most of them concerning an actress named Beverly Silva who'd starred in a series of slasher films. Lori revised her search, adding 'Michigan' after Bev's name. This time the search included links to archived newspaper articles and several forums.

Lori clicked the first article dated from 2008 that appeared.

Ten Years and Still No Answers.

Every year on Beverly Silva's birthday, her mother, father, sister, and grandmother gather on Tanglewood Drive at the edge of the Manistee National Forest to release fourteen yellow balloons.

"Yellow was Bev's favorite color," explains her mother, Carrie Silva.

Fourteen is Beverly Silva's eternal age. The age she was when she walked into the woods with her best friend and never walked back out.

Beverly's friend, also a minor and thus unnamed, told police that Beverly climbed up a large oak tree to watch the sunset. She's never been seen again. Law enforcement has speculated that the girls got separated and Bev sustained an injury of some sort. They theorize she eventually succumbed to the elements. Her parents disagree. They believe something more sinister occurred in the woods that night.

"Bev was an athlete, a runner and a swimmer," insists Beverly's father, Francisco Silva. "She grew up in the woods. We live on thirty acres. She loved to climb trees and swim in the streams. She was a strong swimmer, climber, a strong girl. We believe and we have always believed that something bad happened to Beverly that night."

Cold case investigator Pete Weyland, with the Lake County Sheriff's Department, started looking into the case in 2006, eight years after Beverly vanished. He considered all the theories: an accident in the woods, the possibility that Beverly got lost and eventually perished from the elements, a potential runaway and finally foul play. He declined to commit to any outcome, but said he too finds it very suspicious that no evidence of Beverly has ever been found despite extensive searches that went on for three weeks.

Weyland said, "If Bev had fallen in the pond and drowned, gotten hurt or gotten stuck out there, it's hard to believe one of those searches didn't find her."

Police were informed after nightfall, further complicating initial search efforts.

Despite a decade gone by, Lake County investigators say Beverly's case is open and ongoing.

Lori scrolled further down the page where a video of the news report also appeared. She clicked play. Lori gasped as Bev's mom and dad materialized on the screen. They stood in Bev's bedroom, unchanged though ten years had gone by.

Tears streamed down Francisco Silva's face. "We put all the… the gifts over here in this corner," he said. "People sent teddy bears and flowers and trinkets for when she came home. I still remember when we got this one." He picked up a plush yellow bear. "She collected Beanie Babies, and she didn't have this one. I said to Carrie, 'Oh, she'll just love this,' and I remembered that it had been weeks and maybe she wasn't coming home. She wasn't ever going to see these things. We were piling this stuff in her room like one day she'd touch it and laugh and hug us again, but—" His voice broke and he turned from the camera.

Carrie Silva closed her eyes and reached a trembling hand to her husband's back. When she looked back at the camera, her eyes were filled with tears.

"Rosa," Carrie said, "Francisco's mother, called us the night Bev disappeared. She said, 'Go check on Beverly,' and we said, 'She's at a girlfriend's house, she's fine.' But Rosa was very persistent. She's an older woman from Mexico and… sometime she's quite superstitious. We dismissed her worries." Carrie's hand fell away from Francisco. "I wonder today, if I'd gotten in my car right then and driven to Bev's friend's house, could I have changed everything? Could I have gotten to her first?"

Tears streamed down Lori's face as she watched Beverly's parents, their grief palpable. Accusing, weepy eyes glared at her with the unmistakable question: *Why wasn't it you?*

Lori pushed away from the computer, chair rolling across the room as sobs rocked her body. She clutched her arms around herself trying to hold it all in, keep the emptiness from spilling out. Matilda jumped from her window seat and padded over, rubbing against her legs.

After a time, Lori's cries gave way to whimpers and then to silence. She thought of Jafar's story from the night before. He'd said it had happened in a town near Lake Michigan. Lori had visited those towns with her family in the summers before Bev vanished, before their intact life disintegrated. They'd camped in Ludington and gone further south a few times to hike the sand dunes at Silver Lake. Jafar had said the girl's name was Summer.

Steeling herself against the image of Bev's parents on the screen, Lori moved back to her computer, exited out of the video and returned to the search bar. She paused with her hands over the keyboard, the cursor blinking.

Did she want to know about this second girl? Would she be better off ending the search, grabbing her copy of *Something Wicked This Way Comes*, and escaping into someone else's life for a while? She glanced at the bay window where sun slanted through the open curtains and painted the wood floors in honey.

"No," she murmured after a moment of imagining curling up in the window, book open and disappearing into the pages for hours.

She typed, 'Summer missing Manistee National Forest.'

A series of results populated on the screen. The first included a newspaper article published only two days before.

Twenty Years This Week Since Summer Newton Vanished Without a Trace.

6

Lori cast a final, fleeting look at her book and the bay window, and then she turned back to the article.

It was a warm evening in June when Summer Newton and her best friend, Carmen Shaw, walked into the Manistee National Forest in Manistee, Michigan. The girls talked excitedly about the beginning of summer vacation, which had started the previous week. All was right in the world until they stumbled upon a cabin in the woods.

The cabin was derelict. It had been built during Manistee's boom logging years and long since abandoned. For a time, hunters made use of the little structure as a deer blind. Children crept across the wood floor, daring each other to run all the way in and touch the opposite wall before sprinting back into the forest to safety.

Summer went in for reasons that are still unclear, though her friend later told investigators she had a curious spirit and simply wanted a closer look into the old cabin. Summer's parents would later tell police she was a collector of odds and ends. Stones lined the windowsill in her bedroom and a box contained trinkets she'd found from beach glass to old Coca-Cola bottles.

Summer walked into the cabin and her friend stayed behind, kicking around the forest, and grew frustrated when Summer didn't reappear. Carmen called Summer's name, but the girl did not emerge.

That evening, Summer wore a unique bracelet—a tambourine made of strong leather with zils, or little metal discs, inserted in the leather. It made a jangling sound as she walked. Carmen had heard the bracelet when Summer entered the cabin, but the piece of jewelry had grown silent as the minutes stretched on.

As time passed, Carmen worried that a piece of roof had fallen in on Summer. Carmen had heard no commotion, but she was lost for a better explanation. She began to call Summer's name and finally ventured fearfully into the cabin. Summer was not inside.

Carmen searched the woods around the cabin and then, after a period of a half hour to an hour—reports differ—she returned to her home and asked her older brother Benjamin Shaw to help in the search. Ben, then sixteen, and Carmen returned to the woods. They found no trace of Summer in the cabin or the surrounding forest.

They alerted their parents and then Summer's parents at approximately eight p.m. A search by family turned up nothing. Police were informed of the missing girl at ten p.m.

A large-scale search did not immediately occur. Investigators with the Manistee Police Department were not initially alarmed. It was 1993 after all, and the kids had only just begun summer vacation. Plus, Summer Newton was fourteen years old, hardly a child. They assumed she'd argued with her friend and stalked off.

Summer's parents were less convinced. They contacted additional family and friends and along with the Shaw family resumed their search. The police would not begin their own search, along with more than a hundred volunteers, until the following day, an unfortunate delay considering that night a rain storm swept in from Lake Michigan, potentially wiping away critical evidence.

Summer's case grew as cold as winter long before the snow flew that year. No one had seen anything. There were no confirmed sightings of the fourteen-year-old. Police considered the usual suspects, including a local man with a history of sexual misconduct. They interviewed the residents who lived within two miles of the woods, which in these parts consisted of only twelve houses.

By the fall of 1993, police shifted their focus to Benjamin Shaw, the sixteen-year-old brother of Carmen, Summer's best friend. He claimed he was at home when Summer vanished, but since both parents were away, investigators could not corroborate this. Still, no evidence pointed to Ben other than his proximity to the scene and rumors that he had a short fuse.

Summer's family has not given up hope, but in the years after she vanished, the grief became more than they could bear. They moved south, relocating to a suburb outside of Grand Rapids.

Her parents no longer speak to the press about the case, but her only sibling, a sister named Spring, said this, "I feel like my family has lived two lives—the life when Summer was alive and the life after. The second life is a grayer life, a quieter life, a life marked by grief. If you're reading this and you know something, please tell the Manistee Police. Twenty years is too long not to know what happened to my big sister."

Lori reread the article and searched for the neon glowing link she'd sensed two nights before when Jafar had regaled them with the campfire tale. There were similarities, but were they ground-breaking similarities? Were they merely the tendency of the mind to group slightly similar things to ease the burden on its processing system? Or did Bev and Summer have something more in common? They'd been around the same age. They'd both disap-peared from the Manistee National Forest. Both girls had gone missing in June. They'd both been wearing jewelry that made a tinkling sound. But the girls had vanished five years and more than fifty miles apart.

Lori studied Summer's picture. She was pretty as Bev had been, but she looked petite where Bev had been long and lean with red-blonde hair and dark eyes. Summer had blonde hair and pale eyes, a wide smile with perfectly formed teeth.

"Dude, it's going to be epic!" The shout cut through Lori's thoughts, and she cringed at her downstairs neighbor Kenny's voice.

She stood and walked to the bay window, where she could see Kenny in the backyard with several friends. Thankfully one girl, clad in turquoise pajama pants with the word 'flirty' on the butt, was wandering the yard with a trash bag, throwing beer cans inside.

Another girl held a bundle of Christmas lights. Kenny and a second guy, who stood a foot taller than Kenny and looked like he'd made lifting weights his life purpose, surveyed the back lawn as if preparing for a major renovation project.

"I'm thinking beer pong over here," Kenny said. "Bonfire right there, obviously." He gestured at the firepit.

"We totally need a jello shot station," the girl in turquoise pajamas called. "I mean it's Sydney's twenty-first birthday."

Lori sighed. So much for her relaxing weekend reading in her bay window. It was barely noon, and Kenny was already getting ready for another party.

Lori glanced at her backpack, still sitting inside the door.

She smoothed the fur down on Matilda's head. The cat stood and rubbed against her hand before jumping from the window and padding to her food bowl in the kitchen. She looked back at Lori expectantly. Lori followed her and filled her food and water bowls.

"I promise we'll cuddle tomorrow, Matilda," she told the cat.

Lori slung her bag over her shoulder and walked out the door.

∾

L ori drove the hour north to Clare, to the home her mother shared with her grandmother Mavis. Lori knocked on the front door and then slid her key into the lock.

"Mom, it's Lori," she called, pushing into the entryway. She left her backpack on the floor and walked down the hall into the living room, where she found her mom and grandma watching television.

"It's Lorraine," her mother announced, pushing the handle of her reclining chair forward and standing up. "I didn't know you were coming for a visit." She smiled and gathered Lori in a hug.

"Hi, Mom, Hi, Grandma."

"Hi, Lorraine," Grandma Mavis said. "Don't you look pretty? All grown up. We're watching *Laverne & Shirley*. I love how you can watch any old thing now."

Lori's mother released her and turned for the kitchen. "I made home-made chicken noodle soup and Grandma baked bread and cookies this morning. She had a bug in her bonnet for baking. She must have sensed you were coming our way. Can I get you a bowl?"

"Yeah, sure. Thanks, Mom." Lori sat at the kitchen table as her mother heaped ladles of chicken noodle soup into a ceramic dish. She slathered a hunk of bread with butter and slid the food in front of Lori.

Lori's stomach grumbled. She hadn't eaten carbs in weeks and her body cried out for the food. She spooned a hefty bite into her mouth and closed her eyes, savoring. "This is so good," she whispered.

Her mother beamed. "You always loved my cooking. Your brother, on the contrary, prefers fast food. I swear every time he visits, he's carrying a paper sack of greasy burgers and French fries."

"He is a college student."

"You were a college student, and you still ate dinner like a civilized human being."

Lori nodded, though she'd rarely visited home for dinners in those years. She'd mostly stayed away, surviving on health food bars and air-puffed popcorn, refusing to live perpetually in her pudgy frame. She'd lost the weight too, but had found the only way to keep it off was to avoid her mother's house.

"What's brought you home, honey? Just wanting a visit or issues... with Stu?"

"What do you mean?"

Rebecca shrugged and straightened the plastic placemats, adorned with faded daisies, on the table so they were flush with the edge. "Oh, nothing in particular. I sensed... a bit of distance between you guys at Easter."

Lori sighed. "Stu's fine. He's the same, unchanging Stu."

"Perhaps that's the problem."

"How so?"

"Well, you're turning thirty soon. That's a milestone, moving from your twenties into your thirties. Maybe Stu feels stagnant for you. He's still managing the same restaurant you guys worked at ages ago."

"The restaurant pays good money, and he likes it," Lori argued, though in truth she'd had the same thoughts, but merely buried them.

"Which is fine," Rebecca insisted. "It is. But he graduated with a teaching degree and he's never taught a day in his life. You have a big professional job. You're using your degree."

Lori snorted. "Hardly. I have a degree in humanities with a minor in mythology and folklore. I'm still an HR assistant. I haven't gotten a raise in two years. I'm not progressing either, Mom."

"But I think you want to, honey. Maybe you want to get married and have children."

"No, that's not what I want. Okay? I don't want to get married and I definitely don't want kids."

"Then what do you want?"

"To eat this soup and go take a nap. I'm exhausted."

"Okay. Do you want me to sit with you?"

"No, go watch your show. I'm just going to eat and go lie down."

Rebecca patted her daughter's head and retreated to the living room. Lori felt bad for being short with her, but she didn't want to think about turning thirty or about Stu or her unfulfilling career.

7

Lori opened the door to her childhood room. It was a time capsule. Her mother had barely changed it since Lori had graduated from high school and moved an hour south into the dorms at Central Michigan University.

Lori sat on the bed and surveyed the space, now a keeper of old things and extra things. Cardboard boxes spilled from the wide closet door and stood stacked in one corner of the room. A folding table sagged beneath the weight of her mother's novels, mostly Mary Higgins Clark, and her grandma Mavis's copies of *National Geographic*.

Half of the room still contained the remains of Lori's teen years. Curled posters of 90s heartthrobs hung by tacks on the wall. Freddie Prince Jr and Leonardo DiCaprio's faces had yellowed with time, forever claiming their youth in the glossy images that had once been sold at every mall in the country. Lori and Bev had bought most of the posters together.

Lori brushed her hand over the comforter on her twin bed. It was the same comforter that had covered her daybed in Baldwin at her childhood home. Bev had liked the bedding set, navy blue and decorated in bright stars and moons. She'd told Lori she wanted to ask her parents for a similar one, but she'd never had the opportunity.

Sitting in the little alcove that remained of the girl Lori had once been, she wondered why, in all the years she'd visited her mother and grandma, she'd never stripped off the posters, tossed out the lava lamp that still sat on the bedside table, and brought the room into the twenty-first century.

Her brother, Henry, had updated his room. His former bedroom at their mother and grandma's house no longer contained the race-car bedding or the action figures he'd once propped proudly on his dresser. Before he'd left for college, he'd taken a load of his stuff to the thrift store and returned with a plain navy-blue bedspread. He'd hung two family pictures on the walls and left the rest of the room nearly empty.

Lori leaned over the side of the bed and reached beneath, pulling out a plastic tote that contained most of the stuff she'd set aside when she prepared to leave for college. It contained photographs, two yearbooks, old greeting cards she couldn't part with, and a tangle of cheap jewelry that had seemed important to her as a young girl. In the bottom, she found a neon yellow poster board folded in half. She drew it out and opened it.

At the top of one half it said, 'Bev's Dreams,' and the top of the other said 'Lori's Dreams.' They'd made vision boards before it became popular. Bev's side depicted images of athletic trophies, white-columned mansions, and handsome men.

On Lori's side, she'd pasted exotic locations—pictures of the sugar-white beaches in Greece, the dazzling cathedrals in Europe, and, most of all, the lush Andes mountains.

"Machu Picchu," she murmured, smiling.

That had been the big dream, the one that appeared in multiple pictures, that she always offered when people asked, 'If you could go anywhere in the world, where would you?'

Her desire to visit the ancient civilization had arisen after Lori read *Lost City of the Incas.*

Lori remembered sitting with Bev on her bedroom floor in Baldwin, giggling as they cut out their dreams and pasted them to the board, unaware that they would never come true.

After sliding the poster back beneath the bed, Lori lay down and pulled the covers to her chin.

∾

*L*ori woke to the sound of crunching. She rolled over and sat up, swinging her legs over the side of her daybed, the frilly dust ruffle tickling her bare calves.

Crunch. The sound came again, followed by a grinding and a loud, wet swallow.

"Mom?" Lori called, unable to imagine who could be awake at such an hour and why they'd be eating. "And right outside my door," she muttered, irritated that her sleep had been disrupted. She thought she'd been dreaming, and it had been good, but there were only fragments of a feeling and no tangible details to retrace.

She stood and made her way to her door, wondering if Henry lingered outside. Maybe he'd snuck a snack from the kitchen and sat in their bedroom hall munching away, probably making a mess on the carpet, which their mom would sigh loudly about the next day and then scrub at with a rag on her hands and knees. She wouldn't yell at Henry. She never did.

As Lori stepped to her bedroom door, hand settling on the knob, her eyes drifted down to the sliver of light leaking beneath it. It was an odd light, reddish and misty. She didn't turn the handle, but stood and listened for the crunching sound. It had stopped, and she sensed what lay beyond the door had paused and was listening for her just as she was listening for it, and it was not Henry at all, but something much worse, something hungry.

Though it fed and fed, it was never satisfied.

~

S omeone was screaming.

It broke through the fog in Lori's brain as light filled the room beyond her closed eyelids. Someone was shaking her, fingers digging into her biceps so hard it hurt. Her eyes flew open and she sat up fast, banging her face against her mother's. Rebecca yelped and slid off the side of the bed. As Lori's eyes focused, she registered her mother now on the floor, eyes watering, a hand to her nose.

"Oh, God, Mom. I'm sorry." Lori put a hand to her chin that had struck her mother in the face when she'd jerked up.

Rebecca continued to massage her nose, climbing to her feet. "No, it's okay. I shouldn't have been right over you. You were screaming and thrashing. I was trying to wake you up."

"I was?" Lori's blankets and sheets lay pooled on the floor, as if she'd kicked them off.

Lori's eyes fluttered closed and a flash of the dream came back, something eating outside the door. She looked at her bedroom door. It hadn't been this door, but the door at her old house, her childhood house.

"I used to worry myself sick when that happened to you." Rebecca sighed, stood and wiped a lock of sweaty hair away from Lori's forehead.

"What do you mean? When I had nightmares?"

"Night terrors, the doctor called them. Don't you remember? You went to see that dream doctor four or five times."

"Dream doctor?"

Rebecca sat back on the edge of the bed. "Dr. Childs or Chambers... no, Chadwick, Dr. Chadwick. He had an office in Traverse City, so we drove up there every couple of weeks pretty much that whole summer and into the fall."

Lori frowned, trying to piece together a memory to go with her mother's story. Something vague drifted up—an office with white leather chairs and blue walls and, most striking of all, a gigantic window that looked out on a sparkling lake. Oddly, she couldn't remember the doctor or the conversations they'd had. "I don't remember that. When did it happen?"

"It was the summer after... Bev. A lot was happening. Bev vanishing and then your dad and I splitting up. It was a hard time for you kids, especially for you."

Lori leaned back on her pillows, gazing at the tiny webs of cracked plaster in the ceiling. "What did he do? The doctor?"

"Well, he spoke with you about the episodes, but after we moved here to Grandma's house, they largely stopped and we ended treatment."

"Did I remember what the nightmare was about?"

Rebecca shook her head. "No, I don't believe you ever did. You didn't even remember the screaming. I'd be shaking you and yelling in your ear and it would take a long time to wake you up. It was very scary."

"And I did it again just now."

"Something like it, yes."

8

The following day, Lori tried to work up the courage to call Ben Shaw.

Lori stared at his number on her cell phone, but didn't hit send. What was she going to say? How did you approach someone about a disappearance that had happened decades before? She considered how she'd want to be approached, but the only word that popped in her head was 'politely.'

"Sounds like something Grandma Mavis would say," she murmured, hitting the green button to make the call.

It rang twice and then a man answered. "This is Ben," he said, sounding distracted.

Lori could hear voices and other sounds in the background. "Hi, Ben. My name's Lori."

"Are you the one interested in the bike?" he asked.

"Yes, the bike," she lied, suddenly feeling it would be easier to bring up the missing girls in person rather than on the phone.

"Okay, well, it's still available, but I've had a few calls on it. You can check it out this afternoon. I'll be home between three and five."

"Okay, sure. That's great. Where is that exactly?" She silently prayed he didn't rattle off an address in another state or somewhere hours away.

"732 Clairmont Drive."

"Great, ummm... and what city?"

He paused as if it were a stupid question, and maybe it was. "Clare. Like it said in the ad."

"That's where my mom lives," Lori blurted. "I'm there now."

"Great."

"Okay. I'll see you around three."

"That works, and do you have a bike rack or a truck? The last person who came to buy a bike didn't have any way to get it home."

Lori thought of her Prius, which definitely did not contain a bike rack. "Yep, I do."

"Good."

He hung up the phone without saying goodbye.

That afternoon, Lori guided her car onto Clairmont Drive, a nice subdivision with large tree-filled lots.

She parked in front of 732 Clairmont. It was a two-story colonial with a screened-in side porch and a two-car garage. The garage door stood only halfway open. A green road bike sat in the driveway. As Lori climbed from her car, a man ducked under the garage door and walked to the bike, disengaged the kickstand and rolled the bike down the driveway towards her.

His eyes narrowed on her Prius, and Lori felt color climb into her neck.

He was handsome, with penetrating gray eyes and unkempt sandy hair. He wore faded jeans and a plain gray t-shirt.

"Hi, are you Ben?" she asked the man.

"Yep. And this is the Schwinn. It has new tires and tubes, new cables. I greased it and I've tested it out myself. It's a good bike."

"Is that what you do for a living? Work on bikes?" Lori asked.

"I'm a nurse," he told her.

"Really? That's cool."

He smiled. "I don't know about cool, but it's becoming more commonplace, which is nice."

"What do you mean?"

He shrugged. "That old B.S. that 'men can't be nurses.' That was still pretty rampant when I first started school and I'm grateful it's faded. Let's just say that."

"It seems like a hard job." Lori fidgeted, stuffing her hands in the pockets of her jeans and half-considering commenting on the weather.

"Some days, but it's a rewarding job. I've never regretted it. Anyway, this bike is great for beginners. Not to say you're a beginner, but—"

"Well, umm... I'm not actually here about the bike."

Ben glanced at her car a second time, irritation flickering across his expression. He straightened up. "Okay. Then why are you here?"

"I wondered if you'd be up for talking to me about Summer Newton."

His eyes flashed, and his jaw went tight. He shook his head. "No. I'm not open to talking about that." He turned and started away.

"Wait. Why not? I—" Lori put up her hands, though his back was now to her.

"Listen." He spun around, glaring at her. "I told the police everything that I know twenty years ago. I had nothing to do with Summer's disappearance. My sister had nothing to do with her disappearance. Please, I'm just trying to live my life." He turned and started away.

"I'm not a reporter or anything. It happened to me too. My friend vanished in the woods."

He'd made it halfway up the driveway, but his feet slowed. His back rose and fell as if he were breathing rapidly. After a moment, he returned to where she stood.

"What are you talking about?"

"My name's Lori Hicks. On June tenth, 1998, I went for a walk in the woods with my best friend, Beverly Silva. We lived in Baldwin then. She climbed up a tree and just... vanished. I never saw her come down, and we searched the woods, us and police and volunteers, for weeks. We never found her."

Ben ran a hand through his hair and then left his hand there, massaging the back of his head as if a sudden headache had struck him. "Okay, what then? What does that have to do with Summer?"

"Well, I heard about Summer at a bonfire a couple of nights ago. This guy Kurt told the story. Kurt Hatchell. His brother was friends with you."

Ben rolled his eyes. "Pissant Kurt. Nosy little bugger."

"When I heard the story, I thought he made it up. Like this group of people had conspired to use my story... but then I confronted him. He'd never heard of Bev, but he said this thing with Summer really happened."

"It did."

"It happened to Bev too, and here's what's weird. She had this neck-lace on, a bola, a little bell."

He frowned.

"Like Summer's bracelet," Lori added.

"I see the connection you're trying to make, but—"

"I heard her bell that night and something else too, this far-off screech in the woods, this inhuman sound. People heard the bell later too, people searching the woods, but we never found her and after-wards... people said I did it. Kids at school said I was jealous of her and killed her and buried her out there."

"Assholes," Ben muttered.

"They did it to you too, right? They blamed you and your sister?"

He nodded. "That's what people do in small towns."

"Bev went missing in the Manistee National Forest just like Summer."

"The Manistee National Forest is over five hundred thousand acres. I'm sure a lot of people have gone missing there."

"But under such similar circumstances? Both teenage girls, both wearing a bell-type thing?"

"I'm not sure what you want me to say here. What if they are connected? So what?"

"You don't care?" Lori swallowed the sticky ball rising into her throat, feeling the needling sensation of tears behind her eyes.

He sighed, exasperated. "Believe me, I spent most of my life caring too much, hunting for the truth. Eventually I had to accept that I'd prob-ably never know."

"But two girls missing is more information."

"Then go to the police."

Lori pulled her hands from her pockets and tugged at her t-shirt, feeling desperation sneaking in. "I thought... maybe we could compare notes. Maybe—"

"No." He waved a dismissive hand. "I'm not interested." He grabbed the handlebars of the bike and turned, pedaling it back toward the garage.

"What if they're connected?" she called out. "What if that one piece of information leads us to who took them?"

Lori watched him for another moment and then walked back to her car.

She slid behind the wheel, angry and hurt and mildly chastised. She had been foolish to show up at his house. There were probably hundreds of girls who went missing in Michigan every year. The tiny balloon of hope she'd felt as she drove to his house deflated inside her as she started the engine and pulled away.

∾

B en waited until the woman left. He stripped off his jeans and t-shirt and pulled on his padded cycling shorts and jersey. He strapped his bike helmet beneath his chin and wheeled his road bike from the garage, climbed on and clipped his feet into the pedals.

For three hours, Ben rode, pumping his legs furiously. The road was one place he could silence his mind and he worked hard to do it now, refusing to think of the woman's pleading eyes as she stood in his driveway.

∾

T he ride had emptied Ben's mind, but it fired back on the moment he walked through the door that led from his garage into his kitchen. He scooped an electrolyte mix from the container on his counter and stirred it into twenty ounces of water, drinking it in three gulps. As he walked into his living room, he thought again of the woman who'd appeared at his house, Lori Hicks.

What if she was right, and the girls were connected? What if that one piece of information led him to the person who'd abducted Summer all those years ago?

Ben grabbed his laptop and sat on his couch, propping it on his knees and powering it on. He hadn't looked into Summer's case in a couple of years, but prior to that, he'd get the urge usually around this time, June, the time when she'd vanished. He'd get online and search for her name to see if there'd been any updates. Then he'd search for arrests and crimes in Manistee, Michigan, on the chance that police had arrested someone who might be linked to her. Beyond the occasional anniversary story, there'd been no breaks in the case.

He typed 'Summer Newton' into the search bar and scanned the same articles he'd already read more times than he could count.

Lori had said her friend's name was Beverly something, Silver, he thought. He typed 'Beverly Silver Manistee National Forest.' The search engine corrected the name to Beverly Silva, and a stream of articles about the disappearance appeared.

He started reading, his whole body tensing as the story took him back to his own night in the woods, searching for Summer Newton. He pulled his eyes from the screen and set an alarm on his phone. He had a night shift starting at nine p.m. and didn't want to get so distracted that he arrived late.

As Ben read the articles on Beverly Silva, he crept closer to Lori's conclusion. The cases were similar. The same time of year, same age, same 'without a trace' oddness, same funky little piece of jewelry that made a ringing sound. Both girls had gone into the woods with a close girlfriend who was also their age.

He returned to the blank search bar and typed 'girl vanished in Manistee woods.' Articles for both Beverly and Summer appeared, but as he scanned, he found another name: Peyton Weller.

He clicked the article posted in the Scottville News.

Searches continue for fourteen-year-old Peyton Weller, who went missing two days ago while hiking with her friend in the woods off Ridge Road. Despite searches on foot and by ATV, no sign of Peyton has been found.

Ben looked at the black-and-white photo of Peyton. She was pretty, with wavy dark hair and wide-set hazel eyes.

She'd disappeared in June 2008, five years before.

He found several more articles, but each simply regurgitated the original article's information. The only difference was the passage of time—*twenty-five days since Peyton Weller disappeared, six months since she disappeared*. One final article on the one-year anniversary and then nothing.

He continued clicking deeper into the search engine and found yet another name: Bella Palmer.

Girl vanished from Reed City Woods.

He clicked the link and read.

It's been twenty-two days since thirteen-year-old Reed City middle-schooler Bella Palmer walked into the forest on Peak Road and never walked back out.

Bella, along with her best friend (not named in the press), went to the woods in search of blackberries. According to Osceola County Deputy Tim Harbor, the girls got split up while looking for berries, and Bella's friend was unable to locate her.

Because of the late time of day, only a cursory search was performed the night of Sunday, July thirteenth, but law enforcement assumed Bella might have hunkered down for the night and would reemerge in the morning. However, on Monday, Bella did not reappear, and a larger, more thorough search was conducted. Searches continued including volunteers and police for two weeks, at which point official searches were called off.

If you have information regarding the whereabouts of Bella Palmer, please contact the Osceola County Sheriff's Department.

Ben wrote down the names of the missing girls and the cities from which they'd disappeared. He opened another window in his browser and pulled up a map of Michigan, typed in the locations of each city.

All the cities where the girls had disappeared bordered the Manistee National Forest.

9

As Lori made the hour's drive south to Mount Pleasant on Monday morning, her cell phone buzzed with a new text message.

Ben: Hi. This is Ben Shaw. Call me if you still want to talk.

Lori parked and looked at the clock. Five minutes until she needed to be seated at her desk, reading her daily emails, and she'd not brought a to-go mug of coffee because she'd started out at her grandma's house where they were out of everything except decaf.

Lori texted him back.

Lori: I do, but heading in to work now. Will call you this evening.

As she hurried through the parking garage, her cell phone dinged.

Ben: Working the night shift tonight. I'll call you before ten. Good?

Lori: Sure.

She skipped the elevator, opting for the stairs to take her down the two levels from the parking garage to the lobby.

Inside the Synergy Marketing building, Lori showed her badge to the security guard and crowded into the elevator, full with other employees. The smells of coffee, perfume, and body odor wafted in the stifling space.

Lori's stomach rumbled loudly, and the guy beside her glanced her way. She hadn't forgotten to eat breakfast. She'd avoided the kitchen knowing her mother would have set out a plate of cinnamon toast, some kind of sticky buns and a box of Golden Grahams—Grandma

Mavis's favorite cereal. It was a carb buffet and if Lori had so much as laid eyes on it, she would have felt the old, familiar longing.

When the elevator opened, she beelined for the break room, filled a Styrofoam cup with black coffee and selected a beef stick from the options in the vending machine.

∽

The day passed with Lorraine marking the minutes rather than hours at work. Human resources had never been the most interesting job, but usually the day presented enough challenges to keep her busy.

"Knock, knock."

Lorraine looked up to see Naomi, her supervisor, standing at the door to her office. "You awake in here? It's been so quiet I thought you might have nodded off under your desk."

Lori smiled and yawned, covering her mouth. "Sorry. Nope, not asleep, just trying to get these new employees added to the system." She gestured at a stack of new-hire paperwork.

"Better you than me," Naomi joked. "Want to walk down to the lobby and grab a coffee? I was heading down there."

"Sure. I need to stretch my legs."

Lori followed Naomi down the hall to the elevator. The gray carpet muted their footfalls.

"I am so pumped for this weekend," Naomi told her. "Trevor booked one of those Airbnb things up north. We're taking a wine tour. How romantic is that? Fingers crossed he's going to propose." Naomi's blue eyes sparkled beneath a heavy layer of black mascara.

"Wow, really? Has it even been a year?"

"A year this weekend," Naomi gushed. "I even got a manicure last night on the chance he does." She wiggled her fingers, nails painted a glossy pink.

"And you feel ready to get married?"

"Well, sure, I'm twenty-five. If I'm going to have three kids, I need to get started."

"Three kids!"

Naomi laughed. "Oh, Lori, I hate to tell you, but the rest of the world doesn't move at a snail's pace. My mother always said if you want it, grab it now—tomorrow it might be gone. And I try to live by that. You know? Trevor is amazing. He'd make a great husband and a great dad."

"I bet." Lori watched the descending floor numbers light above them as the elevator dropped toward the first floor.

"I'm getting a mocha to celebrate. Are you working out today?"

Lori nodded. "Yeah, I need to. I didn't all weekend."

"Oh, that's right! Your camping trip. How was it?"

"It was fine."

Naomi made a face. "Fine? That sounds really exciting. Come on, that's it?"

Lori shrugged and stopped at the coffee kiosk. "A black coffee, please," she told the barista.

"Mocha for me," Naomi chirped. "My treat." She handed the guy a ten-dollar bill.

"I'm not a fan of camping," Lori admitted.

"Well then, why did Stu drag you along for that? You should have said you wanted to go somewhere else. Like wine tasting." Naomi grinned and nudged her.

"That would definitely have beat the woods."

"Of course, it would have. What's romantic about trudging through the woods in a plume of bug spray?"

"Not a whole lot."

They got their coffees and started back toward the elevator, Naomi babbling on about her hopeful engagement and all the things that made Trevor 'the one.' Each time Naomi said 'the one,' Lori cringed inwardly. She'd been with Stu for four years and no part of her thought of him as 'the one.' Frankly, she didn't believe the one existed, not for her, not for Naomi and not for anyone. Nothing about the world had shown her such magic except perhaps for books, but at the end of the day, those too were merely words on a page.

Synergy's office had a gym connected by an underground tunnel. It was possible to reach the gym by walking out of the building, across a parking lot and into the separate smaller building the fitness area occupied, but Lori rarely went that way. Usually, Naomi joined her in the gym so she didn't have to walk the tunnel alone. Her shoes slapped against the cement as she walked and the pale yellow lights offered little illumination in the dark hall.

The gym was empty, likely thanks to the beautiful weather. People often preferred to take their workouts outside in the summer months. The emptiness suited Lori just fine. She changed into her workout clothes and climbed onto a treadmill, selecting a forty-five-minute pre-set workout.

∾

Lori rarely showered at the office gym. Nudity in front of anyone was difficult, but especially colleagues she might be sitting in the boardroom across from. But after forty minutes jogging on the treadmill, she was sticky with sweat.

The women's locker room was as empty as the gym itself, so Lori grabbed a complimentary towel and slipped into one of the glass-walled showers. She stripped down in the stall and hung her clothes over the door. Turning the shower to cool, she stepped beneath the spray, sighing as it sluiced down her body.

She thought of Bev, as she had so many times that day, and of Summer Newton. Two girls who'd never lived to become women. Could they possibly have been abducted by the same person?

Lori pressed the soap dispenser and sudsed up. As she rinsed, she heard a sound outside the shower. Another employee at Synergy must have arrived to work out.

Lori shampooed her hair, but as she pulled her head out from under the water another sound reached her. A scratching sound as if someone were walking along the row of metal lockers and scraping something sharp across the surface.

Breath caught in her chest, Lori strained toward the noise, trying to imagine who or what could be causing it. Something in the ventilation system?

She considered calling out. With the shower on, if someone were out there, they already knew where she was. Still, she couldn't bring herself to speak nor to turn off the shower, though she desperately wanted a better sense of what was making the sound.

The screeching dulled and quieted as if growing further away. After several minutes of silence, Lori eased the nozzle to off and stood for another moment, listening. The cool shower no longer refreshed her. Goosebumps covered her from the neck down.

Shivering, she pulled her towel from the hook and wrapped it around her waist, reluctant to open the stall door.

It was the vents or someone stopping to get something they'd left from a locker. The spray of water had distorted the sound, nothing more.

She pushed open the shower door and stepped into the locker room facing the line of mirrors on the opposite wall. She caught a glimpse of herself, pale, wet hair plastered to her head, eyes wide with fear. She smiled as if to reassure herself and turned for the lockers.

The lights went out.

They didn't flicker. The space went from bright to black in an instant.

Lori's heart plunged into her stomach and she gasped. The darkness was so complete in the windowless locker room, tucked into an interior of the building, Lori became instantly disoriented.

She reached into the black, flailing, whimpering. It was as if she'd woken in the night in an unfamiliar place, except it was much worse than that.

Something was in the room with her. She heard it beneath the sounds of her own ragged breath. A chewing, a crunching as if someone sat in the space by the lockers, chomping and slurping.

A little moan escaped her, and the chewing stopped. It was listening for her now. It had heard the sound she made.

Lori backed up, sliding her feet along the tile floor. She pulled her arms in close for fear sharp teeth would suddenly clamp down on her fingers.

Something shuffled in the darkness, coming closer, its own breath a steady huff.

In her terror, Lori couldn't even imagine what it was, what creature had found its way into the locker room and now pursued her in the darkness.

She continued backpedaling and then the cold tile wall met her back and she could retreat no further. She could smell it—like rotted meat and damp earth.

It was closing in.

Lori started to scream.

10

The lights flared on, bright fluorescents washing the gray-tiled room in technicolor.

Lori's scream echoed off the shiny floors and walls, reverberating into the locker room where a woman swooped into her line of sight.

Lori cut off her scream, blinking at the stunned woman, who wore white pants and a pale blue shirt, the uniform for the Synergy office's cleaning crew. She held a mop in one hand.

"Holy Moses, girl! Are you all right?" she asked.

Lori stared, teeth clenched so tight she wasn't sure she could unhinge her jaw and speak.

The woman took a tentative step toward her. "Need me to call somebody? Security?" The woman unlatched a radio hanging on the belt at her waist. The radio crackled, but before the woman could speak into it, Lori shook her head.

"No. It's okay. I'm okay. The lights went off—"

"The lights went off on their own?" The lady frowned, glancing up at the overhead lights.

Lori nodded. "Did... did you see anything when you came in? Like an animal?"

The woman offered a half smile, as if she thought Lori were joking. "I sure hope not. I doubt Synergy would be paying for our cleaning services if we were letting varmints run loose in here."

"A person then? Someone walking out when you came in?"

The woman shook her head. "Not a soul around here except you. I've two other girls, but they're working on different floors. There's still a few people working late, but they're in the main building."

Lori held her towel tight against her, grateful it had not fallen to the floor during the terrifying blackout. "Thank you. I think I'll get dressed now."

"I'll leave you alone for that," the woman said, but Lori shook her head vehemently.

"No, please. You can mop. That's okay."

The woman looked like she might protest, and then she just nodded. "Sure thing."

~

Lori didn't walk through the dim tunnel that connected the building to the parking garage. She sprinted and hit the unlock button the moment her car came into view. She wrenched open the driver's door and jumped in, yanked the door closed.

She sat, catching her breath and staring through the windshield at the shadowy car park.

From her bag, her cell phone rang, and Lori reached for it, her hand shaking.

"Hello?" She heard the tremor in her voice.

"Hey, this Ben Shaw. Everything okay?"

Lori took in a breath and switched the phone to speaker so she could pull out of the garage. "Yeah. I just got in my car, so I was a little breathless."

"Okay. I did some digging yesterday into Summer's case and Beverly's. I found some other girls too."

"Other girls?"

"Yeah. Other girls who went missing in the Manistee National Forest. Maybe it's nothing, but then again, like you said, maybe it's the missing link. If you still want to get together and compare notes, I'm up for that."

Lori maneuvered her car out of the dark garage and onto the street, grateful for the sunlight beaming down. "Yes. I would like to."

"I'm off tomorrow," Ben told her.

"Great. I work until four and then I could meet you. It'll take me about an hour to get there. I live in Mount Pleasant."

"Gotcha. I can meet you if you'd rather."

"No, that's okay. I'll come to you."

"There's a great little café here—the Mulberry Café."

"I've driven by it before. I'll meet you there at five."

"See you then."

When Lori got home, she poured a glass of wine and tried to rationalize what had happened in the gym. It had been her own imagination combined with some electrical failure. But that didn't explain the scratching.

"I was afraid, simple as that," she muttered, opening her laptop and logging into Facebook.

She hadn't logged into her account in weeks. Stu had talked her into getting on social media when they'd both worked at the restaurant, but Lori had never enjoyed the space. It felt voyeuristic, scrolling through the intimate lives of people she hadn't seen in years or, even more strange, people she'd never met who sent her friend requests because they were from her home town or because they knew Stu.

The little icon in the top right listed forty-seven notifications. She didn't click it, but instead went to the search bar and typed 'Ben Shaw.'

Dozens of profiles appeared and none of them looked like the man she'd met. She went back to the search bar and typed 'Carmen Shaw.' Again, multiple options returned, but one was listed with an address in Michigan. Lori clicked it.

The profile picture revealed a woman around her own age with short frizzy brown hair. She held a baby in her arms and next to her stood a man not much taller than her, holding a toddler. Neither child looked at the camera. The little family was all dressed in white and navy blue. It was the kind of picture that had been popular in her own childhood.

Parents and children in matching outfits all piled into the minivan to drive to the Sears Portrait Studio and stand in front of a backdrop of a mountain range or a field of flowers. The photos never turned out the way the mothers hoped. The kids often fought; the husbands looked annoyed. Carmen had managed to get a picture of her and her husband smiling, but no such luck with the kids.

Lori clicked through Carmen's pictures, which mostly included snapshots of her kids. She found one of Ben. He was lying in the grass and the toddler, a little boy, lay balanced on Ben's feet which he'd stuck in the air. He held the boy's hands in his own, both wearing matching grins as the toddler Supermanned above him.

Lori returned to Carmen's profile but didn't see any mention of Summer Newton in the posts. Not that she expected to. She'd never posted anything about Beverly. No one who knew her in her current life even knew that Bev had ever existed, including Stu. Even after four years of dating, she'd never told him the story of the one event that had probably most impacted her life.

Back at the web browser search bar, she typed in 'Dr. Chadwick, Traverse City, Michigan.' She selected the first result, which pulled up a picture of a vaguely familiar man sitting at a large black desk. He had a long thin face and inquisitive blue eyes. His bald head shone in the light pouring through the wide window behind him. Just beyond his slender hands, which rested on the desk, stood a little gold plaque: 'Dr. Arnold Chadwick, Ph.D., Jungian Analyst.'

Services listed on his site included 'Jungian Analysis' and 'Psychotherapy.'

Lori clicked on the 'Contact Us' button and filled out the form including her name, email address and phone number. She added a short note.

'Dr. Chadwick. My name is Lori Hicks. I met with you many years ago regarding nightmares. I hoped we could schedule a session to talk about those things. Please contact me at your earliest convenience.'

~

It was a slow night for Ben in the ER.

After changing I.V. fluids for a patient who'd arrived hours before complaining of abdominal pain, but was now in a deep sleep, Ben slipped into the hall and allowed the door to whoosh slowly closed behind him. At the opposite end of the floor, a young woman was walking away from him. He stared at her, two things striking him funny. One, it wasn't visiting hours, far from it, and this looked like a teenage girl in regular clothes. Two, she looked familiar.

Thick, wheat-blonde hair fell to the center of the girl's back. She wore red and white striped shorts and white sneakers. As she moved further away, turning a corner in the hall, he realized where he recognized the girl from. She looked like Summer Newton. She even wore the same type of clothing Summer had been wearing the night she disappeared in 1993.

Ben followed her, walking quickly to the end of the hall and glimpsing her as she rounded another corner. He sped up, hitting a slow jog, his tennis shoes slapping. As he came around the next corner, he saw her profile as she turned into a visitors' room.

She'd walked into the waiting room they called the Dead Room, coined such because they'd noticed an abnormally large number of patients who coded had visitors in that room. It had become an ongoing joke on the ward that people were drawn to one of the two waiting rooms.

The Kitten Room, labeled thus due to framed photos of kittens playing in a field of flowers, was on the south side of the building and it had a lighter, brighter air. The Dead Room did not. It was darker, the lights often burning out, the coffee always burned. And when someone died in the ER, the nurse or doctor was nearly always directed to the family or friends in this room.

Ben didn't believe the attraction part. More than a few of his colleagues were convinced the room harbored the spirits of the dead. He thought people who were facing the likely death of someone they loved simply chose that room because it was further back, more secluded for their grief.

He stepped into the doorway and scanned the dim room, eyes bouncing over empty chairs and tables scattered with magazines. The single television was off. No visitors sat in the room, none at all, including the girl he'd seen walk in only seconds before.

He walked all the way in, winding through the chairs to the bathroom that sat opposite the coffee counter where someone had spilled coffee grounds and not bothered to swipe them into the little white trash can beside the counter. The door to the bathroom stood open, the light off. It appeared empty, and yet she couldn't have gone anywhere else. Ben knocked on the wall beside the door.

"Hello? Anyone in there?"

No one spoke. He reached through the doorway and flicked on the light. The room illuminated, revealing the white porcelain toilet and sink and the eggshell-colored tile.

He turned the light off and returned to the room, as empty as it had been moments before. On one table tucked into an alcove of the room that he thought of as the crying corner lay a single book.

Ben read the title in dripping red letters: *Strange Michigan: Spine-Tingling Stories from the Mitten State.*

The image beneath the words depicted a man-sized dog, a werewolf maybe, with its mouth stretched in a howl.

Ben picked the book up. He hadn't read a book in ages, but if the evening dragged, it might offer a way to pass the time.

11

Ben woke up around noon, earlier than he liked after working the night shift, but he'd still gotten a solid five hours of sleep and felt refreshed. He'd already decided the night before how he would spend part of his day off.

He drank coffee, ate two pieces of toast, climbed into his car and drove west toward Luther, Michigan.

Ben let off the gas pedal and turned onto Hector Dunn's road. He eyed the house, set far back off the scruffy front yard with its brown grass and scattering of broken-down cars, tires nearly swallowed by weeds, and an old rusted swing set that had been giving Ben the creeps long before Hector Dunn existed as a figure in his mind.

He hadn't driven by the house in years. A pit of fury formed in his stomach as he stared at the dark windows and remembered the man's face when he'd walked out nearly two decades before. He'd looked straight at Ben and smiled. Ben had wanted to kill him. He felt sure this was the man who'd stolen Summer. This sick perv who'd been arrested for trying to abduct another young girl one year after Summer vanished.

But he'd gotten off on a technicality and the police had never so much as searched his rusted Dodge van. As Ben scanned the property, overgrown, mostly buried in a tangle of brush, he spotted the remnants of the Dodge van.

The vehicle now occupying the driveway was, unsurprisingly,

another van, this one as rusted as the Dodge had been back in the day. It was a silver minivan and the rear window was exceptionally dark, as if Dunn had hung something to hide the interior.

Ben coasted his car by and then pulled off the road, killed his engine, and reached for a pair of binoculars he'd tucked into the glove box. He twisted around in his seat and put the binoculars to his eyes. Nothing moved in the dark windows of the house.

In the 1990s, Dunn had lived with his mother, but even then the woman had looked like she had one foot in the grave, rake-thin and perpetually smoking menthol cigarettes. She'd had shrewd dark eyes and lips so thin they receded into the hole of her mouth.

It had been Dunn's mother who'd gotten him off in court. Despite their home, the woman had a nest egg of money and potentially a few connections that allowed her to call in favors when her only child faced a charge of attempting to abduct a minor.

Ben wondered if Cora Dunn still lived.

As he watched, something flickered in a window. Ben focused the binoculars on the side window and realized the curtain which had been fully covering the glass a moment before had a dark slit in the center, as if someone had peeled it back to look out.

At me, Ben thought, glaring through the eyepieces and wishing Dunn could see his face, wishing the man could feel his fury.

"That's right, motherfucker. I'm watching you," Ben muttered.

He lowered the binoculars, intending to step out and stand in the middle of the country road, binoculars to his eyes. He wanted Dunn to know he was being watched, that he needed to look over his shoulder. Before Ben could open his door, his cell phone rang and he saw Carmen's name on the screen.

Frowning and considering ignoring it, he lifted the binoculars back to his eyes and trained them on the window. He could no longer see the dark crevice in the fabric.

"Hey," Ben said, answering the call.

"Hey, Ben, how's it going?"

"Good, what's up?"

"Oh, not much. It's just that Jonas is having a hard time getting clipped into the bike." Carmen laughed. "He's fallen twice now and scraped up his shoulder and elbow pretty bad. I wondered—"

Ben sighed. "I'll come over today. I've got a thing this evening, but I'm off right now."

"Oh, perfect. Thank you, thank you. I do really appreciate your getting him into cycling. He loves to ride once he can get his legs moving without falling." She laughed again.

Ben heard an engine rumble to life. He turned and saw Dunn's minivan backing down the driveway in a cloud of dust. Moments later the van sped by, but Ben couldn't get a glimpse of the man behind the wheel, as the passenger window was so grimy it concealed the driver.

"See you in a couple hours," he told Carmen and ended the call.

He turned his car back on and made a u-turn, cruising slowly back by Dunn's house. It was probably empty. The only vehicle in the driveway was gone with Dunn most likely driving. Ben braked near the driveway and then caught the shape of a vehicle looming in his rearview mirror. It was still too far off to identify, but his gut told him it was Dunn coming home. He'd driven off only to get a glimpse of who was lurking around his house.

"What are you hiding?" Ben whispered, tempted to pull in anyway, to confront Dunn now as a man and let the chips fall where they might.

Instead, he slammed his foot on the gas pedal and pushed it to the floor, roaring away from the derelict little house that Hector Dunn called home.

L ori parked on the street in front of the Mulberry Café.

The restaurant stood on the edge of downtown Clare, where the business district gave way to residential streets. The café occupied a maroon antique Victorian house, likely built at the turn of the twentieth century. The owners had updated it with a wide, wheelchair-friendly wood ramp and sprawling back porch for outdoor seating. Flowers burst from enormous bushes lining the stairs leading up to the front door.

Though Lori had lived in Clare at her grandmother's house after her family had moved from Baldwin, she'd never visited the café. She found Ben on the back porch, seated at a round table beneath a large red umbrella. He waved when she arrived.

Lori took the chair opposite Ben. He'd already ordered a coffee.

"This place is neat," she told him. "I've never been here."

"I come here at least once a week. Amazing coffee, quiche, the works. But you said you don't live in Clare?"

She shook her head. "Mount Pleasant. But I went to high school here."

"How'd you end up in Mount Pleasant?"

"I went to school there, Central Michigan University, and then after I graduated, I got a job, so..." She shrugged.

"What did you study at CMU?"

"Folklore and mythology."

Ben grinned as if she were joking, and then his smile disappeared. "Really? That's a degree?"

Lori blushed. "I think my mother uttered those exact words."

Ben chuckled and held up his hands. "Sorry. I didn't mean to offend. I've just never heard of anyone majoring in that. What do you do? Write fables?"

"I work in human resources for a marketing agency."

"That's quite a leap from folklore and mythology. And you like it?"

"I don't not like it."

"What a lackluster response for your life's passion." He smiled and twittered his fingers.

Lori turned to see a woman walking a little girl down the sidewalk, who waved at Ben.

"Do you know her?"

He shook his head. "Nope." He squinted. "I hope not, anyway. If I do, I'd have likely encountered her in the ER."

"And that's your life's passion? Being a nurse?"

"Yeah. I can't imagine doing anything I'd love more. Not to mention the cafeteria has the best chocolate cake on Planet Earth."

Lori brushed a hand across her stomach and tugged at her shirt, wishing she'd run home and changed. She still wore a pale pink blouse made of a synthetic silk material and she'd begun to sweat. She could see the dark streaks where her perspiration touched the fabric. "I wish I loved my job. It's fine, but…"

"But it doesn't light your soul on fire?"

She laughed dryly. "Decidedly no. So you found other girls?" Lori started, but stopped as the server walked from the café.

"Hi there," she said cheerily, coiffed blonde hair bobbing as she nodded. "Have you been to the Mulberry Café before?"

"No. This is my first time."

"Well, you're in good company with this guy." She nodded at Ben, who smiled back at her.

"Thanks, Deb."

"We have the cinnamon latté on special and for entrées the Reuben sandwich, which is divine. We also have a new salad with feta and chicken."

"I'll take a black coffee," Lori told her.

The woman's pencil-thin eyebrows shot to her stiff hairline. "That's all?" She turned her attention to Ben. "Well, I know you won't disappoint me."

He grinned. "Not a chance. I'll take the quiche and side Caesar salad. Once she sees my food, she'll have to order her own."

Deb walked back into the café.

"Not hungry?" Ben asked.

"I had a late lunch." Lori had in fact skipped lunch and scarfed down a bag of peanuts on her drive to Clare. Her day at the office had turned hectic when a new hire had accused her manager of sexual harassment. Lori's day had been spent sifting through correspondence and meeting repeatedly with the two parties in a boardroom. In the end, they had put the manager on administrative leave.

"If nothing else, consider a piece of pie. It's all homemade right here. I've got a soft spot for the rhubarb, but Deb favors the lemon pecan."

Lori loved pie, but she didn't eat it. "Maybe," she said. "So... tell me what you found."

She was tired, her head a little full-feeling, and a tickle hovered in the back of her throat she feared might morph into a cold. The night before at the gym had ensured a night of tossing and turning, followed by a stressful work day. As much as she wanted to talk to Ben, when she'd left work, she'd also just wanted to drive home and crawl into bed.

Deb returned with her coffee balanced on a little plate piped in red calligraphy.

"Thank you," Lori told her, lifting the cup to her mouth and taking a long drink despite the hot liquid.

"Tired?"

"Yeah. Is it that obvious?"

"You just looked at the cup of coffee like it was a thousand-dollar bill."

"I didn't sleep well last night."

"Because of all this? Bev and Summer?"

"Partially, yeah."

Ben picked up his phone and clicked. "I have a notes app in here that I stored links and names on. Here's what I found yesterday.

"Summer disappeared from Manistee in 1993. Five years later and forty-five miles to the southwest, still part of the Manistee National Forest, your friend Beverly disappeared. Then, in 2003, Bella Palmer went missing in Reed City, which is less than twenty miles east of Baldwin, still in the Manistee National Forest. And finally, in 2008, Peyton Weller disappeared from Scottville, just over forty miles to the west, still in the Manistee National Forest."

"Four girls. Did they all disappear in the woods?"

"Not only did they all disappear in the woods, they were all walking or hiking with one of their girlfriends. They vanished without a trace."

"Holy crap."

"Yeah."

"1993, 1998, 2003 and 2008. That's five years apart for every one of them," she murmured.

"Yep."

Lori leaned back in her chair and stared up into the red umbrella, overwhelmed by the possibility of what Ben had discovered.

"You think one person took all four girls?" she asked. "And he... what, did it on a schedule? Every five years?"

"Possibly. But I don't want to narrow the focus too much. The schedule could mean a lot of things. Waiting five years so the heat cools off. Waiting five years because that's when he comes into town. Waiting five years because whatever sick hunger he has is satiated for that amount of time. Maybe he doesn't even know he's done it every five years."

"Maybe it's not one person."

"True, but there's a lot supporting it being one person. What are the chances there are two people abducting teenage girls in a sixty-mile radius?"

"I don't know."

"Did you ever have any suspects?" Ben asked.

Lori sipped her coffee and shook her head. "No. I... I never even got that far in my thinking. It was just such a big, scary mystery. I didn't think about who so much as what. I remember that night thinking about the Dogman."

Ben cocked an eyebrow. "Seriously? The Dogman?"

"I was fourteen."

"I didn't mean it like that. Well, I did, but not entirely. It's just a bizarre coincidence. I found a book in a waiting room at the hospital, and guess who was on the cover? The Dogman."

Lori's eyes widened. "I'd like to see it."

"It's in my car. I'll show it to you when we leave. I didn't straight away think about people either. I was sure Summer had snuck off to play a trick on Carm, and then she got lost and injured. But after the searches, that got harder and harder to believe."

"Yeah, that was my first thought too, that Bev was hiding and going to jump out and scare me. But then… she never did."

"Who was there that night?" Ben asked. "In the neighborhood, in the search—that kind of thing." Ben took a yellow legal pad from a backpack sitting beneath his chair. He pulled the top off the pen and poised it over the paper.

Lori looked at the paper and then at Ben. "Like everyone? I doubt I could even remember most of their names."

"Well, rattle off anyone you can remember. Just men."

"Why just men?"

"Because in situations like these it's usually men."

12

Lori's face fell. "Oh, okay. Umm... well, the first man who was there that night was Mark Melton. He was our next-door neighbor, and he came to look right away."

"How did he know she was missing?"

"My mom called Charlotte, his wife, to come over and watch my little brother while we went back to the woods. Mark had some kind of survivalist training or something so he joined us."

"And how long was that after she'd disappeared?"

"Less than an hour."

"Okay, that makes it unlikely to be him. After all, he wouldn't have had much time to conceal her or her body. Who else?"

Lori closed her eyes and tried to remember. The moments after Mark had joined them in the woods blurred. "After Mark came, we walked back to the house. My mom thought Bev might have made her way back by then, but she wasn't there. My mom called Bev's parents and then the police. They didn't let me go back to the woods. Within an hour police had a search group out, and Mark had gotten a bunch of the neighborhood guys to join. Some of the women too, but a lot of them had small children at home."

"What about your dad? Did he help search?"

Lori's face pinched, and she opened her eyes. "No. He didn't come home until after midnight. Things had been... strained between my parents. That might have been the night that put the final nail in the coffin for them."

"They split up?"

Lori nodded.

"Where was your dad?"

"Working, he said, and honestly I've never gotten the full story. I think he was having an affair."

Ben looked at her curiously for another moment and then nodded. "What's his name?"

"Brian Hicks. He moved to Florida though."

Ben wrote down his name. Lori's eyes lingered on the name for another moment.

"Anyone who was noticeably absent? Like someone in the neighborhood you'd expect to be searching who never showed up?"

"No. Not that I'm aware of, but since I didn't get to go back out, I don't really know who showed up that night."

The door to the café opened, and Deb walked out with a tray. "Dinner is served," she announced, sliding a plate with a hunk of quiche in front of Ben, who hastily moved his notebook aside. She added the salad beside it.

"Did you decide on anything?" She looked at Lori.

"No, thanks. Just a refill of coffee, please."

"Make that two," Ben said, tapping his mostly empty mug.

"In a jiff." Deb walked back into the café and returned a moment later with a pot of coffee. "Fresh-brewed," she announced.

Ben took a few bites of his quiche and then returned to his notebook. "How about whispers in the neighborhood? Did anyone have suspicions?"

"Not about people. The whispers mostly landed on a couple of swamp spots out there. People seemed to think she'd probably gotten lost, twisted an ankle or something and ended up succumbing to the elements."

"Yeah. That's how we leaned too, but..." He shook his head. "Four girls didn't disappear without a trace after spraining an ankle in the woods."

"Have you ever considered something supernatural?" Lori asked.

"Like the Dogman?" Ben grinned.

"Maybe, or, like... Bigfoot."

Ben took a bite of salad, chewed, and swallowed. "No. I can say with complete honesty the Dogman and Bigfoot never crossed my mind as potential culprits."

"Okay, but did anything not of this world ever cross your mind?"

"No, and based on what you just said, that's why. 'Not of this world.' If it's not of this world, it doesn't exist. If it doesn't exist, it couldn't have kidnapped a girl in the woods."

Lori sighed. "This place doesn't serve any wine, do they? I could use a drink."

"Nope, they're dry as bone."

"How about you? Want to grab a drink after this?"

"I'm also as dry as a bone," he said. "Not in personality, I hope. But in the alcohol department."

"You don't drink?"

He shook his head.

"Is it you don't drink because you had a problem with it or just don't enjoy it?" She realized it was a very personal question after she asked it and almost took it back, but Ben didn't look affronted.

"I don't drink because my dad had a problem with it. Nothing crazy until after Summer went missing and then our entire family became pariahs in Manistee. My dad owned a hardware store in town. People stopped shopping there. It was like they'd held a town hall meeting and vetoed our family because Summer disappeared."

"That's ridiculous."

"Yeah, it is. Summer had an uncle, J.B. Newton. He had a lot of pull in town and he pointed to me right away. I'd gotten into a scuffle with his kid the year before because the little punk trashed my bike after I made out with his girlfriend at a football game. J.B. hung a target on my back, started telling everyone in town that all the signs were there that I'd been a ticking time bomb." Ben set his jaw. "So that's my roundabout way of explaining why I don't drink. My dad started coming home with cases of beer, then he started just drinking them right there in the hardware store, sometimes stumbling out into the middle of the street, inebriated and cussing out the town."

"Her disappearing wreaked havoc on your family."

"Destroyed it. My dad's business closed. My parents got divorced about a year and a half after she vanished. I wanted to move. I begged my mom, but... she was a single mom after my dad left. He's sober now, but he went off the rails for a few years. Now he lives downstate. I see him a couple times a year."

"Is your mom still in Manistee?"

"Hell, no. She got out when Carm and I left for college. She just couldn't afford to get a house with three bedrooms. That was part of why we stayed. After we left, she found an apartment on the east side of the state—Alpena area, it's close to her sisters—and she moved there. This year she got remarried. She lives with Greg now in a little ranch on a golf course. She's doing a lot better."

"How about Carmen?"

Ben scratched his jaw. "Carmen lives in deep denial. She stopped talking about Summer, stopped acknowledging it ever happened."

"I did that too," Lori murmured.

"You did?"

Lori nodded. "Kids at school whispered about me. They said I was jealous of Bev and murdered her and threw her in the pond. It didn't matter that they had dragged the pond." She shook her head bitterly. "You never imagine something like that will happen to you, this crazy, horrible thing, and then somehow the aftermath is even worse. Your life implodes."

"Yep. In the years after, I wondered, what if I'd gone to wrestling practice that night like I'd planned? Would everything have been different? If it had only been Carmen home that night and she'd just run home and called Summer's parents instead of me going out there and looking? Maybe people never would have blamed me and thus my family."

"The evening Bev disappeared she almost didn't come to my house. It was the last week of school and her parents had sent her a note that she could ride the bus home with me. She got a poor grade on her science test and said she'd better just go home—her parents would be mad if she came to my house instead. I talked her into it. 'It's our last week of school, come on, either way you're in trouble, let's have fun before they find out.' If I hadn't talked her into it, she never would have been in the woods that night."

"That's a losing game, the what-ifs. I've played it enough to know. But anyway, just because I don't drink doesn't mean I won't join you."

Lori sighed, pushing her fingers into the hollows by her eyes. "No. I'd better take that back. I have to drive home and work tomorrow. I'm tired and all of this"—she nodded at the notebook—"is taking every bit of brain power I have left to concentrate on. What about you? Was there anyone you suspected?"

"Hector Dunn," Ben told her, picking up his phone. He clicked several things and then handed it to her.

An image of a grizzled man, looking down and left rather than straight at the camera, populated on the screen. Beneath the image was a headline that read, 'Local man arrested for attempted abduction of teen.'

He was bald and his ears were large, protruding from the sides of his head. One of his eyebrows had a line through the center as if he'd had an injury that prevented a strip of hair from growing back. His nose was beak-like, his lips thin and chapped.

"This is his mugshot from 1994. A year after Summer vanished, he tried to kidnap a girl."

"Police arrested him?"

"Yep, he drove up behind a twelve-year-old girl who was riding her bicycle. He tried to force her into the woods. A farm truck carrying a trailer of heifers came along and the girl bolted. The farmer said later he almost hit her, but slammed on the brakes. She jumped into the passenger side of the truck, crawling right up on his wife's lap. They drove her straight to the police. Hector took off, but not before the wife wrote down his license plate number. Cops picked him up that evening at his house and booked him."

"Did he go to prison?"

Ben glowered. "Nope. Hector coughed up some alibi that his mother corroborated. Mind you, she pulled the same stunt back in 1988, I found out later, after someone had accused him of peeping in their daughter's window. 'Oh, no, not my Hector,' his mother said, 'he was right here with me all night.' Lying straight to investigators' faces when they had not only the girl he tried to abduct, but the farmer and his wife who saw Dunn plain as day and wrote down his license plate number. But then the girl got cold feet and didn't want to testify. Dunn got off scot-free."

"That's insane."

"Yep. Our good ole justice system."

"How did you get focused on him for Summer?"

"Luck really. A few people in our neighborhood mentioned seeing a van in the area the day Summer disappeared, a van that looked an awful lot like Dunn's van. I saw his face in the paper that next summer and when I read what he'd done and then the description of his van, I put two and two together."

"Did you tell the police?"

"Yeah, and supposedly they looked into him, but couldn't make a case."

"But you think he did it?"

"Yeah. I do."

Deb returned with their checks.

"I've got this," Ben told Lori, handing Deb his credit card.

"Thanks," Lori said, covering her mouth as a yawn erupted. "What now?" she asked. "I mean, not right now. Right now, I've got to go home and go to bed, but what do we do next with all of this?"

Ben crumpled his napkin and dropped it on his empty plate. "We dig."

"So you want to keep looking into this?"

Ben looked away, his expression troubled, but when he looked back at Lori, he appeared determined. "Yeah. The police will never solve these cases. If we tried to make the link between the four girls, we'd probably get laughed out of town. But if we could find a viable suspect... who knows? Maybe we could put it to rest—the mystery and maybe even Summer."

"And Bev."

"Exactly."

Ben spent the evening hunting online for more information about the missing girls. When he fell into bed after eleven, his brain was a haze of disturbing facts and a collage of photographs of pretty young girls who'd walked into the forest and never reemerged. When he finally drifted off, a vision of Summer danced behind his eyes.

B*en stood in front of the ramshackle cabin, every detail stark and pulsing. He'd never noticed the mushrooms, white and bulbous, growing from the front right corner of the shack.*

He'd walked inside a thousand times after Summer vanished, searched on hands and knees for some scrap of her left behind, some clue that pointed to where she'd gone, but he'd never found so much as a hair. Now, as he gazed at the formidable little structure, a terrible dread laced his blood and traveled to his heart, thumping faster with each passing second.

Though he did not want to go in, his legs carried him through the doorless entryway. He smelled the mildewy interior.

He turned around the single wall that separated the two halves of the cabin, and as he did, he spotted a figure standing in the far back corner, facing the wall as if looking out a window, except no window stood there. As he stepped closer, he saw Summer's long blonde hair above those red and white striped shorts. Tan legs disappeared into white tennis shoes. His mouth fell open and his heart leapt with joy, but still something in him felt disturbed at the sight of her.

She turned haltingly, oddly, and Ben's eyes went wide.

Her face was a pocked pool of withered gray flesh. Worms squirmed from a gaping hole in her right cheek and he could see bits of her teeth clinging to her black gums. Her eyes were two balls of yellow jelly. Her arms hung slack at her sides and he saw much of her flesh had fallen away from the wrists. Her hands were brown and bent like the branches of a tree. Though she didn't look at him, more down and off to the side, he sensed her growing awareness of him.

He tried to shriek, to leap away, to turn and run, but he could not move, could not make a sound, and suddenly she darted like a shadow and closed the gap between them.

∽

Ben's eyes popped open, a whine groaned out of him and his heart heaved against his breastbone.

"Holy fuck," he whispered into the darkness, the image of Summer not trailing away as dreams do, but glaring in his mind's eye as if it had been burned there.

He shuddered and blinked into a darkness so black it instantly troubled him. He gazed into nothingness, unable to discern anything but that which he could feel beneath him—the softness of his sheets and the prickly sensation of gooseflesh running up his legs and arms.

Gradually he understood why the darkness so disturbed him. The light that always trickled in beneath his bedroom door was no longer. This light came not from a single source but from two—the dim bathroom light that he left on and the small halo of light that poured in from the fixture by the front door.

Even the shuttering red light of his fire alarm was invisible in the darkness. His mind scrambled to explain it. A power outage did not explain the battery-operated fire alarm failing.

He stood and groped blindly through the room, hitting his shin on the hard edge of the chair that usually sat tucked into the corner, at times piled with clean laundry waiting to be put away. He cursed and reached into the darkness, searching for the wall that should be behind the chair, but there was no wall, only empty air, and he understood that he'd hit the chair not because he'd lost his bearings, but because it had been relocated from the corner of the room to the empty space between his bed and dresser.

As Ben groped in the darkness, the entire house came to life, lights blazed into the room and sounds boomed.

He smacked into his dresser, the corner poking meanly into his chest, and stumbled back, shielding his eyes as the sounds of television and music and a beeping alarm blared throughout the house.

The room washed in blinding yellow light. The television turned on a loud movie and an actor screamed as if the volume had been cranked to its maximum. The speakers strained under the sound.

Ben heard the radio that sat on the kitchen counter, loud, deafening, and playing a familiar and haunting song—the Police singing *Every Breath You Take*. He might have heard it in the intervening years, but now it transported him back two decades to the first time he and Summer had kissed, and she'd whispered, 'Now this is our song.'

As he tripped downstairs, the lyrics thundered through his house.
Since you've gone I've been lost without a trace
I dream at night I can only see your face

Ben rushed into the kitchen, turning off the radio first, extinguishing lights as he went, coming more fully awake as adrenaline pumped through his limbs. He lurched into the living room where the flat screen blared the eleven o'clock news. Except it wasn't local Clare news, it was news from Manistee.

A reporter stood in front of the derelict cabin in the Manistee National Forest.

"This is the cabin where Summer Newton vanished twenty years ago this past Friday."

The image shifted and a photograph of Summer filled the screen.

She stood on a cobblestone bridge, blowing rainbow-tinted bubbles through a pink stick. Her blonde hair hung over her shoulders in twin braids.

Ben stared at the photograph, walking backwards and sagging onto the couch. He'd never seen the picture before, a photo likely given to the reporter by Summer's mom or sister. Fingers trembling, he picked up the remote and turned off the television.

13

Before Lori left the office, she stopped in to see Naomi, who sat flipping through a wedding magazine. Glossy images of brides in princess-style gowns filled the pages.

Naomi looked up and smiled. "Uh-oh, you caught me." She closed the magazine and set it aside. "You done for the day?"

"Yeah. I'm going to drop by Stu's and see if he wants to go out to dinner. I still need to make amends for bailing on him when we went camping."

"Hardly," Naomi said. "He should be making amends for dragging you into the woods to begin with."

"I need to use some vacation time," Lori said, fidgeting in the doorway. It wasn't a big deal. The company was fully staffed and they had two other HR assistants, but Lori still felt guilty anytime she requested time off.

"Sure, okay." Naomi flipped open her calendar. "What days do you need?"

"The rest of this week and next week too."

Naomi's eyebrows went up. "Starting tomorrow?"

"Yes."

"Okay." Naomi pursed her lips, writing in her calendar. "Is there anything going on? You're not sick or—"

"No. I just... I need some time off."

"Gotcha. Say no more." Naomi closed the planner. "You're off the rest of the week and next week too. Hey"—Naomi waggled her finger from side to side—"next week is your thirtieth birthday, isn't it? Are you planning to run away with Stu and elope?"

Lori swallowed the lump in her throat and shook her head. "Nothing that exciting. But who knows, maybe a little vacation. I haven't thought that far yet."

"Well, whatever you do, ring it in with style."

"Thanks, Naomi. I'll send you an email next week."

"Okay, girl. Be good."

Lori stopped at a convenience store and bought a six-pack of Stu's favorite beer and headed for his house. She'd only spoken to him briefly in the days since the camping trip, and she'd noted his hurt tone the evening before when she said she had an appointment and couldn't meet him for dinner.

Lori used her key to unlock Stu's door. She'd knocked, but he hadn't answered and his car sat in the driveway. He was likely taking a nap after a long day at the restaurant.

As she moved through the house, an unfamiliar sound met her ears, a steady clack-clack-clack. It reminded her of the washing machine when it had too many clothes in it, rocking unevenly against the wood floor, but the accompanying washing machine sounds weren't there. Lori was halfway to Stu's bedroom, where the sound seemed to arise, when she heard a woman's voice. She knew the voice: Nicki. The server who'd been flirting unashamedly with Stu for years.

"Yes… yes."

"I'm almost there…" Stu groaned.

Lori froze, her organs plunging lower in her abdomen.

"Stu… you're so hot. Don't stop…" Nicki shouted.

Lori slumped against the wall, listening to their voices growing louder, merging into moans, coupled with the frenzied clacking, which she now knew to be the brass bed-frame smacking the drywall.

The intensity of their cries gave way to murmurs and the lulling whispers that came after the climax.

Nauseated, Lori forced her feet to move, aware that at any moment the bedroom door would swing open and she'd have a visual to go with the story already playing across her mind.

As she breezed through Stu's foyer, she noticed the keys she'd missed earlier—the hot pink stiletto key chain hanging from the little keyring. She snatched the keys and slipped out the door. On her way to her own car, Lori stopped and dropped them through the grate into the sewer. She barely thought of what she was doing. Her mind had become a tornado of images and sounds coupled with the physical sensations: rolling stomach, dry mouth, shaking hands. She jammed her key in the ignition, started her car, and slammed the gas pedal to the floor. The car lurched forward as the engine shrieked at her mistreatment.

Her mind blanked and, rather than driving home, she maneuvered her Prius onto the highway and drove north. When she arrived in Clare, she bypassed her mother's house and drove to the hospital. Numb, she walked inside, taking the elevator to the basement cafeteria. She put a hunk of chocolate cake on her tray and chose a dim booth in the back corner.

～

"Hey." Ben's voice broke her thoughts, and she looked up to find him in turquoise scrubs, looking at her curiously. "What are you doing here?"

Lori looked from him down to her plate. All that remained of her chocolate cake was a smear of dark frosting. "You said the chocolate cake was the best on Planet Earth."

"So you drove all the way here to try it? That's determination."

"Well, I walked in on my boyfriend of four years screwing his co-worker today, so it seemed like a good time to do it."

Ben's eyes widened, and an expression of pain flitted across his face. "I'm sorry. Do you want some company?"

"Sure." She sighed, leaning her head back against the seat.

Ben slid into the booth, setting his own tray on the table. He had a saran-wrapped tuna sandwich, a bag of chips and a bottle of water.

"No chocolate cake?" she asked.

He shook his head. "I've got another six hours to go. If I eat chocolate cake now, I'll be asleep in the janitor's closet in twenty minutes." He unwrapped his sandwich, but paused before taking a bite. "Are you okay?"

"I don't know yet. Maybe it hasn't fully hit me."

"Did you confront him?"

"No. I just wanted to get out of there."

"That's fair."

"It's weird. I was just talking about Stu with my mother. She was giving me this lecture about unchanging Stu, implying that I needed to take more risks. Obviously, Stu wasn't as safe and solid as she thought."

"Same isn't necessarily safe. I've met a lot of people who never change—stay in the same town, working the same job, dating the same girl—but on the side they're closet alcoholics or they have a gambling problem or they're at the strip club every Friday night."

"You know a lot of people like that?"

He chuckled. "Well, maybe more like a few, but I know some and the impression I've always had is that they're bored, but scared to do anything differently, so instead they find secret ways to get a high, a rush, which usually destroys everything they were trying to hold on to."

"Is that why you ran away from your home town and old life?" she asked.

"I didn't run away. I escaped."

"I thought I did too, but wherever I go, there I am."

"Somehow Stu banging another chick is your fault? Is that what this chocolate cake pity party is about?"

"He's been flirting with that girl for years. Literal years. I never confronted him, never walked away. He's probably been sleeping with her for years. And I've been the clueless idiot still calling myself his girlfriend."

"He's a prick. But you're not an idiot, Lori. Trusting someone doesn't make you an idiot."

"Well, I sure feel like an idiot."

"I recommend you transfer those feelings to him. He's the jerk here. He intentionally lied and cheated behind your back. People get duped by partners like that all the time. We have our lives. How can we expect to be constantly checking up on the person we're dating? We can't. That's how they get away with it. But now you know and that's a gift because you're not married to him and you don't have kids. You guys don't live together, right?"

Lori shook her head. "We talked about it a few times. He wanted to move in, but I always pushed back. Maybe if I had—"

"What? Then he wouldn't have cheated on you? Not a chance.

Instead, you would have found him with this co-worker in your bed instead of his."

Lori cringed.

"I'm sorry to be harsh, but I'm not going to water it down. You need to be shocked right now, pissed. You need to have the courage to get out of that relationship."

"I've always suspected I wasn't relationship material. Maybe I'm finally getting proof."

"Relationships are tough, even the good ones. You just gotta lick your wounds and then get back up and get out there."

"Have you ever been married?"

"No. I've dated a few women seriously. My last relationship ended"—he scrunched his face as if counting back the months—"six, seven months ago."

"Why did it end?"

"She wanted more. Specifically to move in together. We'd been dating for a year. I wasn't ready, but she's in her mid-thirties and wants to seal the deal. We work together, so that's made for a few awkward encounters."

"She's a nurse?"

"No, a doctor actually. She's an anesthesiologist."

"Wow." Lori felt a little twist in her stomach. Jealousy, inadequacy, something. "Who breaks up with a doctor?"

"I didn't. She broke up with me because I wouldn't move into her house. We weren't destined for the long-term. I always knew that and probably shouldn't have gotten serious with her at all."

"How did you know you weren't?"

"Because I know myself. Taylor was great, but we never stayed up all night talking or spent lazy Sunday afternoons reading in bed. That stuff that usually at least happens in the beginning, you know, when the fireworks are flying and you can sit together in a cardboard box all day and still be having fun. It always felt like we were missing a beat together."

Lori considered Stu. Had they ever had those days? All-night chats, lazy days in bed? Their lazy days in bed usually resulted from Stu having a hangover and holding her hostage beside him, so he didn't feel guilty about sleeping half the day.

"How about you? Anyone before Stu? Other relationships?"

Lori shook her head, slightly ashamed by the admission. "No. I went on dates once in a while, but... it always felt so forced. I hated dating. I hate dating."

"It's not my favorite thing either," Ben said. "How about this. While we're playing detectives, we'll give ourselves a break from the dating scene. We can pretend we're too busy to care."

Lori smiled. "Deal."

14

Lori stayed the night at her mother's house, then returned to her apartment the following morning.

"There you are," Stu announced when she stepped from her car. "I've called you like fifty times. Why haven't you called me back?" Stu stood from the front stoop of Lori's house where he'd been sitting. He had a can of beer in his hand. He glanced at it and grinned. "Kenny, your downstairs neighbor, gave it to me. They're pre-gaming here before going out. We could join them, party on campus like old times."

Lori clutched her keys so tightly they dug into her palm. She loosened her grip and searched for her rehearsed speech. "I... No. I'm not interested in going out with the guys downstairs."

Stu shrugged and opened his arms as if to hug her.

Lori lurched back, caught her heel on a crack in the sidewalk and landed hard on her butt. Her keys flew from her hand and clattered on the pavement.

Stu rushed to her side. "Damn. You okay? Here." He offered his arm, but she shoved it away.

Lori closed her eyes, her tailbone throbbing, and climbed gingerly to her feet. "I saw you," she hissed.

When she opened her eyes, Stu's brow was wrinkled, but he seemed to be clueless about what she accused him of. "You saw me? When?"

Lori swallowed the lump in her throat and glared at him. "Yesterday. You were in bed with Nicki. Does that jog your memory?"

The color drained from his face and then he plastered on an incredulous look. "You're kidding, right? Nicki was most definitely not in my bed. I—"

Lori held up a hand, grinding her teeth and fighting the desire to lunge at him, tackle him into the yard and shove his face into the grass.

He seemed to sense her rage and took a step back, holding up both his hands. "Okay, okay. It happened. One time. I swear just one time, and her boyfriend broke up with her a couple weeks ago and she's been so depressed and I just—"

Lori didn't let him finish. She stalked past him, raking her fingernails across his hand when he tried to reach out and stop her.

He whipped his arm back, saying no more as she stormed onto the porch and to her door. She jammed the key in the lock and nearly snapped it off as she twisted it to the side. Forcing herself to calmly wiggle it, she got it unlocked, yanked open the door, and slammed it as hard as she could.

Lori sat on the bottom step that led to her apartment and stared in numb silence at the floor. She didn't cry or scream or feel ripped in half with his betrayal. She felt hollow.

After a while, she got up and walked out to her car. She drove to the party store she could have easily walked to and bought two boxes of Hostess cupcakes and a bag of pretzels, sensing the clerk's judgment. He knew she was going to binge-eat everything that sat on the counter. Lori avoided his gaze as she paid.

Back in her apartment, she turned on a movie and sat on her floor, unwrapping cupcake after cupcake and shoving them into her mouth, eating until she felt sick, tears streaming down her face as a comedy with Meg Ryan played on the screen.

She ate until she felt so full, she could barely breathe, the emptiness within her now bursting.

Lori had once read that eating disorders were a form of control. That people who suffered them were less obsessed with food than a need to have control in a chaotic world. When she thought of all the ways people evolved around her and she stayed the same, she saw that same grasping for control. If she changed nothing then nothing would change. Same apartment, same job, same boyfriend—same, same, same... Same was safe, comfortable, easy.

Discovering Stu in bed with Nicki had jolted her. The carefully built house of cards had tumbled, revealing that it was an illusion, never a house at all, merely an arrangement of carefully placed bits of cardboard waiting for a breath of air to send them flying.

Lori sat on the floor and folded her arms on the bay window seat, resting her forehead on her stacked hands. Tears slipped over her cheeks. It wasn't Stu she cried for, the loss of some great love. It was the illusion, the loss of that safe space, the sense that Stu wasn't the only house of cards in her life getting ready to fall.

~

Though Lori had never been to the Holy Faith Church in Mount Pleasant, it mirrored a dozen others she'd visited during her time recovering from binge eating disorder.

She opened the heavy wood door. The air was stale and smelled of mildew and overpowering perfume, the kind her dad's mother wore that had made Lori recoil as a child when the woman hugged her. Thick dark carpet that led into a tall square greeting space muted her footsteps. Before her, glass double doors led to the pews, but a cardboard sign posted on a metal stand read "Overeaters Anonymous This Way" with a large red arrow pointing toward a closed door on the left.

Lori sucked in a breath and grabbed the handle, pulling it back. The women, all seated at one of four long tables, turned to look at her. The room was bright, with long fluorescent lights shining off the freshly mopped linoleum floor. Along the back wall stood a kitchenette, but unlike most church events where the counter would be arranged with baked goods from the parishioners, the counter stood empty, gleaming bright white.

"Welcome," a woman said, smiling broadly and standing. "I'm Gale. I host the bi-weekly meetings here at the Holy Cross. Come in and have a seat."

Lori half-smiled shyly, and sat on the hard metal chair. "I'm Lori," she murmured.

"Welcome, Lori," the group chorused.

Lori took a seat and crossed her legs, squeezing her hands between her thighs.

"Amber is sharing her story," Gale explained. "Please, go on, Amber."

The girl glanced self-consciously at Lori and then spoke. "I just can't seem to stop." Her face was long and drawn, her eyes bloodshot, likely from the purging, and her voice rasped when she spoke. "I've been watching that Lifetime movie *When Friendship Kills* about the two best friends who both have eating disorders and then one of them dies. I watch it every day, sometimes twice a day, and I keep trying to make the lessons stick. This is bad for you, this will kill you if you keep it up, but I can't seem to stop eating and throwing up. I want to. I really do." Tears spilled over her cheeks, and a middle-aged woman to her right leaned over and clasped her hand.

"Thank you for sharing that with us, Amber," Gale said. "After everyone has told their story, if they'd like to share this evening, we will move into creating positive change. Bethany, would you like to share?"

The woman Gale had spoken to sighed and removed her glasses, folded them and unfolded them and put them back on her face, thick with powdery foundation.

"I haven't binged in a decade," Bethany told the group. "I celebrated ten years last month." The woman held up her hand where a large blue stone glittered on her finger. "I bought myself this ring as a reward and a reminder. It's my mother's birthstone. The last time I binged was when she died. I was so lost and so heartbroken. I ate for days. I didn't leave my house. I was sick, sick in my heart, and I tried to fill the void of her absence with food, but that just made me sicker. I went to a meeting and made the commitment. It wasn't easy. Every day when I thought of my mother, I wanted to eat. I wanted to use food to numb the pain. But I didn't and now it has been ten years and I know you can do it too, Amber. I know you can."

"Lori, would you like to share?" Gale asked.

Lori bit her cheek and stared at the faded linoleum. "I guess it started for me after… after this one terrible year. I was fourteen and one of my friends disappeared and then my parents got divorced and my dad moved away. I'd always struggled with food. It was my happy place, eating, which meant I struggled with my weight, which sucks when you're fourteen. After that summer it got worse and worse. I'd eat entire boxes of Hostess cupcakes or make a full batch of cookie dough and just sit and eat the batter. Sometimes I'd throw up because I'd eaten so much, I felt sick to my stomach. I put on more and more weight.

"I was seventeen when I attended my first meeting. I had a sponsor named Sam who called me every day for six months to check in. It took a long time to stop. Half a box of cupcakes, then only three in one sitting, then two, then one, then none. I moved away to college, and that helped because I didn't buy the food—out of sight, out of mind. I started eating healthy and working out at the university gym and eventually I got better. I've been better for almost a decade. I've had slip-ups now and then, but never like those earlier years. Until today. Today, I ate and ate until I thought I'd throw up. I didn't because I've never been a purger. I saw it all happening again and I... I got online and found this meeting."

"Good for you, Lori. It takes courage to ask for help," Gale said, the other women nodding along with her.

The meeting went on, with more stories and then a round-robin of suggestions. Take a walk, call a friend or sponsor, chew gum, brush your teeth, remember your why. The why behind wanting to stop, needing to stop.

L ori slid behind the wheel of her car, opening her phone to two new email messages. One was from Ben and included links to the news articles he'd found about the girls. The second was from Dr. Chadwick's receptionist with an offer for two potential appointment times. Chadwick had had a cancellation the following day and could see her at noon.

Lori responded accepting the appointment and then sent a message to her mother saying she'd be spending the night again.

Lori texted Ben.

Lori: I'm staying in Clare tonight. Have time to talk?

Ben: Sure. You name the place.

Lori: King's Post.

15

Lori wanted privacy, but King's Post was busy, and every table was full. The only seats available included a couple of barstools shoved beneath the long gleaming bar. Leaving an Overeaters Anonymous meeting and heading for a bar was not healthy transition behavior, but Lori silenced the voice in her head and ordered a gin and tonic.

She watched through the front window as Ben arrived on his bicycle and locked the bike to the rack outside. He wore board shorts, black with a glowing red sun on one side, and a t-shirt depicting two cats kung-fu fighting. He wove toward where she sat and slid onto the stool beside her.

"Nice shirt," Lori told him, grinning.

"Birthday gift from my niece, Allison. I've grown rather attached to it."

"I can see why."

"So, what's up? Feeling a little better than last night, I hope? Your choice of establishment makes me wonder." He cocked an eyebrow at the rows of liquor bottles stacked behind the bar.

No, she wasn't feeling better, but she forced a half-smile. "A little, yeah. I wanted to talk because... well, I guess we didn't come up with a game plan for looking into the girls, so I figured no time like the present." Not true. She'd wanted to talk because after she'd left the meeting at Holy Faith Church she'd felt terribly lonely and even the thought of Matilda in the bay window didn't soothe her.

"Ben, my brotha! How you doing, man?" The bartender, tall and chiseled like a body builder, held out his fist for Ben to bump.

"Hey, Zander, I'm keeping on. How are you, man? Still running bodies?"

"Till the day I die. Been doing more on the day shift though. My old lady is pissed I'm working so much. Had a murdercycle yesterday. Damn if some people just won't wear their helmets. They would if they'd seen what I've seen."

"True that. Widowmaker laws." Ben shook his head. "I'll take a Jones Soda if you have 'em. Vanilla or root beer."

The bartender walked away and Lori looked at Ben curiously. "Did he say 'murdercycle?'" she asked.

Ben nodded. "Zander's a paramedic. 'Murdercycle' is someone killed on a motorcycle. Nasty business."

"I couldn't do it," Lori said, finishing her drink and sliding it back to the edge of the bar. When she caught Zander's eye, she signaled for another.

"It's not for everyone," Ben said.

"When did you know it was for you?"

"When I saved someone's life. That moment pretty well changed me."

"Vanilla soda and another gin and tonic," Zander said, sliding their drinks in front of them. "Hey, we're doing karaoke on Friday. You coming with your crew? Body Runners versus Vampires?"

"Yeah, I'll probably be there."

Zander returned to the opposite end of the bar.

"Vampires?" Lori asked.

Ben smirked. "We draw a lot of blood. A few years back we all started meeting for karaoke and trivia. You need team names for trivia. The paramedics chose the Body Runners and our nursing crew opted for the Vampires. It stuck."

"I don't like the idea of the actual work, but the comradery seems pretty great."

Ben nodded and took a sip of his soda from the glass bottle. "It is, and necessary in our line of work. It's like being in the police force or the military. The ordinary world doesn't get it. You need people around you who understand. If you go home every night and tell your accountant girlfriend about a ten year-old who got rushed to the emergency room so beaten her eye had popped out of her head, it can put a serious strain on your relationship."

Lori flinched.

Ben looked at her apologetically. "Sorry, that was just an example. I've never seen that myself."

"But you know someone who has."

"Unfortunately, yes."

"How do you live with it? With all the death?"

"Live, that's the operative word. I try to live every single day. I've seen how short this life can be. I don't want to miss a second."

"I'm turning thirty next week," Lori said. "And suddenly my life feels... so terribly wrong. A week ago, it seemed fine, not great, but fine, doable. Now... it's like I want to set it on fire and run the other way."

"Maybe your current life doesn't fit anymore."

She pressed her hands on either side of her face. "Aren't we supposed to have this all figured out by thirty? My God, I thought by this time, I'd... I'd..."

"What? Have a husband, couple of kids, little house on a cul-de-sac?"

She squinted at her drink and then lifted it to her lips, downing half. "No. Maybe that's the problem. I never had a plan. I never had a dream of what my life would be. I think I did before Bev, but everything after that was just... one foot in front of the other, you know? It hurt to think too much, to imagine the future because she'd never get a future."

"I can think of one future we can imagine right now. Your birthday, the day itself. How do you want to ring in the thirtieth year of your life?"

Lori frowned and shrugged. "I don't know. Go out to dinner, maybe."

Ben made a face. "Now that's just sad."

"What did you do for your thirtieth birthday?"

"Dressed up in drag and danced onstage at a bar in Toronto. That was after I got a tattoo earlier that day, and let me tell you, that sequined top stung like hell on my freshly tattooed skin." He leaned to the side and pulled up his t-shirt, revealing a staff with a snake wrapped around the top. The bottom of the staff disappeared into the waist of his jeans.

"What is it?" She lifted her fingers to touch it and then quickly tucked her hand beneath her thigh, aware of what an intimate gesture that would have been and flushing at the thought.

"The Rod of Asclepius," he said. "It's a Greek symbol. Asclepius was the Greek god of healing. Back in the day, people used snakes in a lot of healing rituals—staffs too, but I've always had a thing for both. I have a royal python at home."

"As a pet?"

"Yeah. Leia. She's beautiful, about seven feet long, lemon yellow and wicked smart."

"She sounds like a keeper," Lori said, unable to hide the shiver down her spine.

He laughed. "Yeah, most people shudder at the thought of her, but she's really gentle, not a mean bone in her body."

"Are there any bones in her body?"

Ben chuckled. "Contrary to popular belief, there are, yeah. Snakes have hundreds of bones, more than human beings. They've got the central spine like we have here." He leaned forward and traced his finger down the ridge of bone on the back of Lori's neck.

Goosebumps rose over her arms and her breath caught in her diaphragm as his finger traced down her spine through her shirt.

"Hundreds of vertebrae"—he pressed on a knobby spot in the middle of her back and then slowly drew his finger from her spine along her ribcage—"and hundreds of ribs. The skeleton of a snake is amazing. I've seen quite a few." He sat back, taking his touch with him, and Lori tried to concentrate on what he'd been saying.

"I have a cat," she admitted, her cheeks warm and likely pink. "Her name's Matilda."

"Cats are cool. Carm had a cat growing up named Beans."

"What does it feel like? Getting tattooed?"

Ben cocked his head to the side, thoughtful. "Have you ever used a hot tub on a bitterly cold day? The outdoor kind? Where you have to walk barefoot in the snow?"

"Yeah."

"So think of walking out barefoot in the snow, wind whipping your face. You rush up the steps and climb into that water. The hot water needles your feet, your legs as you sink down. It hurts, but it hurts good. Yeah?"

"Yeah."

"That's what it feels like getting a tattoo. It's the kind of pain that keeps you coming back for more."

"How many do you have?"

He closed one eye and scrunched his face. "Twenty-two."

"Twenty-two!"

He pulled up his shirt to reveal his back covered in the ink. Multiple scenes ran together—a man on a bicycle curving down a mountain road, a stairway leading into a sky with a clock at the end, an eagle with a bright blue eye. "There are more on my shoulder and chest, half of one arm, the entirety of the other arm. I also have a full thigh done, but we might get some funny looks if I take off my pants."

She smiled, more warmth flushing her face. "I'd imagine you're right."

"Back to this thirtieth birthday. What's one thing you've always wanted to do? Preferably something you've always wanted to do that scares you."

"I've always wanted to go to Machu Picchu, ride on a gondola in Italy, snorkel the Great Barrier Reef in Australia, but I don't think any of those are going to happen by next week."

"Maybe not next week, but you should do all those things," he said.

"Why do you do stuff that scares you?" Lori asked.

"After my family fell apart, the perfect little family, I was liberated. I quit the football team and joined drama. I stopped wearing my varsity jacket and the cool clothes of the time, and shopped thrift stores instead, buying sixties corduroy bell-bottoms and hitting the surplus store for army jackets and fatigues. I decided I was beholden to no one—least of all myself and those fixed ideals I'd developed that turned out to be little more than ant hills."

"Ant hills?"

"Yeah, these mountains you spend your entire life building only to have one rain wash them away. I've been breaking my own rules ever since. I didn't want to dress in drag on my thirtieth birthday. Frankly, the thought terrified me, but when I dug past the terror, I realized it exhilarated me, and I wanted to challenge myself. I wanted to prove to myself that at thirty I was as willing to escape the box as I'd been at sixteen. Fixed beliefs are a leash for the mind. I'm nobody's dog, especially not my own."

Lori finished her drink, the buzz making her feel light and breezy.

"Go ahead. Tell me what scares you but secretly excites you." Ben gazed at her intensely, his gray eyes catching the light behind the bar.

Lori crossed her legs and folded her arms across her chest, though that didn't stop the tremor that moved down her body at the magnetism hovering in the air between them. Then again, maybe only she felt that pull thanks to her multiple gin and tonics.

"Whew... well..." She let out a long, shaky breath and rubbed her warm cheeks.

As she searched for the things that scared her, the forest loomed in her mind. Not any forest, but Manistee National Forest where Bev had gone missing off Tanglewood Drive, a forest Lori hadn't set foot in nearly fifteen years. She signaled to Zander to bring her another drink. "I'm afraid of the woods."

Ben leaned back, tilted his head and then nodded slowly. "Because of what happened?"

"Yeah."

"Then that's where we'll go."

She shook her head. "I don't think so. I appreciate your"—she gestured at him—"whole take on life, but that's not me."

"How do you know? How do you know if you're unwilling to try? We drive to the road at the edge of the woods, there's time to turn back, we park the car, still time to change your mind, we walk into the trees, we can still turn around and walk back to the car. There's nothing finite in that experience. You won't step off a ledge and start free-falling."

"I'd rather do that," she said. "Yeah. How about bungee jumping or skydiving?"

He grinned. "You'd rather jump out of a plane than go back to those woods?"

She nodded.

"Then the woods it is."

Zander placed another drink in front of her and she thought he gave Ben a wry look, but the alcohol made her unsure and frankly uncaring. She didn't mind anymore that Stu had cheated or that her job was repetitive and unexciting or that she'd binged on Hostess cupcakes after years of food sobriety.

She gulped half the glass of alcohol and stood to use the bathroom, tipping slightly. Ben caught her elbow. "Maybe you shouldn't finish that."

She gazed at him, head drooping forward, and then picked the glass off the bar and finished it.

16

The next morning Ben sat at his kitchen table, sipping coffee and taking notes on a yellow legal pad. He'd printed a map of the locations the girls had vanished from and marked each with an X.

Footsteps padded from the living room where Lori had passed out the night before on his couch. He looked up to find her standing in the doorway.

"Well, this is awkward," she murmured, shielding her eyes from the light streaming through the kitchen window.

"Nah. Awkward would be if you were naked or woke up on the front lawn while my neighbor was watering her flowers. This is pretty typical. Come have coffee. Water first though." He gestured at a pitcher of ice water next to the coffee maker.

He hid his smile as Lori self-consciously patted at her hair and gazed down at her wrinkled clothes.

"Mugs are above the coffee machine," he told her, watching as she selected a mug, gazed at it and then looked at him curiously.

She held it up, displaying the black cup with the large pink heart on it. In the center were two words: 'Go Away.'

Ben chuckled. "Gift from a co-worker who was not a morning person and didn't appreciate the mornings I'd stroll into the hospital, bike helmet in hand, singing a Tom Petty song and telling her to have a stupendous day."

Lori smiled and filled the mug. "Cream?"

"There's coconut milk in the refrigerator."

Lori added milk and started to sit, then went back to the counter and filled a glass with water, drinking slowly and wincing.

"Headache?" Ben asked.

She nodded.

"Bathroom is down the hall on the left, there are meds above the sink. Ibuprofen, Tylenol, aspirin. Take your pick."

Ben returned to his notes. He drew lines between where the girls vanished, using the GPS on his phone to calculate the distance between them.

Lori's scream ripped through the quiet, and Ben jumped to his feet and ran into the hall.

Lori stood plastered against the wall. His python, Leia, slithered along the opposite wall, heading for the living room. Ben squatted and lifted her up.

"Sorry, shit, I forgot I let her out. She's okay." He held Leia out for Lori to touch.

Lori's face had gone pale, but the color started to seep back into her cheeks. "Leia," she murmured. "That's right. I vaguely remember you mentioning her."

"She's harmless, meek as a mouse. Well, she eats those, so maybe not the proper analogy."

Lori ran trembling fingers along the python's smooth scales. "She really is yellow."

Ben grinned. "Thought I made it up?"

"No. I just couldn't picture it at the time."

"I'll put her away, so she doesn't spook you again."

"No." Lori shook her head, stepping toward the bathroom. "I'm okay. I'm going to take some ibuprofen and wash up. Let Leia have her free time."

Ben returned to the kitchen with Leia, releasing her into the screened sun room.

Lori appeared several minutes later, her long hair pulled into a messy top-knot and her face shiny and clean.

"Feel better?" he asked.

"A smidge," she admitted, drinking her coffee. Her eyes drifted to the paper and studied the names written there. "This is about the girls?"

"Yeah," he said, pulling his printed map towards her. "Here's where they each went missing along with the dates." He glanced at the clock. "No work today?"

Lori shook her head. "I have an appointment in Traverse City with, umm... a dream doctor, I guess you'd call him."

"A dream doctor?"

Lori wrapped her hands around her mug. "Yeah, weird, right? When I was young, after Bev went missing, I started getting night terrors, apparently. I didn't remember, but then it happened recently at my mom's and she told me about seeing this Jungian doctor."

"Jungian? Like Carl Jung?"

"You've heard of him?"

"Briefly. During nursing school, we had a psych class and got a brief overview."

"Yeah. He did a lot with dreams as a psychiatrist and there's a whole field of study based on his work. This guy in Traverse City does that work."

"Bizarre," Ben said, thinking of his own recent nightmare about Summer, made worse by the strange explosion of noise and light in his house just after he woke up.

"What?" Lori asked.

"I had a nightmare about Summer a couple nights ago. A really terrible nightmare. I haven't been able to shake it."

"I did too. Not about Bev exactly, but... weirdly, it feels like it was about Bev even though she wasn't in the dream. I dreamed I was back in my old bedroom at our house in Baldwin, the same one I lived in when Bev went missing."

"That's it?"

Lori shook her head. "I woke up in the dream to this horrible crunching sound like something was right outside my door chewing on bones."

Ben shuddered. "What was it?"

"I have no idea. In the dream, I got to the door and I was just frozen with fear."

"That's creepy."

"Yeah, it is. What was your dream about Summer?"

Ben tapped his pen on Summer's name on the map, frowning. He almost didn't want to share the dream—retelling it might bring it back to the forefront of his mind, but it was already there, Summer's wasted face in that dark, moldy cabin. "I was in the cabin in the woods, the one she went into that night, and she was there standing in the corner. She turned and her face was"—he grimaced and touched his cheek—"eaten away. There were maggots coming out of the holes in her skin." He shook his head, a feeling of revulsion washing over him. "Disturbing. It spooked me."

Lori sighed and pinched the bridge of her nose.

"Headache still there?"

"Yeah. I don't think I'll be shaking it anytime soon." She looked at the map. "It is strange, isn't it? Four girls in such a small area."

"Yes. It's more than strange. It's not just the girls going missing. They all went missing in the same way, walking in the woods in the evening with a friend."

"I don't get why someone would target girls who are in twos and only take one of them. It's more difficult, so what's the point?"

Ben stood and refilled his mug of coffee. "Maybe to play head games. He's got a victim to take, but maybe he gets off on the victim he left behind too."

Lori looked stricken at Ben's comment.

"Sorry," he said. "That's not what I meant exactly."

"I think it is what you meant, and you may be right. It's like those killers who send letters to the cops or call the victims' families. They enjoy messing with their heads."

"Maybe… and I hope I'm not about to plant something terrifying in your mind, but maybe... he follows the girl left behind. Not to take her, but just to... relive it or whatever."

Lori had gone even paler.

"Has there ever been anything like that? Anyone watching you, stalking you?" Ben asked.

"I don't know. I mean, never before, but then... well, the night before I met you at Mulberry, something freaky happened at work."

"What?"

"I was in the shower in the locker room at the company gym. I was the only person working out and while I was showering, I heard this sound like"—she bit her lip and scrunched her face as if searching for the right words—"scraping or dragging on the showers. I kind of imagined someone dragging a screwdriver down the locker faces."

"Did you see who it was?"

"No, it got even more nuts because the lights went out, pitch black, but I swear something was in there with me. I started to panic and scream and then the cleaning lady walked in and turned the lights on."

Ben thought back to his own pitch-black night, the terror that had seized him initially upon waking. "That is freaky. Did the cleaning lady see anyone?"

"No. She said I was alone."

"But maybe somebody slipped past her?"

"Possibly, but…" Lori shook her head. "I kind of wrote it off, thinking"—she waved at the map—"that all of this was getting to me."

Ben sighed. "I've wondered that myself, but still, be on the lookout. I don't know why this guy would emerge now if our theory even remotely holds true, but just in case, stay alert."

"Because it's been five years," Lori said suddenly, sitting up in her chair and tapping her finger hard on the names on the map. "The last girl vanished in 2008, that was five years ago."

Ben considered, not sold on the five-year cycle theory, but nodded anyway. "It's possible. And right now, anything is possible, so watch your back."

"You should tell Carmen."

Ben frowned. He hadn't told Carmen anything about reopening his investigation into Summer and he didn't want to. She'd witnessed his manic descent after Summer disappeared and he could already see the expression on her face if he admitted that he'd started considering theories again.

"I messaged the families of the other girls this morning," he said, shifting the subject away from Carm.

"Really?"

"Yeah. Someone in Bella's family has a Find Bella Facebook page, so I reached out through private message."

"Do you have a Facebook page?" Lori asked, remembering her own attempts at finding Ben's profile and coming up empty.

"No. I made one this morning, so I could contact the family. I've got a phone number for someone connected to Peyton Weller. I'll try calling this afternoon. If I can set up times to talk with these people, do you want to go with me?"

Lori looked drawn at the suggestion, but after a moment, she nodded. "Yeah. I do want to hear their stories."

"And theories. I'm hoping to see if a specific person comes up, a man somehow connected to all the girls."

"The guy you mentioned? Hector."

"Maybe him, maybe someone else. I'm not opposed to the possibility it wasn't Dunn, but—"

"You think it was?"

"Yeah."

"Can I borrow your book?" Lori asked, gesturing at the counter where he'd left the copy of *Strange Michigan* he'd found in the ER waiting room.

"Go for it. I flipped through it, but it's not really my thing."

Lori stood and picked up the book. Ben noticed the way her mouth turned down as she stared at the cover.

"I better get going. I'd like to head to my mom's house to take a shower and put on some clean clothes."

"Worried the dream doctor won't take you seriously?"

She smiled, but it looked forced.

"I'm only kidding. It's interesting, the dream thing."

Lori shrugged. "I'm just hoping he can help it stop, honestly. I don't want to have that dream again."

Ben nodded, standing and following her toward the door. "If you figure it out, call and give me some pointers." He took his keys from the hook by the door and Lori watched as if not understanding.

"Are you leaving too?"

He grinned. "I'm taking you back to your car, unless you want to walk the two miles."

Lori put a hand to her forehead. "My car. That's right. I'm sorry about last night. I'm embarrassed. I can't remember the last time I drank that much."

He waved away the apology. "Based on the week you've had, I think a drunken night was warranted."

"Yeah, but you don't drink and—"

"And I also don't judge. I don't drink because that's what's right for me. Most of my friends drink. It's not an issue, Lori."

"Still, I'm sorry for crashing on your couch."

"My couch gets lonely. I'm sure she appreciated the company."

Lori smiled. "Okay, I'll stop. But thank you. I actually picked King's Post because it was walking distance to my mom and grandma's house. Apparently, I was too inebriated to tell you that last night."

"Actually, you did tell me that, but you also told me they go to bed at nine. I didn't want you standing on the stoop pounding on the door for an hour to be let in."

"I have a key."

"I was happy to bring you here. I'm happy I did bring you here. Gave us a chance to talk more." Ben unlocked his car and opened the passenger door. "Your chariot awaits, m'lady."

Lori climbed into her seat and Ben slid behind the wheel, starting the car. The radio blared on. *Every Breath You Take* boomed too loud from the speakers. Ben jumped and cranked the volume to off.

"Not a fan of the Police?" Lori asked.

Ben frowned. "That song must be making a comeback. I've heard it twice this week." He ignored the gooseflesh that had risen along his arms.

"I haven't heard that song in ages. It always struck me as stalkerish."

"Yeah," he murmured, focusing on the road and ignoring the niggling question behind that damn song.

As Ben drove Lori home, she leaned down, head nearly between her legs, and he wondered if she was about to get sick. "Are you nauseous?"

She straightened up and held out her palm. "No. I saw a glint of gold. Looks like someone dropped this on your passenger floor."

He stared at the piece of jewelry on her palm, his own palms instantly sweat-slick and his heart climbing to a crescendo in his chest.

A horn honked and he looked back at the road, swore, and swerved back into their own lane, narrowly avoiding a head-on collision with a pick-up truck, whose driver was red-faced and screaming at Ben as he passed.

Lori gasped, fingers closing around the gold unicorn as she clutched the oh-shit bar with her opposite hand.

Ben steadied the car. "Sorry. I'm sorry. Can you just stick that in the glovebox for me?"

He didn't speak of the necklace again. After he dropped Lori at her car, he drove away and pulled into a parking lot behind a strip of downtown shops.

For several moments he gazed at the closed glovebox, telling himself he'd only imagined it looked like a unicorn. It wasn't, of course. It couldn't be because Summer had been wearing the unicorn necklace the night she vanished. He'd never seen it again after the last night, when it had been hanging beneath the hollow of her throat.

Gathering his wits, he reached for the latch and popped the box open, stretching until his fingers brushed the cool metal. He pulled it out. The gold chain was tangled, but the unicorn with the tiny red eye, a ruby for Summer's July birthstone, was unmistakable.

He'd bought it because it was corny, because they'd laugh about it much the same way they laughed about their song and about the kids at school who took everything so seriously. Summer had gotten him, his wry sense of humor, his refusal to follow the in-crowd.

He sat in his car and stared at it, willing it to make sense.

This was it. Undeniably and yet...

He picked up his cell phone and dialed Carmen.

"Hey, brother," she answered after two rings. He could hear the baby giggling in the background.

"Hey, quick question." He suddenly wished he hadn't called. Carmen didn't talk about Summer and she'd grill him if he asked about the necklace, perhaps fearing he was slipping back into that dark hole it had taken years to emerge from.

"Yeah?"

"Please don't read into this. I'm just curious. Summer was wearing the unicorn necklace when she disappeared, right?"

Silence on the other end and the baby's voice faded as if Carm had walked into another room. "You know she was. It was listed as one of the distinctive things to look for if... if a body was ever found."

"Okay. I thought so. And we never found it?"

"She was wearing it, Ben. Why are you asking about Summer's necklace?"

"I met someone who had a similar experience. She had a friend who went missing in the Manistee Forest in 1998. I'm trying to look at connections."

"Really? Another girl who went missing?"

"Yeah, also fourteen at the time."

"That's scary."

"I know. Don't trouble yourself about it. If I find out anything more, I'll let you know."

"Are you sure that's a good idea, Ben? Getting into all that again?"

"I'm different now, Carm. Okay? It won't ever be like it was."

"Okay. Take care of yourself."

"Carm, wait," he said, before she could hang up.

"What?"

"Have you seen anyone around? Following you or anything?"

The longer he stared at the unicorn the more he thought about Hector Dunn peeling out of his driveway days before and speeding by Ben as he sat watching him. Had Dunn followed him home and put the necklace in his car? Ben flashed on his conversation with Lori. Mind games.

"No, why? What's going on?"

"Nothing, probably nothing. But be careful, okay? Eyes wide open, especially when you're on your own."

"Ben, you're scaring me."

"I don't mean to and I'm probably overreacting, but just in case. I'll give you more details soon."

"Okay, Ben."

17

After a quick shower at her mom's, Lori shrugged into a pair of old jeans and a loose-fitting button-down shirt. She drove to Traverse City to the office of Dr. Arnold Chadwick.

The building stood on a grassy lot that overlooked Traverse City's West Bay. Sun glinted off the windows, turning the structure into a dazzling mirrored cube.

Lori pushed through the glass double doors and into a lobby with a black tiled floor and a wall filled with names and office numbers. There was no receptionist. Next to the names stood a map of the building and beside that a tall stone fountain. Water trickled over the black stones into the basin below.

A memory surfaced for Lori of Henry tugging at their mother's purse, begging for a penny to throw into the fountain to make a wish. Lori glanced into the water, but saw no shining pennies on the dark stone bed.

Nerves and nausea circled within her as she took the elevator to the fourth floor and walked down a hallway carpeted in dark green. She found 4C at the end of the hall. The door read 'Dr. Chadwick.'

Dr. Chadwick did have a receptionist. She sat in the octagonal office at a white desk with a modern-looking computer on its face. The office was clean and bright and Lori knew she'd been in it before, but had no solid memory to accompany the feeling.

"Welcome to Dr. Chadwick's office. Do you have an appointment?" the woman asked, adjusting her green cat's-eye glasses.

"Yes, I'm Lori Hicks."

"Lovely," the woman said, typing on her keyboard. "Have a seat and the doctor will be with you in a moment."

The woman didn't summon the man behind the closed black door and Lori assumed she'd alerted him to a client's presence through the computer.

Lori sat, crossed her legs and then dug in her purse and pulled out the copy of *Strange Michigan*, flipping quickly past the cover and the leering face of the Dogman. She skimmed the pages, glancing at the titles above each story.

The book described a horned creature known as Nain Rouge. It had another story devoted to a water panther. Several stories described haunted houses and hotels. Lori paused on the story of the Dogman and read the first few lines.

Seven feet tall with the torso of a man and the head of the wolf, the Dogman has been giving the fine folks of the Great Lake State nightmares since 1887 when the first sighting of the Dogman was recorded in Wexford County.

She slipped past the Dogman story, skimmed a story about Melon Heads and paused at a black and white picture of a cloaked figure hunched over a tall black cauldron. The drawing revealed only the profile of the figure beneath the cloak, a hideous old woman with a hook nose and a long chin sprouting warts and boils.

The Witch in the Woods

Sources vary regarding the time period when the witch of Manistee was first seen lurking in the dense forests on the west side of the Great Lake State. One legend tells that one morning as two children of a lumber baron played near their home, a tree split open and a woman's long gnarled arms reached out and dragged one child inside. Though the baron hacked the tree down, he found no sign of the witch or his daughter. She had vanished without a trace. Towns-folk would later claim the stepmother of the girl did away with the child, jealous of her husband's affection for his daughter, but there are those who believe the story of the witch.

This writer heard many tales of the Witch of the Manistee Forest, but found few written accounts.

The second story was passed to me by a centenarian named Edith, and for those of you not familiar with the term, that means she was one hundred years old. Edith told me of losing her sister to the witch in 1904. They were girls on the cusp of womanhood, as twelve was in those days, and had been sent to the forest by their mother to collect leeks (wild onions) for supper. As Edith dug in the soil, pulling out a handful of leeks, she glanced up to see a cloaked figure, an old, terrifying woman, reach out and wrap her sister as if in a hug. And then they were gone. Edith did not see the woman drag her sister away. They seemed to vanish into thin air, but stranger still when Edith raced home, nearly an hour had passed since they'd walked into the forest, though she swore only ten or fifteen minutes had gone by. She was scolded for losing her sister and a search was conducted but no trace of the child was ever found.

A trickle of cold sweat slid down Lori's forehead and plopped on her hand. She jumped when the black door opened to Chadwick's office. She dropped the book face-up on the carpet. She'd been so immersed in the story, she'd forgotten she sat in Chadwick's waiting room.

He gazed at her, smiling and revealing two rows of perfect teeth. "Miss Hicks. I'm ready for you." Despite the professional feel of his office, Chadwick wore jeans and a Hawaiian shirt.

Lori bent and picked up the book, stuffed it into her purse and followed Chadwick into his office. It was familiar, though slightly different than what she'd remembered when her mother had reminded her of the visits. The same huge window looked out on the glittering west bay and thick blue carpet muted her footfalls, but the once-white leather furnishings had been replaced with colorful furniture including a long red couch, two sky-blue chairs on stilted legs and, oddly, a fluffy orange beanbag in the corner of the room.

Chadwick followed her gaze and smiled. "You're welcome to the beanbag. It's a favorite among my younger clients, and I must admit to lying there a few times myself for a bit of afternoon daydreaming."

"It looks comfy," Lori said, opting for one of the sky-blue chairs.

Rather than settling behind the large dark desk, Chadwick took the opposite chair.

"Do you remember me?" Lori asked.

Chadwick bobbed his head up and down. "Oh, yes. I remember most everyone I've worked with. Though we called you Lorraine back then and you were significantly shorter."

"And fatter," Lori murmured, not sure why she'd made the statement and wishing she could take it back.

"Ah, well"—Chadwick rested his hands in his lap—"food is often one of the few coping mechanisms available to us as children. Seeking comfort through food is very normal. But I see you were able to deal with that at some point."

"I started going to groups for binge-eaters." Lori looked beyond him toward the window. She felt like a child whenever she spoke about the binge-eating, filled with shame and self-doubt.

"Community is important for long-term healing. Do you still attend meetings?"

"Not really." She didn't tell him about the meeting she'd gone to nights earlier. She was there to talk about dreams, not her penchant for eating a box of cupcakes in a single sitting.

"Tell me, Lori, have the night terrors returned? Is that why you set up the appointment?"

"I didn't even remember I'd had night terrors," she admitted, "or that I'd ever seen you, and then recently I stayed the night at my mom's and I had a terrible dream. My mom woke me up. She said I'd been screaming."

Chadwick nodded. "Much as you experienced in adolescence."

"But I remembered the dream."

"I see. Now that is a new development."

"You remember all that? What we talked about?"

"I tape-recorded all of our sessions. I brushed up before our appointment today. If it's okay with you, I'd like to record this session as well."

Lori shrugged. "Sure."

Chadwick stood and walked to his desk, took a small black voice recorder from a drawer. He set it on the edge of his desk.

"I don't remember much of anything from when I used to come in," Lori admitted. "And I'm a little confused about what exactly you do."

"I look at dreams and nightmares from a Jungian perspective."

"What does that mean exactly?"

"I'll give you the abbreviated version because it takes years of study to truly understand what it means, but Carl Gustav Jung was a Swiss psychoanalyst who viewed dreams as messages from the psyche. Jung put forth a theory that human beings have both a personal unconscious and a collective unconscious. Your personal unconscious is formed by your individual life. Our collective unconscious is the larger assembly of archetypes and symbols that human beings have formed during our hundreds of thousands of years of existence. It's a collective way of interpreting the world, in a sense. The key is that the unconscious is just that—un-conscious. We are not consciously aware of what it knows.

However, the knowledge contained therein can be the keys to our healing, to our individual growth, to overcoming our blocks.

"Dreams are a bridge of sorts from the unconscious, a way for that material to be translated and sent to the conscious so that we might integrate it into our lives and deal with our traumas, fears, et cetera. In the arena of dreams, we can have a lived experience of a trauma and we can overcome it. We can transmute it from something horrific into something benign."

"So nightmares are a way to heal from bad things that have happened to us?" Lori asked.

"In a person who has learned to work with their dreams, yes, they can be that. In a person who is merely dreaming and having nightmares with little thought to their meaning, no. Dreams and nightmares can actually be further traumatizing. If we are abused by a parent and that parent appears each night in our dream and we continue to be the victim and to be abused, the psyche is not distinguishing that experience from the actual abuse. Further trauma ensues. But if we look at the dream from Jung's perspective and see the recurring nightmare as our unconscious saying 'hello, excuse me, this needs to be healed, this needs to be dealt with,' and we then go to that dream and begin working with it for a different outcome, then we can heal the trauma that the dream is attempting to make us aware of."

"How though? I don't have control over what happens in my dreams."

"Well, there's deep work that goes into such things. Lucid dreaming is one way, but many people never master the skill. What we can master is dreaming while awake, going back through the dream in deeper and deeper detail and in our imagination choosing a new outcome again and again. In the case of the abusive parent, we might see that parent stop the hitting and instead hug their child and apologize for how they've wronged them."

"Why not show the child picking up a bat and beating the parent back?"

"It's interesting how many people leap to that conclusion. To me, that is evidence of decay inherent in our society. Trauma is occurring on both sides of the fist. Both the abuser and the abused are traumatized. The goal is to heal, not to create a new form of trauma. The child will not be healed by feeling they have finally beaten the beast. This is a parent, after all. It is hardwired in our biology to seek the love and support of this entity. The healing of that trauma comes from the parent giving love and support."

"Except they don't really give love and support. It's a daydream."

"Yes, but the psyche doesn't distinguish between the two. In fact, Jung often examined dreams from the perspective that every figure in the dream is a representation of the dreamer. The child who was abused has internalized their abusive parent. In a sense it becomes part of their personality. In order to accept themselves, they must integrate the piece of them that embodies the abusive parent."

"Whew," Lori breathed. "I'm feeling out of my depth here. I don't understand how we worked through my dreams when I couldn't remember them."

"There are many ways to work with dreams and nightmares we don't remember. In your case, and in many instances with patients who are also children, we focus on art therapy."

"Art therapy?"

"Yes, it's a way of bringing that which is unknown into the known. We are bypassing the linear left brain and engaging the artistic right brain. The right brain doesn't need to"—he made air quotes with his fingers—"know the material of the dream. It simply works with the emotion the dream is causing. In your case, terror. There are many kinds of art therapy—sand, clay, painting. You drew pictures."

"Pictures?"

"Yes."

"What did I draw?"

Chadwick smiled. "I can show you. I don't have original copies— there'd be art pouring from the windows of this building if I saved the creations of every patient—but I did save it for many years and then when we scanned and saved things digitally, I had an assistant put everything into archives. Give me just a moment."

Chadwick stood and returned to his desk. He drew a very thin white laptop from a drawer and sat it on the desk, opening it.

Lori studied the large paintings hanging on the walls of Chadwick's office. There were two paintings, each at least five feet long and three feet wide. One depicted an enormous watery-looking sun suspended above a village. Sinewy rays came off the sun and it seemed to be held up by a floating figure. The second painting portrayed an old man with white hair and a white beard. Enormous wings protruded from his back and he stood as if perched on the top of a small temple. A huge serpent lay coiled in the woods beside him.

"Those are pictures drawn by Carl Jung himself," Chadwick told her. "He was a magnificent artist with a very creative mind."

Lori stared at the images for another moment, fascinated, but also a bit creeped out by the pictures.

"Here we are," Chadwick said. He stood and walked the laptop to Lori. She took it and settled it on her lap. The picture before her was a crude child's drawing of a tree.

"This is what I drew?"

"One of the many pictures. Click the right arrow and you'll see the others."

Lori clicked the arrow and saw another tree. This time the leaves on the tree were black. In the next picture the entire tree was black. The image after had no tree at all, only a large shadowy blob that looked almost like a figure. The next picture showed the shadow again with more substance. It had legs now, spindly, bony legs and equally bony arms. Four more images matched this one, though the figure appeared to have straggly hair and wore rags. The final image revealed the figure again, but now it seemed to be hunched over and beneath it lay a pool of red that Lori sensed was blood.

18

Lori stared at the final drawing and shook her head. "I don't understand what these mean."

Chadwick took the laptop back. "Shall I print them for you?"

"Yes, please."

"They'll print at Darcy's desk. As for their meaning, that's hard to say. The therapy is not designed to search for meaning so much as to help process the emotion contained within the dream. By taking the dream from the shadow and putting it into being, you reduce its potency. Two of the images of the figures you drew, you burned."

"I burned them? Why?"

"To destroy them. The figure you drew held meaning that you never fully translated, but the emotion was clear enough. You were afraid of her."

"Her?"

"You referred to it as female, yes."

"It does strike me as a woman, even now," Lori admitted, considering the picture one more time.

"Yes, I can see why that connection is there. You said you've been having nightmares again, but this time you remember them. Tell me about that."

"I'm in my bedroom in the house I lived in when I was a kid, the house I lived in when Bev vanished. I wake up in my bed and I can hear someone eating outside the door."

"Eating?"

"Not just eating, crunching, like something hard."

"Hmmm… I see. That is rather unnerving."

"At first in the dream, I think it's my little brother, but then I walk to the door and I'm sure… I'm sure something bad is on the other side, something that will hurt me."

"Do you open the door?"

"No. I woke up before I opened the door."

"I want to unpack this dream further. Let's start with what you think is on the other side of the door. Try to go with your first instinct and not analyze it too much."

"The thing that took Bev."

"Okay, I see. And do you have a visual for that? Is it a man? A monster?"

Lori bit her cheek. "I don't know. A monster, I guess. The Dogman was the thing I thought of when I was a kid, so maybe that's what I'm imagining." She said the Dogman, but she envisioned the shrouded entity from her drawings and her mind coughed up a word: *witch.*

"Okay, I see. And Bev has never been found, so there's genuinely a mystery here regarding what happened to her?"

"Yes, she's never been found. We have no idea what happened to her that night."

"Have you ever tried allowing yourself to believe she left of her own free will?"

"She didn't."

"Okay. So, if that's not something you're comfortable using as a means of shifting the trauma around her vanishing, then the alternative is to accept that something did take Bev that night, in all likelihood someone. Right? If it had been a bear or a forest animal, traces would probably have been found, you would have heard screams."

"Yes."

"So you think an individual took her?"

"That's the logical explanation."

"But the mystery of the event has turned an ordinary person—a sick person, sure, but still an ordinary person—into a monster in your nightmares. In order to process your trauma, I would advise you to go back into the dream from a waking state, a daydreaming state, if you will, and open the door to find an ordinary person on the other side."

"That's it? Imagine I see some guy standing there?"

"Well, not necessarily. Maybe instead you meet Bev there and she has passed on from this life and she is at peace now and whatever took her that long-ago day is no longer important. What's important is that the thing that happened, whatever it was, is long in the past and you reliving the terror over and over is merely your mind telling you that it's time to heal and move on. Might I ask if anything has occurred recently that might have triggered the dream? Some recent change or trauma? Often these resurfacing fears arise due to major change in our lives—breakups, deaths in the family, that kind of thing."

Lori sighed. "I broke up with my boyfriend, but this started before that. It started after I heard a story that was eerily similar to Bev's story."

"A story of another missing child?"

"Yes."

"That makes sense then. It would bring all of that old emotion back to the surface."

"What if the dream is more than that? What if it's trying to show me what happened to Bev?"

"Then I'd ask, do you think you witnessed what happened that night and blocked it out?"

"Not really, no."

"Then how could your unconscious mind give you information it doesn't have?"

"Well... the same way psychics sometimes know where bodies are buried."

Dr. Chadwick crossed one leg over the other, considering her with interest. "Carl Jung had dreams that he considered premonitions, dreams that foretold future events. I have worked with scientists and other doctors who consider such phenomena, but ultimately I am out of my league with such things."

"But you think it's possible?"

"Probable, no. Possible, perhaps. I am reluctant to eliminate anything as a possibility, but I also believe that attaching to unexplainable phenomena can keep us stuck. Healing comes from bringing what lurks in the darkness into the light, the unconscious into the conscious.

"The unknown is always scarier than the known. Have you ever researched the Dogman—looked a bit further into the folklore so you might bring him into the light?"

"He's not real," murmured Lori, thinking about the book in her purse.

"And yet up here"—Chadwick tapped a finger on his temple —"he is."

∼

Lori drove home from Dr. Chadwick's office, glancing repeatedly at printouts of the drawings she'd made fifteen years before. The hunched figure seemed distinctly female, but that didn't make it less menacing. There was something savage about the being, though Lori spotted nothing in the unsophisticated drawing to give credence to her feelings.

She parked at the Mount Pleasant Public Library and walked inside, then paused at a computer kiosk to search for the books she wanted. She searched for Michigan true stories, folklore, and urban legends, jotting down the call numbers for each of the books.

Lori wandered through the stacks of books, double-checking the slip of paper. There were two books on the Dogman himself and an additional two on Michigan folklore that referenced the beast. Lori found all four books and made her way to a corner table tucked behind shelves containing autobiographies.

She skimmed through alleged true stories by people who'd encountered the Dogman. The eyewitness accounts described a creature standing nearly seven feet tall with the body of a man, but the head of a dog. He was covered in thick black fur.

According to one book the earliest sighting of the Dogman occurred in 1887 in Wexford County. Two lumberjacks working in the woods spotted a large creature with a man's body and a dog's head. There were reports of drivers who'd spotted a giant walking dog. Residents who lived near the forest had spotted a half-canine, half-humanoid.

The stories gave her the creeps, but they didn't resonate with her dream or with her sense of what happened that night.

Dr. Chadwick had asked her if she might have witnessed what happened and blocked it out. She hadn't, of course she hadn't, and yet a veil seemed to fall when she tried to examine the moments after Bev had climbed into the tree. The memories were there—smashing the mushrooms, calling up the tree to Bev—but… her dream had begun to seep in and pollute her previously clear memory of that night.

Lori set the book she'd been reading aside and slid another in front of her. On the cover, two glowing red eyes gazed out from a black forest.

The title read, *Those Who Haunt Us and Hunt Us: The Paranormal and Supernatural in Michigan.*

She scanned the table of contents, eye catching on a story listed on page thirty-eight, 'The Manistee Hag.'

She flipped to the page where a black and white drawing showed a haggard woman standing hunched in the woods. Black eyes gleamed from beneath her cloak. In line with the wicked witch images in most fairy tales, she had a long pointed nose flecked with warts and hair. In her bony hands she clutched a skull.

The Manistee Hag

Stories of the Manistee Hag date back to the late 1700s.

Children who played in the woods described a bent woman with black eyes who watched the children from the forest shadows.

In 1906, a lumberman stormed into a nearby village insisting his daughter was taken by the Manistee Hag. The forest was searched but no sign of the girl was ever found.

Today the stories are fewer, but they continue to trickle in. This sighting occurred in 1961.

Two children, sisters, were playing in the forest when they claimed to see a scary-looking old woman emerge from a tree as if she'd been a part of the trunk and simply stepped away from it. Her hair was as wild as brambles, her face as rutted and pocked as the bark, and despite her age she moved so quickly they barely saw her. Suddenly she was just beside them. She reached for one girl child, but the sisters' dog Tully attacked the hag. The hag, or witch as they later called her, screeched and vanished back into the forest.

Lori's mouth had gone dry as she read. She closed the book and took her cell phone from her bag. She texted Ben.

Lori: I've got a weird theory I'd like to pass by you.

Several minutes passed before Ben replied.

Ben: I'm on a bike ride heading south. I can stop by your house. Send me your address.

Lori texted her address, gathered up the books and headed for the checkout desk.

19

Ben biked into Mount Pleasant, following the GPS on his phone to Lori's house. When he arrived, she was standing on the front porch.

"Want to sit out back?" she asked. "On the deck."

"Sure. Let me lock up my bike."

"You can just wheel it back here with us," she suggested.

Ben followed Lori to the side of the house, where she opened the gate in a chain-link fence and led him into the backyard. The yard was nice enough with a couple of mature willows. A line of overgrown bushes crowded the length of the back fence, obscuring the house behind it. On the raised deck stood a glass patio table lined with beer bottles and cans. A copper ring firepit sitting in the yard contained more empties, as did the yard itself.

"Have a party?" Ben asked, raising an eyebrow.

Lori grunted and bent over, snatched up several bottles and walked them to a plastic waste-bin beside the back door. "I put this out here with a bag in it and everything. How hard is it to walk three feet and drop the bottles in? No, I didn't have a party. My inconsiderate downstairs neighbor had a party like he does five nights a week. I barely ever come out here anymore because I have to either sit in his trash or clean it up for him."

Ben grabbed the trash can and carried it to the table. With one swipe, he slid the bottles inside with a crash. "Forget the rest. Let's sit."

She sighed and touched her stomach, a little quirk he'd noticed she did when frazzled.

"Why did you do that?"

"Hmm?" She looked at him, not yet sitting, but still eyeing the cans in the fire pit with barely concealed rage. "Do what?"

He mimed the movement, grazing his fingers across his stomach.

She flushed slightly and shook her head. "I didn't realize I did."

He sensed an untruth in her comment, but based on the color that had risen to her cheeks, he dropped it. "Why do you live here? In student housing, I mean, with a frat boy downstairs?"

She swiped at her stomach again and settled into the chair opposite him. "I just never left. I moved in here my sophomore year at Central. After I graduated, I got a job, years passed. Here I am."

"You've never thought of moving?"

She looked up at a second-story window jutting from the back of the house.

Ben couldn't see inside. The sun glinted off the glass, turning the window into a mirror. A wistful expression flitted across Lori's face as she gazed at the window.

"Matilda is probably asleep in that window right now. My cat. Honestly, I think that window is the single reason I've stayed here. It's a bay window and I love to sit there and read and think. Sounds moronic, right?"

"Moronic? No. It sounds kind of sweet actually, but I bet you could find a bay window that doesn't have a beer-swilling actual moron occupying the space beneath you."

She laughed. "Why do you live in Clare? It's nice, I mean. That's where my mom and grandma lived and where we lived after we moved from Baldwin, but it doesn't seem like it fits your personality."

"Why is that?"

"Oh, I don't know—tattoos, dressing in drag, the list goes on."

"I love small towns," he admitted. "And I like that about myself. Do I also like to escape the small town and get a taste of the rest of the world? Hell yeah. But there's nothing like coming home after a weekend of mayhem, opening my front door and stepping into my place. The hush that takes me in, quiets the chaos I've been submerged in. It's the best of both worlds. I like walking two blocks to Moonie's Diner and grabbing a cup of coffee and a jumbo cinnamon roll after a long ride and having Sadie or Wanda—those are the regular servers—

hassle me about how I'm never going to produce heirs if I keep cycling so much."

Lori laughed. "They actually say that to you?"

"Oh, they don't just say it, they shout it. They're downright hecklers, those two. They make the peanut gallery look like actual peanuts."

"That doesn't bother you?" she asked.

"Not even remotely. I love it. They're great and they don't mean any harm and who knows? Maybe they're right, but producing kids isn't high on my list of priorities anyhow." He caught a flicker of sadness on Lori's face. "How about you? Five candy-smeared, screaming mini-yous in your future hopes and dreams?"

Lori looked back toward the bay window. "I don't know. That kind of life seems to exist in a separate world from the one I'm currently living in."

"True. That's why if you want it, you've got to pack your bags and relocate to that other world. Standing still is a good way to ensure it never happens. You said you've been with your boyfriend for four years? You guys never talked about kids?"

"No, not at all. I never even really thought about it."

"Lori." They both looked toward the voice. A man stood at the side of the property, behind the chain-link fence. His eyes darted toward Ben and narrowed.

Ben surmised this was the cheating boyfriend. He held a single cheap rose in his hand, the kind you buy from the plastic cup at the gas station. His button-down shirt revealed a t-shirt beneath it, something with a surfer catching a bright blue wave.

"Can we talk?" He directed his words at Lori, opening the gate and stepping into the backyard.

Lori stood and took a step toward Stu and then shook her head. "Just leave, Stu. We have nothing to talk about."

"Really? Four years together and that's it? One slip-up and I'm out of the picture?"

"It's over, Stu."

Stu opened his mouth, but Ben could see he wasn't about to grovel. Instead, he looked mad, mean even. "Don't pretend this is some great betrayal. You never let me in. Never." He dropped the rose on the ground and crushed it beneath his tennis shoe.

Ben noticed the way Lori's mouth twitched at Stu's accusation. It was an unconscious confirmation.

But that didn't change what the guy had done. Ben stood, took a few steps across the yard, and bent down, picking up the garden hose.

Stu glared at Ben. "I hope you didn't think you've landed a catch here, man. Look up 'frigid bitch' in the dictionary and you'll see a picture of Lori Hicks."

Ben clicked the nozzle to jet and aimed it at the surfer on Stu's stupid t-shirt. He pulled the lever. A stream of water shot from the nozzle and struck Stu in the chest. Stu staggered backward, yelping in surprise. Shock gave way to fury on his face.

Lori looked equally surprised, but she released a laugh and didn't bother covering her smile.

Stu held up his hands, serving only to deflect the spray into his face. He leaped sideways, but Ben followed him with the stream.

For a few seconds, Stu looked ready to charge, but he shot a final disgusted look at Lori and turned and sprinted back through the gate.

"Yell something at him," Ben called to Lori, releasing the hose nozzle.

"What?" She looked at him, confused.

"Don't let him get the last word."

"Thou art a boil, a plague sore!" she shouted.

Ben looked at her. The absurdity of her words hovered in the warm summer day.

She slapped her forehead. "Shit. That was stupid."

Ben laughed. "I don't know what that was."

Lori turned away from the fence, no longer watching her ex-boyfriend's departure. "A friend of mine at work got me a desk calendar for Christmas. Each day has a new Shakespearean insult. I think that one was from King Lear."

Ben dropped the hose on the ground. "Well, at least it's an insult he won't soon forget."

Lori smiled, but her shoulders sagged when she sat in the patio chair. "What does it say about me that I dated that guy for four years?"

"That you're a glutton for punishment. Forget him. Tell me about your weird theory."

"Yeah, okay." Lori dragged her fingers through her long, wavy hair. Ben noticed her fingers trembling and wished he'd sprayed the asshole ex in the face.

Lori grabbed the blue canvas bag she'd sat on the deck, drawing out two books. Ben saw the copy of *Strange Michigan*. She flipped through the pages and then held the book open for him to see.

"'The Witch in the Woods?'" he asked, reading the title aloud.

"Here, just skim the story."

Ben took the book, eyes trailing over the words of the creepy old woman who stole children in the woods. "Okay, basically a Hansel and Gretel retelling."

"In the Manistee Forest, two children in each story, always a girl child that gets taken." Lori grabbed the second book, flipping it open to a page held by a crimson bookmark. She slid the book to Ben.

This time he read the title silently: 'The Manistee Hag.' Again, he read the stories of a frightening old woman who stole children from the forest. This book offered an origin story for the witch that included murdering and eating her own sister.

Ben frowned. "Disturbing."

"Yeah, and look." Lori pointed a finger to a red circle around the word 'bell.' "She was wearing a dinner bell. Bev was wearing a bell on her necklace and Summer had the tambourine bracelet."

Ben glanced up at Lori to gauge if she was serious. She stared back at him intently.

"Umm... so you think a witch took Bev and Summer?"

"I know it sounds crazy. I do, but... what happened to them was crazy. It defies logic, Ben. Maybe the reason it was mysterious is because... because something supernatural took them."

Ben rubbed his knuckles and tried to choose his words carefully. "Lori, these are urban legends, tall tales. They're not—"

"But they are real. These are people's actual stories. Just because they're not published in a newspaper doesn't mean they're false."

"Don't take this the wrong way," Ben said, "but I have a theory about your theory."

"Okay."

"You said you minored in folklore and mythology in undergrad."

"Yeah."

"Have you considered this suspicion you have about the supernatural stuff might be born of all that stuff you put in your head?"

"You think I'm making this up because I took a few classes about folklore."

"No. I think maybe it's primed you to see things in a different light than you would if you hadn't studied that stuff."

"Do you think working in a medical profession and turning your nose up at anything not explained by science is why you're convinced a person is behind this?"

He sighed. "Don't get pissed."

"I'm not pissed. Why isn't my question as valid as yours?"

"Seriously? Because you're talking about mythical witches and goblins and I'm talking about something we all see on the news every day."

"I never said anything about goblins."

"Lori, a guy did this. A man. If we get sidetracked going down this dead-end road, we'll never get any closer to the truth."

Lori pressed her lips tightly together and closed the books.

"Please, don't get upset. I'm not trying to dash your hopes here, I just… this path"—he gestured at the books—"feels hopeless. But the path that ends with a guy in handcuffs leading the cops to bodies, that's something real. That's something we can work towards."

She sighed and met his gaze. "Okay, you're right. I just read those stories and they sounded so similar."

"I agree. They do, but let's exhaust the logical options first. Then we can start walking into the woods and leaving our trail of cookie crumbs to get back out."

"Very funny. The birds will eat them. We have to leave a trail of stones."

20

"Warren, you got a second?"

Warren looked up from the chart he'd been studying, squinting at Ben and then nodding slowly. "Yeah sure. These eyes need a rest." He took off his glasses and rubbed his fingertips into the concaves of his eye sockets.

Ben eased the door shut behind him and took the chair opposite Warren's desk. "Busy tonight?" Ben asked.

Warren put his glasses back on. They magnified his dark eyes. "Is it a full moon?" Warren gestured at the window where Ben could see little more than their reflections in the glass.

"Yeah, us too, but we're having a rare quiet hour, so I figured I'd pop over."

"Rather than hit the cafeteria and slam coffee and energy drinks with your fellow graveyarders?"

"I'm coffeed out. Trying to cut back, actually."

"Well, I salute you. I've been trying to cut back since I was sixteen and working on my grandpa's cattle farm. Nothing gets you addicted to coffee like four a.m. in the barn on a frigid February morning."

"I'm curious about something," Ben said.

Warren smiled. "And you thought I'd be curious about it too?"

"I rather hoped you might know something about it. The thing where you buy a Volkswagen and suddenly you see Volkswagens everywhere."

"The Baader-Meinhof phenomenon, also called the frequency illusion. Though I'm not sure what you'd like to know."

"It has a scientific name and everything?"

"Most things do. Human beings love their labels."

"Yeah. Well, I'm wondering... let me put it this way. Let's say I once dated someone and then we split up and someone mentions her name to me and suddenly I'm... I'm encountering things that remind me of her. Not just random things either, very specific things. I'm thinking I see her. Songs that we once listened to are playing on the radio. Jewelry that disappeared years ago suddenly reappears."

Warren leaned back in his chair. It squeaked loudly. "Thinking about Taylor?"

Ben scrunched his face. "No, not at all. This isn't about Taylor."

"Not Taylor, eh? Probably for the best, considering the complications of dating within the workplace. I dare say it's a tad late for that conclusion." He laughed. "When considering the frequency illusion there are two major points. The first is that when we encounter something that we term significant, our memory codes that information. Let's use your Volkswagen as an example. I buy the Volkswagen and the process of looking at cars and choosing this particular car and seeing this car every morning in my driveway makes it relevant. I've primed myself to notice the Volkswagen more. The bias occurs when I encounter the Volkswagen in the world and I convince myself that it has appeared largely because of my earlier encounter with it rather than accepting that I simply didn't notice it before."

"You're saying it's there; it's always been there; we just suddenly pay more attention and notice it more."

"Exactly."

"But... what if it wasn't there? Like in the jewelry thing. A necklace that I gave this girl disappeared twenty years ago and then suddenly reappears at the same time all these other things are happening."

"Meaning what? That by thinking of the girl you caused the jewelry to reappear? To miraculously arise where it had not been?"

"Yeah. Have you ever heard of anything like that?"

"That sounds like magical thinking."

"Which means what?"

"At a very basic level it means you're searching for a magical connection between things that are merely simple science. When we are reminded of a person we haven't spoken to in ten years and they call us the next day we might tend toward a magical explanation. It's a simple and very common phenomenon that is in truth merely a coincidence. The odds are against it and that's why it rarely happens. But as superstitious beings who evolved from thousands of years of worshiping all manner of deities and gods and whatnot, it's not surprising that we modern humans still cling to a few of those old beliefs."

"But what about the necklace?"

"The necklace?"

"The jewelry, the thing that appeared."

"I'd imagine you unconsciously took it out of hiding and left it where you'd notice it."

"I couldn't have taken it out of hiding. I literally did not have it anymore. It... it disappeared twenty years ago with a girl who disappeared at the same time."

"The one who got away?"

Ben sighed. "No, she literally disappeared, vanished while walking in the woods with my sister. Gone. She's never been found."

Warren frowned and tilted his head. "That's a traumatic memory. Have you ever spoken with anyone about that?"

Irritated, Ben stood. "Thanks for your help."

"Ben, don't rush out like that. Perhaps we can examine this further."

Ben waved a dismissive hand as he pushed out of Warren's office into the hallway. He didn't know why he'd gone to Warren to begin with. He had a nickname around the hospital—Windbag Warren.

Ben had always liked the psychiatrist. He'd shown up in a pinch on more than a few occasions in the ER on nights such as the one they were currently in. Full moon, a perfect night for crazy-making. But Ben had only ever spoken with him in passing as a colleague. He hadn't liked the way Warren looked at him, his probing questions. Ben felt sure Warren wanted to get him on his couch.

As he rounded the corner back toward his own floor, he ran smack into Taylor. Her coffee crumpled and she shrieked as the hot liquid burned her hand. Ben grimaced as he felt it scatter scalding droplets on his stomach and legs.

"Ugh, damn. Taylor. Shit. I'm sorry. Here." He rushed into the nearest bathroom and retrieved a wad of paper towel, swiped at Taylor's white coat, now mottled with brown-yellow stains.

"It's fine," she said, shoving his hand away and wincing. He saw the glistening red skin on her right thumb.

"I can get you something for that," he told her.

She glared at him. "I'm a doctor, Ben. I can get something for myself."

She stalked off down the hall. He squatted and cleaned up the last of the spilled coffee. He'd heard from more than a few of the nurses that she was still pissed, but not seeing her had given him a sliver of hope that she'd moved on, maybe even forgiven him. Apparently not.

Judy and Kenya stood at the nurse's station. Kenya was sipping from a jumbo energy drink with neon-green font that stated 'Turbo Energy.' Judy stared at the double doors to the emergency room with a deep crease between her eyes.

"Calm before the storm," Kenya murmured.

"Yep. It's coming. I can feel it," Judy agreed.

And come it did. It began with a group of five college students suffering from severe food poisoning. The nurses had gotten only one student into a bed when three more started projectile-vomiting in the waiting room.

Five minutes later an ambulance rolled into the parking lot with a victim of a head-on collision that had occurred on Highway 127. This tragedy was followed by a woman wheeling in her husband, who'd been stabbed by their next-door neighbor.

It was nearly three a.m. when the mayhem subsided enough for Ben to notice the greenish stains down his scrubs and the rancid smell of puke wafting up from them. Besides the vomit, blood coated the hair on his wrists and forearms from the stabbing victim.

Judy looked even worse. Puke stains ran from her shoulder to her waist. Kenya had stayed relatively clean save her once-white sneakers, now vomit-covered with another darker color Ben suspected was feces.

"Fuck all," Ryan Kimner, another ER nurse, grumbled, sagging forward on the nurses' station, head resting on his hands. "I knew I shouldn't have picked up this shift."

"Change quick if you're going to," Kenya said. "This night isn't over yet."

Ben ran to the staff room, stripped out of his scrubs, and crammed them into a laundry bin. He pulled on clean scrubs and started back toward the door, pausing when he saw the girl at the end of the hall, the same girl he'd seen before with her long wheat-colored hair and her red and white striped shorts.

"This one's coding!" Zander, the paramedic Ben had seen at the bar a couple nights before, shouted as he pushed a gurney through the emergency room doors.

Ben spun away from the girl, sprinting to assist.

~

I t was four a.m., and Ben hadn't eaten for his entire shift. Light-headed, he hurried toward the nurses' station, where Judy kept a stash of granola bars. His gaze slipped into room number nine. He saw the teenage girl who'd been brought in during the day shift. A suicide attempt. She'd tried unsuccessfully to slit her wrists. She sat up in bed, staring with oddly glittering eyes straight at him.

Ben slowed and turned into her room, glancing at the chart where her name was displayed. "Everything okay in here, Amanda? Do you need something?"

"She's in the woods, Ben," Amanda whispered, wide glassy eyes locked on his.

"I'm sorry, what—" Ben's words died on his lips as he registered the scissors she lifted toward her neck. Before he could move, she'd jammed the sharp point into her throat.

Blood spurted from the red gash that blossomed on her pale neck. It rained onto the white sheet and the gray linoleum floor, stopping inches away from Ben's tennis shoes.

He didn't freeze, didn't pause at the horror unfolding before him. He lunged across the room, stuffed a palm over the wound and clamped it tight with one hand while flinging the scissors away with the other. They skittered across the floor. He slammed his hand against the emergency call button.

"Stay with me, Mandy, come on now." Her folder had said Amanda, but Ben sensed people who knew her, really knew her, called her Mandy, and he leaned on that now, on the hope that this one tiny connection might bring her back from whatever dark hole she'd plunged into.

Her eyes rolled up, and he could see only the whites. Blood pulsed hot and steady from the wound in her neck as he bunched a handful of white sheet against it.

Kenya ran into the room and then shouted down the hallway for a trauma doctor.

Amanda's other hand flopped open, the one that hadn't been holding the scissors. Through the adrenaline giving him tunnel vision, Ben saw the golden unicorn head, the red ruby eye gleaming.

"What the fuck?" he groaned.

"You okay?" Kenya asked, nudging him aside. "Step out, take a breather. We've got this."

He almost grabbed the necklace. He wanted to snatch it from the girl's limp hand and run to the roof of the building and chuck it into the glowing night, but that would only ensure he'd cross paths with it again when the shift ended.

He turned away from it and stumbled into the hallway.

At six a.m. Ben walked bleary-eyed into the parking lot. More mornings than not he walked off a shift motivated, energized even. Not this morning. This morning he felt as if he'd biked five hundred miles the night before. During a hailstorm. With leg cramps.

He sagged against his car, catching sight of Ryan dragging himself in similar fashion toward his two-door pickup. Ryan offered a half-hearted wave. "Karaoke this weekend?"

Ben gave him a thumbs up, too tired to offer more.

Kenya bounded from the building a moment later. She'd changed from scrubs into a cream-colored business suit and red heels.

"Please tell me you're not going to your second job?" Ben asked as she paused beside her black Saturn.

She grinned, sliding sunglasses over her eyes. "Nothing a few shots of espresso can't cure. Paralegals don't get any more rest than nurses."

"When do you sleep?"

Kenya shrugged. "On my lunch breaks." She climbed into her car, fired the engine, and pulled from the parking lot.

Ben unlocked his door and slid behind the wheel. He started the car and the radio blared to life, though he was sure he hadn't turned it on when driving to his shift the evening before. *Every Breath You Take* by the Police screamed from the speakers. Ben slammed his hand against the radio button before twisting it so hard that he yanked the knob right off the dashboard.

"Shit," he muttered, tossing it on the passenger seat.

He drove home in a fog, walked through the front door and stumbled up the stairs to his bedroom. He needed to feed Leia, take a shower, eat something, but he did none of those things. He lay on the bed, shoved off his shoes, and fell asleep.

21

Lori paused from the witch fairytale she'd been reading when her phone rang. She saw Ben's name on the screen.

"Hey, how'd it go with the dream doctor yesterday?" he asked when she answered his call.

"Pretty good. Interesting. He suggested I try to revisit the dream while awake and imagine a happy ending."

"Huh. Please tell me he's not one of those two-hundred-dollar-an-hour shrinks. I could have given you that advice along with your coffee for free the other morning."

Lori laughed. "His rates approach that. Fortunately, my insurance covers it."

"Listen, I lined up a meeting with Bella Palmer's friend, the one who was with her when she vanished. She runs the Facebook page."

"You're kidding."

"Nope, dead serious. You want to go? I'm meeting her at six over in Reed City. I have to swing by Carmen's house and help Jonas with his bike for the umpteenth time. You can ride along."

Lori stared at the book. She'd highlighted several lines of text and could easily immerse herself in the stories for the rest of the afternoon. She bookmarked it and closed it. "Count me in. Should I come to your place?"

"That'd be great."

Before setting her phone down, she noticed three new emails in her inbox. One was from Stu. She hit delete without opening it. The second was from the office asking her to set up her out-of-office message and the third was from Dr. Chadwick. Lori opened it.

Lori—

Based on our previous meeting, I went ahead and gathered a few names for you: Jungians who work in the deeper archetypal stories. Irene Whitaker is right here in Michigan. Grand Rapids area. She no longer sees clients but works entirely on translating ancient texts, specifically folklore and fairytales. You can reach her at 616-525-9712.

Warm Regards,

Dr. Chadwick

Lori almost set her phone down, followed her usual 'save the uncomfortable things for later' mentality, but then she punched in the number for Irene Whitaker.

A woman, sounding cheerful, answered on the first ring.

"Hi, I'm trying to reach Irene Whitaker."

"This is she."

"Hi, Irene. My name is Lori Hicks and I was given your number by Dr. Chadwick in Traverse City."

"Hello, Lori. Yes, Dr. Chadwick mentioned you. He and I worked together lifetimes ago at the Centre for Analytic Studies in the United Kingdom. I too was interested in the study of dreams. Aren't we all? But ultimately I was called to the stories and that is where I've stayed."

"Do you have time to meet at all? I've been reading some folklore stuff and would really appreciate an expert opinion."

"I can always make time to talk about my passions. I'm in the office most days here in Grand Rapids working on translations. You could come by anytime."

"Okay, great. How about tomorrow, maybe twelve o'clock?"

≈

Ben was sitting on his screened-in porch when Lori arrived. He pushed open the swinging door and walked down the driveway.

"Hey," he called.

"Hi." Lori closed her car door and pushed her hands into her pockets. "Are we officially private eyes now?"

He grinned. "Oh, yeah. We need to hit up a dollar store and get one of those little plastic sheriff badges and a pair of handcuffs."

"Handcuffs?"

He smirked. "Maybe we better skip the cuffs."

"How was your shift last night?" she asked.

Ben glowered. "Rough. Full moons are a nightmare in the ER. I need to get a moon calendar and start taking that day off every month."

"Really? I always thought the full moon hysteria was an old wives' tale."

"Those old wives knew what they were talking about. I've got to grab some tools out of the garage and then we can roll."

He typed a code into a box on the exterior of the garage and the garage door groaned as it slid up.

"Welcome to my church," he said as the door opened, revealing an ordinary garage with cement floors. Shelves stacked with clear totes covered one wall. At the back of the garage stood a long wooden workbench. Tools hung from hooks on the wall above it. A rubber mat in front of the desk held a metal stand that a bicycle hung suspended from.

He walked into the garage, paused beside the bicycle and spun the back tire. "I've gotten on my knees more in this place than anywhere else."

Lori thought of her own recent visit to the overeater's anonymous group, which took place in a literal church. Was there anything about the space that compelled her to bare her soul, to fall to her knees and weep? No. She'd wept in plenty of groups, but it had nothing to do with the structure surrounding them. She could have been sitting in someone's living room or in the community hall of a trailer park—in fact she had been sitting in both places on occasions when she'd found herself sobbing to the group, detailing an out-of-control night when she'd eaten until she'd made herself sick.

But were those meetings her church? The space she clung to when her heart was troubled? No, she didn't think so. The image that rose to her mind was her little bay window with Matilda curled into a ball of fur, clutching the pillow Grand Mavis had carefully stitched in Lori's favorite colors of purple and yellow.

"We used to go to church before my dad left," Lori admitted. "Afterwards we stopped. I'm pretty sure my mom decided God had abandoned her."

"Does she still feel that way?" Ben paused at the worktable, gathering tools into a little blue pouch and folding it closed.

"I don't think so. A few years after Bev disappeared, my mom started talking about how I'd been spared that night—how I must have had a guardian angel." Lori released a harsh laugh that sounded more like a croak. "It was unnerving to hear her say that."

"Why?"

"Because the necklace Bev wore that night—a bola, she called it—was supposed to summon her guardian angel. That's what she told me." She shook her head. "After Bev disappeared, I lost it. I'd never really had it. Who does at fourteen? I was kind of chubby and food had always been a comfort for me. I started binge-eating. By the time I ended my freshman year in high school I weighed almost two hundred pounds. It took a long time to get myself under control. Apparently, I was having night terrors. I don't even remember those, but my mom took me to see a psychologist. Don't remember him either. I didn't realize how much stuff I blocked out."

She stumbled over her words, telling him secrets she hadn't told her own boyfriend of four years.

"I finally got connected with a doctor my senior year who got me into a group," Lori continued. "Basically, AA for binge-eaters. Hardly anyone knows that. I never told Stu. My mom and my grandma are the only people who know. The other day you asked me about touching my stomach." She swiped a hand over her stomach. "It's a throwback thing, a quirk I guess, from my days of being so self-conscious about my body."

As she heard the confession, she laughed dryly. "Maybe this is like a church. I'm sorry to tell you all this. I don't know why I am. I was so ashamed by that, ashamed that I couldn't do it on my own, that I didn't have the same self-control other people had. That's what happened the day I met you at King's Post. I saw Stu and… went into that same old cycle. After it was over, I went to a meeting at the Holy Faith Church."

Ben frowned and carried the tools back out of the garage. Lori walked behind him, wishing she had a time machine that would allow her to erase the last thirty seconds, which in itself was an embarrassing thought. Of all the wrongs she could right with a time machine, her first thought was to erase a moment of verbal diarrhea.

"I lost it too," Ben said. "I did a bunch of crazy stuff the year after Summer disappeared. I broke into her house when her parents were at church one Sunday morning. I was chasing wild theories then. I didn't find anything, but I stole a pair of her socks. Stupid. But they seemed like the least likely thing to be missed.

"I also broke into her locker at school. I keyed her uncle's truck. I tried to get her file at the police office. I went in there under the guise of a school project, said I needed to use the bathroom and slipped off to the evidence room. They caught me, threatened to arrest me. Even after I moved away from Manistee, I kept obsessing. I'm not a drinker, I've never been into drugs, but Summer's disappearance was my drug. I lived on it. I pored over the newspapers every day searching for stories about sex offenders and murderers. I drove all over the state, buying papers and taking notes. I still have a lot of it stuffed into cardboard boxes in my basement. There were years when I hoped a heavy rain would cause my basement to flood and destroy it all."

"How did you stop?"

"I saved someone's life." Ben massaged the knuckles on his right hand. "I was at the pier watching the waves. It was something I did a lot in those days. I'd spend hours reading the papers and then I'd go out to that pier and try to connect the dots, come up with theories. I was out there one day in my early twenties and I saw these kids playing on the pier. It was too cold for swimming. We were coming into the time of year when the water gets icy. This tremendous wave came in and crashed right over the pilings and washed the girl into the water. The boy held his ground. He started screaming for help, and there were no parents around.

"I ran out there and dove in. The water was so cold it took my breath away. It took me a while to find her and when I did, she'd swallowed a ton of water. I got her onto the shore and bent her over, beating on her back. I thought she was dead. Her skin was ice-cold and gray and she wasn't breathing, but I didn't stop. I did mouth-to-mouth, and suddenly she gurgled and spit up.

"For the next two days, I didn't think about anything except saving that girl. I didn't think about Summer one single time. I'd found it, the path out of the obsession, and I felt like I had this one shot. I had to run it down and not look back. I enrolled in college the next day, did an accelerated program, applied to nursing school and now here I am."

"And then I showed up and dropped the obsession at your front door."

He shook his head. "It's different now. It doesn't have the same hold on me it once did."

L ori and Ben arrived at a modern farmhouse with a wrap-around porch and a wooden swing set in the side yard. Lori felt a little jangle of nerves at the thought of meeting Ben's sister.

"That's Carmen," Ben told her, gesturing to a woman sitting in the front yard with two small children. "And that"—he pointed at the garage where a man was biting his lip and staring in frustration at a bright yellow road bike—"is Jonas, who calls me over here twice a week to help him with his bike."

Lori smiled. "He looks like he's trying to solve a complicated algebra equation."

"Now that he could do in a cinch, but changing the gears on a bicycle? Not so much."

Ben parked, and he and Lori climbed out. "Hey, Carm," Ben called. "Go have a chat. I'll be over shortly."

Lori walked toward Carmen, who sat on a yellow and red checkered blanket. A baby, wearing only a blue onesie, lay on her back with several toes from her right foot inserted in her mouth. Another child, this one a little boy in the toddler range, sat coloring a picture of a cow, scribbling huge streaks of pink across the cow's backside.

Carmen smiled and struggled up to her feet, wincing. "I'm embarrassed to admit that at thirty-three, it's a lot easier to get down there than back up. Hi, I'm Carm." She extended her hand and Lori took it, noticing something warm and wet pass from Carmen's hand into her own.

Carmen pulled away and looked at her palm. "Oh, Jesus, peanut butter. I'm sorry. I swear it's not baby poop. Here, let me grab you a wipe."

"No big deal," Lori assured her, holding her hand out so she didn't unconsciously swipe it on her pants.

"So, you've been chumming around with my big brother. I hope he's treating you well."

Lori flushed. "Well, not... I mean, we're not dating or anything. We've just both been looking into the disappearances."

Carmen's smile fell, and she stepped back toward her children, leaning down to ruffle her son's red-blond curls. "Here, Thomas, have a drink from your sippy cup." She bent over and grabbed a blue cup decorated in whales and held it out to the boy, who continued coloring with one hand while guiding the lidded cup to his lips with the other. He didn't even look up.

"He's determined," Lori said.

"He sure is. A lot like his daddy. Jonas insists on cycling, but nothing about it comes naturally to him. Every time he goes for a ride, he comes home with road rash."

"Ouch," Lori said. "I'm afraid I'd have a similar experience."

"Do you want some iced tea? I have a pitcher on the porch."

Lori glanced toward the garage.

"They'll probably be twenty minutes," Carmen explained. "Ben's big on giving Jonas a lesson every time he comes to show him something on the bike."

"Sure." Lori followed Carmen up the porch, accepting the tall glass of tea she poured. "This place is really beautiful," Lori told her, noticing the matching rocking chairs on the porch engraved with words 'His' and 'Hers.'

"You lost a friend too? In the woods?" Carmen asked, her expression pinched.

"Yes, my best friend, Beverly Silva. We were both fourteen."

Carmen stepped to the porch rail and busied herself brushing pollen off the wood. "It's such a terrible thing, to lose a friend like that. I had to forget. It was the only way I could move on." She forced a smile, eyes flicking toward the garage. "Ben acts like I sold out, gave up. He thinks that's why I live this life, married with kids, doing the mom thing, but you want the truth? Ben's the one who's afraid. Not me.

"Well, that's not quite true. I am afraid. I'm terrified of something happening to the people I love, most of all my children, but I still had them. I still got married. I'm the one who's invited genuine love and vulnerability into my life. Ben acts like he's the risk-taker, but the truth is he's running from vulnerability. He has been ever since Summer disappeared. Did he tell you he and Summer were going out?"

22

Lori's eyes widened at the sudden outpouring of information. "No."

"He acts like everything's on the table, everything's transparent, but in reality, he picks what you see and paints it like it's the complete picture. They were. I was pissed as hell when it started because I was losing my best friend to my brother. Summer would come over and they'd sneak off to the garage to make out. It drove me batshit crazy.

"But what do you do? Forbid your best friend from dating your brother? It's the oldest fight in the book and nobody ever wins. It would probably have fizzled. She was fourteen, he was sixteen. Those things rarely last, but then... then she disappeared, and that changed everything. She was frozen in time.

"And Summer going missing was just the beginning. It got so much uglier, so much harder on Ben most of all because people in town blamed him and that extended to our family. My dad started drinking, his business went under, foreclosure, divorce... Ben fled. He's a runner." Carmen turned to face Lori, shaking her head. "I'm sorry. I shouldn't be saying this stuff. I love my brother. I adore him, but... sometimes I feel judged by him, like he thinks I sold out somehow."

"This looks like a pretty enviable life to me," Lori said, looking beyond Carmen to her two children.

"Meeting Jonas reminded me of what it felt like to feel safe again, loved unconditionally. Was I scared of falling in love with him? Yeah, definitely, but I was more afraid to turn into Ben. That's a horrible thing to say, but it's true. I saw how he ran away from anyone or anything that really touched him. He chased all kinds of stuff that gave him a thrill, but anything that offered something deeper than that, something more, he hopped on his bike and pedaled away as fast as his legs could carry him."

"I really don't know him that well," Lori murmured, feeling awkward talking about Ben when he was standing just across the yard.

"I hope you get to know him, Lori. I hope he's finally ready to let someone in."

"Mama, come see," the little boy called, waving his picture in the air.

Carmen walked back down the steps, kneeling on the blanket beside her little boy. "Oh, Thomas, that's so pretty, what is it?"

"Uncle Bem!" he announced.

He held the picture high. Lori saw a round circle with several squiggles coming out of it.

"That looks just like Uncle Ben." Carmen laughed, winking at Lori. "Sit, relax." She said patting the blanket.

Lori sat down, crossing her legs and sweeping her fingers through the fragrant grass.

"I rarely talk about Summer because what is there to say?" Carmen said, frowning at Lori. "I've told the story a thousand times. I've mulled over what might have happened, but none of my imaginings gets me closer to the truth, and I don't want to be trapped in the past. I want to live my life here and now, with these two, with my husband, with this sky full of pink clouds.

"It's not that I'm afraid, it's that I'm no longer deluded into some skewed idea that I'm Nancy Drew and I'm going to unravel the big mystery. People disappear. They get taken, sometimes they're never found. I won't be one of those people who squander the lives they were given chasing a phantom. I got to live. Me. There were two of us that night and I got to live. You did too, Lori. You are alive."

The baby bent over and reached for the plastic tray of food. She popped a large, round grape into her mouth.

Carmen's eyes bulged and she screamed. "Maddison, no!"

Lori fell back as Carmen lunged for her daughter and wrenched the child's mouth open, fished the grape from the girl's cheeks and flung it away as if it were a live wasp. She clutched her daughter against her chest, rocking and moaning and patting the girl's head. Maddison's bottom lip trembled and she started to cry, calming only when Carmen handed her a bottle.

As if remembering Lori, Carmen looked up and color rose into her ashen cheeks. She released her baby carefully. The girl rolled onto her back, clutching her bottle with both her hands and feet. Carmen stood, smoothing out her skirt and tucking her hair behind her ears.

"I'm sorry. I…" She gestured at her daughter. "Grapes are one of the most common foods babies and small children choke on. I hate them. That's a weird thing to say. Who hates grapes? But I do. I hate them. And marshmallows too. Choking is the leading cause of death for kids under four years. Jonas insists on buying them and our nanny Brenda, even though I've told her a million times not to, puts them in the kids' premade lunches. I'm sorry."

"No, it's okay. It would scare me too."

Carmen smiled, watching her daughter, but her spine stayed rigid as if she were on red alert for the next catastrophe awaiting her two beautiful children. "That's the price, I guess, and maybe the reason Ben doesn't have children or a wife because if you lose them… they're gone." Her voice trailed off on the last two words.

Ben and Jonas stepped from the garage.

"Did somebody scream?" Ben asked.

Carmen waved at them. "It's fine. I panicked when she put a grape in her mouth."

Jonas shot Ben a look as if to say, *You know Carmen.*

Ben wiped his hands on a dirty rag and walked toward the yard with Jonas beside him. "Lori, this is Jonas."

"Hi," Lori said, getting to her feet and offering her hand.

He shook it. "What are you kids up to tonight?" He looked between Ben and Lori. "Not another Scientology potluck, I hope." Jonas muffled his laughter, while Carmen grabbed another grape from the container and threw it at him.

"Not funny, Jonas." She laughed.

"Ha-ha." Ben rolled his eyes. "Officially the one and only time I'll let the two of you set me up on a blind date. No potlucks for us this evening, we're doing some digging into a missing person's case over in Reed City."

Carmen made a face. "That's romantic."

"Really? Not another girl?" Jonas asked, curious.

"Yeah, remember I told you I'd found some others? This is one of them."

Carmen got to her feet, swinging the baby up with her. "Time for a diaper change," she announced, walking toward the porch. She turned back. "Nice to meet you, Lori. Be careful, you guys."

They watched her disappear into the house.

Jonas grabbed Ben in a half-hug. "Text me when you're home safe. I don't want to be up half the night thinking you're out there chasing a serial killer."

Ben hugged him back, grinning at Lori over his shoulder. "Yes, Dad."

Jonas draped his arms over their shoulders, walking them toward Ben's car.

"Bem, Bem!" Thomas shouted running after them with his drawing in hand.

Ben squatted down. "What do you have here, Sir Thomas?"

"It's you."

Ben took the drawing and nodded. "I'll cherish it. Thanks, man." He gave Thomas a high five and then stood and followed Lori too the car.

As Ben drove away from the farmhouse, Lori watched him gazing at Jonas and Thomas in the rearview mirror.

"They're really nice," she said.

"Yeah, they're great. Carmen gets a bit high-strung now and then, but it's just her mama bear coming out. Did you have a good chat?"

Lori bit her lip, wondering if she should mention what Carmen had told her. She knew if she didn't it would consume her brain until she blurted it out in some less appropriate moment. "Why didn't you tell me you were going out with Summer when she vanished?"

Ben glanced at her. "Didn't I?"

"No."

He looked out the window. "I don't know. I figured I had. Everyone knew. I assumed you read it in a newspaper article or something."

He said no more about it and they drove the rest of the way to Reed City in silence.

～

"I think that's her," Ben said when they walked into the Sunset Grill. "She told me she'd be wearing an MSU Spartans t-shirt."

Renee Douglas sat at a high-top table drinking a glass of red wine. She wore a green Spartans shirt with stone-washed jeans. She was short and heavier-set, her small feet dangling high above the ground.

"Renee?" Ben asked.

Her eyes lit at the sight of Ben and she quickly brushed her curled brown hair away from her face, smiling shyly. "You've found her."

"I'm Ben," he said, offering his hand. "And this is Lori."

"Hi." Renee shook both of their hands. "Great to meet you both."

"You too, Renee. I appreciate your taking the time to talk with us."

"You're welcome. I already finished a glass. This is number two. I haven't told the story in a long time. I thought it'd be no big deal, but then when I was driving here tonight and remembering what happened, I realized I needed a couple of adult beverages to retell it."

"I'm right there with you," Lori said, glancing at the cocktail menu.

"Did it happen to you too?" Renee asked.

"Yes," Lori told her. "In 1998. My friend went missing when we were walking in the woods."

Renee nodded, eyes flooding with tears. "Bella was my very best friend in the whole world. She was pretty and popular and none of those other girls ever gave me the time of day, but Bella did. She had a heart of gold, and I don't say that because she's gone. You know how people do when someone is gone... She just loved everyone and everything. Including me." Renee lifted her glass to her lips.

Their waiter, a slim kid with a bad case of acne, stopped to take their order.

"Gin and tonic, please," Lori told him.

"Ginger ale for me," Ben said.

"Ugh." He scratched at a crater in his face and then quickly dropped his hand, eyes darting toward the bar as if he'd been reprimanded more than once for picking at his face while on the job. "Is Vernors okay?" he asked Ben.

"Yeah, thanks."

The kid wandered back to the bar, and Renee returned to her story.

"We wanted to make blackberry cobbler," Renee said. "We'd learned how to make cobbler in home-ec class in school before summer break and we couldn't wait to pick our own berries and make the cobbler at home. We played in the woods a lot back then. All the kids in town did. That evening we went later than usual because Bella had dance class, and then I walked to her house afterward. We took plastic buckets and went to the woods and started looking. I don't know when we got separated. We'd been chatting but then drifted off on our own and next thing I knew she was gone.

"I kept listening for her whistle, thinking she'd blow it when she realized we'd gotten separated and not seen each other in a while."

"Her whistle?" Lori asked.

"A rape whistle," Renee explained.

"Why was she carrying a rape whistle?" Ben asked, leaning forward in his chair.

"Her mother insisted she wear it every time she left the house. Bella's mom was great, but she was a little kooky. She lived in terror of anything happening to her kids. She had fire-drill plans posted in every room of the house. She used to lecture us a lot on never going with strangers. The summer before Bella vanished, her mom made her wear a lifejacket our whole time at summer camp. She was twelve, for Pete's sake."

Lori frowned. "Did she blow it that night?"

Renee nodded. "Yeah, she did. A few times just for fun and then... well, later I heard it, I thought, but... they never found any sign of her, so..."

"Was she wearing anything else? A bell or—"

"Gin and tonic and a Vernors. You guys want some apps? The loaded potato skins are totally addictive." The waiter arrived, notepad ready.

"I think we're good," Ben told him. He turned his focus to Renee. "Were there any men around that night, Renee? Any men loitering in the area?"

She shook her head. "The police asked that too. I didn't see anyone, but... I was distracted. One of my other friends had called that morning and said this boy in our grade liked me. Jared was his name, and no boys had ever liked me. I was gushing about it to Bella. The boys always liked her. She was gorgeous with long chestnut hair and really pretty green eyes. It seems so stupid now. I probably wouldn't even recognize Jared if I ran into him these days." She shrugged. "Such is the mind of an eighth-grader."

Lori lifted her glass, got a whiff of the alcohol, and put it back down, her stomach curdling. The queasiness that had followed her after her last night of gin and tonics coursed through her and she pushed the cocktail away.

"How about guys around town?" Ben asked. "Guys who got in trouble for messing with underage girls? Or guys people whispered might have been involved?"

Renee tilted her head, thoughtful. "We sometimes thought the school janitor was a little creepy, but I don't think he ever got in trouble. He died in a car crash when I was in high school. No one else I can think of."

"Other than the whistle, did she have anything on that made noise? A bell-type thing?" Lori asked, sensing Ben stiffen beside her. She ignored it.

"A bell?" Renee shook her head. "No. Just the whistle. But people heard it after she vanished. It was weird because several of the searchers heard the whistle and tried to track it, but never a sign of her. Really, there were a lot of strange things that happened during the searches."

"Really? Like what?" Lori asked.

"More than a few people got lost during the searches. My mom told me later about this woman named Gina. She was in a line, you know, walking within arm's reach of people on either side, and then suddenly her husband noticed she wasn't there, so then the group was calling for her. They couldn't find her.

"She ended up out on the interstate waving down a farm truck passing by. He drove her back to the lot where everyone started the search. She said one minute she'd been walking in the group and the next minute she was alone in the forest, kind of dizzy, with no clue how she'd gotten over there, how much time had passed. It was weird—so weird her husband insisted she go into the emergency room and get checked out. He was afraid she'd had a stroke."

"Had she?" Lori asked.

"Nope. Doc said she was right as rain. No fever, heart rate and blood pressure were good. They ran labs just in case. Didn't find a thing."

"And there were other stories like that?"

"A handful. People getting separated from the group, feeling light-headed. I wasn't there for most of that, but my mom told me about it later. She said the woods gave her the creeps."

They said little as Ben drove back home. Lori mostly stared out the window. He glanced at her profile now and then and thought he saw the quiver of her chin as if she were struggling not to cry.

He parked in his driveway and turned off the engine. "Are you okay?" he asked.

She faced him, nodding, though her face looked drawn. "I'm worn out. I need to sleep for about twelve hours."

"You're welcome to stay if you're too tired to drive."

"No." She shook her head. "I need to be in my own bed. Thank you, though."

"Okay." He opened his door and waited until Lori had climbed out as well. "So, I got an email back from Gertrude Weller this evening. She's Peyton Weller's aunt and she said she'd be happy to talk to us. She's over in Scottville."

"Wow, okay. When?"

"Are you sure you're up for it?" Ben asked.

"I'm sure."

"I'm going to take a long ride tomorrow. Want to meet here again? Say four o'clock and then we'll drive to Scottville?"

"I'll be here."

23

Lori pulled her pillow over her head to mute the sound, but it seemed to make no difference.

Crunch, crunch, crunch…

Gnawing and pulling and slurping and all of it right outside her door. She'd kill Henry for waking her up. She let her arm flop to the side where the pillow fell from her hand to the floor.

The chewing continued and she couldn't imagine what he could be eating that would make so much noise.

She sat up in her daybed and stared across the room, eyelids heavy and wanting to slip closed. But she'd never fall back asleep with him out there. She stood and started for the door, stepped on something hard and yelped in pain. She reached down and felt along the carpet, eyes adjusting to the dark. It was a little metal ball. When she lifted it, it tinkled. Lori held it in the fragment of moonlight that had gotten past her curtains. It was a little round bell with pretty designs etched in the surface and something in her belly throbbed at the sight of it—so familiar, and yet… crunch.

She pocketed the ball and continued toward her door, reaching for the handle. It was warm and almost wet beneath her palm. The crunching had stopped. Lori lowered her eyes and stared at the bit of strange light spilling beneath the door. It carried with it a reddish-brown fog that seeped slowly into the room.

Lori's fury at Henry shrank down and another emotion replaced it—fear. She was suddenly sure whatever had been eating had heard her wake up and *approach the door. It stood just on the other side, perhaps its long nose tilted up, trying to catch her scent. Its maw hung agape, its meal growing putrid in the warmth.*

Another sound arose, beginning at the top of her bedroom door. A grating screech as if whatever stood on the other side had long pointed nails and had begun to drag them down the face of the door.

～

"Yo, dude, maybe you better call 911."

Lori woke to a mass of voices, many talking over the others, unfamiliar and disjointed.

"She may be having a seizure—"

"At least the screaming stopped—"

"Bro, I totally have E downstairs. Let me get out of here before you call the cops."

"Lori, hey, Lori." Rough hands shook her shoulders, and she blinked and clamped her eyes shut when the bright lights of her living room fixture blinded her. She shoved both hands over her eyes.

"She's awake," a girl said.

"Lori. Hey, it's Kenny. You okay?"

The voices subsided, and when Lori pulled her hands from eyes, she saw Kenny, her downstairs neighbor, kneeling beside her and no fewer than ten of his friends loitering around her apartment. Most of them held beer cans. One was smoking a lit joint, the tendril of smoke swirling into the air above the kid's head.

"What are you doing in my apartment?" she asked, trying to raise her voice, but it came out as a croak.

She sat up, wincing at the ache in the left side of her neck, for which she could thank falling asleep on the couch. As she sat up, her eyes caught her bare legs, and she snatched a throw from the back of the couch, settling it over her pale thighs.

It had been warm when she'd returned from her outing with Ben, and she'd lain down in a pair of old, elastic-less underwear that she usually wore during her time of the month and an oversized t-shirt with a faded picture of Buffy the Vampire Slayer on the front.

"You were screaming," Kenny explained, standing up and grabbing a can of beer off her coffee table. She saw the ring of condensation he'd left behind on her hardcover copy of Wally Lamb's *She's Come Undone*.

"What are you talking about?" she asked, still groggy, her throat hoarse. She wanted a glass of water, but sure as hell wouldn't be getting up and trotting across the room in her holey underpants to get one.

"It was crazy," a girl wearing a cut-off CMU t-shirt that left her midriff bare chimed in. "Like, we were all partying and drinking and somebody said, 'Hey, quiet, do you guys hear that?' and we all went quiet and it was like—"

"You were being murdered," a guy with a ball cap pulled low on his forehead finished.

"Or raped," Kenny said. "We came barreling up the stairs, ready to kick the guy's ass. Your door was locked, so we had to bust in. Sorry about that."

Lori looked beyond him to where her door hung ajar, dangling crooked on one hinge.

"But then there was nobody in here. Just you lying there screaming and, like… you didn't stop," Kenny said.

Lori dropped her eyes to her lap and rubbed her forehead. She could feel the warmth burning in her cheeks, and she wanted to pull the blanket over her head and make everyone in her apartment simply disappear. Normal people already would have left, she thought. They'd have realized she'd just been having a nightmare and taken their leave, but these were drunk people. A few of them had even begun to chitchat as if they weren't standing in the middle of her apartment.

"I must have been having a bad dream," she said finally.

Kenny bobbed his head up and down. "More like a nightmare. I mean when I touched you, you were like so hot. You maybe need to go to a doctor."

"Yeah, thanks." She raised her voice, though it hurt to do so. "Umm… thanks, everyone. I appreciate your coming to my rescue, even if the bad guy was just in my dreams."

A few of them chuckled, but they still didn't mobilize toward the door.

"I think I'd like to get back to bed now," she told Kenny.

"Oh, yeah, sure thing. I was gonna say 'don't lock your door in case it happens again,' but"—he gestured at the door—"that thing won't be locking anyway."

Lori pressed her lips together and nodded. "Thanks again, Kenny."

Kenny waved at his gaggle of drunken friends. "All right, guys and gals, let's take this party back downstairs."

They slowly trooped from the room and disappeared into the hallway. One of them made a half-hearted attempt to close her door, but it remained open a crack. Lori stood, wincing at the pinch in her neck and massaging it as she made her way to the kitchen. She poured a tall glass of water. Two beer cans remained on her kitchen table.

She remembered Matilda and scanned the space, looking for her kitty. "Matilda. Here, kitty, kitty," she called, but the cat didn't materialize.

Lori finished the water and limped to her bedroom. Not only did her neck ache, her feet ached.

"Jesus, I'm not even thirty and this is happening," she muttered, bracing her hands on the side of the bed as she lowered onto the floor. She peered under the bed, spotting two glowing yellow eyes tucked into the far back corner.

"There's my girl," she murmured. "Come here, honey. Come out. It's okay."

After a minute of coaxing, Matilda shimmied out from under the bed. Lori picked her up and snuggled her, then set her on the mattress.

"Let's lock this, shall we?" Lori said, moving back to her bedroom door and turning the lock on the handle. It was a flimsy lock, easily broken, and she hoped Kenny wouldn't be making another appearance that night.

The thought of it made her cringe and she didn't want to sleep knowing she might have another nightmare and find herself trapped somewhere, her body shrieking while her mind did God only knew what.

The dream repeated on a steady and disturbing reel in her head—the crunching and slurping—and though she hadn't opened the door in her dream, she felt convinced that the figure she'd drawn so long ago stood on the other side.

Lori lay awake, listening to the throb of the music in the backyard blending with voices. She tried not to sleep and managed it for an hour, but then exhaustion took hold and pulled her under.

24

Ben slipped on his padded spandex shorts and his dry-fit shirt. He velcroed his cycling shoes and lunge-walked to the garage while circling his arms.

He rode west on 10, a highway that eventually ran through the Manistee National Forest, turning onto back roads to avoid traffic.

As he rode, the pavement unrolled in a sinewy strip, gradually muting his mind. He concentrated on his breath, on the steady thrum of his legs as they scissored beneath him.

On either side of the road, the forest bunched against the ditch, casting a streak of shadow that he tried to stay within to keep his body temperature a few degrees cooler.

Ben wasn't sure when he sensed that something was off. He'd been so focused, so empty of thought, but gradually noticed the hairs on the back of his neck prickling. He peered down to see his forearms too were covered in gooseflesh.

He glanced toward the dark woods and had the unnerving sense that something watched him from within them, but something couldn't watch him. He was pedaling nearly twenty miles per hour. Anything in the forest would have to be running at top speed to track him from the woods. There were animals that could do it—wolves, foxes, even deer—but they'd be dodging trees and foliage.

Still, the sense that something tracked him and continued to pace him only deepened as he pumped his legs faster. He was on a long stretch of country road, a stretch he'd ridden before, and he knew the next signs of human life lay at least five miles away, the next town more than fifteen.

He pedaled harder, but turned and skimmed the forest as he did so. Something flashed in the trees, a whirring shadow that was in fact moving. Or was it stationary and his momentum caused everything in the trees to have the illusion of movement?

Whatever it was, it stalked him. It wasn't a benign, curious being watching from the safety of the trees. It was something malevolent, and alarm pinged in his head. He tried to shake it off and return to his empty mind, but he could not make the feeling dissipate, as if his body sensed the danger and refused to let his brain shut it out.

Lactic acid accumulated in his legs and, though he hadn't had a cramp in years, one seized him. Ben took one hand off the handlebars to knead the taut flesh in his side. His breath huffed, and he'd stopped the rhythmic breath necessary for a long ride and started panting—the type of breath that caused blackouts if it went on too long. He needed to stop, take a break, catch his breath, but he sensed that whatever pursued him in the woods would attack, and he'd be alone and vulnerable on the roadside.

Gritting his teeth, Ben pedaled harder, sweat pouring down his face, entire body moaning in protest.

When he spotted the Red Light Tavern, he broke wide open, pumping his legs, breath singing through his teeth. He swung into the dirt parking lot, hopped off his bike, allowing it to crash to the ground. He didn't kickstand it or chain it up. He fled into the bar, panting and limping.

Ben inhaled the spirits, the beer smells that comforted him and reminded him of his dad, though he hated that the primary scent he associated with his father was draft beer. Warm yellow lights softened the edges of the room and the lined faces of the men occupying the bar stools. Most of them looked at him curiously when he entered, but soon returned to their drinks and conversations.

A middle-aged woman with black hair streaked white drifted down the bar. "Hey, sugar. What can I get ya?"

Ben swallowed the bile rising into his throat. He thought he might throw up and held up a hand, unable to speak for a moment. When the sensation passed, he walked on trembling legs to a barstool and collapsed into it. "Ginger ale and a glass of water, please, and some paper towels."

"You all right, honey? Your face is red as a tomato. Not having a heart attack, I hope. Young thing like you."

"I biked here. Just overdid it, I think."

He mopped his face with a paper towel and downed the entire glass of water in one gulp, slid the glass back for a refill. After fishing his phone from the back of his shirt, he dialed Carmen's phone number.

"Hey, Ben," she answered.

"Uncle Bem, Uncle Bem," Thomas called in the background.

"Hi, Sir Thomas," Ben said. "Carm, could you or Jonas come pick me up?"

"Thomas, please stop trying to hold the kitty. She's going to claw you," Carm said, distracted. "Did you say pick you up? Where? Did your car break down?"

"No, I'm at a bar called the Red Light Tavern somewhere off of highway ten. I biked out here, but started feeling sick to my stomach. I don't want to risk trying to make it back."

"Huh, guts of steel is having stomach issues. That's hard to believe."

"Yeah, for me too."

"I'll come. I just need to load up the kids."

"Bring Jonas's bike rack."

"Okay. Give me a half hour and I'll be there."

Ben hung up the phone and sipped his ginger ale. The sickness in his stomach subsided, but the terror he'd felt on his ride lingered. Nothing could have been chasing him in the woods, and the more he thought about it, the more he wound back to Lori's fears about the Dogman or a witch in the woods. Her superstitions had gotten to him. That was all.

And yet… the image most prominent in his mind was Amanda, the girl in the hospital, who'd slit her own throat after saying the words 'she's in the woods.' Who was in the woods? And more bothersome still, how had Amanda gotten the unicorn necklace? Unless of course he'd hallucinated seeing it there in her hand. Strange nights—full moons in the E.R. Murphy's Law ruled those nights.

A woman sitting with a man at a little table in the back stood and sauntered to the jukebox. She wore jeans so tight her belly spilled over the top and an equally tight red top showed off her bulging cleavage. She primped her poufy blonde hair as she walked, leaned seductively over the box and turned to blow a kiss at the man at the table. He caught it, but rather than putting it to his mouth, he made a show of reaching for the crotch of his pants.

"I'm in hell," Ben muttered under his breath.

A moment later the jukebox kicked on, the song sending an icy trail of gooseflesh up Ben's spine.

Every Breath You Take by the Police started, their signature electric guitar sound pumping out the chords.

Ben stood and stumbled to the bathroom. He braced both hands on the grimy sink and stared at himself in the smudged glass.

Too many nonsensical things were happening, each testing Ben's ability to stay focused on the obvious truth. A person had been abducting and likely murdering girls in the Manistee National Forest. It wasn't a great mystery. Once the killer had been unveiled, all the little illogical pieces would slide together, but for now the inexplicable kept rearing up, drawing him away from the truth.

Even as he explained it all away, he saw her behind him. Summer, but not the Summer he remembered. This was the Summer of his nightmares with her face a mask of putrid flesh. He spun around, but there was no one there.

25

Lori woke late, emerging from sleep to the undiluted light of mid-morning. Matilda lay curled on the pillow beside her.

Yawning, Lori reached for her phone. It was nearly nine a.m. and she had a missed call from her mother and a text message from Ben.

Ben: Heading out for my bike ride. We still on for meeting this afternoon?

He'd sent it an hour earlier.

Lori texted back.

Lori: Yep, I'll be at your place at four.

She had to be at Grand Rapids by noon to meet Irene Whitaker, and it would take an hour and a half to drive there, which left an hour to get ready. She stood, nuzzled Matilda's back, and then made for the kitchen. She brewed coffee, peeking into the backyard and grimacing at the mess of cans and beer bottles left by Kenny and his crew. A pair of polka-dot thong underwear dangled from a bird feeder Lori had hung in the backyard.

"I've gotta get out of this place," she grumbled, taking her mug of coffee with her to the shower.

Lori ran the water cool. The dream from the night before hovered, and no amount of coffee or cold water uprooted it from her befuddled mind.

~

Irene Whitaker's office was located in an old section of Grand Rapids where brick ran amok and ivy crawled up the faces of the buildings. The building that held 486 Kensington had two display windows darkened by heavy black curtains. The door did not open when Lori pulled the handle, but a large green button beside the door said, 'Ring for Service.'

Lori pushed the button and waited.

Several minutes later, a woman opened the door and peered up at Lori as if the midday sun were difficult to look into. "Lori Hicks?" she asked.

"Yes, that's me. Are you Irene?"

"Yes, I am. Do come in out of that glare."

Irene stood less than five feet tall. Bouncy black and gray curls framed her petite-featured face. She wore red glasses and a bright blue shirt with a beaded neckline. A black skirt, so long it hid her feet entirely, brushed the floor as she moved. She closed the wood door and slid the deadbolt into place.

"Pause," she told Lori, putting a hand on her arm. "And breathe." Irene took a deep breath through her nose. "Smell that? That is the smell of ancient secrets, of papyrus and paper that has seen the passage of time, worn leather and glue and the oils of millions of fingertips brushing the pages, of ink and lead and paint. For me it is the most intoxicating scent I have ever encountered."

Lori closed her eyes and breathed. She did not know how to describe the smell—musty, but warm and soft, inviting. The smell reminded her of the little library in Baldwin where'd she sometimes sat as a girl, tucked into the kids' corner, reading paperbacks while her mother searched for sewing patterns and magazines and occasionally a Harlequin romance.

"It is very homey," Lori said.

"It is. Which is why, much to my husband's frustration, I have filled our house with old books. They are decadent. Some of the pages are so worn they are as soft as silk." Irene sighed dreamily. "On we go," she said, opening her eyes and urging Lori forward. "This is my work space and the closest thing I have to an office. Shall we sit?"

They walked deeper into the room, which was long and narrow and filled with bookshelves as high as the ceiling. Books lined every surface.

A wooden table with two padded chairs sat at the back of the space. A single book lay upon the table next to a notepad and pencil.

"I do all of my translations here," Irene explained. "I hear the voices of the ancestors when I work, the voices in all these books telling me to see clearly what the author meant to convey."

Lori pulled out a chair as Irene sat in the one opposite.

"Tell me what ancient figure you seek to know."

Lori glanced at the book on the table. The title had long since rubbed off from the dark leather cover. "Witches, I guess. I'm wondering about witches."

"Ah, yes." Irene's eyes shimmered in the soft yellow light. "Witches have come into vogue, as they say, or don't they say that?" Irene chuckled. "I'm never one to keep up with the lingo in this fast-changing world. Regardless of the verbiage, the mistrust of witches is long behind us. The empowerment of women and the shifting of the scales from patriarchy towards matriarchy is redefining the witches of history. As well it should.

"But let me also tell you this. There were powerful women who learned to work their own kind of magic and then there were the hags of the forest. They were rare, nearly always lived in total isolation, and the magic they sought was not to increase the harvest or honor the cycles of the moon. There's a reason the truly old tales are filled with a certain kind of witch, and that witch was not kindly or beautiful. She was as evil as the most vile of men—the men who tore into homes and raped the wives and children and killed the livestock and burned the field to ensure the family would not survive the winter. She had malice and greed and most of all hatred in her heart.

"The word 'witch' derives from the old English word 'wicca,' which means sorceress or female magician, but later this word would come to be associated not only with magic but with a purpose linked to the devil, a woman who deals with the devil or whose magic comes from the devil.

"Now the devil is a whole other entity, much broader in scope, which I dare not get into or a week from now we'll still be sitting in these chairs. Suffice it to say the term 'witch' had a negative connotation not simply because men detested women in power, which many of them did. It became soiled in part because some very nefarious individuals walked this earth and they had abilities that seemed to defy the intellect of mortal men and women. Since they used these powers for evil rather than good, the source of their power was attributed to the devil."

"Do you believe that's where their power came from?" Lori asked, thinking of the doorway in her dream and shuddering.

"Do I believe that?" Irene mused. "How are we to know the source of such extraordinary power? We live today in a world of science. We move further and further from mystical explanations for good and evil. Now we look upon brain chemistry, parental attachment, life experiences. We pinpoint those things as the reason for evil acts, but still those explanations do not satisfy most because we inevitably come upon the outliers.

"The well-adjusted boy with loving parents who was never teased in school but still mutilates and murders other human beings. The bright young woman who poisons her entire family. There are many who still believe it is the war between good and evil carrying on beneath the surface, and that we've merely taken on new, less frightening words to describe it."

"But what do you believe?" Lori insisted.

"I believe there is free will among human beings and some of them will do evil acts for their own benefit. I also believe there is magic, there has always been magic, and there will always be magic and we, perhaps, are not a species that will ever be able to distinguish between the two."

"Then you believe that evil witches existed?"

"Surely, yes."

"Could they still exist?"

"Anything can exist. There will always be a limit to our perception as human beings. There are sights we cannot see, sounds we cannot hear."

"What about here in Michigan? Do you think a witch, an evil witch, could live here in Michigan?"

"There are hundreds of thousands of homes in our state, twenty million acres of woods, more than ten thousand lakes. Plenty of places for something to hide. There are places that people never go. Is that by design? By something that is capable of steering them away? I think it's possible, yes."

"Have you ever come upon old texts about evil witches here in Michigan?"

"There are stories, yes. Books less so. You must remember that Michigan and all of the United States is young. The old stories come from Native Americans. They passed their stories through spoken word and reenactments, but even so, they too shared stories of witches or hags. Now in other countries we see a much larger emphasis on the witch as both archetype and figure in history.

"In Russia, Baba Yaga is the dark witch most known in Slavic folklore. We first see her appear in writings in the late 1700s. Baba Yaga is a hag who dwells in a hut on chicken legs. She possesses magical powers and is said to bestow wishes upon those who do her favors. In the study of Jungian psychology, we examine Baba Yaga as part of the crone or even the wild aspect of the female psyche. But in the old stories, Baba Yaga was a cannibal witch whose victims were primarily children.

"We similarly see a story appear in the Grimm Fairytales, which were first published by German brothers Jacob and Wilhelm Grimm under the name *Kinder- und Hausmärchen*, which translates to *Children's and Household Tales*. The story of Hansel and Gretel appeared in their book, and that story originated with one of the brothers' wives, Henriette Dorothea Wild. These were not merely brothers who told tall tales. They were medievalists who were intensely interested in mythology and they collected German folklore.

"It is said that the story of Hansel and Gretel arose in part due to the great famine that struck the Baltic region from 1314 to 1322. This famine struck more than thirty million people and is estimated to have ended the lives of a quarter of the population in the region. Many families abandoned their small children, and it is said that some were cannibalized. Others still pointed to hags who waited in the forest for these abandoned children, drew them into their homes, and ate them."

Lori's hands had grown clammy and she rubbed them together beneath the table.

"Then there is Jenny Greenteeth," Irene continued, "also known as Ginny or Wicked Jenny. The origin of this witch appears in England in the 1800s. Small children were told to stay away from the water or Jenny, a terrifying water witch with green skin and teeth and hair, would grab them and drown them merely for her own pleasure."

"Those are all very disturbing," Lori murmured. "And so many of them focus on children."

"Yes, they are the stuff of nightmares. If we look at them as real beings the focus on children is twofold. One, children are easier to capture and manipulate. Two, children often possess the traits these beings might desire—eternal youth, etc. If we consider them merely as urban legends, it's plain to see why their victims are children. The tales are meant to make children behave. 'Eat your dinner or the Baba Yaga will come for you.' 'Don't play by the pond or Jenny Greenteeth will drag you in.' That kind of thing."

"Is it possible that they were real? These witches?"

"Some aspect of them was likely real, but stories take on a life of their own. Do the witches exist first or do they arise from the mythology, being born into being from the terror in the hearts of the children imagining them? It's an intriguing line of thought. Sometimes I sit at this desk for hours not writing a word but thinking deeper and deeper into those strange possibilities."

"My friend disappeared in the Manistee National Forest in 1998," Lori said. "A friend and I have discovered four other girls who vanished in the area. All of them were between thirteen and fifteen years old, pretty, and wore something that made a sound—usually bells, but one had a whistle. They've gone missing every five years since 1993. After my friend vanished, I started having nightmares about a shrouded being in the woods. I've come to think of her as a witch." Lori reached into her bag and took out the folder she'd tucked her drawings into. She laid them on the table.

Irene considered them, flipping through each thoughtfully. "Every five years, you say? Manistee National Forest... Hmm... One moment." She stood and disappeared into the stacks.

Irene did not return with a book, but a massive three-ring binder so overflowing with papers it could not be closed. She dropped it on the table with a thud and settled back into her chair, deftly flipping the pages, though Lori could see no headline or tabs to distinguish the sections.

"The Manistee National Forest, here we go."

"What is that?" Lori asked. "The binder?"

"This is my western Michigan binder. I have a separate binder for southern Michigan, eastern, and an additional one for the Upper Peninsula. This is the place where I store anecdotes. My work is in literature, scholarly articles, printed texts, but I also collect personal stories. All mythology must begin somewhere, after all. I have a story you should read."

Pushing hard on the metal tabs, Irene opened the binder. She extracted a sheet of paper protected by a clear plastic sleeve and slid it across the table to Lori.

May, 17, 1963

Many years ago, my great-grandmother told me a story about a person she called the Hag of Manistee.

In this story, there were two sisters. One was beautiful and fair, with golden hair and brilliant blue eyes. The other was homely and round, with dark stringy hair and muddy brown eyes. The two sisters loved to play in the Manistee Forest, braiding daisies into crowns, swinging from the branches of the oak tree and swimming in the shimmering pond filled with green lily pads and pink and white lilies.

The girls did not know that an evil witch lived in the woods, lured by the sound of the dinner bell, which always hung about the beautiful sister's waist, for she was in charge of summoning the men in the evenings away from the farm and to the dinner table. The witch heard the bell and the girls' laughter and she crawled out from her lair beneath the earth and started to watch the sisters from the shadows of the forest. She grew more and more obsessed with the children, who reminded her of her own sister and herself.

The hag had once played in the forest with her own sister. As a child, the hag had been short and homely with lank hair and dead eyes. Her sister was beautiful, blonde and blue-eyed and the envy of all the girls in their village. In her jealousy, the ugly sister murdered her beautiful sister and consumed her flesh, believing that she would absorb her beauty and grace. Instead, she was exiled by her family and banished to the forest.

As the witch watched the girls, she became desperate to absorb the beautiful sister she now watched, much as she'd consumed her own sister years before. She watched and waited until one day the beautiful sister waded into the pond to swim alone. The witch reached one gnarled hand up through the cold mud and into the shimmering water. She grabbed the sister's ankles and yanked her through the mud and into her hut.

The girl lived there for five days as the witch consumed her piece by piece, adding her slowly to her black cauldron and stirring her into nothing.

A bead of sweat slid between Lori's shoulder blades, though it was cool in the room. "I don't like that story," she murmured.

"It's not a likeable story," Irene agreed. "But in it we see the number five appear, which is interesting based on your experience. Too, we see the dinner bell—also fascinating based on your experience."

"Do you think it's real? This story?"

"The story is real, but is the witch real? Well, can we prove that she is? And at the same time, can we prove that she's not?"

26

Lori arrived at Ben's just before four p.m. The drive to his house had been a blur. She'd ruminated on the story of the witch in the Manistee National Forest. It both unnerved and excited her to have spoken with a woman who believed in the possibilities Lori had been entertaining. What she'd discovered, however, was that Ben's theory was less terrifying than a mystical witch who ate children.

Ben walked out of the house as she parked. "Feel like driving?" Ben asked. "I'm spent."

"Sure, yeah. Hop in," Lori told him through her open window, not bothering to get out of her car.

Ben settled into the passenger seat, holding a stack of printed articles.

"Not feeling well today?" she asked.

He looked out the window but gave her a nod. "I'm not sure I've recovered from my last shift. Then I took a long bike ride today, or attempted to anyway, but..." He didn't finish his statement.

"You felt sick?"

"Kind of. I felt off... let's just say that."

Lori tucked her hair behind her ear. "Me too. Not sick, but I had the nightmare again last night. Kenny, my downstairs neighbor, and about ten of his friends came busting in because I was screaming. Let's just say it was not a restful night."

"Damn, they came right into your apartment?"

"Yep, broke the door down basically."

"Maybe I should have driven."

Lori smiled. "No. It's good for me. I get more tired if I'm riding."

As Lori drove, Ben summarized the articles he'd printed, which included men in Michigan who'd been arrested or convicted of kidnapping, sexually assaulting or murdering young women or girls.

"Leslie Allen Williams abducted and murdered girls in the fourteen-to-sixteen age range, but he was incarcerated in 1992, so he was off the streets before our girls vanished," Ben murmured, flipping through his pages. "The problem with everyone I found online is they were in prison before 2008 when Peyton went missing. I come back again and again to Hector."

"Why did you print all those when you're convinced it's Hector?"

"Maybe I'm wrong. I don't want to ignore other possibilities."

Lori thought of the witch again and almost brought it up, but she already knew Ben's thoughts on the theory. Most people would agree with him. Even Lori's common sense agreed with him, but something deep in her gut kept coming back to the belief that something much darker than either of them had ever encountered had taken their friends.

Peyton Weller's aunt Gertrude lived in a modular home on a small lot surrounded by other modulars in Scottville. A deck and wheelchair ramp clung to the front of the yellowing exterior. Potted plants lined the porch rail and a dozen or more bird feeders hung from the house's eaves and from trees scattered throughout the yard.

Lori and Ben climbed from her car and walked to the front door. The screen door was closed, but the interior door stood open. Lori heard the sounds of the Dr. Phil show playing on the television.

Ben knocked on the screen door. A heavy woman in a billowy green dress lumbered toward them, wiping a lock of sweaty hair from her forehead. "Hold on, I'm comin'."

Her face appeared red from the effort, and she paused in front of a whirring fan that sat on her kitchen counter. She leaned into the fan and waved and mopped her neck with a hand towel. She continued to the door, struggling to catch her breath.

"Sorry about that. This heat is just about killin' me." She pulled the screen door open. It screeched on its hinges.

"Hi. You're Gertrude?" Ben asked.

"Yep, come in," she told them. "It's not much cooler in here, but it's a smidge."

Ben and Lori followed her. The living room lay only a few steps from the kitchen. Gertrude collapsed, winded, into a worn La-Z-Boy chair and grabbed a remote control from the armrest, muting the set. She waved at her crimson face for another moment. The overhead fan buzzed at full speed and two smaller fans droned from surfaces around the living room, but they did little to cut the stifling heat.

Ben and Lori took the checkered sofa.

"I'm Ben and this is Lori," he told her.

"Hi. Nice to meet you," Lori said, feeling her own forehead perspire.

"I figured you was," Gertrude told them. "Ain't got many visitors around here no more."

"Are you still up for talking about Peyton?" Ben asked.

"Sure am. I talk to her every day. Seems only right I should talk about her now and then."

"You talk to her?" Lori asked.

Gertrude gestured toward a hanging shelf arranged with four framed photographs. The images in the newspaper of Peyton Weller did not do her justice. The girl had been beautiful, with long caramel-colored hair, dreamy hazel eyes, and an infectious smile. In one photo, she stood in front of a stone fountain wearing a glittery gold miniskirt and a jean jacket. She looked closer to eighteen years old than fourteen.

"She was very pretty," Lori said.

"Sure was. Where she got them genes, I don't know. Her daddy, my brother Gary, was pretty good-lookin', but Rita, Peyton's mom, always had that street hustler look about her. Peyton coulda been a model."

"Is that what she wanted to be?" Lori asked, thinking back to her own teenaged years and how she'd often thought Bev could be a model, though her best friend only laughed when she mentioned it.

"Jesum crow, no!" Gertrude grabbed her towel from the TV tray beside her chair and mopped her glistening forehead. "She wanted to go to a big-time school just like that little girl in *Gilmore Girls*. Have you two seen that show? Peyton and I watched it all the time. She just loved it, especially Rory, the daughter. Rory wanted to be a reporter, one of them kind that goes into wars and things, so that's what Peyton wanted to be. Coulda done it too. She was sharp as a tack, that girl. Coulda done anything she set her mind to. Don't know where she got them brains either. A gift from God."

"It must have been a terrible loss for you," Ben said.

Gertrude lowered her voice as if someone else were in the house. "Ripped our family plum apart, destroyed it. Peyton's mom blamed Gary because he'd gotten involved in drugs and she was sure somebody had grabbed her over an unpaid debt or some such thing. Gary blamed Rita because she was off with a boyfriend that night. Things had been unraveling for them for a while. Peyton goin' missin' just was the straw that broke the camel's back.

"There's a video out there somewhere, shameful. They let a reporter from the weekly paper come into their trailer for an interview after Peyton went missin'. That reporter started askin' questions about the drugs, which sent Rita spewing hate towards Gary, and he spewed it right back. Rita jumped on him in that tape, raked her nails across his cheek. It was terrible, and we were all angry, angry at Rita and Gary for makin' such a spectacle, because it caused everybody to focus on them instead of Peyton. Not to mention it got everybody saying, 'With a home like that, what fourteen-year-old girl wouldn't have run off?'"

"Can you tell us about the night itself, everything you know about what happened the evening she disappeared?" Ben asked.

"Fern Bowman was with her that night. They was real close, those two. Been chums since diapers. They both lived in the trailer park. Fern's ma used to work with me at the Buckeye Tavern, but then I got on the disability after a car accident. Fern and Peyton liked to walk the trails. They went just about every night in the summer. That or the kids would find a ride out to Hackert Lake to go swimmin'.

"Fern said she and Peyton were hikin' along and Peyton had to go pee, so she slipped off into the woods and then... nothin'. She didn't come back. Fern started hollerin' for her, but Peyton kept stayin' gone. After a while, Fern got a little cheesed off and went stompin' outta them woods in a huff. She went on home to her trailer, but around ten or so, Rita called her up and asked where Peyton was. Fern told her she'd taken off on her in the woods, but that wasn't like Peyton, and once Fern knew she hadn't come home, that's when everybody started worrying.

"So Rita called Gary home from wherever he was—some bar, I think. Gary called me and we made some more calls and a group of us headed out there in our cars and some went into the woods. Rita called the cops the next day, but they wasn't too concerned. Kids from the trailer park had a habit of takin' off, but not Peyton. We kept on lookin', but the cops didn't for probably two weeks. By the time they sent out searchers any trace of her was long gone."

"Did you suspect anyone?" Ben asked.

"Of takin' her?" Gertrude pressed her lips together grimly. "She was real special and there's a lot of perverts out there. If any of 'em got their eye on her, it woulda been an easy place to nab her, but I can't see how Fern never saw or heard nothin'. But then maybe she'd been scared into keepin' her mouth shut."

"Was Fern open about that night? Did she talk to police?" Ben asked.

"Yeah, she did, but then her mama packed her up and moved her out of town not two months after Peyton went missin'. Seemed strange to me, but what could I do?"

"This might sound odd, but was Peyton wearing anything that night that you know of that made a sound?" Lori asked. She glanced at Ben, who looked exasperated at her question. "Like a bell?"

Gertrude gave her a curious look. "That is a funny question, because yeah, she was, though I don't think they ever printed that in the paper. She had on this pretty silver anklet that had little clumps of bells on it. It was adorable, and she cherished that thing. A boy at school had given it to her for her birthday about a month before she disappeared. She had a birthday party at Riverside Park. I made a strawberry cake from one of them Sara Lee mixes. That was her favorite.

"Her dad didn't show for the party, and her mom was ranting on her phone every five minutes, calling to scream at him for being a deadbeat. It could have ruined Peyton's day, but she was the kind of girl who didn't let things get her down. You know? Sometimes I wondered how Gary and Rita produced such an angel. I love my brother, but he's been a hard person all his life. Not mean or anything. Just prone to getting into things he shouldn't, getting involved with women he shouldn't."

"Where are Peyton's parents now?" Ben asked before Lori could probe further into the anklet.

"Gary's living in a motel down by the border of Indiana that rents by the week. He's been in rehab three times, but can't seem to make it stick. Last I heard of Rita she'd met some guy and followed him out west, Vegas, but who knows where she's at now."

"But there's still an open investigation into Peyton's case," Ben pushed.

Gertrude shrugged. "They say there is, but nothing ever happens. We're really alone out there. That's what it comes down to. People think if someone goes missin' the cops will swoop in and turn over every rock." She shook her head. "No, siree, not for our Peyton, anyway. Like I said, they took one look at Gary and Rita and started muttering the apple doesn't fall far from the tree."

"So she had an anklet that made a sound, but Fern never heard the sound after Peyton went into the trees?" Lori asked.

"Nope, not that she said anyway, though I did hear from one of the gals out lookin' that night that she followed the sound of a bell for a half-hour deeper and deeper into the woods until she got so turned around, she panicked and started runnin' back the way she'd come. She ran into somebody who led her out to the street, but that had her in a tizzy."

"Have you ever heard of a person named Hector Dunn?" Ben asked.

"Oh, sure, Hector frequented the Buckeye back in the day. I hated servin' him. He was a terrible tipper. Course he tipped if you were young and skinny as a pole."

Ben grew taller in his seat. He leaned forward. "You knew Hector personally?" Ben's eyes glittered.

"As well as you can know a man like Hector. He was a queer fish, that one."

"How so?" Ben asked.

"Oh, he'd come in, nurse a beer for three or four hours and just sit and watch people. Girls mostly. If a pretty girl walked in, he'd stare at her without even pretending not to. He almost took a beating a few times when a boyfriend or a father took to noticing his watchin'. He gave me the heebie-jeebies. Never was so grateful I was a big, ugly woman than when Hector Dunn came through the door. What's got ya wonderin' about him?"

"I think he could be responsible for the girls disappearing," Ben said. "He tried to abduct a girl not far from where my friend vanished in 1993 and we've linked him to other girls who went missing."

Gertrude scratched at her chin. "I sure hope not. I don't wanna think of Peyton spending her last moments with that creep." She shifted her bulk in the chair, visibly uncomfortable at Ben's suggestion. "You think Hector Dunn took my Peyton?"

"I know nothing for certain, but your knowing him strengthens my belief."

"And what about you? Is that what you think?" Gertrude fixed her solemn, dark eyes on Lori.

Lori swiped at her stomach and then glanced at Ben, who seemed equally curious about her response.

"I think it's very possible, yes," Lori murmured. And she did. Her theory about the witch was quickly crumbling in the face of Hector Dunn, who'd now appeared in several of the girls' cases.

"Oh, God," Gertrude moaned. "God, no. Please God." She looked up at the ceiling, watermarked from a leaky roof. "Please God, don't let it have been Hector who got her."

"Gertrude, when was the last time you saw Hector Dunn?" Ben asked.

Lori wanted to silence him, to suggest they take their leave, as Gertrude had begun to breathe rapidly and her face had turned to deepening shades of red.

"I don't know," she murmured, turning her head slowly from side to side. "Please, dear God, don't let it be him. Let her have run off like everybody said. Let her have planned it all and be livin' down in Florida with a rich husband and two beautiful children." A tear slipped down her cheek.

Lori stood and went to the woman, kneeled in front of her and took her hand. "It might be that, Gertrude, okay? We don't know anything for certain, so if that's what you've believed... it's okay to keep believing it."

～

B en sat in stony silence as they drove away from Scottville.

"What?" Lori demanded. "Did you want to keep pushing her until she had a heart attack?"

Ben looked at her as if surprised by her tone. "No. I think you were right to end it. I'm thinking about Hector Dunn and how to nail him."

"Oh," Lori said, slightly embarrassed that she'd assumed he was mad at her. "She was wearing a bell," Lori murmured.

"And she knew Hector Dunn," Ben countered. "Seriously though, what's up with the bell thing? You really think that's important?"

Lori held up her hand, ticking off her fingers. "Summer wore bells, Bev wore a bell, Bella had a whistle, Peyton had an anklet with bells."

"Okay... which in my opinion just made it that much easier for Hector to find them."

"Maybe."

"But that's not your theory because you're still hung up on the witch thing."

"No," she snapped, swiping her hand over her stomach. "I'm not hung up on anything. It's just a bizarre aspect that I can't shake."

"It is bizarre. It's all bizarre. I just don't want to get sidetracked by red herrings."

"Listen, we're going to pass Baldwin on our way back. I'd like to… just drive by a few places."

"The woods where Bev disappeared?" Ben asked.

"Yeah, and the Silvas' house," Lori said. The desire to go back to Baldwin had struck her suddenly as they'd left Gertrude's home.

"Let's do it," Ben said.

27

"The Silvas' house is just down here," Lori said, turning onto the street where Beverly had grown up, the place Lori had spent so much time. "It's that blue one." Lori gestured at the two-story robin's egg blue house with white shutters. It was mostly unchanged save for a new brick mailbox where a plastic one had been in their youth. Trees that had been only saplings planted by Bev's mom Carrie in their younger years had grown large and bushy at the sides of the house.

"They must be having a party," Ben said, gesturing at three red balloons that floated on ribbons from the mailbox.

Lori coasted to the curb, leaving the engine idling as she studied the house.

"Are you okay?" Ben asked.

Before she could speak, someone rapped their knuckles on the driver's side window. Lori jumped, turning to peer at a woman with glossy red hair swept over one shoulder. For an instant, Lori saw Bev, aged fifteen years, and then the face before her focused.

"Zoe," she whispered, hitting the button to roll down the window.

"Lori! My God, is that you? It is. I thought so, but... Well, come on, get out and give me a hug."

Lori, shock still rendering her mute, opened the door and climbed out, her surprise growing when she took in Zoe in full.

It wasn't merely the resemblance to Bev that had unnerved her. Zoe was very pregnant, her huge belly sheathed by the billowy yellow dress she wore.

Zoe hugged her. Lori felt the firm mound of her unborn child pressed against her own soft stomach. She hugged back, smelling Zoe's peach-scented shampoo. The baby gave a little kick, catching Lori in her right hip. She started, and Zoe laughed, pulling away.

"She's a feisty one," she said, putting both hands on her belly. "It's so good to see you, Lori. Did my parents invite you?"

Lori glanced at the house where she and Bev had run through sprinklers in the backyard and caught fireflies at night. "No. I..." She trailed off, catching sight of Bev and Zoe's parents. They hadn't seen her. They were standing in a group—Bev's mother Carrie with the same red-gold hair her daughters had inherited, Bev's dad Francisco, dark in complexion and hair. Lori remembered how she'd watched them as a girl, thinking they were so beautiful. No wonder they'd produced a daughter who looked like Bev. "No, they didn't. I just... I was in the area and thought I'd drive by."

"Well, my tia Rosa would say that's destina—fate. Today is my baby shower, and you were meant to be here."

Ben climbed out of the car and offered a wave. "Hi. I'm Ben," he told Zoe.

Zoe looked back at Lori, eyes gleaming. "Is this your husband?"

Lori laughed and blushed. "No. We're just friends."

"Oh, okay. I see. Hi, Ben. I'm Zoe, and growing up Lori was my only line of defense against my big sister who would tickle me until I peed." She laughed and then grimaced. "Uh-oh. Gotta keep the laughing to a minimum these days for the same reason. Though it has more to do with this baby sitting on my bladder than Bev's tickling."

Lori smiled. "I forgot about that. She loved to tickle-torture."

Zoe groaned. "It was the worst. Come on." She tugged on Lori's hand. "You guys come out back. We have a massive buffet. I wanted Chinese food, but Rosa insisted on some authentic Mexican dishes too. There's so much food. Come, come. My parents will be overjoyed to see you."

"You're so grown up," Lori said, allowing Zoe to pull her around the edge of the house.

"Yeah. It's weird sometimes. I look in the mirror and wonder who that woman is staring back at me."

"You look a lot like her. Like Bev."

Zoe glanced back, smile widening. "People tell me that a lot, but... I can't always tell. I guess it's harder when you're looking at yourself."

"How about Collin? Is he here?" Lori asked, thinking of the brother who was a year younger than Bev and a year older than Zoe.

"Unfortunately, no. He got married and then took a big software job out west. He and his wife join us in Mexico City every year for Día de los Muertos, but he hasn't been back here to Michigan in two years."

Lori watched the expressions on Bev's parents' faces as she slid into view. Every muscle in her midsection tensed and a part of her expected them to bellow at her to get out, she wasn't welcome there.

Bev's dad saw her first. The smile slipped from his face and then came back, larger, his eyes curious. Lori couldn't be sure, but she thought he squeezed his wife's hand or gave her some signal to look their way because Carrie's gaze swiveled toward her. For a moment, she just stared as if not sure who this stranger was that Zoe was dragging into their backyard, and then recognition registered.

Lori saw her speak her name, her lips form the word 'Lorraine,' and then both parents were moving toward her. They did not look angry. They both smiled.

"Look who I found," Zoe announced.

"Lorraine? My goodness." Carrie took her hands. "You've changed so much."

Lori smiled, remembering the girl they'd known with her pudgy body and limp dark hair.

"You look the same," Lori told her. "The most beautiful mom at school. We all thought so."

Carrie smiled and crushed her in a hug. "Hardly, but I thank you for saying it. It's so good to see you."

"This is my friend, Ben," Lori told them.

Francisco continued to watch her as if unsure what to say.

"Hi. Great to meet you both." Ben shook Francisco's hand and then Carrie's.

"Well, come on, these beverages won't drink themselves," Zoe said, leading them away from her parents toward two long tables stuffed with so much food the red tablecloths beneath were barely visible. "Virgin piña coladas in that one and piña colada sangria in that one. I wish I were drinking from the sangria option, but I think this little baby bun would not approve."

Zoe drifted off to greet more family. Ben opted for a bottle of water while Lori took a cup from one of the women working the buffet. She was likely an aunt or cousin. The Silvas had a vast family, many of who had immigrated to Michigan from Mexico over the years.

A woman with pale blonde hair, holding the hand of a little dark-haired girl, stepped up beside her. "Here, Quinnie." She handed the little girl a plastic cup of virgin piña colada and then took a sangria for herself. She drew in a deep breath, as if gathering herself to turn back to the posse of family behind them.

"Hi," Lori said, when the woman caught her eye.

"Hi there. This is quite a baby shower, huh?"

"It sure is."

"Are you a school friend of Zoe's or family?" the woman asked.

"A school friend. I actually, um…" Lori wondered if speaking Bev's name would draw a curtain across the sun, casting the merriment of the party into gloom. She lowered her voice. "I went to school with Bev. She was my best friend."

The woman's eyebrows knitted together. "I'm sorry. I never met Bev, but I've heard she was lovely."

"She was. Zoe looks a lot like her. It's startling really."

"I'm Rowan," the woman said, extending her hand.

Lori shook it. "I'm Lori and this is…" She started to introduce Ben, but he was no longer beside her. He stood in the center of a gaggle of kids who watched him, mesmerized, as he inserted a piece of long grass between his lips and made it whistle.

"Mr. Popular," Rowan said, as her own little girl walked toward the bunch.

"Is that your daughter?" Lori asked.

"Yep, my Quinnie girl."

"She's beautiful."

"She astonishes me every day. That's my husband over there, Garrett, and our new little one, Morgan."

Lori followed Rowan's gaze to a dark-haired man laughing and rocking the baby on his hip. Several Silva family members stood around him cooing and making faces at the baby.

"Are you related to the Silvas?" Lori asked.

"I'm married into this crazy bunch," Rowan admitted. "Garrett is Francisco's cousin."

"I was always so envious of Bev's enormous family."

Rowan chuckled. "I get that. They're a sight to behold when they all get together like this. It's good though. I don't think Francisco and Carrie have done a big celebration in a very long time."

"You don't know if... the police have ever found anything?" Lori asked. "It's just, I don't feel comfortable asking Carrie and Francisco, especially not today. I was with Bev that night, the night she disappeared. It's haunted me all these years."

Rowan frowned, eyes flitting first toward her daughter, then toward her husband and son. "I don't believe so, but it's not a topic the family discusses much. I think if there'd been developments, we would have heard something."

"Hora de cenar," a bent old woman called in Spanish.

A younger woman standing beside her yelled, "Time to eat. Come on people."

Ben and Lori joined the buffet line. "Doing okay?" he murmured, leaning closer to her.

"Yeah," she said, taking a paper plate and adding a spoonful of beans. "Is this okay with you? Hanging out here?"

"Absolutely. Look at all this food!"

After they ate, they watched Zoe opening gifts, her husband standing and displaying the items with a goofy grin, holding up little onesies and snuggling plush toys. When they unwrapped an antique-looking bassinet, the little girl Quinn ran over and tried to climb into it. Rowan pulled her away, tempting her with a handful of caramel popcorn.

Someone handed Zoe a tiny box wrapped in silver paper with a white bow on top. Zoe unwrapped the gift, revealing a little white jewelry box. She opened it and drew out a long silver chain. The charm on the necklace tinkled.

A jolt of alarm streaked through Lori's body. It was a bola, the same type of little bell Bev had been wearing the night she disappeared. Lori had never seen one again after that night and as she gazed at it, she struggled to catch her breath.

The color had drained from Zoe's face and from Carrie's as well. They both stared at the necklace, transfixed, as if looking into the etched silver orb had cast a spell rendering them as statues.

"It's a bola," a woman with a long dark braid plaited down her back announced. She swept across the grass, her purple skirt swishing, and plucked the necklace from Zoe's hand. "You wear this to invite the baby's protector. Here, let me help." She looped the silver chain around

Zoe's neck.

Zoe's eyes darted toward her mother, but some of the color had come back to Carrie Silva's face and she reached a hand to her daughter's wrist, giving it a squeeze.

The old woman who'd stood behind the buffet hobbled to Zoe and leaned close to her, whispering in her ear. Then she lifted the charm from Zoe's neck and kissed it before making the sign of the Cross. Lori realized who the old woman was—Bev's grandmother Rosa, who the Silvas used to visit in Mexico.

"It's beautiful, Maria," Carrie told the woman who'd given Zoe the necklace. "She'll cherish it."

Lori stared at the silver ball catching the sun as it rested on Zoe's chest that rose and fell rapidly. Zoe's husband took the place of Maria, putting large hands on her suddenly frail-looking shoulders. He leaned down and nuzzled his face against her cheek. Zoe visibly relaxed, reaching a tentative hand toward the ball and clutching it for a moment.

"This one is from me," a girl, no more than seven years old, announced, running across the grass. She tripped, and the present flew from her hands, landing at Zoe's feet. The girl stood, brushing off her dress. "I'm okay, I'm okay. Go on, Cousin Zoe. Open it."

Zoe's husband bent over and grabbed the gift, likely not trusting that his pregnant wife wouldn't tumble out of the chair if she leaned too far forward. He handed it to Zoe.

Lori's own breath had slipped back in, expanding in her lungs, which moments before had felt no larger than peas. Ben, as if sensing her upset, scooted his chair closer and gave her a reassuring smile.

Zoe pulled at the rainbow-colored wrapping. From the tissue paper, she extracted a bright orange onesie with the words, 'I get it from my mama.'

Zoe burst out laughing, and the little girl grinned. "See, Mom?" she called out to a woman sitting near the buffet.

The woman smiled. "I see, Jenny." She directed her attention to Zoe and winked. "She wouldn't leave the store without it."

"It's adorable. Thank you, Linda."

~

Many of the party guests lingered as Lori and Ben wished Zoe the best and started back toward the car.

"Lorraine." Carrie caught up to her in the driveway. She took Lori's hands in her own. "I've wondered about you so many times over the years. I'm so glad you came today."

"Thank you, Mrs. Silva. I appreciate your welcoming us like this. If I'd known you were having a shower, I wouldn't have dropped in out of the blue."

"No, I'm delighted you did. I'd love for you two to come back in the house for a little while. We didn't get much time to talk during the party."

Lori glanced at Ben.

"Please," Carrie said. "You were such a good friend to Bev. I'm sorry if we never told you back then. We were so lost in our pain."

"You don't owe me an apology," Lori assured her. "Bev was my lifeline. You guys were like my second family."

Carrie looked at the ground. "We all lost so much, didn't we?"

"Mrs. Silva, I'm sorry to butt in," Ben said, "but did you or your husband know a man named Hector Dunn?"

Lori bristled at Ben's question. She felt protective of Carrie Silva and suddenly didn't want her to know anything at all about their little sleuthing expedition.

"The name doesn't sound familiar. Why do you ask?"

"My sister's best friend, Summer, disappeared in Manistee National Forest in 1993 and we never found her. There have been other girls. Lori and I may have uncovered a link. Hector Dunn. Police arrested him in 1994 for trying to abduct a girl near Manistee."

The color drained from Carrie's face as Ben spoke. Lori maneuvered her away.

"You don't have to think about all this now," Lori insisted. "We don't want to ruin your night."

"Lori, we're here. That's why we came here," Ben said.

She turned and glared at him. Ben closed his mouth.

"A link?" Carrie asked, looking from Lori to Ben. "You think this man was involved in Bev's disappearance? You think he took her?"

Lori and Ben spoke at the same time.

"No," Lori said.

"Yes," Ben announced over her. "We've talked to the aunt of another girl who vanished who also had a connection to Hector Dunn."

Carrie's chest and neck grew blotchy, and she pulled at the collar on her dress. "Let me just... catch my breath. Ever since..." She took a few steps away from them, swayed, and collapsed.

28

Ben shot forward and caught Carrie Silva before she hit the ground.

"Oh, God," Lori moaned. "Mrs. Silva, are you okay?" Lori held her hand as Ben laid her on the grass.

Carrie's eyelids fluttered, and she sucked in tiny sputtering breaths.

"I think she's having a panic attack. Go get her husband," Ben ordered, maneuvering Carrie on her side in the grass and rubbing her back. "Just breathe, in through the nose, out through the mouth. Notice the blades of grass. Everything is okay. Just breathe."

Lori ran to the backyard, where Francisco stood talking to Zoe's husband. "Mr. Silva," Lori blurted. "Hurry, come with me. Mrs. Silva's fainted."

"She fainted?" he demanded, but he'd already pushed past Lori and started toward the front lawn, where Ben had gotten Carrie Silva into a position on her hands and knees.

Francisco knelt beside her.

"I'm fine, Fran, okay, honey? I just had one of those little anxiety things."

Francisco smoothed his wife's red-gold hair back from her face where it had pulled away from her French braid.

A moment later, Zoe appeared. "Mom, what happened?" Zoe tried to get down to her mother's level, but her husband clutched her elbow.

Carrie waved a hand. "Don't sit down, honey. It's okay. I'm fine. Here, Fran, help me up." She held onto Francisco's shirt as he wrapped

175

an arm around her slender waist and helped her stand. The redness in her face abated, and she released a shaky laugh. "That was unexpected."

Lori stood, hands shoved into her pockets, angry at Ben, angry at herself for even showing up.

"Lorraine and her friend gave me some startling news and apparently this old body of mine decided it wasn't up for hearing it."

"I'm really sorry, Mrs. Silva," Ben told her, glancing at Lori, who refused to meet his eyes. "I shouldn't have sprung that on you like that."

"No, not at all, and call me Carrie. Let's go in the house. It's warm out here and all day in the sun has left me feeling weak in the knees," Carrie said. "I want to hear everything. We all need to hear it as a family."

Lori didn't move from her spot. Her feet seemed cemented to the ground. Tears battled behind her eyes. In the presence of the Silvas, she felt like a child again. The ugly little girl their beautiful daughter had befriended. The last person to see her alive.

The Silvas started toward the house. Ben looked back and waved at Lori to follow them, but she couldn't make her feet go. As they traipsed inside, Francisco lingered behind. He returned to her, his face unreadable. Lori expected an admonishment, a confession that he blamed her and that he was furious she'd ruined his only living daughter's baby shower.

He touched her elbow and squeezed gently. "Come on, Alice. You can flip through some photo albums Zoe has made over the years. There's an entire one devoted to you and Bev."

Tears spilled over Lori's cheeks and a sob slipped from her lips. Francisco had nicknamed her Alice when she and Bev were little girls. Lori had loved *Alice in Wonderland* as a child. She'd carried a battered copy with her everywhere she went and watched the movie dozens of times.

Francisco wrapped her in a half hug. "I know," he said. "I know."

As he led her to the house, Lori swiped at her tears, which tried to start anew when she stepped across the threshold into the Silvas' familiar kitchen with its red and white tiled floor. The kitchen table was different and stood stacked with dishes from the baby shower. A family picture of Carrie, Francisco, Bev, Collin and Zoe hung above the table. The sisters had been young. They wore matching yellow bib overalls and pink t-shirts.

In the living room, mostly unchanged since their childhood, Carrie and Zoe sat on a long couch. Carrie patted the space beside her. "Come, sit," she said to Lori.

Lori walked on stiff legs, her face still wet with tears, and sat beside Carrie, who squeezed her knee. Ben had chosen a burgundy club chair, and Francisco settled into the opposite one.

Ben caught Lori's eye and mouthed 'sorry' at her. She smiled.

"I'm going to head back to the party," Zoe's husband told his wife, kissing the top of her head.

"Don't let those kids eat all the cake," Zoe called after him.

"Okay." Carrie rested her hands in her lap. "I'd like to hear what you guys have discovered, Ben. We've lived in limbo for fifteen years. If there's anything at all that might bring answers, we want to know it."

Ben nodded, leaning forward in his chair. "In 1993, my sister and her best friend, Summer, both fourteen, went for a walk in the Manistee National Forest over in Manistee. Summer disappeared. We searched and searched." He glanced at Lori and then went on. "I don't know if it's relevant, but she was wearing a tambourine bracelet—a bracelet with little bells on it like a tambourine—and searchers heard it in the weeks after she vanished, but never found her."

"This was in 1993?" Francisco cut in. "Five years before Bev went missing?"

"Yes. Then in 2003, thirteen-year-old Bella Palmer vanished in the Manistee National Forest in Reed City. She was walking with her best friend, Renee. They were picking berries and got separated. They never found her."

"She had a rape whistle," Lori added.

"And you feel that's important?" Zoe asked, wincing as she adjusted her position on the couch.

"We don't know," Ben said, "but if nothing else it's a way to find them. If someone was watching for girls going into the woods, it would be a lot easier to find the girl who had something that made a sound, a bell or a whistle."

"Like Bev's bola," Carrie murmured.

"Three girls have vanished from the Manistee National Forest in fifteen years? That's pretty far apart," Francisco said.

"Four girls," Ben said. "In 2008, Peyton Weller, fourteen, went for a walk in the woods with her friend in Scottville and disappeared. No trace ever found."

"Four girls?" Carrie's face paled, and she reached for Zoe's hand, curling her fingers through her daughter's.

"Four girls, but in twenty years and miles apart. I mean, Reed City to Manistee is what? Seventy miles?" Francisco asked.

"Yes, but anyone with a vehicle can cover those miles in an hour or less."

"You think one person took all four girls?" Zoe asked, looking to Lori for confirmation.

"We think it's possible," Lori admitted. "It feels too coincidental that four girls all vanished from the Manistee National Forest, all under eerily similar circumstances."

"And this man you mentioned, Hector," Carrie said. "You think he's involved?"

"I got wind of him a year after Summer went missing," Ben explained. "He tried to force a girl into the woods, the Manistee National Forest no less, who was riding her bicycle on a country road outside of Manistee. He lived with his mother in Luther, Michigan, which is pretty close to smack dab in the middle of all the cities the girls disappeared from."

"Other than the attempt on the girl riding her bike, was there anything else connecting him?" Francisco asked.

"Yes. In Summer's case, someone who knew Dunn saw him in Manistee the day Summer went missing and another person spotted a van that looked like his in the vicinity where Summer and Carm went into the forest. Police questioned him, but his mother gave him an alibi. She also gave him an alibi for the girl on the bicycle, even though three witnesses placed him at the scene."

"Was he charged in the case?" Francisco asked. His hands had moved from his knees into fists.

"No. The girl refused to testify. She was afraid. The case got dropped."

"What the hell?" Zoe muttered.

"I know," Ben agreed.

Lori had said little. It was enough to be with them, back in the Silva home where she'd spent so much of her youth, and a tumult of memories and emotions swirled through her as she gazed around the room.

"We've also found a connection between Dunn and Peyton Weller. We spoke to Peyton's aunt today and found out that Dunn used to go to the bar where Peyton's aunt worked."

"I've never heard of him," Carrie said.

"But that doesn't mean he wasn't around that evening," Zoe cut in.

"And it doesn't mean he was," Francisco said.

While Ben and Francisco continued their conversation, Carrie took Lori upstairs to show her the nursery.

"We kept Bev's room exactly the same for fourteen years," Carrie told Lori, leading her up the stairs. "And then Zoe got pregnant, and we decided it was time…" She pushed the bedroom open.

Gone was the violet-colored bedspread and mess of stuffed animals strewn across the pillows. Gone was the dresser Bev and Lori had spray-painted hot pink one summer after Mrs. Silva had brought it home from a garage sale. Gone were the posters of teen actors and musicians, the pinned-up Polaroids of Bev and Lori, the faux-cheetah rug that sat under Bev's vanity, always scattered with beads from her homemade jewelry.

In the place of Bev's former life stood a cherry-wood crib with lemon-yellow bedding. A mobile of stars and moonbeams hung over-head. They had painted the walls a soft gray color, and watercolor images of owls and hummingbirds hung in white frames. A glider with a floral cushion sat in the corner holding a small pink teddy bear with black-button eyes.

"It's beautiful," Lori murmured, and it was, though it also broke her heart to see it. She had never again stepped in Bev's room after the night her friend had vanished, and now Lori wished she had gone to the Silvas just once so she could stand in the room and commit every detail to memory.

Lori stepped back into the hallway and turned away from the room, catching her breath.

"I know," Carrie told her, touching her on the small of her back. "It took fourteen years for me to change that room and even now I feel sick whenever I open the door."

"Bev would have wanted you to," Lori murmured, and it was true, but it hurt just the same.

Lori and Carrie walked back downstairs. Ben sat on the couch beside Zoe, flipping through an album.

"That's Lorraine and Bev with their homemade Slip 'N Slide that was a total disaster," Zoe explained.

Lori looked at the image, and her stomach somersaulted. There she was, short and thick with her tangled brown hair and her ugly navy blue one-piece standing beside Bev, long-limbed with golden-red hair brushed behind her. They'd taped black trash bags together and angled them along a slope in the backyard, aiming the hose at the slick plastic.

Lori had gone first, getting a running start and belly-flopping onto the bags. They'd immediately ripped apart and bunched beneath Lori as she slid and then rolled down the hill. Bev had joined her at the bottom, and they'd sat laughing as they untangled Lori from the bags.

"You look so happy," Ben said, gazing up at her and smiling.

Lori faltered, glancing back at the picture, looking this time at her face instead of her imperfect body. She was smiling, her grin so wide it lit her entire face. She did look happy.

Lori sat beside them, momentarily lost in the nostalgia of the photographs.

"Remember this?" Zoe asked, pointing to a picture.

"Oh, my gosh," Lori murmured. "Halloween. I went as Alice in Wonderland and Bev went as the Red Queen."

"And Collin dressed as the Mad Hatter and I wore a Cheshire Cat costume!" Zoe laughed. "I refused to take that costume off until it was threadbare and my mom finally threw it away."

"That was so much fun," Lori said.

Beyond the windows, the sun set, casting an orange glow across the yard.

"We probably should get going," Lori said, tearing her eyes from the images and looking at Ben.

Ben glanced at his watch. "Wow, it's after nine. Yeah, okay." He stood and stuck out a hand to Zoe. "Great to meet you, Zoe. And good luck with the baby."

"Likewise, Ben, except for the baby part," Zoe joked. "Unless…?" She waggled her eyebrows at Lori.

"Very funny," Lori said, hugging her. "It was so good to see you, Zoe."

"You too, Lori, and don't be a stranger. I'm serious."

Lori hugged Carrie and Francisco goodbye next, promising to keep them updated on anything they discovered.

As Lori walked to her car, a tremor of tears bubbled in her chest. She hadn't expected the overwhelm of emotion as she left the house. She felt as if she'd found some piece of Beverly, a piece that had been lost along with her friend all those years before.

"Let me drive," Ben said, brushing a hand down her back. "You relax for a bit."

"Thanks." Lori handed him the keys. She climbed into the passenger side of the car and rolled down the window, watching the house for the last moments as Ben started the car and pulled away. She wondered if she'd ever see it again, or if this was that final shred of closure she'd needed with Bev's family.

"Should we still—?" Ben started.

"No," Lori blurted before Ben could finish. He was going to suggest going to the woods, but she didn't want to be anywhere near them at nightfall.

Ben turned off of the Silvas' street and onto the wooded road that led back to the highway. He watched the trees roll by. "How far were you from here?" he asked.

Lori peered out at the dusky woods and shuddered. "About two miles west of here off of Tanglewood Drive."

In an instant the car shut down. The lights extinguished and the thrum of the engine died. The car slowed, coasted, and rolled to a stop.

"What the hell?" Ben said, staring at the wheel and then the dark dashboard, mystified. "What did I do? Is there, like, an off button on this thing?"

Lori stared at the dashboard, equally puzzled, but her confusion was quickly overshadowed by another emotion—fear.

"How do I pop the hood?" he asked, leaning forward and searching for the latch beneath the wheel. He found it and pulled it. As Ben reached for his door handle, Lori's hand shot out and depressed the lock button, locking all the car doors.

"Don't get out," she said, eyes peeling wider as she swiveled her head, trying to see through every window at once.

"Lori, I have to get out. The car just died."

"There's something out there," she said, grabbing Ben's arm so hard her fingernails dug into his skin.

He squinted toward the windshield and then through her passenger window. "I don't see anything. It will take me two minutes. Maybe a spark plug came undone or something."

"No," She shook her head hard from side to side. "That's not it, Ben. It's not. Do not get out of this car."

He looked like he might disagree, but closed his mouth, staring beyond her into the shadowy woods.

She turned and followed his gaze. The silhouette of something stood there watching them. She could see only the outline, like a person, but misshapen, perhaps hooded.

"Oh, God, it's her," she whispered.

"Her? Her who?"

"What do we do?" Lori unbuckled her seatbelt and twisted around, hands frantically searching the seat, backseat and floor.

"What are you looking for?" he asked, not taking his eyes from the silhouette. He leaned further toward Lori's side of the car as if trying to make out what occupied the woods.

Lori's fingers closed on the Maglite she'd kept in her backseat for years, but her hands trembled so badly she dropped it and yelped when it landed on her foot. "Ouch, oh, damn. Ugh."

"Are you okay?" Ben leaned forward and grabbed the light.

"Yeah, I'm fine. That thing is heavy."

"Do you have Triple A?"

"Yes—oh, good idea. Or the police? Maybe I should just call the police."

Ben shook his head. "Not if you have Triple A. Just take a breath and call them. I'm going to shine the flashlight out your window."

Lori shrank away from the window, grabbing the lever on her seat and pushing herself into the far back position.

Ben turned on the light, aiming it through the glass.

Lori's spine went rigid and she couldn't help but follow the beam of light and prepare herself for what it revealed.

Nothing was there. Not a person. Not even a tree in the shape of the thing they'd been looking at.

Lori held her phone with an iron grip, but she hadn't dialed. "It's gone," she whispered.

Ben angled the light from side to side, searching for anyone in the trees. Nothing moved except the shuddering leaves.

"Call Triple A," Ben told her.

Lori started to dial and then paused, deciding, for reasons she did not understand, to lean over Ben and turn the key. The engine purred on.

Ben looked from her to the hood of the car. "How'd you do that?"

She shook her head. "Let's just get out of here."

29

When they finally reached Ben's house it was nearly ten p.m.

"You can stay," he offered.

"I'd better not. My mom's place isn't far. I'll head over there for the night. I've got a lot on my mind. I feel like sitting with it for a while."

"Yeah, me too." He leaned in and hugged her, a surprising gesture, but it felt good. When he pulled away, he held her eyes for a long moment. "I'm sorry about the thing with Bev's mom, bringing all that stuff up when you clearly didn't want me to."

"They needed to hear it. Sometimes I make things worse trying to pretend everything's okay," she admitted.

"Well, I'm also sorry if I didn't take your fears seriously tonight about the thing in the woods."

"No, it's better that you didn't. If we both panicked that'd be way worse."

Ben slipped out of the driver's door. Lori met him outside the car.

"You're sure you're up for driving home? I'd hate for your car to stall again."

"I'm fine. I have my cell phone and if I break down, I won't be far away from your place or my mom's."

"Okay, good night." He leaned in and kissed her cheek, which again surprised her. As she climbed behind the wheel, she touched the spot of warmth where his lips had been. They were friendly gestures, nothing romantic per se, but... they'd still felt good.

Her car did not stall as she drove to her grandmother's house and though the experience in Manistee had unnerved her, she had the niggling sense that it wasn't a mechanical problem that caused the car to die. Something bigger was at work, something that operated outside the laws of ordinary reality.

The house was dark and quiet when she arrived. She flicked on the kitchen light and her stomach grumbled at the sight of the box of mini-chocolate donuts sitting on the table. She moved to her grandmother's wall calendar, where she kept a meticulous record of all her comings and goings.

'Free Night at the Soaring Eagle,' her grandmother had written in neat cursive.

Her mother and grandmother wouldn't be home for the night. Once a month they usually stayed at the Soaring Eagle Casino in Mount Pleasant. Her grandmother enjoyed gambling—her favorite game was Texas hold 'em—and as a result of her frequent visits to the casino, they gave her a free night in their hotel every month.

Lori didn't mind the time alone. Though she wasn't elated about the empty house, her thoughts skittered across the experience of seeing the Silvas. If Lori's mother were home, Lori would have felt obligated to tell her all about it.

She grabbed the donuts from the table, mentally promising herself she'd eat no more than four. She walked into the living room, going to the selection of DVDs that her mother and grandmother had amassed. There were hundreds of them. Lori searched through the Disney movies, selected a copy of *Snow White* and slid it into the DVD player.

~

L ori jumped when someone cleared their voice loudly in the living room doorway.

"Jesus, Henry, you scared me half to death," she muttered when she whirled to see her little brother grinning behind her.

"Okay, this is wrong on multiple levels," Henry said. "First of all, you're watching *Snow White*. Second of all, you just jumped like you were watching *Saw*."

Lori released the pillow she'd been squeezing and let it drop to the floor.

"What are you doing here?" he asked. "Mom implied I was going to have this place to myself tonight. How can I have a raging kegger when you're up here getting crazy on Disney movies and donuts?"

Lori grabbed the pillow from the floor and chucked it at him. It bounced off his torso.

He pounded one fist on his chest. "See that? Pecs of steel. Been hitting the gym every morning at six for three months. It's paying off."

Lori leaned forward and grabbed a chocolate donut, took a big bite and smiled through her chocolate-smeared teeth. "I'm carb-loading for the marathon."

He cocked an eyebrow. "For real?"

She rolled her eyes. "Nope. Just doing the thing my therapist told me not to do, eating my feelings." She didn't mention that each of the three donuts she'd eaten had left her racked with guilt and shame. Henry knew little of the binge-eating disorder that had plagued his older sister and she preferred to keep it that way.

He grinned and grabbed a donut. "Sometimes you just need a little sugar, sis, and it's not more complicated than that."

"Easy for you to say," she grumbled. "You've never had an ounce of body fat."

"Bullshit. Look through Mom's albums. In middle school I was a veritable potato with hair. The other kids called me Hippo Henry."

"They did not."

He laughed. "Well, my best friend Brad did a few times, but that's because I called him Bacne Brad."

Lori sighed, finishing her donut and returning her gaze to the movie, where the black-cloaked witch offered Snow White the poisoned apple.

"Joking aside, whatever possessed you to select *Snow White* as your feature film this evening?"

Lori shook her head. "There aren't enough hours before my bedtime to explain. What are you here for anyway?"

"Lasagna, duh. I spent my entire check on fifths for a party last weekend. You think I had money for groceries?"

"You realize you're twenty, right? In the future, food will probably need to take a slight precedence over beer. Not to mention rent."

Henry waved a dismissive hand and walked to the kitchen. "Mom and Grandma would happily give me my old room back. I can be the professional jar-opener and dude who carries wood from the shed to the fireplace."

Lori listened to him opening cupboards and drawers. He waked back in with a heaping plate of lasagna and three pieces of garlic bread stacked on the edge of the plate.

"I hope you're not serious."

He laughed. "Not if every house on the planet burned to the ground. I'd live under a tree before I'd move back in. No offense to Mom and Grandma, they're the bee's knees, but living here..." He shook his head. "The knitting and the vacuuming and the Lifetime movies? Nah, no thanks. Really though, I didn't blow my check on beer. I'm saving for a loft in Detroit. I met this woman." He closed his eyes as if talking about her caused him physical pain. "She's a mortgage broker down there, thinks she can get me an interview at her company." He forked a bite into his mouth. "She's twenty-four, a total cougar."

"I'm pretty sure twenty-four does not a cougar make."

He laughed. "I know. She wants to strangle me when I call her that, but seriously, I'm crazy about this girl."

"'Drop out of school' crazy?" Lori asked.

"I'd transfer, do part time to finish my degree, work full time."

"Why not just move in with her? Why save for your own place?"

He stared at her. "This coming from the woman who's been with her boyfriend four years and you still haven't moved in together. Where is Stu? He didn't join you on this fabulous adventure at Mom's?"

Lori almost grabbed another donut at the mere mention of Stu. Instead, she clenched her hands together in her lap. "I caught Stu cheating on me last week. It's safe to say we're over."

"No shit?" Henry used a piece of garlic bread to wipe up the sauce and cheese still clinging to his plate.

"None, unless you count the shit I've been eating as he lied through his teeth to me for the last however many months or maybe years."

"What a dickwad. What happened?"

"I don't want to talk about it."

"You are so much like Mom." Henry sighed.

"What's that supposed to mean?"

He shrugged and licked his fingers one by one. "That's just something she does whenever I bring up... complicated things."

"And by complicated things you mean Dad?"

"Mostly Dad. Yeah."

"It's not surprising, is it? He cheated on her, pretty much abandoned her with two kids. You were only five."

"I know. I do. I know all of that, but I'd like to know other things too. I'd like to know what life was like before... all of that happened."

"They fought a lot. We've talked about this."

"Come on. That's it? That's all you remember?"

Lori grabbed a blanket from the back of the couch and wrapped it around her. "No. There were good years when I was little. When Dad was still working at the appliance store. But then he got that marketing job and he started being gone a lot. By the time they had you, Dad was like an idea more than a reality. He was there for big stuff, Christmas, Easter, but... not the normal day-to-day stuff. He was gone a lot. For the first six months after you were born, he was around, but then it started all over again. Working late, weekend business trips. Mom just seemed to get more and more sad, stressed, fed up."

"What did you guys do? You and him during the good years?"

Lori smoothed her hands over the pilled blanket. "A lot of putt-putt golf. That was one of his favorite things. And he loved dogs, but Mom was allergic so we never had one, but we'd go to the animal shelter and look at the dogs or we'd go to his friends' houses and play with their dogs. He'd roll in the grass and the dogs would pounce on him and lick his face."

Lori smiled, remembering her dad with his ash-blond hair and his pale blue eyes. Henry looked a lot like him. She remembered the sheepdog his dad's best friend had owned, named Hooligan. Her dad had loved the dog and once after a drunken bonfire he'd even crawled into Hooligan's doghouse and spent the night with him. That was a story Lori had heard about later. She'd been too young to attend that party and had spent that weekend with Grandma Mavis.

"I love dogs," Henry said. "When I have a house someday, I want a German shepherd."

"That's a big dog."

"Go big or go home."

She smiled. "Hmm, what else? He made these really delicious home-made pizzas with all kinds of funky stuff on them—pickles or taco fixings. They were crazy good."

"I think I've tried a few like that when I was stoned, but I'm not sure I'd go for pickles on a pizza sober."

"Don't knock it til you try it," Lori said.

"I wonder about him sometimes," Henry admitted. "Why he so completely erased himself from our lives. If it's what he wanted or if—"

"Mom made him?"

"Yeah. I know that's a shitty thing to say."

"It wasn't her. I contacted him twice. He moved to Florida, got remarried, had two new kids. He replaced his whole life. Her, us, and he even got the dog he always wanted."

"How do you know that?"

Lori sighed. "I took a Greyhound bus there right after I finished my senior year in high school. I missed him being at my graduation. I had a birthday card he'd sent me for my sixteenth birthday with his address on it. I took the bus and I called him and he came and picked me up at the Greyhound station. It was surreal. He lived in this neat little Cape Cod with his pretty blonde wife. They had a two-year-old and a six-month-old. Lola and Harvey."

Henry's face darkened. "That's a joke, right? You're not telling me he had two children and named them—"

"Variations on our names. Yeah, that's what I'm saying, and that's why Mom doesn't like to talk about him and that's why I don't like to talk about him. I lost all faith in him the instant I set foot in his new life and realized how much I was not welcome. He had me on a plane back to Michigan before dinner."

Henry leaned his head back. "Screw him. What a bastard."

"Pretty much."

He puffed up his cheeks and blew out a loud breath. "Want a beer?"

Lori cocked her head. "You actually think Mom and Grandma have beer?"

He chuckled. "I leave a secret stash in the garage fridge tucked way in the back. I'll get us one."

"Thanks." Lori grabbed the remote control and powered off the TV.

Henry returned and handed her a beer. She popped the top and took a sip.

"What's with *Snow White*, for real?" Henry asked, gesturing at the now-dark screen. "Not plunging back into your witch fixation, I hope."

"What do you mean?"

"The witch thing. Remember? When we were young. You kept reading all those stories about witches and watching the movies, but then you'd be scared and want to sleep on Mom's bedroom floor. She finally forbade it."

Lori frowned. Much like the revelation of the dreams, the story struck her as true and yet not solid, a memory that had slipped between the cracks and could not be easily wrenched from beneath the floor-boards. "I remember that, kind of anyway. When was that? Was it—"

"After Bev," Henry said quietly. "Those months before we moved to Grandma's. I'm not surprised it's a blur. That was a weird summer. I have some really clear memories, but then nothing about other things. I don't remember packing our stuff to move here to Clare to live with Grandma Mavis. I don't remember the last time I saw Dad."

"Do you remember the day Bev disappeared?"

He nodded. "Our neighbor Charlotte came over to watch me and brought her daughter, Daisy. Ugh, I couldn't stand her. She was so bossy and always stole my toys. I remember you coming home and then you and Mom going back out. After that it's blurry. I'm not sure if it was all one day or a series of days. People coming and going, police, Bev's parents."

"It's a blur for me too," Lori admitted. "The day itself is crystal-clear, but everything that came after is a haze."

30

Lori turned the doorknob, warm and pulsing beneath her hand, and drew it slowly open. The familiar hallway of her childhood home did not lie beyond the bedroom door. Instead, she stared into the forest off Tanglewood Drive. Though she knew it was that forest, she also saw the lighting wasn't right, and the trees weren't right either. Everything had a reddish hue. The trees did not merely cast a single shadow, shadows surrounded the trees, and they did not match the trees at all, but seemed to wriggle and twist though there was no wind.

The crunching started again, more frenzied now, a slurping sound accompanying it. Lori walked forward, her bare feet sinking into the ground that too was unlike the forest by Tanglewood Drive. It was soft and mushy and though the air seemed full with a wet chill, the ground was warm and wet like the earth in a tropical rainforest.

All these things tried to distract Lori from that steady crunching, but she could not ignore it. She continued, though she was so terrified her entire body shook. It did not merely tremble, but quaked, her hands slapping against her thighs, her knees clacking together painfully.

She grew closer to the sound, closer still, and saw the oak tree Bev had climbed into. A creature hulked beneath it, bent over, eating and crunching and swallowing with that wet gulping sound. Its back was covered in mismatched animals' pelts. Black tangled hair protruded from the top, human hair. It was not an animal, but a person standing there, eating.

Lori took another step and something squished beneath her feet. The soft

*flesh of a crimson mushroom oozed between her toes and discharged a scent like
rotted meat. Lori froze as the thing at the tree slowly straightened and turned.*

*The woman, if she could be called that, had a face so lined and grooved it
nearly blended with the bark of the tree beside her. Her hair was as twisted as
branches, her eyes two black pits in her gruesome face. Blood coated her chin
and ran from her lips. Bones and flesh filled her cupped hands.*

*Lori looked down at the woman's feet, at the thing lying there, the long
blonde hair and the red and white striped shorts. Everything else was a bloody
blur and she opened her mouth and began to scream.*

≈

"Lori! Wake up!"
Lori's eyes shot open and she gasped for breath.

Henry, looking terrified, stood above her, a pitcher of water in his
trembling hand. It was tilted at an angle as if he were about to dump it
on her face.

She put her hands up to block him. "No. Don't. I'm awake."

He set the pitcher on the dresser and then offered his hand to help
her sit up. "Jesus," he muttered, raking both hands through his hair.
"Holy Christ, you scared the living shit out of me. I walked through the
front door and you were screaming like... like..." He shook his head.

Lori leaned back against the headboard, her dream raw and real, the
room around her slowly sinking into focus. "It's okay," she whispered,
her voice raspy.

After Lori reassured Henry multiple times that she was fine, he
retreated to his own room. She sat and remembered the dream, the
woman devouring the girl on the ground. It had not been Bev, but
Summer Newton lying on the ground. Summer with her blonde hair
and her red and white shorts.

≈

In the morning, Lori ate a quick breakfast of instant oatmeal,
treading lightly through her mother's house so as not to wake
Henry. She left a note that she wouldn't be back later as she had to go
home and check on Matilda. First, however, she wanted to visit Manistee, the place where Ben had spent his youth and where Summer had
gone missing.

Lori walked through the quaint downtown of Manistee. Purple flowers hung in overflowing pots descending from the antique-looking light posts.

The sidewalks were abuzz with people, mostly tourists, Lori assumed based on their flip-flops and beach bags. Not to mention it was midday on a business day when most people were chained to their desks for another five hours.

After walking the length of the town, she doubled back and walked into a hip gastropub with gleaming wood floors and waitstaff dressed in craft beer t-shirts. The smells were intoxicating, but she turned and left. She needed someplace older and less appealing to visitors. She wanted a locals' place, a dive.

She found it the next street over—Moriarty's Pub, a bar and restaurant that occupied the lower level in a building that looked like it had been built in the early 1900s and not cared for much since. The windows were dark except the glowing 'Open' sign.

When Lori pushed through the door, the bar was dark and filled with shadows. Smells of warm wetness assailed her—spilled whiskey and puke and sweat. Six people were seated at the bar, four men and two women, and not a single one of them wore beach shorts or had sunglasses propped on their heads.

Lori chose a seat, self-conscious, an outsider who'd walked into their lair, but the people at the bar paid her no mind. The counter was sticky and Lori pulled her hands away too late, because both palms had the gooey residue lingering from where she'd touched the surface.

The bartender, a grizzled, pot-bellied man somewhere in his fifties, slapped a paper napkin in front of her. "What'll it be?"

"Um… a beer," she said, searching for the most relaxed drink. The 'you can trust me with your secrets' drink.

"Which one?" He gestured at the tap.

"The blue one." She squinted at the tap. "Budweiser."

He turned, filled a tall, cloudy-looking glass and plunked it on the napkin. Beer foamed from the top and instantly soaked the tiny napkin beneath it.

"Have you lived here long?" she asked, pulling a ten-dollar bill from her wallet and setting it on the counter.

He didn't answer her, just lumbered to the register, popped it open and extracted eight dollars in change.

She considered asking again, but it had been hard enough the first time around. She sounded like she was trying to pick the guy up.

Lori took the cash, stuffed it back in her purse, and dragged her beer closer. The bartender had gone off down the bar where he was topping off shot glasses for two middle-aged men, both hunched over and talking with their heads close.

He returned a moment later, wiping the bar and plopping two more flimsy napkins beside Lori's beer. "Yeah," he told her. "Way too long."

Lori swallowed, almost not sure that he was talking to her. She steadied her hands on the cool glass of her drink, took a sip and tried not to grimace. Drinking beer always tasted like licking an aluminum can—not that she'd done it, but she imagined a similar metallic aftertaste.

"I wonder... did you ever hear about the disappearance of Summer Newton?" She hadn't intended to jump straight to that question, but she sensed this was not a man of many words. If she tried to engage him in small talk, she'd be there all day.

He paused mid-wipe and appraised her, eyes narrowing. "You a cop?"

"Ha." She laughed, and her face grew warm. "I'm flattered that you'd think so." His face darkened, and she backpedaled. "I mean, not that I'm impressed by cops. I just, well, I've always thought of myself as kind of a weak person. Not weak, but... not strong."

Shut up! the cool calm voice that wasn't a blithering idiot told her, but she carried on.

"What I mean is, cops always seem to have that... like, authority thing, not just because they carry a gun, which I don't, obviously."

"Why you askin' then?" he asked gruffly, pinning her with his beady blue eyes.

She closed her mouth and formulated her next words carefully. "I knew her. I met her as a kid and someone recently told me she'd vanished when she was fourteen. It got under my skin, so I thought I'd see if anything ever came of it. I'm not a police officer though. I work in HR actually. That's human resources."

"I know what it is," he muttered. He stepped away, heading back down the bar where the two women sat.

"Give us another round, Blondie," one woman cackled leaning far over the bar as if attempting to swat the bartender on the backside.

He moved away from her, leaned into the drink well and pulled out two bottles of dark beer. He popped the tops and put the beers in front of the women.

Lori wondered about the nickname. Had the bartender once been blond? He was bald now, the kind of bald he wore proudly—freshly shaved and shined like the bumper on a new sports car.

He disappeared behind the bar for several minutes and when he returned he held a sheet of paper in his hand. He slid it in front of Lori.

It was a missing person's poster. An old one, from the looks of it, spattered with pin holes from where it had likely clung to a corkboard, and marred with more than few stains.

Summer Newton smiled out beneath the words 'Have You Seen Me?'

"Had this hanging on the board since it happened. Ain't nothing come of it," he said.

"Are there theories? Word around town, that kind of thing?"

He shrugged. "Sure, ain't there always? Stickiest one is the boyfriend did it. The brother of the girl she'd been with the night she went walkin'. Ben Shaw."

"Did you know him?"

"Nah. Saw him around town. His dad owned a hardware store. I heard a few people talkin' here an' there, said he was a punk, liked to start trouble."

"Have people speculated about why he'd hurt Summer?"

The bartender leaned closer. Lori could smell pickles on his breath, and liquor, whiskey maybe. She wondered if he slipped off to the backroom now and then for a shot.

"Some people said he wanted to lay her and she wouldn't put out." He leered at Lori, a sudden gleam in his eyes as if he delighted in telling her such a sickening secret.

Lori leaned so far back from him, she nearly tumbled off her barstool. His hands shot out and grabbed her by the forearms as she started to fall back. His grip was hard and sticky, much like the bar itself. Lori tried to hide the shudder that rippled through her at his touch. "Thanks, wow. Almost fell on my back."

He raised both eyebrows. "Best place for a woman to be."

Lori blinked at him, words failing her. "Well, okay," she managed. "Thanks for all your help."

She hopped off the barstool and bolted for the door. When Lori burst back onto the sidewalk and the world outside of Moriarty's, she felt like Persephone stepping from the underworld back into a field of flowers and fruiting trees. She staggered a few feet, caught her breath and pressed a palm against the brick wall beside her.

31

Ben woke thinking of Hector Dunn. He skipped his usual routine of coffee and breakfast and breezed out the door. On the drive, he pulled into a donut shop and bought a to-go coffee and an egg sandwich.

He reached Dunn's road just after nine a.m. and drove by Hector's house, not slowing, but looking for a suitable pull-off space where the man wouldn't notice Ben's car. He found it a few hundred yards past Dunn's house. A seasonal road branched off to the right. Ben followed it, his car bumping over the uneven ground, high grass scraping the exterior.

He parked and climbed out, stayed in the woods as he backtracked toward Dunn's house. He walked until he could see the house. The paint on the single-story ranch peeled in curls. The windows were dark, covered by curtains. A back porch hung lopsided from the back of the house, the rail mostly broken away. In addition to a two-car garage connected to the house, a barn, also in disrepair, stood further back on the lot.

Ben stared at the back of the barn and wondered what lay inside. He moved closer, scanning for anything that might prove his suspicions about Dunn, but he knew he'd see nothing. The man might be deranged, but he sure as hell wasn't stupid. If he had abducted and murdered the girls, he'd hidden them well.

The back door swung out and Dunn stepped onto the back porch wearing only a pair of yellowed boxer shorts that sagged low, revealing his hairy belly. Dunn lit a cigarette and slumped into a rusted metal chair. He sat and smoked and stared at the trees that ran behind the house. As his eyes roved across the back of the property, he paused. Ben froze, unsure if Dunn had locked eyes on him.

The man stood and lumbered back into his house, emerged moments later with a rifle.

"Oh, shit," Ben whispered, ducking low and hurrying back through the trees.

Behind him the sound of the gunshot exploded the quiet morning. Around him birds squawked and took flight.

Something crashed through the forest. Ben spun around to catch the backside of a deer fleeing deeper into the forest.

"A deer," he murmured, bracing a hand on a tree to catch his breath.

He peered back toward the house. Dunn had leaned the gun against his house and resumed his cigarette.

Ben didn't bother watching further. He rushed back to his car and climbed behind the wheel.

~

Lori glanced back at the door to Moriarty's Pub, half-expecting Blondie or whatever the hell his name was to follow her out. He didn't, and after she made it back to the main street in downtown Manistee, still bustling with people, the hammering in her chest subsided.

She walked through town, some of her resolve giving way. Somewhere in the distance a bell tower began to count the hours. It was noon.

Ahead of her, a woman stood on a ladder on the sidewalk, arranging letters on a movie theatre marquee board. Lori read, 'Welcome Manistee High School Class of 1993.' The woman started down, bending to pick-up a purple leather bag.

"Excuse me," Lori said, pausing in front of her. "Were you part of class 1993?"

The woman, dressed in white capri pants dotted in tiny red cherries, grinned and curtsied. Her golden-blonde hair had the sun-kissed, wind-blown look of a day on the lake. She was beautiful, and Lori felt instantly plain standing beside her.

"I surely was. And the Michigan Apple Queen to boot. Magnolia

Fairchild at your service. Tell me you were not in the class of 1993? I never forget a face and you look far too young to have been one of my classmates."

"No, I graduated from high school in Clare, but I'm in town looking into something that happened in 1993, a disappearance."

Magnolia's guileless blue eyes went wide. "Summer Newton. Is that who you're referring to?" She touched her forehead with the back of her hand as if she were a damsel from a country-western film who might faint at any moment.

"Yes. Summer. Did you know her?"

"Oh, goodness me," Magnolia said, taking Lori by the hand and pulling her toward the theatre doors. "Let's get out of this blazing sun. I'm a summer girl from my crown to my toes, but this humidity has got my blouse as slick a second skin. Ugh. I'm hoping it eases back before the party, but Michigan, being the volatile gal that she is, probably won't let up until we've all melted like the Wicked Witch of the West."

Lori followed her through glass double doors into the cool, dim interior of the theatre lobby. It was quiet. Heavy maroon curtains shielded the larger theatre from view. No lights shone behind the snack counter, no ticket sellers or ushers occupied the space.

At the edge of the lobby sat a red sectional with a movie poster beside it advertising a new Tom Cruise action movie.

"We can sit here. My brother manages the theatre and they agreed to let us do a slideshow and cocktail party here before the reunion. I was tickled pink. So many fond memories of this theatre. It's a shame how many of the small-town marquees have closed right down. Just boarded-up buildings now," Magnolia lamented.

"There used to be a drive-in theatre in my old home town," Lori said, "but it closed before I was born. My mother used to tell me about packing into a car with a group of friends and watching the double feature."

"Drive-ins are so magical," Magnolia said dreamily. "I've been to the Cherry Bowl Drive-In up by Benzie County a time or two. I always fall asleep before the second movie, but it's a hoot anyway, sittin' in your car, eating a hot dog and watching the show."

"I'll have to try it out one of these days." Lori reached into her bag and pulled out an article she'd printed about Summer. According to the caption beneath the picture, the photo had been taken on her last day of school. She stood at the end of her driveway waiting for the school bus wearing olive green shorts and a white v-neck t-shirt.

Magnolia crossed her legs and leaned toward the article, rotating a gold bracelet on her right wrist as she scanned the headline. "I still remember that summer so vividly," she started. "I'd graduated, which already made it a memorable time, but when Summer Newton disappeared, the whole town just went topsy-turvy. Her family was known around town—her uncle especially, but also her cousin Jimmy. Within twenty-four hours, we were all out looking, searching the woods, the quarries, the beach, the lakeshore. We were all thinking about that show *Twin Peaks* that had been so popular a couple years before. Did you ever see that? The one with the prom queen found dead on the beach."

"I did see it," Lori said, remembering watching the show with Bev. They'd been riveted waiting to find out what happened.

"Instead of playing volleyball, we were walking the beach looking for her body wrapped in plastic or some horrible thing. I get the chills thinking about it." Magnolia held out her arm as proof. "We never found her though. Thank God. I know that's a terrible thing to say, but I just don't know how people recover from things like that. Finding one of their own..." Magnolia fiddled with the zipper on her leather bag, gazing at Summer's photo. "May I ask what has you looking into Summer's disappearance now? I mean it's twenty years. I just can't believe it's been that long."

"I heard about Summer on a camping trip recently. I couldn't stop thinking about it, so I figured I'd look into it. I was trying to see if I could get a sense of what might have happened, spur some interest in the case again. I wonder if you ever heard rumors, anything like that?"

Magnolia looked thoughtful. "The boyfriend, Benjamin Shaw. That's what everybody said. Maybe something happened between them in the woods. Maybe she broke things off and he murdered her in a rage, then forced his little sister to make up the story and help him conceal her body."

Lori frowned. "And people believed that?"

"Some people did."

"Kids at school?"

"Yeah. Some did and then others, people who knew Ben, said he'd never have done anything like that. I didn't know him well, he was two years behind me, a sophomore when I graduated, but... I thought there might be something to the rumors."

"Why is that?"

"I saw them arguing once. Ben and Summer. It was after school had let out. They'd kind of kept things a secret, you know? That they were going out, but then word got around like it does. Anyway, I was jogging one afternoon and saw them parked at this lovers' lane spot. It was the middle of the day, so no one else was there, but I could hear him yelling in the car. I sort of slowed down, not eavesdropping, but, you know, I was curious. She jumped out and ran into the woods crying."

"Do you have any idea what they were arguing about?"

Magnolia shook her head, pink lips pursed together. "No, but I told the police about it after she went missing, and I wasn't the only one. A girl who was friends with Summer claimed she saw Ben shove her once."

"Other people in town also thought Ben was involved?"

"Yes, on account of his temper. He'd also gotten in fights at school. He punched Jimmy Newton in the face one time. That was Summer's cousin. I can't say Jimmy didn't deserve it—he was always stirring up trouble—but who walks up and punches someone in the face? That's a man with impulse control if you ask me."

"Were there ever any other rumors?"

Magnolia took to circling her bracelet again. "My dad thought Summer's disappearance was related to the disappearance of that girl down in Free Soil who'd gone missing some years before. I was only a wee thing then and don't remember much about it. My dad had grown up in Free Soil before he opened a car dealership in Manistee. His brother still lived in Free Soil and mentioned years before that a girl disappeared over that way."

"What was her name?"

"You're testing my memory today." She steepled her fingers at her lips. "Her name started with an M. Miranda or... Meredith. That was it, Meredith Abram. I think she was around Summer's age, maybe a little younger, twelve or thirteen. Went off walking in the woods and never came home."

"Was she by herself?"

"Nope. Had a little friend with her. The friend came back, but Meredith never did."

A s Lori drove home, she thought of Magnolia's words. The town really had blamed Ben, their suspicions bolstered by more than one possibly violent interaction between the sixteen-year-old Ben and the fourteen-year-old Summer. It bothered Lori. It bothered her that her own suspicions had been raised by the woman's admission.

32

At home, Ben retreated to his garage and spent the early afternoon doing bike maintenance. He fixed two bikes that co-workers had dropped off. One needed new tires and another a new chain. Then he tuned up his own bike, cleaning the chain and adjusting his brakes. His hands moved mechanically, but his brain chewed on Hector Dunn and the bits and pieces that connected him to the missing girls. Nothing substantial had appeared, no smoking gun, per se, but plenty of connections. Enough of those connections and he might be able to get a detective interested in digging deeper.

As he worked a text came in from Ryan Kimner, a fellow nurse.

Ryan: Karaoke tonight. Be there or be square.

Ben: It's on like Donkey Kong.

He finished his maintenance and then rolled the bike out of the garage. He thought of Lori and fished his phone from the pocket of his jersey and texted her.

Ben: Interested in joining me for karaoke tonight? Give Sherlock and Dr. Watson a break.

Her reply was immediate.

Lori: That depends. Am I Sherlock or Watson?

He grinned, straddling his bike before texting Lori back.

Ben: Obviously, having a medical degree, I'm Watson and your love of cigars destines you to be Holmes.

Lori: I don't love cigars. They smell like manure.

Ben: Then perhaps I'm Agent Scully and you're Agent Mulder.

Lori: ??? Shouldn't I be Scully, seeing how she's a woman?

Ben: Oh, no. That's just biology. We're talking real traits here. Scully is the skeptic (and the doc)—Mulder is the believer in all things weird and wonky.

Lori: So I'm the nutcase?

Ben: I like to think of you as the crunchy peanut butter to my smooth grape jelly.

Lori: Crunchy peanut butter—i.e. nutcase.

Ben laughed out loud.

Ben: You coming tonight?

Lori: Sure. What time?

Ben: Seven.

Ben rode the Pere Marquette Trail, opting to go west rather than east in the direction of the Manistee Forest. He rode for two hours, the thrum of his tires on the pavement lulling him into a meditative state. He didn't think about Hector or Summer or things that lurked in the forest.

He returned home, showered and changed into loose-fitting khaki pants and a dark t-shirt. He searched the drawers in his bathroom and spritzed cologne on his neck. Ben couldn't remember the last time he'd worn it and wrinkled his nose after he sprayed it. Taylor had picked out the scent and it smelled overpowering. He wet a washcloth and scrubbed at his neck.

He checked on Leia and tidied up his living room, throwing laundry in the bathroom hamper and loading coffee mugs he'd left on the coffee table. As the minutes clicked closer to seven, he felt his nerves amp up.

When Lori arrived, he watched her through the front window. She wore a light summer dress, white with gray flowers. It was the first time he'd seen her in a dress. Her long brown hair was pulled over one shoulder and she brushed at her stomach self-consciously as she hurried up to his door.

"Hey," he said, pulling it open before she could knock.

"Hi." She smiled, looking surprised. "Thanks for inviting me."

"My pleasure. I figured we needed a night off."

"There's another girl," Lori blurted as he stepped out his house.

"Another girl? Who disappeared?"

Lori nodded. "Yeah, Meredith Abram. She went missing from Free Soil in 1990."

"Three years before Summer."

"Yeah."

"Huh, that kind of kills the five-year thing."

"Unless it's unrelated. Or maybe there's no five-year cycle at all."

"How did you find about her? Nothing ever came up in my searches."

Lori tugged at the hem of her dress. "I was just searching around online and came across an old article."

"Dang, okay. Did you find any contact information for the family?"

"Yes. I sent her mom an email. She's willing to talk to us tomorrow."

"Okay." Ben held up his car keys. "Let's say we go kick some ass at karaoke and then we can figure out our next steps."

Ben sipped his ginger ale and half listened to the screechy rendition of *Addicted to Love* coming from Holly, an ICU nurse, on the karaoke stage.

"Anyway," Zander continued, leaning across the table towards Lori, "I was standing around there one night chatting with a few of the vampires after a drop-off when suddenly I heard this door slam from a room at the end of the hall and then footsteps pounding toward us. I kind of jumped to, like ready to face the emergency, but nobody appeared. The vamps started laughing at me like I missed an inside joke. Finally, Kenya here"—he winked at Kenya, who was sitting back with her feet propped on the back of another nurse's chair—"told me that it was just the three a.m. ghost."

Lori looked at Ben, who rolled his eyes at her. "Really?" she asked Zander.

Zander took an ice cube from his glass and flung it at Ben. It struck him in the neck and slipped down his shirt, freezing a trail toward his pants. Zander directed his attention back to Lori. "Yes, really. Come on, Kenya, back me up."

"It's true," Kenya said, adjusting the straps on her tank top. "Ben's the emergency room cynic. He's heard it too, but he's always giving us some song-and-dance about footsteps echoing from other floors."

Ben dug the ice cube out of his shirt and shot it back at Zander. "A healthy dose of skepticism comes in handy in our line of work. Remember Ginny, that rotating nurse last year who wouldn't go in room eleven because the toilet flushed on its own?"

"To her credit," Kenya cut in, "she was on duty the week before when the patient in room eleven died." She leaned toward Lori. "While on the toilet."

"No?" Lori looked horrified.

Ben reached over and tucked Lori's tag into the back of her dress, his fingers brushing against her warm skin. "Yes." He smirked. "But I can tell you definitively that toilet had been flushing on its own for months."

"Oh, come off it, Ben. You've seen some spooky shit in there," Ryan said, pausing to take a long swig of his beer. "In fact, I have it on good authority you were the first one who saw Mrs. Hardy."

"Of course I saw her. I was her nurse."

"You were the one who saw her after she died," Ryan said, casting Lori a significant look.

"You did?" Lori stared at him.

Ben smiled at her and shook his head. "I must have confused the nights. I thought I saw her, but then it turned out she'd died on the day shift... so I guess I confused which night I saw her."

"I call bullshit," Kenya said.

"I second it," Ryan added.

"Thirds," Zander agreed. "Holly's done. Lori, you're up, girl. Get up there and show off that sultry Carly Simon sound."

"If Carly Simon has a twin sister who can't hold a tune, I might be on par with her," Lori said.

"She looks a bit like her, don't you think?" Zander asked Ben. "Carly Simon circa 1975."

"Carly Simon suffers in comparison," Ben murmured, winking at Lori as she stood.

Ben watched Lori take the stage. She looked nervous, brushing at her stomach and tucking her hair behind her ears. She also looked beautiful, her sundress swaying above her shapely legs.

"Sing *I'm Too Sexy*," Kenya shouted.

Lori grinned and held up her gin and tonic, glancing at Ben, who gave her a thumbs up.

The song started and Ben's smile faltered and disappeared. Her voice was husky, sexy, but the music and the words were all wrong.

"Every breath you take..." she sang.

Ben stood abruptly, and the chair he'd been sitting on careened over, crashing into a woman standing beside the pool table. She shrieked and the man she was playing against, a bearded goliath who stood a foot higher than Ben, strode around the table angrily.

"You just hit my girl," the man shouted, jabbing a thick finger against Ben's chest.

"Back off, gorilla. I was getting ready to apologize," Ben snapped, trying to lean over and right the chair. He looked at the woman, who stared at her boyfriend with a mixture of fear and awe. "Sorry about that," he told her.

"You don't talk to her, you talk to me," the man growled, moving so close to Ben's face he felt the bristles of his facial hair.

"You trying to kiss me, man? Because I don't normally swing that way. For you, I might make an exception."

The man cocked his fist back and Ben ducked as he swung. The guy's fist caught air, sending him stumbling sideways.

"Whoa, whoa, dude." Zander shouted. He, Ryan and two of Zander's paramedic friends stood up, creating a wall between the gorilla and Ben. "Chill out, man," Zander told the guy, who'd righted himself and seemed ready to fling every person in his path aside to get to Ben.

"Hey," Jerry, the owner of the bar, shouted. "Take another step and I'm calling the cops. Take two and I'm pulling out the gun I keep behind my bar." His eyes drilled into the gorilla, who still glared at Ben.

The gorilla's girlfriend grabbed his hand and tugged him away. She picked up her purse and slung it over her shoulder. "Let's get out of this dump," she snarled, shooting a final menacing stare at Ben, who was tempted to yell a farewell that would have gotten him pounded for sure.

In the scuffle, he'd forgotten about Lori, and more importantly the song she was singing, but it reasserted itself in his head. He looked at the stage, where she'd stopped singing, likely because she'd caught sight of what was unfolding on his side of the room. She was telling something to the DJ and trying to fumble the microphone back onto its base.

"I'm done," Lori said, turning to the DJ who operated the karaoke.

"What?" he yelled, pointing at his thick headphones.

"I'd like to stop now," Lori shouted, trying to return the microphone to the stand. She missed and it dropped to the floor, releasing an ear-splitting screech of feedback. Lori scrambled to pick the microphone back up and put it in place.

"Thanks for stopping that guy from mopping the floor with my face," Ben told Zander, who was still watching the door the gorilla had disappeared through. "We're going to split."

Zander put a hand on his arm. "I wouldn't just yet. That guy is liable to be lurking outside waiting to finish what he started."

"We'll be fine," Ben said as Lori arrived at his side. "Let's go."

She said a quick goodbye to his friends and followed him toward the door. When he pushed out of the bar into the warm night, he paused, looking up and down the street.

"What happened in there?" she asked.

"That halfwit wanted to kick my ass because I knocked over my chair and it hit his girlfriend. It's fine." He was walking fast, faster than necessary, and he could feel her struggling to keep up.

"What's wrong?" Lori asked, though he barely heard her. His footfalls were deafening on the pavement. She grabbed the back of his shirt. "What's wrong?" she shouted.

He slowed and turned, his pulse jumping, and he didn't know if it was the encounter with the gorilla or the damn song. "Why did you pick that song?"

Lori stared at him. "In the bar? The karaoke song? I don't know. It was on the screen and I clicked it."

Ben studied her, searching for some other explanation, and then he clapped his hands together hard, startling her. "What in the actual fuck is happening?" he said, face tilted to the sky.

"You're freaking me out right now," Lori said. "What's happening? What was wrong with the song?"

He shook his head because he didn't want to tell her and then laughed and threw up his hands. "Why not, right? Why not tell you? Okay, well…" He paced away, staring at the cracked sidewalk. "That was mine and Summer's song and I've heard it now four times in a week. Before that I couldn't tell you the last time I heard it—years, most likely. And that's not all, folks, I've seen her. She's always walking away, disappearing around a corner, but it's unmistakably her and let me not forget the necklace I gave her with the unicorn. The necklace you found in my car appeared again in the hand of a girl who slit her own throat at the hospital. The necklace Summer was wearing the night she vanished. I'm either losing my ever-loving mind or something seriously fucked is happening."

"It's her," Lori said. "It's the witch."

"Jesus, Lori!" Ben shouted and started away from her again.

She didn't follow him. He heard her turn and start in the other direction.

"Damn it," he muttered, spinning around and chasing after her. He'd almost caught her when ahead of them on the sidewalk stepped the gorilla. He stood wide-legged, hands fisted at his side. He reminded Ben instantly of Bebop and Rocksteady, the bumbling idiot supervillains from *Teenage Mutant Ninja Turtles*. Ben might have even cracked a joke if Lori wasn't walking directly into his path.

"Lori, stop!" Ben commanded, and she must have heard the warning in his voice because she looked up and froze.

"No buddies and no bartender. Who's going to protect you now, pretty boy?" the man growled.

He stepped toward Lori and Ben ran forward, ready to throw himself between Lori and the gorilla. Lori's hand lifted and she shoved something in the man's face. The gorilla shrieked and lunged away, swiping at his face.

"Run," Lori screamed, whirling back towards Ben and taking off down the sidewalk. Ben raced after her.

They didn't slow until they'd reached his car. They both jumped inside. Ben started the engine and threw it into reverse, squealed out of the parking lot and down the street.

"What did you do? Mace him?" Ben asked, looking at her, incredulous.

"Flea and tick spray," she admitted, an uneasy smile on her face. "I had some in my purse because I picked it up for Matilda. I'd forgotten to take it out."

"Brilliant," he whispered. "Bloody brilliant."

She laughed and pulled her dress lower toward her knees. "Or really stupid. If it hadn't done the trick, we might be getting our heads bashed together right now."

Ben looked at her. "I would have taken the head-bashing so you could get away."

She smiled. "My hero."

"I'm sorry I reacted that way about the witch thing," he said. "I don't want to believe it. Is that so terrible? I want to think it's all a screwed-up coincidence."

Lori faced him. "I understand being skeptical, but at what point do you take the lid off your closed mind and open up? Huh? I heard the stories of your friends. You yourself have had those experiences. Denying it doesn't make you smarter, Ben. It makes you vulnerable. If we're going to face this thing, we have to believe it's real."

"Like Santa Claus?" He smirked and then immediately held up a hand in apology. "I'm sorry, that was out of line. I'm a skeptic by nature."

"There's a fine line between being skeptical and stupid," she murmured, unable to hide her smile.

He glanced at her. "That's such a Mulder thing to say."

$\sim$

He had invited Lori in, wanted her to come in, and she'd wanted to say yes. She almost had, but a voice in her head urged her not to. She wanted to believe it was a protective voice, a voice that wanted to keep her safe, but she wondered if it was the voice always reminding her she wasn't good enough.

As she drove to her mother's house, Lori thought of Ben and the words he'd spoken and the way he'd looked at her. It could be real, his feelings, and it could also be a spell cast over them by the forced closeness, the misconception that having experienced a similar tragedy made them in some way compatible. They weren't compatible. Ben was a risk-taker, a thrill-seeker, an outdoor enthusiast, a skeptic. Lori was a homebody who liked to read books and daydream. Even if they managed to start a relationship it would fizzle out when their differing personalities started to clash. When Ben wanted to spend their Saturdays mountain-biking, Lori would want to lie in bed and read.

It was destined to fail.

She parked in the driveway and pushed into the house. Her mother and grandmother hadn't heard her come in. They were in the kitchen talking in hushed voices.

"Henry said he had an affair," her mother continued.

"Poor Lori," Grandma Mavis said. "Why does this world keep throwing obstacles in her path?"

"I don't know, Mom," sighed Rebecca.

Lori leaned against the wall, listening to the women who loved her most in the world quietly grieving for her.

"Her thirtieth birthday is the day after tomorrow. Maybe that will cheer her up."

"Did you order her gift?" Grandma Mavis asked.

"I did. I just hope we can get her to go."

Lori frowned, feeling guilty for eavesdropping. She opened the front door and closed it loudly. The women went silent.

Lori walked into the kitchen, where her mother and grandmother sat at the table.

"Hi, dear," Rebecca told her, smiling. "Staying the night again?"

"Yeah. I took some time off of work."

Grandma Mavis stood and hugged her. "Good. You deserve a little break. Can I make you a plate? I cooked spaghetti."

Lori yawned and shook her head. "I'm beat, but I'll see you right here for coffee in the morning."

"Good night, Lorraine," her mother said as Lori started out of the kitchen. "Oh, honey, could you keep your door open tonight?"

Lori turned back. "Sure, why?"

"Just in case you have a bad dream. I'll hear you sooner."

"Thanks, Mom. Good night."

33

Lori drove to Ben's the following afternoon for their planned trip to meet Meredith Abram's mother.

She parked and climbed from her car.

"Road snacks," she told him when he walked from the garage. She held up a plastic container of muffins. "Coconut cranberry, a Grandma Mavis specialty."

"Ooh, thank you, Grandma Mavis," he said, as she handed him the container. He peeled off the lid and grabbed one out, eating half a muffin in a single bite. "Mmm… wow. That's a good muffin."

~

Ben drove to Free Soil to the home of Meredith Abram's mother Margot.

Margot lived in a two-story cedar-shingle house located on a deep, wooded lot. Ben parked near the garage.

Lori climbed from the car, admiring the well-manicured lawn and the elaborate landscaping. To the side of the house a massive wildflower garden bloomed in vivid shades of red, pink and yellow. Along the stone walkway that led to the front door stood little fairy houses and ceramic garden gnomes and frogs.

A woman opened the front door and stepped out. She looked like she belonged in the house. She wore a pink and yellow floral bandana covering her pale hair. Her floor-length yellow dress matched her bandana. She waved at them. "Come in, please. I've put on tea."

Lori walked up the path with Ben following. The interior of the home was as whimsical as the outside. The walls were painted a pale orange with bright flower wallpaper borders butting against the ceiling. The floors were honey wood, covered in vibrantly colored rugs.

"I'm Margot Abram. You must be Lori," the woman said, taking Lori's hands.

"Yes, thank you for having us. And this is Ben."

"Welcome." Margot turned and led them through the bright hallway into a sun-filled kitchen. The kitchen cabinets were painted white and an old-fashioned yellow oven matched a vintage ice chest. In the center of the round kitchen table stood a vase overflowing with fat pink and yellow flowers.

"I picked those from my garden this morning," Margot said, gesturing at the flowers. "Please, sit. Get comfortable."

A large square window overlooked the garden, and Lori spotted bird houses and hummingbird feeders hanging from wrought-iron poles throughout the plants.

"You have a lovely home," Lori said, leaning forward to smell one of the flowers. It was sweet and pungent.

"Thank you." Margot filled delicate teacups from a silver tea-kettle. "I have some wonderful herbal teas—blueberry hibiscus, ginger peach, honey ginseng or perhaps a more standard black or green tea."

"I'd love to try to the blueberry hibiscus," Lori told her.

"Make that two, please," Ben added.

Margot poured their teas and carried them to the table. "This house used to have dark carpets and gray walls," she said, sliding the cups to them. "Two years after Meredith disappeared, I did a complete over-haul. It's my homage to her, my way of honoring her life. She loved flowers and bright, sunny things."

"It's a wonderful tribute," Lori said.

"It is," Ben agreed. "So many people turn away from life after such tragedies. It seems as if you've turned toward it."

"I've done my best," Margot said. "We lost Meredith's dad seven years ago to a heart attack. That was hard, but not as hard as losing Meredith. I find peace knowing they're together now. And I still have my other children, Mickey and Bernadette, they're both grown and living their lives, but I see them often."

Margot turned back to the counter, picked up three framed photographs and brought them back to the table before she took a seat.

"My glowing girl," Margot murmured, tracing the line of Meredith's face in the picture. "That summer she was so happy. She'd aced all of her classes, talked her dad into paying for horse-riding lessons, and her cousin, Allie, my sister's daughter, was coming to visit for two weeks in August. They lived in Georgia. This was taken just days before." Margot held up a photo of her daughter sitting on a park bench eating an ice cream cone. Meredith's hair was arranged in a side ponytail. She wore bright yellow and pink high-top sneakers. "She begged us for those shoes for her thirteenth birthday. She was wearing them when she disappeared."

"Can you tell us what you remember about that day?" Ben took out his notebook and pen.

"Sure. I remember that day better than any that has come since or before. It's burned in my mind. It was a Thursday. The kids were on summer break. My son Mickey was at camp up at Crystal Lake near Frankfort. Cal, my husband, worked for the gas company. He was out that day like usual and I was home with my youngest, Bernadette. She'd turned four the previous March. Meredith had a girlfriend come over, Annie Miller. They'd been building a fort in the woods nearby. They gathered up a hammer and nails. I gave them my usual 'don't leave your dad's tools in the woods or he'll tan your hide' lecture. Meredith gave Bernie, that's what we call Bernadette, a kiss on the forehead and promised she'd play with her later. Bernie hated it when Meredith left. She loved her big sister so much. Off they went, and I never saw her again."

"When did you realize she was missing?"

"Four thirty-three. I remember looking at the clock just a minute or two before Annie walked through the door thinking they'd been gone an awful long time, but I wasn't worried. In those days, kids would go off all day, but usually they'd run in and out, come back for popsicles or snacks, but that day they didn't. Annie came in and asked if Meredith was home. I said, 'No, isn't she with you?' Then Annie got scared and started to cry. She said they'd been playing hide-and-seek and got separated. It had been more than an hour since Annie had seen Meredith. She'd walked through the woods calling her name, but couldn't find her."

"Did you call the police?"

"Oh, God, no. Not right away. In those days, you just didn't jump to those kinds of conclusions. I thought she got turned around out there. We waited at the house for another half hour, then I called my mother and asked her to come and watch Bernie while I went back to the woods with Annie. I felt sick in my stomach. I didn't realize what it meant then, that my girl was gone, but later I did. We searched until my back and feet were screaming, then we walked home. I called Cal and asked him to come back, and I called Annie's parents and asked them to come pick her up. By nightfall we had fifty people in those woods."

Margot picked up the framed photograph of Meredith and smoothed her fingers along the gilded edges.

"You realize grief is a marathon. If you're going to survive you can't spend it all in a day. The problem is you don't get to choose. It pours out of you, it renders you hunched over and gasping for breath, but on you go and go and go. We've been running with this grief for twenty-five years, the hope passing like sand through our fingers, but even now, more than two decades later, if I unfurl my palm, I see a pebble or two remains."

"We both know how that feels," Ben said. "We didn't lose a child. That seems unimaginable. But we both lost close friends, and you never stop hoping that someday—"

"She'll walk through the door," Margot murmured, looking toward the hallway that led to the front door. "But of course, she never did. The police didn't start a search until four days after she vanished. We were furious. My husband walked into the station and screamed and hollered and they almost arrested him. They thought she'd run off and Annie had helped her and they'd created the whole story about a fort in the woods to give her time to get away.

"Utter nonsense. What thirteen-year-old girl runs away with nothing but the clothes on her back? Her little Thundercats wallet with three dollars in it was sitting on her dresser. She'd never have run off. Meredith was such a good girl."

"Were there ever any suspects, Margot?" Ben asked.

"Suspects…" she murmured, lifting her own tea and sipping it. "No. There was never anything at all, never a trace of what happened to her. In so many cases there are sightings, there's a shoe left behind, a toy, some evidence of something. Not with Meredith. It was as if she vanished into air."

"How about rumors around town?" Ben asked. "I don't mean to push the subject. It's just that people usually talk."

"I did hear a disturbing story after she went missing, but it wasn't about Meredith. It was about the woods. A guy I'd gone to high school with, Adam, told me about a scary experience he had in those same woods as a boy.

"He said that he and his sister Georgina were walking in the Manistee Forest looking for morel mushrooms. It was the season, late spring, and there'd been a week of rain followed by hot humid days, perfect weather for those little critters to start popping up. They were excited, took out their paper bags hoping to find the mushrooms. He said they hadn't walked for more than fifteen minutes when they both got really tired. He related it to the way he's felt when he's had medical procedures as an adult where he was given anesthesia. He said it was the feeling when the sedative is just starting to take you under. They both ended up sitting down against a tree and falling asleep.

"It was after dark when he woke up to the sound of Georgina crying. She'd had a dream that something was chasing her through the woods. She stood and started running and ran smack into a big oak tree. Shattered her nose, broke one of her eye sockets, if that tells you how hard she was running, how scared she was. Adam's dad belted him that night. He thought Adam had scared Georgina, but Adam also sensed that his dad was frightened of the woods. He'd lived there since a boy and his daddy before him. He was always telling Adam and Georgina to stay on the edge, not go too far in, but their mother would override him while he was at work and say, 'You kids go play, just be home before Dad gets back.' And they always were, except for that day."

"Did Adam say what Georgina dreamed was chasing her?" Lori asked. Her legs had begun to shake beneath the table, causing their teacups to clink against the plates. Lori steadied them.

Margot shook her head. "He said they talked about it a lot those first weeks, but Georgina couldn't put her finger on it. Something that wanted to eat her. That's all she could remember."

Lori felt cold all over.

"That's a pretty dark story to share with someone whose daughter disappeared in the woods," Ben said.

"Yeah, he didn't want to tell me. I forced it out of him. Then afterwards I wished I hadn't," Margot admitted. "I had terrible nightmares about Meredith running from whatever it was that had been chasing Georgina."

"Was she wearing anything that made a sound that day?" Lori asked. "Something with a bell on it?"

Margot frowned and shook her head. "No, nothing that I can think of. The girls were into toe rings back then. She might have had one of those on, but I'm really not sure."

"Does the name Hector Dunn mean anything to you?" Ben asked.

Margot looked at him, surprised. "Well, sure. He was our handyman for ten years. I used to see his mother from time to time at the church potlucks over in Luther. That's how we found Hector. He did work for us on occasion—painted the shed, trimmed back the trees, nothing extraordinary. His mother Pearl passed on a few years ago. Why do you ask?"

Lori could see a vein pulsing in Ben's neck and he held his teacup so tightly in his hands, she thought it might shatter. He set it down carefully.

Margot looked at him, puzzled, a frown creasing her thin mouth. "Hector hasn't been implicated in some way, has he?"

"We've found links between Hector Dunn and multiple girls who have vanished from the Manistee National Forest."

Margot blinked at him and then looked at Lori, who reluctantly nodded to confirm his statement.

"What sorts of links?"

"He was in the area or knew family members of victims. He was also arrested for trying to abduct a girl on a bicycle a year after my friend Summer disappeared in the woods. She was fourteen. She was never seen again."

"Hector? He was always such a nice man, quiet. He loved the kids…" Margot's frown deepened.

"Did he show a special interest in Meredith?" Ben asked.

The color drained from Margot's face and for a long moment she stared at the garden beyond the window. Finally, she nodded. "He brought her gifts sometimes. Little trinkets." She turned suddenly to look at Lori. "Earrings once. Little red and green Christmas bells."

"Was she wearing them that day?" Lori asked.

Margot shook her head. "No. I still have them somewhere in Meredith's stuff. It's all boxed up in the loft over the garage."

~

"That was proof positive it's Hector," Ben said as they drove back to Clare. "I'm going to write something up tonight that details everything we've found that points to him. Zander's brother is a cop. I'm thinking he can suggest a detective who might be interested in digging deeper."

"There's something unusual about the Manistee Forest, Ben, something we can't explain."

He glanced at her. "What do you mean?"

"People getting disoriented, walking in one spot then suddenly in another. That girl's nightmare of something chasing her, her and her brother falling asleep in the woods. It all implies... I don't know. Something supernatural, maybe."

"I disagree," Ben said. "I think it points to pollution and toxicity. I mean, take a look at industrialized America pre-1970s, before the EPA started regulating what factories could dump into the ground and water. In all those cities around the Manistee National Forest there were factories dumping their waste. Paper mills, paint factories, salt plants. The list goes on. That stuff doesn't just magically disappear. Instead, it seeps into the ground water. Get enough of it accumulating down there and percolating for a few decades and poof, you've got some kind of noxious gas rising up from the earth that no one is aware of."

"That might explain the disoriented stuff, but it doesn't explain the disappearances."

"Because there's a man behind those, Hector Dunn. Who knows, maybe he's aware that the forest is polluted and people get off kilter when they go in there. Maybe that's why it's his hunting ground."

"I really don't think so."

"Lori, I'm talking cold hard facts here and you keep reaching for something from a fairytale."

"I met with a woman in Grand Rapids a few days ago, a Jungian Analyst who studies folklore. She's collected stories from right here in Michigan, stories about child abductions in the Manistee National Forest that happened decades ago, long before Hector Dunn was alive."

"Of course there were. Look at any city in the history of the world and you'll find murders and abductions. That doesn't mean something supernatural is at work."

"There's something wrong in those woods."

"I hope you're not setting up an excuse to get out of our trip to the forest tomorrow."

Lori scowled. "Tomorrow? What are you talking about?"

He cocked an eyebrow. "Yeah, tomorrow, your thirtieth birthday."

Lori shook her head. She'd honestly forgotten about his insistence that they visit the woods on her birthday. "I'm thinking I'd rather spend the day eating ice cream in bed, plus my mom and grandma are making dinner—"

"We'll go after. Why don't I join you for dinner? I'd like to meet the woman behind these fabulous muffins." He kept one hand on the wheel while opening the Tupperware and taking out another muffin. He winked at her.

"You can come to dinner, but afterward we should just go catch a movie or maybe play putt-putt golf."

"Not a chance, birthday girl," he told her, setting his muffin down so he could squeeze her knee. "Tomorrow we're facing some fears."

34

"This is thirty," Lori murmured, staring at herself in the bathroom mirror.

She looked the same, much as she'd looked the same on every birthday for the entirety of her life. But she felt different. Maybe it was the anticipation of the day ahead, in particular the hike in the woods off Tanglewood Drive. Maybe it was the recent events that had her feeling her life had been tossed into a washing machine on spin-cycle.

She'd slept late, read in bed for an hour and made a single serving of pancakes. Now, as she left, she kissed Matilda on the head, and gazed longingly at her bay window before leaving her apartment.

As she opened her driver's door, a voice rang out behind her. "Lori, wait. Happy birthday!" Stu jumped out of his car, a bundle of daisies wrapped in purple crepe paper held in his hand. "Happy thirtieth," he said, jogging across the street to her and holding out the flowers.

"Thanks, Stu." She grabbed the flowers and tossed them onto her passenger seat as she climbed behind the wheel and slammed the door.

He opened his mouth, but she ignored him, started the car, shifted into drive and pulled away. She glanced at him, open-mouthed in the rearview mirror, and grinned.

"Catch ya next time, Stu," she said to his reflection.

~

Lori arrived at her mother's house and walked in to the smells of beef stew and carrot cake. Balloons hung suspended from the backs of the kitchen chairs. Her mother and grandmother wore matching pineapple aprons.

"It's the birthday girl!" her mother exclaimed, hurrying to Lori and taking her by the shoulders. "My goodness, you get more beautiful every day." She kissed her cheek. "Happy birthday, honey."

"Thanks, Mom."

Grandma Mavis set down her ladle and grabbed Lori in a hug. "I added peppers and garlic, but no onion to the stew, just the way you like it."

"Thanks, Grandma. Is Henry coming?"

"No, he wanted to, but he's got some big exam on Monday. You know Henry."

"That's fine. I have a friend who's going to join us."

"Not Stu?" her mother asked, eyes widening.

"No, Stu and I broke up."

Her mother feigned surprise, exchanging a look with Grandma Mavis.

Her grandmother shrugged. "Good riddance. We never liked Stu anyhow."

Ben arrived carrying a small box wrapped in brown paper and decorated with a hand-drawn picture of a grinning cat.

"That's some serious artistry." Lori laughed.

"I tried to channel Matilda for that one," Ben told her, leaning in to kiss her cheek. "Happy birthday."

"Thanks. Are you sure you're up for this?" She opened the door wider so he could walk into the house.

"Meeting your mom and grams? Heck, yeah. If they're anything like you, this will be an afternoon to remember."

Lori led Ben into the kitchen where her mother had set the table and hurried around ladling stew into the bowls.

"Mom, this is Ben," Lori told her, feeling an instant blush rising into her face.

"Ben, hello. I'm Rebecca. This is my mother, Mavis."

"Three generations," he said. "I'm honored."

Rebecca smiled and pulled out a chair. "Have a seat, kids. Dinner is ready."

They sat and talked. Ben spoke comfortably, regaling them with harrowing stories of life as an E.R. nurse.

"Enough about me," he said after a while. "Let's talk about Lori, the guest of honor."

Lori smirked. "There's nothing these ladies don't already know about me, Ben. You're a far more interesting topic."

"Oh, I don't know about that," Rebecca said. "What's this Ben mentioned about your going to Baldwin later for a walk in the woods?"

Lori glanced at Ben, who mouthed the word 'sorry.' He must have told her mother and grandmother when she'd gotten up to use the bathroom.

Lori brushed a hand over her stomach. "Yeah. We are. It's time to go back there. It's been fifteen years."

Rebecca reached for Lori's hand, rubbing her fingers over her knuckles. "I'm proud of you, honey."

"Thanks, Mom."

"But be careful," Grandma Mavis insisted. "If you'd like, you can borrow my Swiss Army knife."

Lori smiled. "I think we'll be okay without the knife, but I appreciate the offer, Grandma."

They sang Lori happy birthday, and then Lori leaned in and blew out her candles, wishing silently that all the families of the missing girls had answers.

Her mom handed her an envelope closed with a gold seal. Lori opened it and pulled out the paper inside, reading it.

"Mom?" Lori studied the ticket, puzzled.

"It's a plane ticket. Well, a gift certificate for a plane ticket. It should cover anywhere you want to go. I was in your room and saw that old dream board. You wanted to go to so many places. Machu Picchu— remember you talked and talked about wanting to go there? I'm thinkin' it's about time you do that."

Lori lunged out of her seat, grabbed her mother and burst into tears. The emotion poured up and out of her in a rush and she couldn't quell it.

"My sensitive girl," Rebecca murmured, petting her daughter's hair. "I'm so proud of you."

Lori sat back down. Ben handed her a napkin and she wiped away her tears. "Thank you, Mom. I can't believe you did that. It's too much."

"Oh, no, it's not," Grandma Mavis said. "You best send us pictures, and not that kind you put on the interwebs, understand? Real ones I can put in a frame on the mantel."

"Grandma had the final say," Rebecca told her. "I was afraid to buy the ticket, afraid of you going off somewhere, but then—"

"Then I told her we'd never met a stronger, more brilliant, more beautiful woman," Grandma Mavis declared. "And that woman needed a passport full of stamps."

Lori pulled away from her mother and hugged her grandma. She sat back in her chair, smiling at Ben, embarrassed. He grinned and handed her the gift he'd brought.

Lori peeled off the paper to reveal a small white box. She lifted the cover to find a beautiful gold compass on a black leather band.

"You wear it like a watch," Ben told her, taking it from the box.

Lori held out her arm and he secured it to her wrist.

"Now, you'll never lose your way."

～

Ben chatted as they drove to Baldwin. Lori offered directions, but couldn't manage much small talk. Cold sweat broke along the back of her neck.

"This is it," Lori whispered as Ben coasted to a stop on the grassy fringe of Tanglewood Drive.

The forest awaited her, unchanged despite the passage of years.

"Ready?" he asked.

Lori's mind blanked. She thought panic might seize her and render her incapable of stepping from the car.

"Hey." Ben took her hand.

She looked at him, the fugue cleared, and she nodded.

Lori stepped from the car and stared at the trees. Nothing about them appeared threatening, but goosebumps prickled along her arms as she walked closer.

Ben met her, taking her hand a second time. "No big deal. Just an afternoon stroll in the woods."

Lori swallowed and allowed him to lead her down the embankment and into the trees. Nothing extraordinary happened. The witch did not swoop from her hiding place to devour them. Hector Dunn did not step from behind a tree with an axe clutched in his hands. Of course, even in the horror flicks, there was some build-up to the horror, some period of tranquility before the creature struck.

"So far so good?" Ben asked.

"Yes."

They walked on, Lori searching for familiarity amid the trees.

"It's strange," she murmured. "I don't remember which tree Bev climbed. I thought it'd be seared in my memory, the location and the tree itself, but..." She shook her head. "They all look similar. I can't remember anything distinct about it."

"Shall we climb one?" Ben asked.

He released her hand and jumped onto a low branch. Lori's breath caught. He'd scurry up the tree and disappear. She'd be left to make her way alone out of the woods.

He turned. "Come on. We'll do it together."

"I'm not great with heights."

"We'll go slow. The minute you want to stop, we'll climb back down."

Lori nodded, remembered the shame of not being able to get into the tree as a girl, and took his hand. The first branch was low enough to step on. The others were spaced close and their girth large, so she could easily move from one to the next, following Ben up the tree as if it were a clunky spiral staircase. Fifteen feet off the ground, the branches grew narrower and leafier.

"Here, sit on this one," Ben said, patting a thick limb, "straddle it, back against the tree. I'll hold open the leaves, so you can look out."

Lori sat, dropping a leg on either side and squeezing the branch to keep from falling. As Ben peeled open the branches, she saw the slope of trees beyond them, the flock of green that reached the horizon. She caught her breath. No orange-pink sunset lit the sky, but the blue of the world above was punctured by hundreds of voluminous white clouds. They looked like mountains in the sky.

"It's stunning," she murmured.

Ben gazed out at the sky, but turned back to watch her. Her heart thumped against her breastbone.

He let the leaves fall into place and straddled the branch so that he faced her, their knees touching. "I think if I kiss you right now, it will help to rewrite this place. Give you a new memory, a bit like what the dream doctor described."

"If it's a therapeutic suggestion, how can I say no?"

He leaned into her, braced his hands on the trunk behind her and pressed his mouth against hers.

She hadn't kissed another man besides Stu in years. Ben tasted like cinnamon gum and his lips were soft and inviting. He didn't smash his mouth against her face the way Stu had. The kiss left her breathless, and when Ben pulled away, Lori glanced down and teetered before Ben righted her.

They both laughed.

"That was a very memorable first kiss," she said.

Ben held her legs, squeezing her thighs. "I look forward to the ones on the ground."

"Why do you like me? Not saying that you do, but—" Lori started, warmth creeping up her neck.

"I do."

"You do?"

He smiled. "Yes, I do. I did just kiss you."

"Okay, but why?"

"You can't see yourself, Lori. A lot of people can't. You're real. That's what I like about you. You don't pretend to have everything together, to have the world figured out. I like that."

"Except you seem to have the world figured out."

He laughed. "Hardly. I'm just a stubborn ass who refuses to follow the rules."

Twigs cracked beneath them and Lori stiffened. "Did you hear that?"

Ben leaned over and looked down.

"Adrian!" someone yelled.

Ben glanced back at Lori, offering his hand. She took it and followed him down, still breathless, feeling the lingering warmth on her mouth from his.

"Adrian!" a man's voice yelled again.

"Hey," Ben called out as they descended from the tree.

The sounds of crunching twigs stopped for a moment and then started again. A man moved toward them. He was older than them, but not by much, early forties. He wore sweatpants and a Detroit Tigers t-shirt.

"I'm searching for my friend's daughter. Her name is Adrian. Did you see anyone come through here?"

Lori lurched back and tripped over a root in the ground. Ben caught her elbow before she fell. "No, we haven't seen anyone. Where'd she go missing?"

The man turned back the way he came and gestured. "A mile back probably. I've been walking for over an hour. We can't find her anywhere. It's the strangest thing."

Ben's hand had slipped from her elbow to her hand. Lori's was slick and cold. She wanted to scream.

"How old is she? Adrian?" Ben asked.

"Fourteen," the man told them. "She's a little under five feet tall, long blonde hair. My daughter Diane said she's wearing shorts and a t-shirt, tennis shoes."

"What were they doing in the woods?" Ben asked, and Lori heard the strain in his voice, fear and disbelief.

"Beats me—hiking, talking girl stuff."

"We'll help you look," Lori blurted.

Ben nodded.

"I'm Percy," the man offered.

"I'm Ben, this is Lori."

35

Somehow Ben got separated from Lori and Percy. They'd been holding hands and then he'd stepped away to look inside a dead tree that had half-fallen. The hollowed-out trunk was large enough to hold a hiding girl, but only if she was tiny. Only ashy bark lay in the center.

"Lori?" he called, looking behind him. No sign of her.

He ignored the nagging sense of déjà vu, and the voice in his head reminding him this had been his idea and now he was separated from Lori in the woods that had terrified her since she was fourteen.

Ben walked, listening as the leaves rustled in the breeze. The wind was picking up as the day dissolved into evening. He heard another rustling sound as he moved forward and paused. Rather than leaves, it sounded distinctly like paper.

He continued on, the sound growing louder. Ben stepped into a clearing of trees. In the center stood the strangest-looking tree he'd ever laid eyes on. It was short and fat with twisted branches jutting in every direction. The bark appeared faded, as if the tree had died many years ago and been slowly bleached by the sun.

He started toward it and then paused, eyes drawn to the trees surrounding the clearing. It wasn't the trees he stared at, but what had been nailed onto the trees.

Hundreds of missing person's posters hung from the trunks. They flapped and scraped with the wind. As he stepped closer, he saw the faces beneath the big block words 'MISSING.' Summer's face was the first to register. Summer with her golden hair and inquisitive eyes, with the dimple on only one side of her smile. And then his eyes trailed to the other faces and he knew he was looking at the girls who had disappeared in the Manistee National Forest. Beverly Silva, Peyton Weller, Bella Palmer and others he didn't recognize.

Ben's heart thundered in his chest and he forced his eyes to the ground. He studied the blades of grass, the fanning leaves of the ferns. When he looked up, the posters would be gone, merely a figment of an overactive imagination. He lifted his head. They weren't gone. Instead, they seemed to have multiplied. The trees beyond the clearing flapped with the posters. The wind lashed against them, threatening to tear them away.

Someone had done this. Here in this desolate place, someone had gathered all of the girls' missing posters and nailed them on bent and rusted nails. The wind intensified and the pages flapped harder. One ripped free and struck Ben in the back of the head. He jumped and jerked the paper away, watching it disappear into the forest.

Ben turned and ran, lungs catching as his feet pounded the soft ground. "Lori," he yelled.

Tree branches lashed against his face and the wind roared in equal measure with his blood.

He wanted to get a grip, to stop panicking, but his body had bypassed his brain. It refused to calm down. He ran until his legs burned and sweat poured into his eyes.

"Ben!"

He heard Lori and skidded to a stop, momentarily off-kilter at the sudden calm in the forest. The wind had simply died. Ben stared at Lori, his breath erratic. He knew he looked wild by the expression in her eyes.

"What?" she said, face paling as she looked past him, behind him as if expecting something pursued him, something with razor teeth and dead eyes.

Ben took a deep breath and hitched a thumb over his shoulder. "I found something totally screwed up."

"What was it?" She'd taken a step or two away from him back in the direction of the road. At least he thought it was the direction of the road, but he realized standing there he'd gotten turned around. His usual stellar sense of direction eluded him.

"Come with me. You need to see it."

"Oh..." Lori swiped a hand across her stomach, again peering past him. "I don't know. Tell me first. Okay?"

"Where'd he go? Percy, the guy?" Ben asked, staring beyond her, wondering suddenly if he'd imagined the whole ordeal—the man, the posters, all of it.

"He's at Tanglewood Drive, it's just back there. He went to meet more searchers." Lori crossed her arms over her chest as if chilled.

"There's no wind," Ben muttered. "Was there? Just a few minutes ago?"

"Wind?" Lori shook her head. "No, not that I noticed."

"There's a grove of trees back there covered in missing person's posters. I mean covered, like ten on each tree and they're... the girls. It's posters of our missing girls."

Lori reached a hand for Ben's and tugged him back toward the road. "Let's go. Okay? Let's just get out of here."

"It was all the girls, Lori. All of them. That means someone else has connected them, someone came out here and hung those posters up."

"But why would they do that? Why would they put the link out there knowing it could get them caught?" She turned quickly to look behind her.

"You have to see it. I need you to see it."

"I don't think—"

"Please," he insisted. "Please. I need... It's important for me that you see it." He didn't add because it felt unreal, like a nightmare he'd temporarily slipped into. He needed validation that it was real.

"Okay," she sighed, following him slowly.

Ben led her back toward the grove of trees, searching for the familiar sound of the wind passing through paper, but only the crunch of twigs under their feet met his ears.

"Maybe this way," he said, turning abruptly after they'd already walked a hundred yards in the direction he thought the trees lay. "I really thought they were this way, but maybe..." He turned again, backtracking and taking another direction. "They were here, I swear to God."

"I believe you," she murmured.

Something in her tone unnerved him and he turned to look at her. She was pale and her forehead was slick with sweat.

"Are you okay?" he asked.

"I don't know. I'm not feeling well all of a sudden."

"It's him. It's Hector Dunn," Ben muttered. "He's fucking with me. I know he is. He put the posters up." He continued searching the trees, spinning in circles.

"Please, let's just go," Lori murmured. "I think I might be sick."

They trudged out of the woods, meeting Percy and another group of searchers walking in. Lori apologized for not helping search, saying she didn't feel well, and Ben could see that she didn't. Her skin had grown warm and feverish.

"Lean your seat back," he said when they climbed into his car.

Lori hit the lock button before she reclined her seat and closed her eyes.

Ben started the car, but watched the forest for several long moments, wondering if Hector Dunn had gone into the forest that night to hang the posters and walked out with another girl.

Ben parked at the curb in front of Lori's mother's house. "You could stay with me tonight," he said.

Lori wanted to. She wanted to spend the next eight hours with Ben wrapped around her, but she shook her head. "Not tonight. Some night, I hope. But not tonight."

He angled across the seat and kissed her. She leaned into the kiss, but pulled away before the kiss turned into more.

"Thank you for today."

He laughed dryly. "I'd hoped for something memorable, but not so strange."

"It was memorable and it wasn't entirely strange."

"Call me tomorrow?" he asked.

"I will." She opened the car door and climbed out, waving goodbye before disappearing into the house.

Ben didn't drive home. He steered his car west for Luther, Michigan.

It was dark when he arrived at Hector Dunn's house. Lights blazed behind the covered windows.

Ben parked at the same seasonal road he'd driven on days before. He slipped from his car and crept through the woods, alert for the sounds of a girl's screams. As he drew closer, he heard voices and broke into a run.

At the side of the house, he slowed and snuck to a window. Blue light spilled out from a television. The window was mostly covered, but the bottom right corner offered a limited view of the interior. The room he looked into was dark except the television. He studied the shapes in the room, a couch and other furniture. A distinctive silhouette reclined on a chair. It was a large man, and though he couldn't make out his features, Ben was sure it was Hector Dunn.

The voices had come from the television. There was no girl in the room with Dunn unless she was hidden from view.

Ben snuck around to another window. This one looked into the kitchen. Again, Ben found a gap in the fabric covering the window. He made out a table and three chairs. A clump of browning bananas sat in the center of the table. Dishes lay piled in the sink and on the surrounding countertops. The trashcan was overflowing with garbage, a pizza box resting on top.

As Ben scanned the space, movement caught his eye and he ducked lower as Dunn walked into the kitchen, shirtless, scratching at his groin.

The man opened the refrigerator and stood staring at the contents for a solid minute before selecting a can of beer. He popped the top and guzzled it, tossed it toward the trash, where it bounced off the pizza box and rolled across the linoleum floor toward the window where Ben stood.

Ben slipped away from the window, moving around the house, listening. He could see the small rectangular windows that looked into a basement, but when he got on his belly and tried to peer inside, they were covered with something thick and dark. He tapped lightly on the glass, hoping if a girl were trapped inside, she'd hear him and call out.

Silence.

36

Lori drove home from her mother's house the following morning. She fed Matilda and then powered on her computer to check her email. She had a message from Irene Whitaker.

Dearest Lori,

I enjoyed our meeting the other day and hope you have uncovered more intriguing paths to follow in your hunt to find the witch.

As part of my ongoing research into mysterious figures both known and unknown, I keep an email where people submit their stories.

One arrived yesterday that I thought might be of particular interest to you.

A man by the name of Hank Loomis sent me a message about a strange figure he has captured on his trail camera in the Manistee National Forest. He describes this person as a 'bag lady.' Perhaps you are interested in following up with him?

His contact information is below.

Best of luck to you.

Kind regards,

Irene Whitaker

Lori grabbed her cell phone and dialed the phone number listed for Hank Loomis.

"Heller?" a man answered.

"Hi, is this Hank Loomis?"

"Yeppers."

"Hank, my name is Lori Hicks. I'm calling about the email you sent regarding the image on your trail camera."

"Huh, ain't that a hoot. Had to trek down ter the library to send it. Ain't never sent an email in my life."

"Well, if you're open to it, I'd like to see the video."

"I'm as open as a box with no lid. Come on by."

"Can you tell me where you're located?"

"Yessum, right on the Loomis Junkyard, south side of Furback Trail in Idlewild."

Lori jotted down directions and ended the call. She dialed Ben, but her call went to his voicemail. She texted him.

Lori: Hey, I'm going to see some guy who has a video of something odd in the Manistee Forest. He lives in Idlewild. Want to join me?

After his trip to Hector Dunn's house, Ben had returned home the night before and stayed up until nearly midnight writing a detailed summary of Hector Dunn's connection to the missing girls. He thought of Adrian, the one who'd vanished the evening before. He hoped she was an anomaly, a strange coincidence, and she'd already returned home safe and sound.

He drank coffee and changed into his cycling outfit, wheeled his bike out of the garage and onto the road. His head was a cyclone of thoughts and voices all fighting to be heard. He needed to turn it off, but as he climbed on his bike, another voice cut in, this one reminding him of the posters in the woods. *Stay away from the Manistee Forest*, it seemed to say.

He shut it down and started his ride. The trees were as they'd always been—neutral, neither positive or negative, an aspect of his environment that he encountered every day, necessary for human survival, but of little interest during his bike ride. He moved too fast to notice them deeply, to worry about what their leafy boughs might conceal.

Cycling had been his meditation, his process to bypass the shit that life threw his way, and he'd be damned if fear and superstition stole something so integral away from him.

He took a different route, pedaling away from his house and heading east rather than west.

There was a lake out that way that had once held a resort. In the summer, families flocked from Detroit Metro, packed into their station wagons, ready for a weekend at the warm, weedy lake. The kids would do cannonballs off the docks and the parents would sit beneath umbrellas and straw hats, the dads sipping Scotch and the moms drinking highballs.

Before Ben's dad took the plunge into full alcoholism, he'd told Ben stories of vacationing with his own parents at the now-abandoned resort. He'd amused Ben with tales of his first French kiss with a Jewish girl from Rhode Island who'd spent summers at the lake visiting her grandparents. He'd spoken of the time when he'd gotten banned from the lake gift shop for throwing a water balloon at the owner.

The stories had always struck Ben as the kind of golden realities that only existed in retrospect. If he could have zoomed in on his father's life during those years, he would probably have seen a station wagon filled with fighting kids, his dad pulling his sister's hair. His grandfather white-knuckling the steering wheel as his wife badgered him to slow down.

Ben's grandfather had also been an alcoholic, but they never called him that despite his death at sixty-two from cirrhosis of the liver. Drinking had been viewed differently in those days, as acceptable for everyone, even pregnant women. The term 'alcoholic' was relegated to bums drinking from brown bags on the street. Regular Joe Schmoes with day jobs and families were just kickin' back, relaxing after a long day, week, month.

As he rode, Ben's thoughts grew narrow and then vanished. He breathed, noted the passing pavement and geography, but went blank for a while.

He wasn't sure when he became aware of the engine behind him, the sound of tires eating pavement, going faster than even the cars who sped on the back roads like they were drag racers, not rusted old Chevys and Fords. The opposite side of the road was empty, plenty of space for the car, or truck from the sounds of it, to swing wide around him. Still, Ben inched closer to the shoulder, careful not to angle onto the dirt where his wheel might slide out.

He sensed the vehicle moving closer, heard it. It wasn't passing. It had decelerated, but not much, only enough to keep from slamming into Ben's back wheel, but it was bearing down.

Ben glanced over his shoulder and glimpsed a dark green pickup, a Ford, gaining on him.

Ben swept an arm forward, signaling for the driver to pass. The truck slowed, and then the tires squealed as it accelerated fast. It was coming up close now, so close that Ben could feel the heat of the truck's engine against his back.

He looked back again, but the truck's windshield seemed to be tinted and the glare of the sun obscured anything he might have witnessed behind the dark glass.

"Go! Pass!" Ben shouted, waving his arm again, angrier now. He'd dealt with aggressive drivers before. They were nearly always white guys driving big trucks who were infuriated with the mere concept of a bicycle, let alone having to share the road with one.

Ben pedaled harder, faster, but it was no use, even at his fastest he couldn't outrun the truck.

Ben slowed. He'd pull to the side, park his bike and wait for the asshole to pass. Maybe he'd even memorize his license plate number and report him to the police.

As he decelerated, the truck's bumper nipped his tire.

"What the fuck?" Ben screamed and turned, but the truck hadn't backed off. It was still coming, harder and faster, and Ben felt the impact as the truck slammed into the back of the bike.

Ben went airborne, arms and legs flailing as he sailed toward the ditch. He heard the crunch of metal as the truck devoured his bike, but it was far away, the other sensations taking center stage as he landed with a sickening thud on his shoulder. He heard and felt the snapping of his own bones, the sound merging with the frame of his bicycle being crushed.

The truck screeched to a stop, taillights glowing red in the hazy afternoon sun.

Ben lay crumpled on the roadside. Flames lit the right side of his body, his ribcage and hip especially. Warmth oozed from his chin where it had struck something sharp in the ditch, a rock or broken glass. Still, the physical pains came secondary to his focus on the truck.

The driver had hit him on purpose and now sat idling in the road, contemplating, Ben imagined, finishing him off. Perhaps throwing the truck in reverse and backing right into the high grass at the roadside where Ben lay struggling for breath.

The brake lights glowed, and Ben couldn't wait a second longer. He heaved himself to a crouch and, screaming between his clenched teeth, he hobbled into the woods. Blood roared in his ears and a spell of dizziness swept over him. He staggered against a tree, clutched it for a moment and then moved on, limping, pain searing through his midsection. His right knee pulsed with the beat of his heart.

Behind him, he heard the door of the truck slam. The driver had gotten out.

Sweat poured into his eyes, burning. Everywhere he felt the burning, but he plunged further, dropping to his knees when the pain became too much and crawling on his belly into the ferns that stood nearly two feet high. He lay, unmoving, struggling to rein in his breath and hear, above his own body's outcry, the sound of the man from the truck.

He thought he heard the crunch of twigs underfoot, leaves crackling, but he couldn't be sure and after a while he heard nothing at all.

37

Lori arrived at the Loomis Junkyard and found the weedy driveway to Hank Loomis's trailer. The Prius nearly bottomed out on a hollow in the two-track, but she managed to keep it going.

She parked and climbed out, surveying the trailer suspended on stacks of cinder blocks. A rusted aluminum roof had been erected above the structure and stood on wooden stilts. Lori could see the grooves in the aluminum, thick with dead leaves and grime, and she thought she spotted a tuft of fur, but tried not to look too closely.

A man wearing a grimy ball-cap and equally soiled t-shirt lumbered through the front door and down the steps. "Yous here about the Toyota parts?" he called.

"No. I'm Lori Hicks. I called this morning about your trail cam video."

"Ah, okay. I tried ter tell them po-lice, but them's thinkin' another a'those Loomis boys causin' trouble. It's trespassin is what it is, but theys don't care." He chuckled and leaned a thick hip against a rusted-out pickup. "Ain't never stirred up trouble m'self, but Rocky and Boyd's been kickin' up dirt since they could walk on two legs."

"What did you see in the trail cam?" Lori asked.

"I'll show yer, come on." He straightened up and trudged back toward the front door.

Lori did not want to walk into this man's trailer and yet her feet carried her forward up the rickety wood steps.

Hank opened the screen door, which let out a shriek of metallic protest, and held it open for Lori to walk inside. She considered leaping backwards off the stoop and sprinting back to her car, but the sheer politeness that had been drilled into her would not allow such a rude act, so she stepped into the musty little trailer that stank of over-full ashtrays and cat piss. The likely culprits of the piss, two matching black cats with yellow eyes, jumped down from the counter and twisted around Hank's legs, meowing loudly.

"Git. Go on, git," he barked at the cats, leaning down to shoo them out the door.

He was surprisingly gentle with the cats, running his dirty hands over their sleek backs as they both darted from the trailer and made for the woods beyond.

"I have a cat," Lori admitted, searching for small talk and fighting the urge to plug her nose.

"Them's Black and Blackie. Shown up here years back and never left. They're all right."

"My cat's name is Matilda," Lori said.

"Never understood folks namin' their beasts after people." He continued across the room to a sitting area with a sagging couch. A stack of cardboard boxes took the place of a coffee table. Hank plucked a plastic camouflage box from the surface, flipping open the top to reveal a small dark screen inside. "Boyd bought a dozen a' these last year fer the yard. I put two in the woods to catch thems deer spots, but saw more than thems deer." He clicked around, his thick fingers surprisingly deft on the small buttons. "Ain't used this one since the thing. Thought I'd best keep 'er on here."

Lori watched the screen. A fuzzy gray video appeared. Lori could make out the trees and in the dark background two glowing eyes.

"That's a porcupine," Hank said. "But watch here."

A minute passed and then two. The stench in the apartment made Lori's head swim and she rocked on her feet before reaching for a wall to steady herself.

Hank didn't seem to notice. "'K, here we go."

As Lori watched, something moved in the darkness of the trees, something she could barely see, though it was larger than an animal. It shuffled into view, moving slowly and hunched over. It took her several moments of staring to make sense of the shape. It appeared to be a person walking bent over with a dark tattered blanket over its head.

Except blanket wasn't right. It was more like a cloak made of animal pelts.

Lori thought of the figure in her dream, the woman covered in animal skins and furs.

"Saw this three nights back. Night before that girl went missin' down yonder."

"The girl in Baldwin?"

"Yessum. Might be nothin', might be something.'"

∾

B en heard someone creeping towards him. He blinked his eyes open to see a hunched figure shrouded in animal hides. It seemed to be sniffing at the air. He squinted, but the figure blurred, sweat and maybe blood running into his eyes. He blinked, but the figure was gone. He was not sure if it been there at all.

He had no sense of the passing of time, but the light in the forest looked different. Hours might have gone by.

After a while, he again heard the rustle of leaves.

"Anybody in here? Hello?" a man's voice called.

Ben tried to roll onto his back, but the sting in his hip shouted in angry protest, and Ben groaned. He hadn't passed out exactly, but lay suspended in a red room between waking and sleeping where the forest appeared tinged with a crimson glow and the plants and trees throbbed with the pounding in his temples.

"Help," he gurgled, his mouth filled with saliva.

He thought he might vomit, and clenched his mouth and eyes closed. His interior world rolled and nausea coursed through him. He retched onto the forest floor, recoiling from the smell. Aching, he dragged himself away from the puke.

"Did you hear that?" A woman's voice said.

"Yeah," the man agreed.

Ben heard the man and woman moving closer.

"Here," Ben croaked, lifting one arm awkwardly above the ferns.

The footsteps grew faster, and then he felt a hand touch him gently between the shoulder blades.

"Holy shit, man," the guy said. "We saw your bike and thought, *This is not good*. But you're alive. Esther, go call 911."

"Okay," she said. "Hang in there," she called to Ben.

He heard her retreating. The man's hand still lingered on his back, the touch gentle, reassuring. "How you doing? You okay?"

"Mm-hmm… fractured ribs, possibly fractured hip, I hope not. Meniscus tear on my right knee." Ben huffed the words out, every breath excruciating, but it gave him something to focus on, something beyond the pain itself.

"Okay, okay," the man said. "I'm Tom. Are you a doctor or—"

"Nurse," Ben murmured.

"What's your name? And if it hurts too much to say, then just lie there and be quiet."

"Ben."

"Okay, Ben. I'm sorry this happened to you. Did someone hit you?"

"Yeah."

Another surge of nausea rolled up, and Ben turned his head to the side and puked. He scooted away, grunting in pain. Tom tried to help him, but he could feel the man's fingers were hesitant to take hold of him, as if they might cause further damage.

"They're on their way," the girl yelled.

Minutes passed. Tom didn't speak, and neither did Ben. The girl had returned to the roadside to flag down the ambulance.

Ben counted his breaths, but lost track around six hundred and fifty. He heard the siren in the distance.

"Here we go," Tom murmured, again lighting fingers on Ben's back. "They're almost here. Esther and I were on our way to adopt a dog up in Harrison. It's a mutt, but real sweet-tempered, according to the lady at the shelter. A boxer-pit mix. We were thinking about calling her Custard. We own a little ice cream and custard shop down in Rosebush. Maybe once you're all patched up, you can come in and get a custard— on the house."

Tom talked on, and Ben appreciated the distraction. Soon more bodies were moving through the woods and paramedics laid a spinal board in the grass beside him.

Hands and fingers groped along his back.

"No spinal injury," he told them. "Unless I'm missing it somehow."

"Ben?" Zander's voice spoke.

"Yep, it's me," Ben muttered.

Large, powerful hands gripped Ben and carefully positioned him on his back. The two paramedics lifted him onto the spinal board and strapped his forehead, chest, hips, and legs in place.

Zander looked pale as he worked, glancing at Ben's face now and then.

"Almost done," Zander said as he took one end of the board.

"Ready?" the second man asked.

"Yep, one-two-three-lift," Zander said.

They hoisted the board up, and Ben saw Tom and Esther standing to the side. They were his age or younger, maybe late twenties, and wore matching tie-dye shirts with the words 'The RoseBush Custard Cup is the Place to Be' in blue block letters.

He twitched his fingers at the couple, unable to move any other body parts. "Thank you," he told them.

"Sure thing," Tom said. "I'm so grateful we found you."

"Me too," Ben murmured, though he could no longer see them as Zander and the second paramedic carried him to the ambulance.

"What happened, Ben? Hit-and-run?" Zander asked.

"Yeah," Ben said, as they pushed him into the back of the ambulance. "I got hit by a truck."

And though he hadn't seen the man behind the wheel, he knew who had been driving: Hector Dunn.

38

"Ben…"

He heard Lori's voice and opened his eyes. The sharp pains in the early hours after the accident had dissipated, replaced by something dull and aching. He cringed as he smiled, drawing in a shuddering breath.

"Carmen called me," she told him, squeezing his hand. "I came right away. Does it hurt?" She gestured at his bandaged ribs.

"Less than a lobotomy, worse than a root canal."

"Less than a lobotomy? Have you had one of those?"

He smiled, but only halfway. Any more movement hurt. "No, but if it means I won't feel this anymore I might request one."

"Don't do that. Who's Scully without her analytical brain?"

He raised an eyebrow. "Someone not getting run over by psychopaths."

"You think it was him? That Hector Dunn hit you?"

"I do. I talked to a detective who said they'd be contacting police in Luther to question him, but… I don't know. My faith in their ability to bring him in is suspect. Still no developments on Adrian?"

"No. How long will they keep you?"

"Two days and they're going to release me. I'm pretty banged up, but no major injuries. Guess I was lucky. My bike sure wasn't."

~

L ori followed the news in Baldwin, but they'd still found no trace of Adrian. Two days after the accident, she picked Ben up from the hospital and drove him home.

He sat in her passenger seat with a bag of prescriptions in his lap. "Don't take me home," he said suddenly as she turned onto his street.

"What? Why?"

"He's in for questioning today. He goes in at eleven o'clock."

"Who? Hector Dunn?"

"Yeah."

"What does that mean then?"

"It means he won't be home. I want to go to his house."

Lori shook her head. "That sounds like a terrible idea. Have you looked at yourself lately? You're not exactly in breaking and entering condition."

"I don't want to break in. I just wanted to look around. There are two places he could hide a pickup truck—the garage and the barn. I want to peek in and see if it's there. In and out, five minutes tops. I'll snap a picture with my cell phone and we'll be on the road back here."

Lori thought of Adrian. Her family had posted pictures of her on social media—images of Adrian playing Frisbee with her golden retriever, or wearing her gymnastics leotard. They told stories about how she wanted to be a special education teacher when she grew up, how she volunteered at the animal shelter. Already Lori would have recognized her if she passed her on the street, with her wavy white-blonde hair and her childlike blue eyes. If Hector had taken her, there was a chance, albeit slim, that she was still alive, that she was in his house, bound or trapped.

"Okay," she said.

"Yeah." Ben sat up higher in his seat, slapping his hands together. "Okay, let's do this. What changed your mind?"

"If it's him, if he took Adrian, this might be our only chance to save her," Lori said, driving them out of town.

"That's assuming he doesn't kill them within hours," Ben said. "But you're right. Even if she'd dead, he's not likely to have gotten rid of all the evidence by now. There has to be some trace of her left behind."

39

"You don't have to be involved in this," Ben told Lori when she turned the car onto Hector Dunn's road. "You can drop me off. I'll hobble around to the windows and barn. See if I can find anything."

Lori tilted her head, wanting to say yes, but shaking her head. "No. I'm in. I started all this after all."

"No, you didn't. Dunn started it. And it's time to finish it. If you change your mind, you can wait in the car."

They drove down the desolate road, the house sliding into view.

"That's it?" Lori whispered, though there was no one to overhear them.

"That's it," Ben confirmed. "His van's gone. He should just be sitting down to questioning. Here's what we've got to do. I need you to drop me off by the house, then stay on this road. Just up there, you'll see a two-track on your right. Park there, that way your car is hidden. It's not a long walk, but it's further than I can go quickly right now. I'll meet you back here at the house."

Lori swallowed, sweat trickling down the back of her neck as she turned into Dunn's driveway. Ben climbed out and limped toward the garage.

She drove back onto the road, found the two-track and parked. Lori ran through the woods, wishing she'd worn tennis shoes that morning rather than sandals. When she made her way back to the house, she found Ben peering through garage windows.

"Anything?" she asked.

He shook his head. "It's filled with crap, but no vehicles."

Lori walked to the door at the back of the house, climbed onto the porch and tried the knob.

"It's locked," she whispered to Ben when he came around.

"I figured it would be. Let's check the other doors. I thought we could break a window, but if we do that and find something then he'll know we were here and he'll move it."

"Well, if it's Adrian, we're taking her out of here with us."

"Yeah." Ben spoke the words, but Lori knew he didn't believe they would find Adrian alive in the house.

~

Ben searched for unlocked windows, but found none. He discovered Lori at the side of the house. She turned the knob on a door. It creaked open.

"Holy shit," Ben murmured as it swung in.

"I'll check the house, you go check the barn," Lori said. "Let's meet back here in five minutes."

Ben shook his head. "I don't think we should split up."

She held up a hand. "It's fine. This is faster. Five minutes. Okay?"

He frowned, but nodded. "Be careful," he told her.

Lori slipped into the dim interior of the house. Ben hobbled toward the barn at the back of the property. The doors were closed, but not padlocked. He doubted Hector would hide anything—or anyone, for that matter—inside. Too easy for someone to break in and find it.

Still, he wanted a look in that barn for one very particular reason. He peeked between the slightly ajar barn doors into the gloomy space. It was cluttered. Tools and cardboards boxes and old furniture lay strewn along the edges of the barn's interior on the dirt floor. But in the center stood a large vehicle covered by a dark tarp. The tarp was frayed and holey.

~

L ori crept up the stairs from the laundry room into the kitchen. The house stank of garbage and mildew. She wrinkled her nose, moving through the kitchen and down a dim hall that opened into a living room.

"Adrian?" she called softly.

The only sound was the ticking of a clock.

She opened a door that led to a cellar and hurried down, stepping lightly on the narrow wooden stairs that descended into the darkness. The dirt floor and craggy walls were barely illuminated by a sliver of basement window not coated in grime. There were three windows in total. They'd been covered in black tape. On one window some of the tape had pulled away. It dangled in a slimy-looking black curl that reminded Lori of a snake.

As she searched the murky space, her eye caught on a tall backless bookshelf that blocked a large hole in the wall. Lori stepped closer to the shelf. The book titles startled her: *The Devil in the Shape of a Woman, Satanism and Witchcraft, Grimm's Fairytales.*

"What the hell?" she murmured. Why did this man have no fewer than twenty books about witches?

Lori took a worn leather book, titled *Surviving the Witch,* from the shelf and flipped it open, reading silently.

The witch in a fairytale must be redeemable in some way in order for a lesson to be valuable to the village, but in the truth of life, a cannibal witch who consumes the youth she covets, who steals girls she sees as inherently undeserving of their good fortune, does not need to be redeemable. In fact, on principle, someone who commits such horrors would never be redeemable in the eyes of human beings. So why would such a witch let the children go? What benefit would come to her?

That's why there are few stories of children who have survived such a witch. It would be a great hazard to the witch to release such a child and it would render the witch's original purpose void.

We must also consider how such a child might react if they did escape a cannibal witch. If they survived such an ordeal, we should not underestimate the power of their own mind to make it all go away. To lock such an experience in that dark basement known as the shadow where so many of our repressed memories go. There it will fester until it is ultimately transformed into some other future trauma—such as an inability to enter the woods, to be close to older women, etc. But I would hazard to say that in all likelihood a child taken by this witch never returns.

How long the witch would keep the child is a question I've often pondered. In all the stories of mythical witches, the child must perform certain tasks. In Vasalisa the Wise, the girl must clean Baba Yaga's hut, prepare her meals and separate the rotten corn from the good corn. In Hansel and Gretel, the witch keeps the children to fatten them up. This period of holding implies that it does not satisfy the witch's appetite if she consumes her victim immediately.

Lori flipped to another page and read on.

In fairytales, to face the witch and survive, the heroine must show no fear. The heroine will not beat her, not in the usual way. Instead, she must face her, serve her, and do it with clarity and strength. In a sense, she must impress the witch, earn her respect. The witch can see through layers of the psyche, into the heroine's conscious and unconscious mind, into her darkest desires and her deepest fears.

On the floor above Lori, the clock chimed and she jumped, dropping the book.

~

B en slipped inside the barn and moved to the tarp, grabbed a corner with one hand and lifted it high. A dark green Chevy pickup sat beneath the tarp. Ben's breath left him in a rush and a ripple of wooziness coursed through him. He leaned his good hip against the truck, fighting for breath. He hadn't expected the reaction, the almost panic that arose at seeing the truck again, at reliving the impact as it struck him from behind and sent him airborne.

He registered a sound behind him and straightened up, dropped the tarp and stepped back to the barn door. Through the opening, he spotted dust flying as someone drove fast into the driveway and slammed to a stop.

Hector Dunn had returned.

~

L ori bent and picked the book up. As she placed it on the shelf, she got a whiff of something rancid drifting from the hole in the wall. She reached for her cell phone to use the flashlight, but found her back pocket empty. She'd left it in the car.

She turned and walked the perimeter of the basement, found an old box of long wooden matches. She returned to the bookcase and lit a match, reached with trembling fingers between the shelves so she could illuminate what lay in the hole.

She moved closer, peering into the opening. It was a hollowed-out space, much too low for standing, with a dirt floor and walls. On the floor lay a heap of dirty-looking sheets. Lori stared at them for a long time.

Something poked from beneath the corner of one sheet. Gradually she understood that it was a girl's tennis shoe, a pink and yellow high-top sneaker faded with time. She'd seen the shoe before and she knew where. It had been the shoe Meredith Abram had been wearing the day she vanished.

As she stared at the shoe and the shape beneath the sheets, Lori started to sway from side to side. Black dots danced behind her eyes and the scared voice, the Lorraine in the woods voice, screamed at her to run, to get out. She was standing in the house of a murderer staring at what had to be the body of a thirteen-year-old girl who'd vanished decades before.

In a distant part of her mind, Lori registered the sound of a door banging open above her. Footsteps hammered across the floor and she knew it was not Ben, could not be Ben, because he was injured and couldn't walk fast.

She lurched away from the bookshelf, searching for someplace to hide, looking again at the tiny windows. If she could manage to get one open, she doubted she could fit through to get out.

Lori heard him moving down the hallway above her. The door to the basement had been closed. Lori had opened it, and she searched her memory for whether she'd closed it.

Lori didn't think so.

Her body quivered with fear as she shuffled to the wall, pressing her back against the cold stone. Her bladder felt heavy, her knees weak, and again child Lorraine pleaded with her to try for the window, bash the glass and wriggle to freedom, but Lori knew she'd never fit through.

Above her the footsteps stopped and then they started again, but not across. They were coming down, one heavy boot-fall after the next, pounding down the wooden stairs.

Hector's shoulders were hunched and his face was red. Anger

twisted his features, and Lori froze as he stepped off the last stairs into the basement.

Her breath wheezed out, and his head jerked up, his eyes bulging when they landed on her. He didn't move, didn't speak, and then after a long, sickening span as he appraised her, he smiled.

"Ask and he shall receive," Hector muttered, fingering the zipper on his jacket. Up and down, it went, his hands and legs fidgety as he bounced, locking her in place with narrowed, predatory eyes.

Lori stood statuesque, as if by not moving she would vanish before him, but she didn't. She was pinned in place. He didn't have a weapon, but he did have a hundred pounds on her. He wasn't fit, but was tall and barrel-chested. Her eyes drifted down to his large, cumbersome work boots. One kick and she'd be unconscious.

"I… my cat is missing," she stammered. "I live just down the road and she… she tears people's screens and breaks in sometimes. She… she's a real piece of work." The lie sounded even less believable when it spilled from her lips.

Hector Dunn cocked his head to the side, nodding as if he bought it. He stepped closer, his bulk taking up more of the space than seemed possible. "Here, kitty, kitty," he sang.

Lori started toward him. She'd just brush by and make a run for it.

He almost let her, but before she'd made it to the steps, he caught her upper arm hard in his meaty fist.

"Hold on there, little kitty," he whispered, his breath sour. "Don't I know you from somewhere?" He pushed her against the wall, pressing a knee between her legs, trapping her. He stared down into her face. "Yeah… I think so. I think you were one of them girls, them girls in the woods."

Lori clenched her eyes shut, panic seizing her. She couldn't run, couldn't fight back. Her only hope was Ben, who could barely walk. An unbidden image rose in her mind of two more bodies tossed beneath those dirty sheets, two more bodies that would never be found.

She searched for a way to stall him. "Why do you have the books? The ones about witches?" she sputtered, gesturing toward the book-shelf. She instantly regretted the question. She'd just given away that she likely knew what lay behind it.

He stared at her for a long time, unblinking, and she sensed his mind churning behind his dark eyes. "Of all the things you might have come to ask, you're interested in some books."

"Did you take Bev? Was it you? Or…"

"Or what?" He smirked. "Was it something else? Something that makes me look tame in comparison?"

He lifted a callused finger and traced it down Lori's cheek. She squirmed beneath his touch.

"My mother loved to read," he murmured gazing toward the books. "You might have even called her obsessed with stories. She read all the time. A lot of people thought she was an only child." He shook his head. "No, no, she had a sister. A prettier sister, smarter, faster."

"What happened to her?" Lori whispered, fearing she already knew.

"One day she didn't come out of the forest," he said, "and my mother was not so very sad. For days her sister was gone. They searched and searched and then on the fifth day, she appeared. She was not beautiful anymore. Her hair, once glossy and black, was white and dirty like the wool of a lamb who'd been out to pasture. Two fingers of her right hand had been severed as well as her right foot. Her face, her once-beautiful face, was withered and gray."

"I don't understand," Lori whispered.

"Don't you?"

"What… what took her?"

He moved his face close to her. His breath blew hot on her cheek and he sniffed her neck. "I think you already know."

Lori screamed and reached her free arm up, jabbing her fingernails into Hector's right eye. He howled and brought his head forward hard, smashing it against hers. A dazzle of black spots exploded behind her eyes, but she twisted sideways, falling on her hands and knees.

He grabbed her long hair and jerked her back. Lori cried out, trying to wrench away. He didn't release her and she shrieked at the tearing sensation in the back of her skull. She thought he'd tear her hair from her head.

He dragged her, hand sunk into her hair, up the stairs. Lori stumbled to stay on her feet, holding his fist in her hands and trying to loosen his grip.

Hector topped the stairs and stepped through the doorway, yanking Lori behind him.

"Please," she murmured. "I won't tell anyone. I swear." She knew her words fell on deaf ears.

As he dragged her into the hall, she caught sight of Ben.

Ben held a rifle in his hand, lifting it high.

Hector didn't have time to react. Ben swung the handle of the rifle and smashed it against the side of Hector's head. Hector teetered, releasing Lori's hair. He tried to take a step toward Ben, but his right leg gave out and he crashed into the wall.

Ben turned the gun around and pumped the rifle.

"Move and you're dead," he told him.

Lori crawled past Hector, who seemed to have lost consciousness. Blood rushed from the wound in the side of his head, pooling on the floor.

In the distance, she heard sirens.

40

The day passed in a blur of police and questions and a brief stint in the back of an ambulance, while a paramedic gingerly touched Lori's hair and declared that Hector had not actually ripped more than a few strands from her scalp.

After what felt like hours in the too bright police station, Lori and Ben, both haggard, walked to her car in the dark parking lot.

"Look up," Ben said as she opened her driver's door.

The vast night sky was lit with a billion flecks of silver.

Lori let out a shuddering breath and stared up, the horror of the day slipping away for a moment as the infinite swept her out of her small world.

She shifted her attention back to Ben.

He smiled. "Let's get out of here."

$\sim$

When Ben asked her to spend the night, she said yes.
            They walked in, both exhausted, and collapsed on his bed fully clothed.

Lori fell into a fitful sleep, waking the following morning with a headache and a tender spot on her forehead where Hector had smacked his skull against hers.

She slipped from the bed and walked downstairs, overhearing Ben on the phone.

"There were two though? I see. Okay, and no chance he's getting out? Good. Call me if you hear anything else. Thanks. Bye."

Lori walked into living room, rubbing her sleepy eyes. Ben sat on the couch.

"Hey, you're awake," Ben said, smiling.

"Any news?" she asked.

"Yeah, that was Zander. His brother has a friend on the force in Luther. They're keeping a tight lid on it and obviously it's early, but so far, they've found two sets of remains in Dunn's basement. They've tentatively identified one as Meredith Abram based on clothing, but it will take weeks for dental records."

"Only two though?" Lori asked, sitting on the couch beside Ben and folding her legs beneath her.

"It's a huge piece of property. The important thing is that piece of shit is sitting in jail and he won't be walking free again in this lifetime."

"We got him," Lori murmured.

"Yeah." Ben sighed, staring into space. She saw a shadow of something pass over his face, sadness perhaps.

"You finally caught the bad guy, so why do you look bummed out?" she asked.

Ben gazed at her, unblinking. "I guess... in some weird way, I don't want it to end."

"The search? The hunt?"

He shook his head. "Us. You and me and this whole insane last couple of weeks. It's been mad and yet... I almost feel sick that it's over, that tomorrow I won't be texting you to say we need to jump in the car and drive west to Scottville or Reed City."

"It's not over yet. There's a long path ahead now. Questioning, an eventual trial."

Ben took her hand and rubbed his fingers across her knuckles. "And maybe some fun stuff too."

She smiled. "I'll stay with you again tonight if you want," she said. "Play nurse to your patient. Though I'm afraid you'll have to tell me what to do."

He grinned and kissed her. "Sponge baths mostly."

The kiss was long and Lori wanted more when it ended.

"Let's go upstairs," she said.

Ben stood and took her hand. "Are you sure?" he asked.

"Very."

∼

The following day, Ben insisted on making breakfast, though Lori wasn't hungry and his throbbing knee caused him to sit every few minutes, which left her to flip the pancakes. She enjoyed it, the ease with which they'd woken together.

Memories of the day before scattered through her thoughts. Both of them touching each other so gingerly, afraid to hurt the other. And after they'd made love, he'd slept holding her hand. They'd spent the entire day in bed.

As Ben finished making pancakes, he talked excitedly about places they would go when his body was healed. "You've never been to Kitch-iti-kipi?" he exclaimed. "Oh, we're going. As soon as my knee heals up. You've never seen such clear water."

Lori's cell phone rang and she answered it. "Hi, Mom," she said.

"How are you, honey? Did you sleep okay?"

"Yeah, thanks." Lori had called her mother the day before and filled her in on all the harrowing details. Rebecca had wanted her to come right home, but Lori had insisted she was staying at Ben's.

"And today? Are you coming here to my and Grandma's house?"

Lori wandered out of the room and onto the screened-in front porch. "Probably not, Mom, but tomorrow for sure and then I'll give you more details."

"All right." Her mother sighed. "They haven't... they haven't found Bev at that man's house, have they?"

"No, not yet, but if I hear anything I'll call you first."

Lori walked back into the kitchen. Ben had finished his pancakes and two of her uneaten ones as well.

"I've got to go see my mom today. She wants to hear about every-thing," Lori lied.

"Sure, yeah. That makes sense. I'm going to hang out here, I guess. Do some of that R&R the doctor recommended."

∼

Lori had found the woman online. She was mentioned on the Find a Grave website for Hector's mother, who had died years before. The obituary for his mother read, 'Survived by her son, Hector William Dunn, and her sister, June Kimberly Dunn.'

41

Lori found an address for June Kimberly Dunn at the Hidden Pines Retirement Home in Harrison, Michigan. When she requested to see June Dunn at the reception area the woman looked at her as if she'd gone mad.

"June Dunn?" the receptionist named Heather, repeated back to Lori.

"Yes, please."

"One moment." Heather picked up a phone and dialed. "Miss Dunn? Yes, I'm sorry. I know that, but you have a visitor. Can she—" The receptionist frowned and set the phone on its case. "She hung up on me, but she didn't say you can't come up. Take the elevator to the fourth floor. Miss Dunn is in room 406."

Lori rode the elevator to the fourth floor. The hallway floors had been freshly mopped and plastic caution signs were located every few feet as she walked to June's room.

Lori knocked and waited. Minutes passed with no answer. She knocked again.

Finally, the door creaked open and a bony woman with a wilted face glared out at her.

"Hi, Miss Dunn. My name is Lori Hicks. I'm so sorry to bother you. I hoped to ask you a few questions."

The woman leaned heavily on her cane as she moved from the front door of her apartment back through the kitchen and into a dark hallway. She said nothing, but Lori followed behind her.

Miss Dunn shambled into a dark sitting room and collapsed into the only chair that occupied the space. Lori hovered by the television that played an old black and white movie on silent.

The woman pinned Lori with her shrewd gray eyes. Her tangled, yellow-white hair clung to her mottled scalp. She was rail-thin and her gnarled hands clutched her cane in front of her. "Go on then. What do you want?"

"Well, it's a long story." Lori smiled, but the woman's glare only deepened. "I guess I'll just get straight to it. I met your nephew, umm… Hector, and he said, well, he said that when you were a child something happened to you."

"Not something," the woman hissed. "The witch."

"It's real then?" Lori said, feeling suddenly breathless. "Did you beat her?"

The woman sneered. She rested her cane against the wall and pulled up the bottom of her skirt, revealing one leg that ended in a gnarled stump. "Not before I fed her."

Lori stared at the missing limb in disgust, unable to hide her revulsion and disbelief. "But you got away. How?"

"I took her eye."

Lori shuddered.

The woman laughed and shook her head. "You're not ready for her. I can smell your fear. So can she." The woman started to stand, pushing her scrawny arms on the armrest of her chair.

"Wait, please. A girl just vanished. Adrian Kranz." Lori fumbled in her bag and took out the picture she'd printed of Adrian. "Please, if there's any chance she's still alive—"

"Oh, she's still alive," the woman rasped, staring at the photo, though her features did not soften. "Five days. Five days until she'll be ready, but you… you're not strong enough. You're weak and empty and filled with doubt."

"How do I find her? How did you find her?"

The woman cackled. "You don't find her. She finds you."

"The police arrested your nephew. Did you know that?" Lori asked, sure she was violating some confidence by telling the old woman.

"Good," she muttered.

"Do you know why?"

The woman glared at her. "Because he likes to play witch."

"I'm sorry, he likes to play witch?"

An ugly smile creased the corners of the woman's mouth. "When I was a girl, we played a game called Boogeyman. One child was the boogeyman and the other children ran and screamed and hid. In Hector's life the Boogeyman was not a man at all. The boogeyman was the witch... Some children grow to fear such things, others long to become them."

"Hector murdered girls so that he could be like the witch?"

The woman scowled. "Some children are born rotten. They will only ever be rotten."

"Did he... help her somehow? Help the witch find little girls?"

The woman slammed a fist on the arm of her chair, startling Lori. "You think she needs Hector Dunn? That good-for-nothing worm?"

Lori heard hatred in the woman's voice, but also a certain grudging admiration for the witch.

"He had contact with some of the girls, with their families..." Lori murmured.

"The world is small, girl. It's small and filled with evil. The kind of evil that knows all, sees all, and takes what it wants."

∾

B efore Lori returned to Ben's house, she visited a novelty jewelry shop that sold cheap costume jewelry as well as purses and hair pieces. She searched among the necklaces, found the one she wanted and paid cash at the register.

When she arrived at Ben's, he was in the kitchen cooking dinner.

"Shouldn't I be doing that?" she asked when she walked in. "I did sign up to be the nurse after all."

"The sponge-bath nurse," he said. "And I might need one of those later."

Lori smiled and stopped in front of him, taking a deep breath and gathering herself for what she wanted say.

"What is it?" he asked, forehead creasing.

"Today I met with June Dunn. She was Hector Dunn's aunt and a long time ago she was playing in the woods and the witch abducted her."

Ben had been opening a packet of shredded cheese. He stopped and set it on the counter, studying Lori. "Are you serious right now?"

"Completely. She showed me the stump where her foot used to be.

When I was in Hector's basement there was a shelf filled with books about witches. I asked him about them. He told me about June. I don't think Hector took Adrian Kranz. I think the witch did and I think she's still alive, but not for long."

Ben laughed. "Do you hear yourself? You can't possibly believe that an evil forest witch is behind the abductions. You said yourself it was Dunn, we nailed him."

"What kind of human being could have abducted all the girls?" Lori demanded. "Bev was in a tree, thirty feet off the ground. What man could have climbed into a tree and kidnapped a fourteen-year-old girl without making a sound or leaving a trace?"

"Lori, twenty-five thousand kids go missing in this country every year. I bet if we looked into those cases, there'd be a hell of a lot who disappeared without a trace."

"It wasn't Dunn. He didn't get Bev. I know it."

"You found Meredith Abram in his basement. What further proof do you need?"

"Meredith was the one girl outside the five-year cycle. He had those books, Ben. His aunt, his mother's sister, she... she lived through it."

"He's a pedophile, a liar and a murderer. You can't believe anything he says. He's filling your head with this shit to throw you off the scent, to keep you from finding—"

"From finding what? It's not in our hands now. Detectives are searching his property. What would be the point of his misdirection?"

"It's a form of control. He likes to manipulate people. He wanted to scare you down there. He wanted you to question what was right in front of your eyes."

"It's so much more than that, Ben. I was drawing that witch after Bev disappeared. I've been dreaming about her. I visited a guy in Idlewild who had a video of her on his trail camera."

Ben stared at her, puzzled. "I'm sorry, what? You met someone who claimed to have a video of her?"

"Yes."

Ben frowned and touched his ribs as if they felt tender.

"Are you okay?" she asked him.

"Yeah, just due for another painkiller. I might have to go lie down for a bit."

"I'll finish this," Lori said. "You go rest."

42

Ben woke, startled. His stomach twisted inside. From downstairs he heard the radio playing. He couldn't make out the words, but he knew just the same...

Every step you take...

His palm hurt. Something sharp poked into the soft flesh and when he lifted his fist and opened it, the unicorn necklace fell onto the bedspread. A pinprick of blood ran from his palm where it had cut into his flesh.

He lumbered down the stairs and into the kitchen. Lori had left a note, a single sheet of paper folded in half with the words, 'I have to try...'

He stared at her message, willing it to make sense, and reluctantly he understood. She'd gone to Baldwin, back to the forest. She'd believed the crazy stories of Hector Dunn and his aunt.

"Damn it," he muttered, sinking onto a stool and staring at the papers on his counter.

Lori had been doing her own research. While he'd been hunting for sex offenders and pedophiles, Lori had been hunting for proof of the witch.

Ben gazed at the stories, each occupying its own neat square on the table. Caricature witches leered at him, their crooked teeth and warty noses comical and unnerving. The one thing every image had in common was an ugly misshapen tree looming in the background. As he considered the trees, another tree arose in his mind.

The tree in the center of the clearing surrounded by the missing person's posters. The deformed tree that looked like it had been dead for longer than it was alive.

How much of a headstart did Lori have? How long had he been sleeping? It didn't matter. It was a fantasy, a disturbing one, but Lori would drive to Baldwin, get spooked by the night forest and return. He could sit and wait.

But he couldn't.

He stuffed his feet into his tennis shoes and walked to his car, cursing her under his breath.

∿

Lori parked on Tanglewood Drive and turned off the engine. The murky woods hulked beside her. She took the necklace from the box, gazing at the shimmering bell before sliding the chain over her head and stepping from the car.

As she cut through the trees, she lifted the bell and rang it, shuddering as the tinkle echoed softly in the forest. The rational part of her mind reminded her of how ridiculous this venture was. The frightened part of her mind shrieked for her to run back to the car. But she shut the voices down, set her jaw and continued forward.

She thought of what Dr. Chadwick had said about active daydreaming, about going back into the dream. She thought she might be able to put herself there and by doing so step from this world into the world of the witch.

She let her eyes drift half-closed and conjured details of the dream, the red misty forest, the sound of crunching…

Floating, barely aware of the night sounds around her, Lori walked on. Now and then she heard the tinkle of the bell around her neck, though she hadn't lifted it.

Gradually, she registered that the warm red mist no longer occupied her imagination. It surrounded her now, as real as the sky above and the earth below. It was the same forest and yet it was different.

In front of her, a hut sat atop a nest of gnarled roots. Skulls loomed from stick-spikes surrounding the house.

Lori walked up the roots like steps to the outer door. She did not knock, but pushed inside.

～

Ben parked behind Lori's car on Tanglewood Drive. He'd dialed her number a dozen times, but she'd never answered and now, as he walked by her car, he spotted her cell phone lying on the passenger seat.

He trudged through the woods, flashlight scanning, creeped out by Lori's stories despite his best efforts to write them off as centuries-old myths written to scare little children into behaving.

He walked to the tree, to the spot he thought it had been, but it wasn't there.

"What the heck?" He'd been so preoccupied with thoughts of the stories he'd not been paying as close attention as he'd thought and must have gone the wrong way.

～

Lori's breath caught as she stepped into the hut.

The witch sat in a crude wooden chair, gnawing a bone, gristle still hanging from the tip. Her sharp yellow teeth, moldy green at the gumline, poked and plucked at the meat. Above her maw, a dull black eye watched Lori. The other was a pit of shriveled flesh. The witch's good eye was quick. It darted around the strange hut, a swiveling snake eye that moved in ways human eyes could not.

Long curled fingernails, brittle and brown, extended from her crooked hands and she tap-tapped them on the arm rest of her chair. Her tongue was coated in moss, hair like tangled branches, brittle and sharp, a medusa of the forest.

As in the fairytales, a black cauldron hung above a hearth filled not with wood, but bones. Darkness stirred in the black fatty liquid. It released a putrid odor, a smell of death and fear, a scent that made Lori's stomach twist and churn.

～

B en walked on, a fever stealing in. Sweat rolled down his face. His knee and hip throbbed and the ribs on his right side hummed.

He thought of the stories of the hikers, of Lori's own experience of growing sick when they walked through the forest, and he sensed what it was. A defense, a way to keep him back, turn him away from what lay ahead.

Saliva filled his mouth and he spit it in the grass. He walked faster, though his knee shrieked and his hip muttered and his ribs tried to keep the breath out. The nausea hit in a deluge and he bent over and vomited. He wiped his mouth with the back of his hand and continued forward.

"Ben..." The voice came from behind him, small and girlish, but oddly grating. It didn't sound right, the distorted voice so familiar and yet altogether not.

He turned, dread and anticipation lighting firecrackers in his head.

Summer stood in the forest behind him. Her form was tremulous and shifting, her face solid and then decayed and then bone and back to solid. Her lips moved but her words didn't line up and he saw a blackness so dark between her lips that he stumbled back. His stiff leg and hip didn't appreciate the sudden movement and he grunted as they seized and sent a molten flash through the right side of his body.

He fell backward, horrified as Summer streaked toward him. Ben landed hard on his butt and elbows. Pain pinged through the bones of his elbows and into his shoulders, but the fern-covered ground cushioned his fall.

He snapped his eyes open, expecting her to be gone, but she loomed over him. The stench of her rolled over him and he clamped a hand over his mouth and nose. She smelled like something dead, rotten, but sickly sweet. He gagged, but didn't throw up, crawling away from her.

"Don't go, Ben. Come with me. Come with me and we can be together forever." Her whisper came out louder, fiercer, but he struggled back to his feet and ran, though his right leg barely bent and he groaned with every breath. He ran until he could no longer smell her or hear her.

∼

L ori searched the hut for Adrian, but could not find her.
The witch extended her fingers and curved her long finger-

nails around the arm of the chair. For a moment they seemed to grow thicker and sharper, losing their curl and extending out toward Lori like knives.

"Do you know why I chose these girls?" the witch asked, and her voice rasped in Lori's head like a thousand hornets jostling against a windowpane. "I chose them for their wild spirit, untamed, unhindered. That is a gift that comes easily, unfairly to beautiful girls. But the ugly girls, they must take it, wrestle it out of the black void and consume it."

Lori wanted to clamp her hands over her ears, but knew she would continue to hear the witch's voice in her head. Lori was in her world now and the rules of the ordinary world no longer applied.

"You know me, girl," the witch went on. "You know this hunger. But they will fill you up, fill you up in ways that nothing ever could, fill that gaping black pit in your soul. You'd never want again. Never hunger again."

Lori's eyes flickered to the pile of bones and though she tried to look back at the witch, things had begun to take shape and she could not tear her gaze away. Strips of fabric clung to the bones, manes of glossy hair to sightless skulls, and then other things, little colorful things, trinket and shiny bits.

And then there amidst the bones, Lori saw Adrian. Tear-streaked, eyes swollen, frozen in terror. It was the girl Lori had seen in the posters and yet... she looked as if she'd aged. She held one arm against her chest. Lori stared at the hand resting against Adrian's t-shirt, realizing two of the girl's fingers were gone. All that remained were bloody stumps where her pinkie and ring finger had been.

Terror sharp and bright blazed in Lori's chest and she stared, dazed at the bloody knuckles on Adrian's hand. Her mind, moments before a torrent of thoughts, went blank.

Haltingly, Lori dragged her gaze from the gore and back to the bits of jewelry tangled in the bones. Her eyes bore into one piece, a shiny silver orb. Beverly Silva's harmony bell, her angel caller, lay in the carnage.

On stilted legs, Lori walked to the bones and fell to her knees. She lifted the bell and started to ring it.

43

At last Ben gazed upon the ugly tree with its twisted branches and its thick trunk. Wart-like nodules protruded from the rotted bark.

Wincing, Ben climbed up the tree and shined his light down into the center, into the hollowed-out trunk. Ashy clumps of bark met his gaze, but as he studied it, he realized it was not bark, but bones that filled the hollow in the tree.

Bones and cloth and hair. The topmost hair was pale, almost as white as the bones themselves. Tangled within that hair, he saw a discolored whistle, once red, now faded to a pale pink.

He stared and stared, paralyzed, transfixed, his legs as thick and dense as the other trees in the forest. He was unable to think through to the next step, unable to tear his eyes from the horror hidden in the ugly old tree.

And though it was impossible, he heard the far-off tinkle of a bell and knew it was down, down deep beneath the bones.

～

The witch did not appear to move, but suddenly she was there beside Lori. She bypassed her, reached a skeletal hand for Adrian, clutched her and dragged her toward the cauldron. Adrian screamed and writhed and though the witch looked little more than bones, she was stronger than any human man.

"No," Lori screamed and stood, searching for the way to beat the witch. She grabbed hold of Adrian's other arm and pulled.

Adrian shrieked, tears pouring down her face. The witch's face was not a mask of fury, but of pure delight. She delighted in Adrian's screams, in Lori's fear. They would rip Adrian in two if they both continued to pull.

Lori let go of Adrian's arm and dove toward the pile of bones. She swept the trinkets, the witch's trophies, in her arms and plunged through the doorway out of the hut.

∼

B en heard the ringing of the bell and he reached into the tree and dug. He pulled out bones in handfuls and let them rain onto the earth behind him. He gagged when pale hair slid off a sightless skull. He scooped bones and bark until he was bent over, his top half upside down in the tree, but he didn't dare go further. He'd get stuck. He could die that way.

Ben cursed and climbed out of the tree, searched the ground until he found a strong, sharp stick.

He hacked and tore at the rotten tree, bark crumbling away, bones falling from the hole he'd created, and still that far-off tinkling beckoned him deeper and deeper.

∼

A s Lori fled the hut, she heard an inhuman shriek behind her. The witch was furious that Lori had stolen her trophies.

Lori tripped and fell, the jewelry skittering across the moist ground.

The witch materialized in front of her. Her mouth a gaping black hole. The scream that had started in the hut continued. Lori thought her skull might burst and she clamped her hands over her ears.

The witch grabbed hold of Lori's arms. Her touch blazed against Lori's skin, singeing her flesh.

Lori grabbed at the ground searching for anything to use as a weapon. Her fingers skittered across the jewelry and landed on the tiny golden unicorn with its sharp horn.

As the witch dragged Lori to her feet, Lori jammed the horn into the witch's good eye. The witch released Lori as purple-black blood spurted from her eye-socket.

The witch spun back toward her shack.

The hut and the roots beneath it shook and crumbled. The entire structure collapsed in clumps of bark and bone.

Adrian leapt from wreckage.

Lori ran to her. "Run!" she screamed into the girl's ear.

Lori pulled her away. Behind them the witch continued to howl.

Ben's fingers closed around a spinal cord and a gleam shimmered in the flashlight. He stared at it. It was gold. The head of a unicorn, its once bright ruby eye dulled and dark. He dropped the spine and fell heavily to his knees, but he didn't stop.

He dug at the roots of the tree that were black and rotted. An overwhelming stench poured from the hole and bile rose into Ben's throat, but he swallowed it back and dug.

They ran until Lori's legs were so weak, she had to slow. Adrian's hand was slick in her own and her wails had turned to whimpers.

Lori blinked ahead of them. She could hear something, panting, but the forest had again changed. The red mist no longer sheathed the ground. It was the forest she knew again, dark but familiar, and a light shone up ahead.

"No," Adrian whispered, trying to tug away, but Lori urged her on.

They stepped into a clearing. Ben sat on the ground, face glistening and dirty, a flashlight discarded at his side. A black hole lay before him and behind it a pile of bones.

44

Ben leapt to his feet grabbing Lori around the waist.

"No," she murmured. "Help Adrian. Her hand."

He pulled away. Adrian still clung to Lori, but she allowed Ben to look at her hand.

He said nothing though dismay flashed across his face. When he took Adrian's wrist in his fingers, she winced, but didn't cry out.

"They're not bleeding anymore," he murmured, tilting her hand to the side. "But we need to call an ambulance. Do you…" He glanced at Lori, "have the missing appendages?"

Adrian eyes drifted closed and she gave a slight shake of her head. "She ate them," she whispered.

~

Lori blinked at the ground in front of her, the bones and dirt coppery red and rancid-smelling. Ben had stepped away. He was on the phone with the police, telling them to come to the woods off Tanglewood Drive. They'd found skeletons, several of them.

"What do we tell them?" Adrian whispered, holding Lori's hand so tight her fingers had gone numb.

. . .

"I don't know…" Lori murmured, looking at the forest beyond them. Her fear had gone and she could not say why. Had the witch been annihilated when Ben destroyed the tree or had she merely fled, moving undetected through her own world to take up residence elsewhere?

"They'll never believe us," Adrian continued, tears streaming down her cheeks. "They'll say we made it up, that we're insane."

"We both saw it. It's pretty hard to deny a story when two people experienced it. And your hand. How can we explain that away?"

"It's not that hard. I don't think we should tell. Okay? I want you to say you found me in the woods and I was out of it and… I'll just say I don't remember. Maybe I had an accident and lost my fingers. The blood loss made me disoriented."

"Adrian. Why?"

"Because!" Her voice rose higher. "Because my… my mother says I exaggerate and I make things up and if we tell them this… they'll say I made it all up and I'm trying to get attention and—"

"Okay… shh." Lori hugged Adrian closer.

~

It was a hard story to tell and it fell to Ben to do it Among the three he was the most level-headed and, ultimately, he hadn't been there, he hadn't stepped into that other world.

"We were walking," Ben told the investigator, "and we saw this strange, creepy-looking tree. We were looking for Adrian. We'd been hiking in this forest the evening she went missing, so we decided to come back. I knock down dead trees all the time. It's something I learned to do as a kid with my dad. You knock them down safely so they don't fall on some unsuspecting guy who's taking a stroll in the woods. Anyway, I started trying to knock this one down and it began to crumble and bones started falling out. We kept pulling it apart and more appeared."

He swallowed and glanced at Lori, who sat on the ground beside Adrian, her arm wrapped tight around the girl's shoulders.

"While we were breaking apart this tree, we heard someone calling for help. That's when we found Adrian. She was crying and she'd been injured."

Another policewoman stood at Lori and Adrian's side. She'd tried twice unsuccessfully to get Adrian to speak with her privately, but Adrian refused to let go of Lori.

The policewoman squatted down, resting a hand on Adrian's arm. "Do you remember anything, honey? Anything before they found you?"

Adrian shook her head. "I... no. It's just blank. I was walking in the woods with my friend Diane and then there's nothing until tonight."

"Okay. Maybe some of it will come back. Right now you need medical attention." The policewoman shifted her gaze to Lori. "You're welcome to ride in the ambulance."

45

Lori sat in her bay window gazing for a few final moments at her apartment. Cardboard boxes sat stacked against the wall.

"Knock-knock," Ben said, opening her door and stepping inside.

"Hi." Lori stood.

"You're all packed? I told you I'd help."

"I know, but I needed something to fill the time. Now I'm trying to psych myself up for moving back in with my mom."

"I told you to move it with me." Ben kissed her.

"Maybe someday."

"Should we start loading these then?" he asked.

"Wait. Did you talk to Zander's brother about what the police found in the woods?"

He nodded. "How much do you want to know?"

"All of it."

"Okay... in total they found nine skeletons in the tree."

"Nine?"

"Yeah," he said. "They haven't identified all of them. Six are still Jane Does, but they've been able to use dental records to confirm Bev, Summer, and Bella. They don't have dental records yet on Peyton. They're trying to track down her parents. Five of the nine skeletons were older, all likely girls who were murdered in the 40s and 50s. No identification, but they do have a unique piece of jewelry connected to a twelve-year girl who disappeared in 1944. Marilyn Ashwood. They're trying to track down her parents to get a DNA sample, but they don't know if they're living or deceased."

"What about the... the old woman?" They'd stopped referring to her as the witch in the days after that night. Each time Lori spoke the word she feared she might conjure the evil back from wherever she had gone.

"One hand and a few teeth from a very old skeleton is all that Zander's brother knew. I think the rest of her skeleton just... turned to ash when I was pulling out the others. "

Lori sighed. She'd already known that. Ben had told her and she'd seen it for herself, but still she'd hoped that investigators would uncover something that proved the witch had existed.

"They've also identified the other body in Hector Dunn's basement."

"Who was it?"

"A girl from the upper peninsula. Her name was Polly Snyder. She disappeared in 1996 after going for a bike ride."

Lori sighed. "I guess it's finally over."

Weeks had passed since that terrifying night in the woods. Lori and Adrian had spoken daily. Adrian's family knew nothing of what had transpired during Adrian's absence. Adrian clung to the story that she remembered nothing, but in secret she told Lori about minutes that crawled like years and hours that passed in seconds.

Her time with the witch had been so bizarre it was nearly impossible to retell. Some of it was tedious and some of it was delightful, hours shoveling black flesh into the cauldron followed by hours sitting down to a feast of fresh fruit and wine. The witch never spoke, but Adrian had heard her thoughts and likewise the witch had heard Adrian's. Some moments the witch had been kind and consoling, in others she had been cruel and venomous.

Adrian remembered vividly the loss of her fingers. She'd woke to find the witch crouching beside her. Before Adrian could move, the witch had lifted Adrian's hand to her mouth and bitten both fingers off at her knuckle.

On the final day, Adrian had known her end was coming. She had resigned herself to death long before Lori arrived.

Now Lori parked the car and turned to Adrian. "You're sure you're up for this?" she asked.

Adrian nodded, fiddling with the little bell Lori had given her that night. It was the bell Lori had worn into the forest, but it no longer made a sound. "Yes. I need to do it. It's starting to fade. Everything that happened... it's slipping away."

"For me too," Lori admitted.

Lori climbed from the car, walked to the office door and rang the green buzzer.

Irene Whitaker opened the door wearing a jewel-colored tunic over black leggings. "Come in, come in. I was so happy you called, Lori. And you must be Adrian." She took Adrian's uninjured hand and held it tight, looking into her face. "You are a very brave girl."

They followed Irene to her table in the back and began to tell their stories.

EPILOGUE

"Sixty-two days until we meet in Italy," Ben said, picking up Lori's carry-on bag.

"I'm looking forward to it," she told him.

"But you're off to Machu Picchu first," he said.

"Yep. Time to face some of those fears, live some of those big dreams," she murmured, leaning into him as he rested his cheek against hers.

"Okay, then this is goodbye for now," he whispered.

"Goodbye for now."

He kissed her, but she didn't melt into him in the way she wanted. She was leaving on a two-month solo trip and, though it had been hard, she'd refused to get lost in Ben Shaw. She needed to find herself first.

As he drew away, he paused, kissed her ear and whispered, "Stay out of the woods."

She smiled, picked up her bag, and blew him a kiss as she walked backwards to check in for her flight to Peru.

Sixteen days later, Ben opened his mailbox, drew out his mail and flipped past an ad for used cars, a bill for his internet, and lastly a postcard.

He gazed at the photograph of the ancient Incan civilization of Machu Picchu. He flipped it over and read Lori's words.

Ben,

I can't believe I waited so long to see this place. It's glorious. I rode the Inca Rail from the Sacred Valley up the mountain. It was otherworldly, in a very much 'of this world' kind of way. You'll be happy to hear I'm savoring every moment.

Forty-six days until Italy. I'm excited to hold your hand in a gondola.

Adiós,

Lori

P.S. I miss you.

Don't Miss the Next Novel in the Troubled Spirits Series:
Ashwood's Girls

THE TRUE STORY THAT INSPIRED DARKNESS STIRRING

On April 18th, 1943, four boys were bird poaching in Hagley Woods in Worcestershire, England. They came upon a strange-looking tree known as a wych elm. When one boy climbed into the tree, he looked down into the hollow between the branches and made a disturbing discovery. Tucked within the tree was a human skull.

The boys notified police. Investigators found a full skeleton shoved into the wych elm. The skeleton still had bits of the person's clothes attached, as well as a wedding ring, tufts of hair, and a single shoe. A medical examiner discovered the skeleton belonged to a woman who had been dead for approximately eighteen months. After finding fabric in her mouth, he surmised she had died from suffocation. The skeleton was also missing one hand, which was later discovered a short distance away from the tree.

The case took a strange turn when respected anthropologist Professor Margaret Murray announced that the woman looked to have been killed as part of a black magic execution.

Investigators searched for the identity of the woman in the wych elm, but repeatedly came up empty. However, one year after the discovery of the body, graffiti appeared in Birmingham. It posed the question 'Who Put Bella Down the Wych Elm?'

The skeleton discovered in the wych elm has never been identified. For a deeper look at this story, visit my blog.

ALSO BY J.R. ERICKSON

The Troubled Spirits Series

Dark River Inn

Helme House

Darkness Stirring

Ashwood's Girls

Or dive into the completed eight-book stand-alone paranormal series:

The Northern Michigan Asylum Series.

Do you believe in ghosts?

ACKNOWLEDGMENTS

Many thanks to the people who made this book possible. Thank you to Team Miblart for the beautiful cover. Thank you to RJ Locksley for copy editing Darkness Stirring. Many thanks to Will St. John for beta reading the original manuscript, and to Travis Poole And Emily Haynes for finding those final pesky typos that slip in. Thank you to my amazing Advanced Reader Team. Lastly, and most of all, thank you to my family and friends for always supporting and encouraging me on this journey.

ABOUT THE AUTHOR

J.R. Erickson, also known as Jacki Riegle, is an indie author who writes ghost stories. She is the author of the Troubled Spirits Series, which blends true crime with paranormal murder mysteries. Her Northern Michigan Asylum Series are stand-alone paranormal novels inspired by a real former asylum in Traverse City.

These days, Jacki passes the time in the Traverse City area with her excavator husband, her wild little boy, and her three kitties: Floki, Beast, and Mamoo.

To find out more about J.R. Erickson, visit her website at www.jrericksonauthor.com.